GOETHE

JOHANN WOLFGANG GOETHE was born in Frankfurt-on-Main in 1749. He studied at Leipzig, where he showed interest in the occult, and at Strassburg, where Herder introduced him to Shakespeare's works and to folk poetry. He produced some essays and lyrical verse, and at twenty-four wrote *Goetz von Berlichingen*, a play which brought him national fame and established him in the current *Sturm and Drang* movement, *Werther*, a tragic romance, was an even greater success.

Goethe began work on *Faust*, and *Egmont*, another tragedy, before being invited to join the government of Weimar. His interest in the classical world led him to leave suddenly for Italy in 1786, and the *Italian Journey* recounts his travels there. *Iphigenie auf Tauris and Torquato Tasso*, classical dramas, were begun at this time.

Returning to Weimar, Goethe started the second part of *Faust*, encouraged by Schiller. During this late period he finished his series of *Wilhelm Meister* books and wrote many other works, including *The Oriental Divan*. He also directed the State Theatre and worked on scientific theories in evolutionary botany, anatomy, and colour.

Goethe was married in 1806. He finished *Faust* before he died in 1832.

David Luke was born in 1921 and is Tutor in German at Christ Church, Oxford. He has published articles and essays on German literature and various prose and verse translations, including Kleist's *The Marquise of O and Other Stories* (1978) for the Penguin Classics, Thomas Mann's *Tonio Kröger and Other Stories* (1970), Goethe's *Roman Elegies* (1977) and Jacob and Wilhelm Grimm's *Selected Tales* (1982).

GOETHE

INTRODUCED AND EDITED BY

DAVID LUKE

*

WITH PLAIN PROSE TRANSLATIONS
OF EACH POEM

PENGUIN BOOKS

Penguin Books Ltd, Harmondsworth, Middlesex, England
Viking Penguin Inc., 40 West 23rd Street, New York, New York 10010, U.S.A.
Penguin Books Australia Ltd, Ringwood, Victoria, Australia
Penguin Books Canada Ltd, 2801 John Street, Markham, Ontario, Canada L3R 1B4
Penguin Books (N.Z.) Ltd, 182–190 Wairau Road, Auckland 10, New Zealand

—

First published 1964
Reprinted 1969, 1972, 1981
Reprinted in Penguin Classics 1985

—

—

Printed and bound in Great Britain by
Cox & Wyman Ltd, Reading
Set in Monotype Fournier

TO NEVILL COGHILL

GENERAL EDITOR'S FOREWORD

THE purpose of these Penguin books of verse in the chief
European languages is to make a fair selection of the
world's finest poetry available to readers who could not,
but for the translations at the foot of each page, approach
it without dictionaries and a slow plodding from line to
line. They offer even to those with fair linguistic know-
ledge the readiest introduction to each country's lyrical
inheritance, and a sound base from which to make further
explorations.

The selections in each book have been made by the
anthologist alone. But all alike reflect contemporary
trends in taste, and include only poetry that can be read
for pleasure. No specimens have been included for their
historical interest, or to represent some particular school
or phase of literary history.

J. M. COHEN

CONTENTS

CONTENTS

CONTENTS

x

CONTENTS

CONTENTS

CONTENTS

CONTENTS

CONTENTS

INTRODUCTION

'GOETHE'S smaller poems, numerous as the sands of the sea, we have neither time nor inclination to criticize in detail. Most of them have some sort of whimsical originality, many have considerable pathos, and all are more or less immoral.' The words are those of an English critic in 1814 – a date incidentally at which about one third of the poems, including a large number of the greatest of them, were still unwritten. The puritan disapproval is characteristic of that period of Goethe's reputation in England; it was a chorus in which Wordsworth and Coleridge had heartily and uncritically joined. In our own day it is less loud, and the image of Goethe in the English mind, though still not altogether well focused, is less distorted than it was. We are prepared now to acknowledge that the poems belong, with *Faust*, to the peak of his achievement and contain the very marrow of his genius. The book by which, in Europe generally, he was most widely known in his day – *Die Leiden des jungen Werthers* – is not one that commends itself easily to present-day taste, and the same may be said of his other novels, *Wilhelm Meister* and the mysterious *Wahlverwandschaften*. His dramatic work is curiously unsatisfactory as such. In the obstinately imperfect masterpiece *Faust*, written piecemeal over a period of sixty years, we look in vain, despite its many poetic and dramatic beauties, for an overall dramaturgical unity and logic; and even in the chastely classical *Iphigenie auf Tauris* and *Torquato Tasso* it is not sheer theatrical effectiveness that we most admire. These dramatic works belong to Goethe's poetry; and it is in his poetry – if we understand this word in a fairly inclusive sense – that Goethe is clearly at his greatest. There are many other Goethes too: the sage and aphorist, the scientist, the critic, the autobiographer, the letter-writer, the conversationalist, the statesman, and the man of the world. But it is as Goethe the poet that he most surely holds his place among the supreme European élite. And, nevertheless, as Goethe the poet he is least European of all, in the sense that the frontiers of language, notoriously, are hardest for poetry to cross.

The present volume is thus conceived in terms of an impossible task: to represent, somehow, Goethe at his most poetic – which is also, by definition, Goethe at his most untranslatable. In *Faust*, as has often been discovered, he is least translatable of all; I have attempted nevertheless to represent *Faust* here by interspersing extracts from it among the selected poems. It has of course long been a common practice to include in Goethe anthologies the various incidental songs or self-contained set pieces from his plays, such as Gretchen's *König in Thule* ballad, her soliloquy at the spinning-wheel, the watchman's song, Iphigenie's 'Song of the Fates', Klärchen's song in *Egmont*, and so forth; in addition to these, however, I have also included a number of excerpts from monologues or dialogues in *Faust*, for the sake of their exceptional poetic interest. It may seem illogical in principle to do this without also cutting slices from *Iphigenie*, *Tasso*, the epic masterpiece *Hermann und Dorothea*, or for that matter from other lesser-known longer works. *Faust*, however, is in a number of ways unique: its lyricism is exceptionally pervasive, even seeming (as Professor Barker Fairley* suggests) to predominate over dramatic functionality; its dialogue is less integrated and indivisible than that of *Iphigenie* or *Tasso*, and indeed often reads rather like two or more lyrical monologues at cross purposes. At the risk of arbitrariness I have therefore treated it as lawful prey for the anthologist, and have brought some eight hundred lines of it into the scope of a selection which must in any case be no more than an incomplete and inadequate aid to those who wish to look for what Goethe has to offer as a writer of poetry.

It is true, of course, as Mr T. S. Eliot has pointed out,† that Goethe does not qualify for the status of 'great European' only by being a German poet of the highest rank, and that he would not so qualify even if he were more translatable

* These points are discussed in his *Goethe's Faust: Six Essays* (Oxford, 1953): see also the introduction to his selection of the poems (Heinemann, 1954).

† *Goethe as the Sage* (1955).

than he is (and had been as well translated, say, as Shakespeare has been by Schlegel and Tieck). The 'great European' (Dante, Shakespeare, Goethe) must also have other qualities such as those which Mr Eliot calls amplitude, abundance, universality, representativeness, and wisdom. Goethe has these. And it must be admitted that for a proper understanding even of the phenomenon 'Goethe the poet' a purely aesthetic or poetry-centred approach is a too narrow one. Goethe is by no means a self-effacing artist who shrinks into insignificance behind the body of his writings. He seems to stand constantly beside them; and this not only because his life is so much more fully documented than that of any other of the world's great writers. It is a commonplace of Goethe criticism to insist on the unusual closeness of his work to his life; a commonplace to recall his habit of letting himself overflow directly into art, of writing poetry as another man might keep a diary (though Goethe often kept diaries as well); a commonplace to quote his own famous description of his literary writings as so many 'fragments of a great confession'. Considering his life and his poetry together, we can see not only that there is something lastingly remarkable about his life as such – something that remains for our ill-balanced age exemplary in its human wholeness – but also that it is precisely his highly unusual combination of longevity with vitality that accounts for the continued originality, *Ursprünglichkeit*, of his poetry. Goethe was copious, but he was also various. It may well be possible to find in his whole work that profound 'unity' which Mr Eliot postulates as a further necessary condition of great-Europeanship; but this is of course very far from meaning that in his verse he was the monotonously self-repeating master of a single style. His poetry went on living, changing, developing unabatedly for sixty years or more; and being always a part of himself, growing as he grew, it remained 'original' even when it was most imitative. Originality is after all not absence of models, but what one can make of one's models; it is the recognition of kinship and the capacity to transform; above all it is the refusal to imitate oneself. Goethe wrote in the style

of north-European folksongs and popular ballads, and in sophisticated Italian verse-forms; he imitated the hexameters of Homer, the elegies of Propertius, the epigrams of Martial, the classical lyric poetry of Persia; and when he had done what it was his to do with these idioms, he would drop them and turn to something else. After the age of about fifty he virtually stopped writing in hexameters and elegiac distichs; he felt for a year or two the need to use sonnet form; the Persian phase occupied his latter sixties and then came to an end; at seventy-eight he was trying his hand at imitating Chinese poetry. He worked his models first into his system, then out of it. He was resilient, able to forget, willing to leave things behind, deep enough to be inconsistent, big enough to be both personal and universal, alive enough for his life to be art and for his art to be life.

The sixty years or so that extend from the time of Goethe's first maturity to his death in 1832 are recognized as the great age of German literature and culture; to Germans they are, simply, the age of Goethe, *die Goethezeit*. Outside the German-speaking world it is common for Goethe to be labelled a 'romantic', and in the European perspective of the various types of romanticism – in so far as they are types of the same thing at all – this description contains a limited truth. German literary historians, preferring narrower perspective and preciser classification, have always been at pains to exclude Goethe from the category *romantisch*. The 1770s were the epoch of pre-romanticism, to which Germans and Germanists continue to give the odd but traditional name of *Sturm und Drang* (Storm and Stress) epoch. Blake and Burns were then still in their teens, and Wordsworth and Coleridge still children. Goethe's first original work fills this decade, while at the same time transcending it: he was, in fact, in his twenties writing poetry of a kind that had no parallel in any European literature in that generation. But equally without parallel was the work that came of his further maturity and anti-romantic reaction in the 1780s, after he had moved to Weimar. This phase, which may be said to last until 1805, the year of the death of Goethe's friend and literary

partner, Schiller, is for German literature the epoch of high classicism (*Klassik*); it includes much of Goethe's and all of Schiller's finest work. The German romantic movement (*Romantik*) properly so called, though it overlapped with Weimar classicism, did not begin until 1797 or 1798, when Tieck, Novalis, and the Schlegel brothers were forming a school and Hölderlin (if we count him as a romantic) was writing his mature poetry. Goethe's relations with the German romantics seem on the whole to have been antipathetic. His younger contemporaries represented to him a human and artistic stage through which he felt he had already passed. The odd historical position of Goethe is that he had, in certain important senses, repudiated romanticism in advance, before it had properly got under way – certainly before it was ever called 'romanticism'. Later, when the label had become current, he defined *das Romantische*, in a much-quoted saying, as a disease (*das Kranke*). And in the meantime the somewhat pathological genius of Hölderlin – whose finest work, admittedly, he never saw – had quite escaped his notice. It is one of the tragi-comic ironies of European literary history that so much mutual ignorance and disesteem separated the most distinguished writers of that age. The year 1798, which saw the publication of the *Lyrical Ballads* of Wordsworth and Coleridge, can also be said to date the beginning of the English romantic movement; yet the two schools, German and English, developed simultaneously in virtually total isolation from each other. As for Goethe, now in his fifties, he had even less knowledge of Wordsworth and Coleridge than they had of him. Blake, to whom he was in some ways akin, was at that time an unknown quantity even in England. It was not until a generation later that admiration was exchanged between Goethe and Byron, and that Shelley was moved by enthusiasm for *Faust* to translate two scenes of it; the author of *Faust*, however, considered neither Shelley nor Keats worthy of his attention.

Johann Wolfgang Goethe was born in 1749 in Frankfurt-am-Main into a well-to-do upper-middle-class family and remained

in comfortable circumstances all his life. He was granted personal ennoblement as 'von Goethe' by his patron the Duke of Saxe-Weimar, whose service he entered in 1775. His father, a cultivated, pedantic, disappointed man, at first educated his son at home and then sent him at the age of sixteen to the fashionable university of Leipzig, then an important cultural centre. It was mainly during his three years here that Goethe's juvenilia were written, in the current debased rococo (called for no good reason 'anacreontic') style – a kind of frivolous drawing-room-and-boudoir verse, derived from French models, the trivialized literary equivalent of mid-eighteenth-century Meissen porcelain. 'Anacreontic' poems were brief, dainty, erotic in an impersonal, quite unlyrical, archly playful way, and usually calculated to end in some kind of neat witticism (the so-called *pointe*). As an example this selection includes one of the pieces that Goethe wrote in French during this Leipzig period. The next two poems also show the influence of anacreonticism, though the second of these (*Mit einem gemalten Band*) was written three years later, at a time when Goethe was undergoing a poetic transformation.

In April 1770, after an illness which had kept him at home for nearly two years, he went to study law for eighteen months at Strasbourg. It was here that he met Johann Gottfried Herder, the eccentric Protestant clergyman whose voluminous critical and philosophical writings were so important a factor in the German pre-romantic and classical revival. In Herder's mind the Enlightenment, Rousseau, humanism and Christianity mingled in a confused and stimulating ferment. He infected the young Goethe with his literary enthusiasms, which at this time included in particular a passion for collecting and translating folk-songs and ballads – a practice which was already becoming fashionable in England and Scotland. Herder and Goethe between them were responsible for re-establishing in Germany a creative connexion between the long-despised folk-song and the language of the cultivated lyric; the later Romantics further explored this vein. Goethe's verse also took from the environment of Strasbourg an unprecedented infusion of strongly felt landscape imagery;

and an additional appropriate experience of 1770 and 1771 was his passing sentimental attachment (to which Goethe-criticism traditionally ascribes a probably exaggerated importance) to Friederike Brion, the daughter of a country parson who reminded the poet of Goldsmith's Vicar of Wakefield.

What may broadly be called his Frankfurt period (after Leipzig and before Weimar) was the springtime of Goethe's art, in which, having discarded false urbanity and debased convention, he plunged boldly into suddenly expanded possibilities of poetic diction. The naïve tone of folk-poetry was one to which he was to return occasionally in later years as well, bringing it to its unsurpassed perfection in Der Fischer (1778) and Erlkönig (1782) in which the potent brew of the Scottish border ballads seems to mingle with the eerie incantations of Coleridge's Ancient Mariner (1798) or Keats's La Belle Dame sans Merci (1819). Goethe also, in the Frankfurt period, revived and perfected the traditional so-called Knittelvers of German popular verse-narrative: a rough, vivid, freely syllabified line of four stresses, commonly rhymed in couplets. In this metre he wrote parts of Faust and various other comic-satirical pieces and fragments, which often employ an archaizing German impossible to convey in translation (Legende, Diner zu Koblenz, and Rezensent are three minor examples). He also at this time frequently used an exclamatory rhapsodic free verse (thinking, though mistakenly, that in so doing he was imitating the odes of Pindar). The best pieces in this manner are Ganymed and Prometheus, well known in the settings by Hugo Wolf, whose music wonderfully develops their expressive power. Mahometsgesang is a further example. There is, however, no single predominant style of the Frankfurt period – Goethe still had, as he himself remarked later, no style, only styles. His deepest need in the early 1770s was to experiment, to explore what sometimes turned out to be blind alleys, to remain (both in his poetry and in his life) uncommitted, idiosyncratic, free-lance. His manner of living and educating himself was still wayward and dilettantish to a degree notorious among his friends; his legal studies and brief professional prac-

tice meant little or nothing to him. He had picked up at least smatterings of half a dozen languages, and dabbled in several other subjects, particularly in the visual arts; he had read extensively though not intensively. The vitality and variousness that were to be his permanent assets manifested themselves in these years as impulsiveness and caprice. His fluttering genius settled on many perches but hardly ever for long; he made many literary plans which he carried out only partly or not at all; he wrote innumerable verses, doggerels, sketches, and fragments. Among his longer works completed and published before the move to Weimar are the rough-hewn pseudo-Shakespearian chronicle-play *Götz von Berlichingen* and, of course, the all-too-famous *Werther*. This semi-autobiographical letter-novel shocked and fascinated Goethe's contemporaries in and outside Germany as a comparatively realistic study of unhappy love and a seeming apologia for suicide; today it is a less fashionable but still beautifully written and perhaps underrated work. There can be no doubt, however, that by far the most important thing achieved by Goethe in the 1770s, for all its characteristic fragmentariness, was the early germinal version of *Faust*, the so-called '*Ur-Faust*'. This really consists of several separate sketches, in various kinds of verse and in prose, for different parts of what is now known as '*Faust*, Part One'. It contains above all, as a coherent sequence of scenes, the famous tragedy of Margarete or Gretchen – an episode which despite its prominence in the finished *Faust* has little or nothing to do with the Dr Faustus story as such, but which remains, with its brief balladesque intensity and especially in its poignant childlike central figure, one of the supreme creations of all poetic drama, excelled by nothing in Shakespeare and never subsequently equalled by Goethe or any other writer. It might well have been published as a lyrical drama on its own in the 1770s, with incalculable effects on the development of German literature (the theme of the seduced and abandoned girl was a favourite one of that epoch, though only Goethe handled it with such poetry and subtle understanding). But by another historic irony, Goethe

withheld it, taking all his *Faust* manuscripts with him in 1775 to Weimar, where they lay untouched for many years; and the text of the *Ur-Faust* (in the form of a contemporary transcription of the lost original) was not discovered until more than a century later.

The *Sturm und Drang* epoch has also been called by German literary historians the *Geniezeit*, in ironical allusion to the prevailing and at that time novel conception of natural genius as something that sprouted like a plant or gushed like hot water from a geyser, through the sacred medium of the artist's idiosyncratic personality. Goethe himself expresses this aesthetic in *Künstlers Abendlied* (1774) in terms of something very like a secularized Protestant hymn; he was friendly at this time, though not later, with pietistic evangelical circles whose emotionalistic religiosity was in fact in some ways a parallel phenomenon to the pre-romantic anti-rationalistic theory of genius. Among his *Sturm und Drang* contemporaries, however, Goethe was certainly the only authentic *Genie*. Not by calculation, but by a profound creative instinct, he was then already performing his historic linguistic role: that of being (with Luther and perhaps Nietzsche) one of the two or three greatest originators and perfectors of Modern High German as a literary medium. In the 1770s the German language as we now know it was still at a formative stage; Goethe precipitated and crystallized it, and developed it as well. The many untranslatable neologistic compounds first used in his Frankfurt and early Weimar poetry ('Blütendampf', 'Blütenträume', 'Nebeltal', 'Gipfelgänge', 'schlangenwandelnd', 'freudebrausend', 'vollschwellend', 'leisrauschend', 'Wissensqualm', 'Lebensfluten', 'Goldwolken', 'Dickichts-Schauer', etc.) are only one aspect of this linguistic creativeness. He pushed forward frontiers of vocabulary and grammar, invented and altered usages, and transformed simple words by new imaginative juxtapositions. In the history of eighteenth-century German poetic diction some timid steps had already been taken in these directions by the pallid verse of the pious and pompous Klopstock; but it was Goethe who poured

out the true wine. Goethe certainly also had, in a marked degree, the capacity of genius for 'inspiration' – that is, for verbalization and composition at the pre-conscious level. In the memoirs of his youth he recalls how he would frequently make poetry in a state approaching somnambulism or trance, sometimes waking and leaping out of bed in haste to scrawl down what had come to him before he forgot it, as he often did. The lines beginning *Über allen Gipfeln* ... (1780), probably the most famous of all German lyrics, were suddenly scribbled on the wooden wall of a mountain hut. This gift of spontaneous poetry had not left him even in his old age: the solemn and mysterious stanzas *Um Mitternacht ging ich* (he tells us) emerged ready-made into his mind on a moonlit winter night of 1818, unheralded and un-explained.

After Goethe settled in Weimar, however, a quite different style came to predominate both in his writing and in his life. The elements of conscious reflection and control, acceptance of con-vention and self-limitation, assumed increasing importance; the explosive idiom of the Frankfurt period, and its corresponding philosophy of the sacredness of impulse and the absolute value of the passing moment, began to ebb away. When Goethe accepted in 1775 the invitation of the eighteen-year-old Carl August, ruler of the small Duchy (later Grand Duchy) of Saxe-Weimar-Eisenach, to join the cultured circle of his court, he did not at first intend that Weimar should become, as it did, his home for the rest of his life. Within a year he was a member of the Duke's privy council and saddled with heavy, various, and unaccustomed responsibilities. He came, however, to look upon these, despite their frequent irksomeness, as a disciplinary ex-perience of immense value. *Torquato Tasso* (finished in 1790), a dramatic study – the first such in European literature – of the romantic dilemma between the demands of the aesthetic and of the practical life, largely reflects and symbolizes Goethe's ex-periences and self-criticisms in his early Weimar years. Another of the most important of these experiences was his extraordinary, much-discussed, intense, and prolonged attachment to Charlotte

von Stein, the intellectually interesting but by no means beautiful wife of one of the court officials. A considerable number of Goethe's poems (as well as other works) between 1776 and 1784 refer directly or indirectly to her (whom he sometimes calls 'Lida'); half a dozen of these appear here in the group beginning with *Warum gabst du uns die tiefen Blicke*, a nostalgic meditation on the contrast between ideal love and disillusioning actuality. The relationship between Goethe and Charlotte, it seems, was entirely platonic, but came to a rather undignified and embittered end as a result of Goethe's flight to Italy in 1786 and its sequel.

Goethe's loves before 1786 were habitually impossible, frustrated, or inconclusive: Friederike, Lotte Kestner (the original of Werther's Lotte), the elegant Lili Schönemann (the 'Belinda' of the groups of love poems written just before the move from Frankfurt to Weimar), and above all the sisterly Lida. The succession does not end here; but after the Italian journey a different and complementary pattern emerges. Christiane Vulpius, whom Goethe met in Weimar almost immediately after his return from Rome, contrasted with Frau von Stein in a number of particulars. Despite her social inferiority to Goethe, she lived in his house like a wife, to the scandal of Weimar society. Of his children by her, only one, August (1789–1830), survived infancy. The association, which lasted devotedly until Christiane's death in 1816, became a legal marriage in 1806, during the Napoleonic disturbances. The *Römische Elegien*, which rank among Goethe's supreme achievements, were written after he had begun to live with Christiane, though they retrospectively synchronize, by a wholly appropriate poetic fiction, this newly found personal happiness with the poet's intellectual experience of Rome. For Goethe the visit to Italy, and to Rome in particular, was a self-liberating gesture, a hegira, a turning-point in his life, a human and artistic transformation, of which the Elegies were the first-fruits. In them he attaches himself to a quite un-Germanic stylistic tradition, that of the Latin elegiac poets such as Propertius, Catullus, and Tibullus (the 'triumvirate of Cupid' mentioned in the fifth Elegy). Romantic mood-lyricism

and indefinable longings are replaced by sovereign urbanity and unashamed sensuality, though deep feeling remains. German mountains, waterfalls, and mists give way to the intense sunlight and clear outlines of a Mediterranean pre-Christian world. In the elegiac distich, or rather its German prosodic equivalent which Goethe, and after him Hölderlin, brought to perfection, Goethe had discovered what was to remain for over a decade his natural medium, one in which he could combine spontaneity with the observance of convention. (Unlike Hölderlin, however, he never wrote in the more difficult convention of strophic odes.)

The *Venezianische Epigramme* reflect a brief and rather disillusioning return visit to Italy in 1790. A vein of cynicism and indecency is obvious in a number of these, which editors usually suppress; I feel that to continue this policy only falsifies the mature Goethe and encourages the all-too-easily formed image of him as a pompous, stuffy, and humourless Olympian. The same considerations apply to the more violently anti-Christian or anti-clerical gibes in this collection; they are revealing rather than brilliant, but should offend only the under-faithed, who find it necessary to treat the externals of religion in a spirit of permanent deadly seriousness. Continued protest against Procrustean doctrinalism and fig-leaf squeamishness was an essential feature of Goethe's religious development. The weird if somewhat contrived ballad *Die Braut von Korinth* (his adaptation of an ancient ghost story) is a variant of the same polemic, and so in a sense is its complementary companion-piece *Der Gott und die Bajadere*. Both this and the later very remarkable (though again usually suppressed) poem *Das Tagebuch* (1810) reveal the power of Goethe's art to transform potentially scabrous themes into something human, subtle, and delicate.

Artistically perhaps the most perfect of his longer works, and an apex of his classicism, is one which can here unfortunately be only minimally represented: the epic in nine cantos *Hermann und Dorothea* (1796), the enchanting and moving idyll of German small-town middle-class life set against the disturbed political background of Europe in the 1790s – a suspended timeless poetic

vision of elementary human relationships. I have given one short extract from it, as better than nothing. The epic as a whole has many affinities to the shorter elegiac idyll *Alexis und Dora*, written in the same year; a more tragic note is struck in the elegiac lament *Euphrosyne* (1798).

After the two years leave of absence which he had taken in 1786, it was agreed that Goethe's official duties should be confined to cultural matters such as the directorship of the Court theatre. His former administrative activities, however, had themselves borne intellectual fruit: their practical demands had stimulated in him an intense, and since the earlier Weimar years steadily increasing, interest in various branches of natural science. By one of his refreshing creative errors, Goethe himself seems to have valued his writings on geology, mineralogy, anatomy, botany, meteorology, and especially his vast treatise on optics and the theory of colour, at least as highly as his literary work. Their exact status and significance, scientific and otherwise, is still a matter of dispute. Goethe was an untiring collector and careful classifier of mineralogical and anatomical specimens, and in general a meticulous naked-eye observer of natural phenomena; from the point of view, however, of strictly empirical science in the modern sense, his observations were usually misinterpreted and his factual results therefore incorrect as such and as stated. In particular his lifelong polemic against the accepted Newtonian theory of the nature of light appears, if taken at its face value, as an obstinate aberration. But Goethe and the scientific establishment were and are at cross purposes. By implication and in tendency, his scientific work was essentially a protest against the materialistic presuppositions of modern science, the mathematical abstractness of its methods, its puristic departmentalism. Such a protest can today still serve as a corrective; it belongs to the perennial tradition of human values in revolt against dehumanizing abstraction and the cold lust for neutral fact. It was Goethe's basic conviction, expressed both in his scientific and in his literary works, that man and nature are bound to each other by a profound correlation, that nature is a

whole, that its processes are gradual and orderly, that its laws are also those of human life and of art. Goethe's was, in fact, the type of mind which demands a synthesis between scientific and the various non-scientific modes of thought, and which abhors irreducible antinomies and unbridgeable gaps. His discovery in 1784 (independent though not unanticipated) of a recognizable *os intermaxillare* or snout-bone in the human species pleased him particularly as a victory against orthodox rationalistic theology, which had held the supposed absence of this bone to mark a fundamental distinction between man and the lower animals. But to Goethe man was part of the natural continuum, and all nature indivisibly divine. To the rationalist passion for endless differential classification (in anatomy and botany, for instance) he opposed his sense of an organic unity underlying the diversity of phenomena. His quest for a synthetic or holistic view and for a fusion of scientific and poetic discourse is reflected in his two 'Metamorphosis' poems, which revive a style reminiscent of the scientific-didactic verse of Lucretius or Virgil. The first, *Die Metamorphose der Pflanzen* (1798), is related in content to Goethe's botanical treatise of the same title (1790) and adopts the formal convention of expository address to the poet's mistress. (Christiane's occupation, before she met Goethe, had been the manufacture of artificial flowers.) The second, *Metamorphose der Tiere*, is especially revealing. (This poem, possibly a fragment of a larger project, is commonly dated 1806, though on inconclusive evidence; for a number of reasons it is more likely to have been written before 1800.)

The concept of discoverable timeless natural and aesthetic laws dominated Goethe's 'classical' years, and especially those (beginning in 1794) of his close intellectual partnership with Friedrich Schiller. The latter, ten years younger than Goethe, a lesser poet but a more conscientious dramatist and philosopher, lived in Jena and after 1799 mainly in Weimar. Goethe and Schiller shared many ideals: they hoped not only to create classical, living, symbolic, canonically beautiful works of art, but between them to re-educate and civilize the German public,

to clarify principles and standards, to discover the specific requirements of the different literary genres and the abiding structures of the human imagination. Their ambitions as to the wider influence of Weimar classicism were to remain unrealized, but their association was of incalculable value to both of them; Goethe felt the loss of Schiller in 1805 acutely and lastingly. In particular it seems improbable that without Schiller's persuasion he would ever have resumed work on the fragmentary *Faust*.

A revised but truncated version of the '*Ur-Faust*', with one or two new interpolated scenes, had appeared in 1790; between 1797 and 1806 the gaps were filled in and the complete 'First Part of the Tragedy' was published in 1808. The 'Second Part', however, was not finished until the very last years of Goethe's life, and appeared posthumously. There are thus three main stages in the composition of *Faust* as a whole: in Goethe's twenties, in his early fifties, and in his late seventies; these correspond sufficiently to the three main chronological phases into which the present selection of his verse is divided, and I think it more useful and revealing to keep the *Faust* extracts in their separate historical places than to pretend that they are parts of a successfully unified and indivisible dramatic composition.

The examples (Section Three) of poetry written after 1800 begin with a group of seven which might be called poems of renunciation; there follow sixteen miscellaneous lyrics and ballads all written before 1820. The outstanding event of these two decades however occurred when at the age of nearly sixty-five Goethe found himself, to his own great surprise, striking a fresh and powerful lyrical vein. He had discovered a new and inspiring model and forerunner: the great fourteenth-century Persian poet Mahommed Shams-ud-din, known as Háfiz. Goethe read his work in a recent German translation in 1814, and proceeded to an intensive study of Persian poetry. The result was the *West-östlicher Divan*, written during the next few years: a wonderful fusion, again, of personal with traditional and conventional elements – this time a more alien and exotic tradition than that of Latin and Greek poetry. The *Divan* (the

word means 'assembly' or 'collection') is divided into sections
with titles such as 'The Book of Háfiz', 'The Book of Suleika',
'The Book of the Cupbearer', or 'The Book of Paradise'. The
'Suleika' of most of the love poems was the beautiful and cul-
tured Marianne von Willemer, herself a poet and former actress;
she had married a Frankfurt banker, at whose house Goethe
stayed when in 1814 and 1815 he revisited the Rhein-Main dis-
trict and the scenes of his youth. She returned his love, and even
successfully imitated his poetry, but their brief idyll was ended
by renunciation and permanent withdrawal on Goethe's part.
Nevertheless, even a poem written in 1828 (*Dem aufgehenden
Vollmonde*) refers above all to Marianne, and the eight-line
Vermächtnis (1831) accompanied her letters to him, which he
returned shortly before his death.

The *West-östlicher Divan*, being full of more or less concealed
literary allusions, has called forth more learned commentary
than any of Goethe's major works except *Faust*. I have tried here
to select the more immediately accessible of these poems, also in-
cluding some from the remarkable 'Cupbearer' cycle in which
Goethe adopts with sympathetic ease the pæderastic convention
of Middle Eastern poetry, and enters, presumably even more
easily (for he was a heavy and enthusiastic wine-drinker even by
the standards of his age) into the spirit of Háfiz's drinking-songs.
Of Háfiz's celebrations of wine and love it was disputed from
the outset whether they should be interpreted hedonistically or
mystically. So far as Goethe is concerned, certain passages of the
Divan suggest that he found an oriental style and setting particu-
larly appropriate to the expression of a sense (increasingly
characteristic of his old age) of the dissolving boundary be-
tween earthly love and the love of God, as well as of the mani-
festation of the divine beauty in nature generally. In the famous
Selige Sehnsucht (based on a favourite Persian parable of the
moth and the candle-flame) sexuality becomes mysteriously
transparent; the same is true of *In tausend Formen* and of
Höheres und Höchstes. Goethe's two ballads based on Indian
legends (*Der Gott und die Bajadere* of 1797 and the extraordinary

Paria trilogy of 1823) also share the theme of the continuity and contiguity of the lowest with the highest. Such poems, as well as the 'Elegy' (1823) of the *Trilogie der Leidenschaft*, complement and counterpoise the Roman Elegies and *Das Tagebuch*, just as the mystical ending of Act V of *Faust* Part Two complements and counterpoises the pagan nature-worship of Acts II and III.

The *Divan* well represents the freer, more nonchalant and inventive style of lyricism to which Goethe returned in his 'post-classical' years, but which at the same time was never in any narrow sense 'romantic'. How far above a merely passive cult of 'inspiration' was the poet who in the strict *ottava rima* of the *Zueignung* to *Faust* could feel himself to be 'lisping' like 'an Aeolian harp', and who in *Lied und Gebilde*, announcing the *Divan* programme of greater fluidity, could see the 'liquid element' solidifying to a ball of crystal in his 'pure hand'! In the poetry of the last two or three decades of his life, Goethe advances and intensifies the expressiveness of German in a manner often even bolder than that of his Frankfurt period; yet his language now possesses an indefinable tranquillity and ripeness, as well as the characteristic conversational ease which he could always combine even with solemnity. In poems such as *Sommernacht, Vollmondnacht, Paria*, or the final magical lyrics of 1827 and 1828 (*Dämmrung senkte sich . . ., Früh, wenn Tal . . ., Dem Aufgehenden Vollmonde*, and *Der Bräutigam*) there are strange grammatical liberties, compressions, and dislocations (Goethe himself compared the tough, condensed language of *Paria* to 'a damascene sword-blade forged from steel wire'). In the last-written parts of *Faust*, above all, this tendency (as well as the invention of compounds – 'grünumschränkt', 'Zitterperle', 'Erfüllungspforten flügeloffen', 'Pappelzitterzweige', 'Wallestrom', 'Zackenhaupt', 'Säuselschweben', 'Dauerstern', etc., and numerous hyphenated forms) is pushed far enough to invite comparison with modern symbolist and expressionist techniques. In *Faust* Part Two Goethe's language reaches never-surpassed heights of sensuous power in the

'Arcadia' speech and final chorus of Act III, and of limpid ecstasy in the closing scene on the fringes of Heaven.

Goethe's verse epigrams are extremely numerous and contain, besides polemic, a good deal of humour and wisdom. Apart from those in classical distichs, they mainly belong to his sixties and seventies but are usually not more exactly datable. I have put a selection of them into something approximating to a thematic order. These are preceded by a group of (for want of a better word) philosophical pieces, mostly written between 1815 and 1821 (*Vermächtnis* was added in 1829). Goethe, in his own final edition, grouping his philosophical poems together under the title *Gott und Welt*, not inappropriately included among them the two *Metamorphose* pieces, the nostalgic *Dauer im Wechsel*, the ecstatic *Wiederfinden* in which the Suleika of the *Divan* becomes involved with Neoplatonic metaphysics, and the solemn, oracular *Urworte, Orphisch* (1818): this I have placed after the end of the selection of epigrams, as being Goethe's most impressive achievement in the didactic vein. Less abstract, and distilling an even greater lyric force, is the beautiful meditation on Schiller's exhumed skull (1826). The sombre, plangent notes of this poem and of the *Trilogie der Leidenschaft* are rare in Goethe. The latter (1823/4) was not originally conceived as a group. Its centre-piece, usually called the 'Marienbad Elegy', was inspired by the poet's sudden passion for a young girl, Ulrike von Levetzow: it is the profoundest of his love-poems, deeply individual and yet deeply generalized – an old man's symbolic farewell to the last of his loves and to the world which only love can make significant.

To read such a poem is to be reminded again how nearly impossible it is to generalize about Goethe – about the outlook on life expressed by his poetry and suggested by the vast but of course still utterly inadequate biographical evidence – about his happiness or otherwise, his 'Olympian balance' or neurotic imbalance, his sense of the tragic or his 'avoidance of tragedy'. It seems unsafe to venture beyond the necessary platitude that his poetry is extremely wide-ranging – 'probably', as Professor

Barker Fairley has said, 'the most wide-ranging body of lyrical poetry that ever came out of a single mind'. Wide-ranging in theme and mood, wide-ranging in form and imagery – there cannot be said to be any characteristically 'Goethean' imagery, landscape, or setting. This *breadth*, of course, in itself helps to make Goethe (as Mr Eliot points out) a great European such as neither Wordsworth nor Hölderlin can be, though their *heights* are no less than his. A comparison of Goethe with Hölderlin is particularly instructive. It reveals Hölderlin's limitations; and if we are bold, and set aside exceptions, we can say that – like comparison with various other poets of high distinction – it also reveals Goethe's. Hölderlin's remote, rapt, visionary, hymnic, prophetic tones, his glittering hyper-language, are on the whole quite alien to Goethe. Goethe was not a prophet, not possessed by a vision, not steeped in metaphysics, not poised in intense incandescence over schizophrenic decay. Unlike Hölderlin and many other younger contemporaries, he was uninspired by patriotic or nationalistic sentiment. Unlike many romantics and later neo-romantics, he professed no self-conscious philosophy of Poetry or cult of Beauty. 'The Muse', he wrote at the end of his life in tones of admonition, 'can be a companion, but not a guide'; and his scapegoat-hero Torquato Tasso receives (though he does not take it) the deeply Goethean advice, 'Der Mensch gewinnt, was der Poet verliert' – 'what you lose as a poet you will gain as a human being'. Goethe was not an aesthetic per-fectionist or a determined explorer of the rarefied and exquisitely refined. As we also learn from *Tasso*, he understood the roman-tic obsession, the romantic dream and death-wish and nostalgia; but he is not the poet of these things. He is not a brooding self-tormentor or shrill self-mocker, not an irony-haunted *poète maudit*, not a minstrel of despair. In his lyric poetry he nearly always avoids the expression of extreme tragic emotion – at most, this appears in lyrics attributed to fictional characters (Mignon and the Harp-Player in *Wilhelm Meister*) or in his dramatic poetry (Faust and Gretchen – in fact the youthful Gretchen drama is the only work in which Goethe really achieves

unmitigated tragedy). In his writing, the affirmation of life is made to predominate.

On the whole, too, Goethe certainly cannot be claimed as a Christian poet. His religiosity, though genuine, was eclectic and ethically unproblematical. He appears to have been no more troubled by a Problem of Evil than Spinoza or Leibniz were. He accepts evil as necessary but does not ponder it particularly deeply or assign to it any very effective role in his essentially monistic cosmos; his Devil, as we see in *Faust*, is on friendly visiting-terms with God. Sin, as a concept, apparently scarcely existed for him. He refused to think of man or nature as fallen or radically corrupt; he had no use for Revelation, Incarnation, Redemption, Christ's '*Jammerkreuz*'. Christ was unnecessary. Whatever may have been his private feelings, he does not express in his poetry, at least, any acute sense of the reality of death: it is conceived as transformation rather than extinction; there is something indestructible about all genuine existence ('How can I perish?' exclaims Werther. 'How can you perish? Do we not *exist*?'). To Goethe, God was immanent rather than transcendent, and it seemed obvious to him that the world, and the process of creation, were eternal; time and nature were not, as in Christian theology, created *ex nihilo* and subject to eventual reannihilation. God was apprehended by Goethe not as supernatural Judgement or Grace, but very positively as the Creator or creative force perpetually at work in the natural order and virtually identical with it – as '*Gott-Natur*', as Spinoza's *Deus sive Natura*. 'Pantheist', like 'humanist', is a label that often suggests itself to the reader of Goethe as a near-enough general description of this thinker who took such elements as suited him from the general stock of philosophical and theological tradition (Christian, Neoplatonist, Gnostic, and otherwise) and who could feel himself poetically, as at the end of *Faust*, into attitudes or beliefs not characteristic of him. Goethe was never a strict and logical abstract thinker; his intellectual and even his artistic conscience were healthily accommodating. He even seems to have regarded logical consistency as rather

neurotic, rather '*hypochondrisch*'. He could take life, art, and religion less than seriously and yet was far from being fundamentally frivolous or uncommitted. A German poet and critic of this century has suggested that, when in our attempt to reassess and redefine Goethe, we have done sifting and balancing antithetical 'isms', we are left confronted with what he calls 'Goethe the poet of created Being'.* Goethe's last irreducible substance is his sense of the absolute positivity, the meaningfulness, the 'truth' of visible reality – a reality which, unlike Nietzsche's self-transcending and self-exploding world, is still something created – still holy, as 'everything that lives' was to Blake; the kind of reality of which Spinoza had said that 'the more we understand particular things, the more we understand God'. As a scientist and poet, Goethe's piety was of this sort; if indeed 'piety' is a word that can be used of him – for somewhere between 'pious' and 'impious' he again slips through the net. But it was, as Holthusen remarks, 'a piety of the *Te Deum laudamus*, and not of the *De profundis*'.

Goethe is optimistic, though not an 'optimist'. His wisdom goes beyond optimism and pessimism, as it goes beyond rationalism and irrationalism. He saw other creatures as well as Reason in the human aquarium. His frighteningly exact understanding of neurotic mental conditions is embodied in the cold corrosive whisperings of Care to the aged Faust. 'Demons', he knew, 'are hard to banish.' Faust's replies symbolize Goethe's determination not to lose his nerve; to remain faithful to his philosophy of perpetual development and unflagging activity ('in the beginning was the Deed'); to preserve his balance, however precarious, between many opposites and not least between brutal vitalism and pallid asceticism; to remain central and whole. What saved Goethe as a human being, thinker, and poet? Tact; inexhaustible energy; and above all, perhaps, the continued readiness to love. This last is not so much a question of the number (exaggerated by popular and romanticizing biographers) of 'women in Goethe's life', or of the fact that

* Hans Egon Holthusen, *Goethe als Dichter der Schöpfung* (1949).

youthful incarnations of the Eternal Feminine could fill him with agonies and ecstasies even in old age, or of how often or how seldom he was loved in return. It is simply that Goethe appears to have continued to be prepared to give himself to this kind of experience in one way or another – to find the world of visible creatures, and especially of personal creatures, lovable and beautiful: that he was profoundly disposed, no doubt by his earliest childhood memories, to associate love with happiness and to feel himself secure and at home in the world.

> 'Zeugest mir, daß ich geliebt bin,
> Sei das Liebchen noch so fern.'

This surely was the deepest root of his confidence, of the tenderness, the *Innigkeit* of his poetry, of his sense of the goodness of life. A fitting epigraph for him might be made of some words used by Nietzsche, but more applicable to Goethe than to himself: 'we love life, not because we are used to living, but because we are used to loving. There is some madness in all love; but there is some reason in all madness.'

*

The German text of the present selection is based on the 'Gedenkausgabe' of the complete works (Artemis Verlag, 1949 onwards) in which the two volumes of the *Gedichte* are edited by Emil Staiger and the *Faust* volume by Ernst Beutler. I have made only a few minor departures from this edition: for example, for about half a dozen of the epigrams I have adopted readings from Staiger's three-volume annotated edition (Manesse Verlag, 1949); for the poems from the *West-östlicher Divan* I have taken the punctuation and a few other details from the later edition of this work by Max Rychner (Manesse Verlag, 1952); and occasionally I have used titles from sources other than the 'Gedenkausgabe' (these are enclosed in square brackets; in the case of the *Faust* extracts they are partly of my own devising). As already indicated in the foregoing Introduction, my arrangement of the poems selected represents a compromise be-

tween the chronological principle and that of significant group-ing. Partly for this reason and partly because the composition-date of so many of Goethe's poems is unknown or uncertain, I have refrained from any detailed dating of the poems, either in the text or in the table of contents. The order of the poems with-in each of the three main sections can serve as a rough guide, and I have attempted to observe these three main chronological divisions as strictly as possible. The division of the *Faust* ex-tracts into three groups is for reasons already explained. It must further be pointed out that for purposes of the *text* I have in nearly all cases used Goethe's final versions of the poems and of *Faust* (as represented by the above-mentioned editions), while basing the *arrangement* (in so far as it is chronological) on the dates of his original versions, where ascertainable. Thus in the case of the first group of *Faust* extracts I have not used the so-called '*Ur-Faust*' text but the final (orthographically and other-wise revised) *Faust* Part One (1808); the speech of Helen in the second group follows the Part Two text (1832) and not the 1800 sketch; and the scene between Faust and Care is necessarily given in its finalized form, though it was probably in all es-sentials written in the 'classical' period, to which (like the Helen episode) it belongs in spirit. Similarly, the poems of 'the younger Goethe' are given in the revised form which Goethe used for the collected editions of his poems (beginning in 1789). In one case (*An den Mond*) where the differences between this and the original form are more than trivial, I have given the latter as well: comparison of the two draws attention to still unsolved problems affecting the interpretation of this famous poem. The text of two juvenilia in English verse, which I have included as curiosities, is that established by Dr Richard Friedenthal.

The translations do not aim at word-for-word literalness; the grammatical structure and rhetorical traditions of German are different from those of English, and to eschew paraphrase too rigorously would lead to results as absurd as in literal cribs of Latin or Greek texts. This is especially the case with the highly distilled grammar of Goethe's last period (with its genitive

absolutes, ellipsis of articles and pronouns, etc.). It is often necessary to translate one German word by a whole phrase, and this applies not only to the compound nouns, compound participles and so forth in which German, like Greek, is so fertile. Consequently I have attempted in these translations to write something resembling English prose rather than anglicized German. Where there appeared to be ambiguities (intended or unintended) in the original, I have if possible made the corresponding English words ambiguous in a similar way. Where these versions seem to be inexact, I must ask the well-disposed to believe that there has been a specific linguistic or stylistic reason; where they in fact unwittingly distort or obscure Goethe's meaning, I must apologize to the experts for my lack of discernment. But a prose translation of poetry can in any case never (and a verse translation hardly ever) pretend to be more than a crude propaedeutic guide to what has obviously no substitute: the original text.

In making these versions I have owed much to the annotations provided by the German editions, particularly those mentioned above; and for the Introduction I must further acknowledge a general indebtedness, which will be perceived by the learned, to the writings of Professor Staiger. I have also, among a number of patient colleagues and friends whose valuable suggestions have contributed to the emendation of the typescript or the proofs, to thank most especially Professor E. M. Wilkinson and Mr W. H. Auden for their constant encouragement and expert guidance on many problems.

I

THE YOUNGER GOETHE

(1766–86)

A SONG OVER THE UNCONFIDENCE
TOWARD MYSELF

THOU knowst how heappily they Freind
 Walks upon florid Ways;
Thou knowst how heavens bounteous hand
 Leads him to golden days.

But hah! a cruel ennemy
 Destroies all that Bless;
In Moments of Melancholy
 Flies all my Happiness.

Then fogs of doubt do fill my mind
 With deep obscurity;
I search my self, and cannot find
 A spark of Worth in me.

When tender freinds, to tender kiss,
 Run up with open arms;
I think I merit not that bliss
 That like a kiss me warmeth.

Hah! when my child, I love thee, sayd,
 And gave the kiss I sought;
Then I – forgive me tender maid –
 She is a false one, thought.

She cannot love a peevish boy,
 She with her godlike face.
O could I, freind, that thought destroy.
 It leads the golden days.

And other thought is misfortune
 Is death and night to me:
I hum no supportable tune,
 I can no poet be.

When to the Altar of the Nine
 A triste incense I bring,
I beg let Poetry be mine
 O Sistres let me sing.

But when they then my prayer not hear
 I break my wispring lyre;
Then from my eyes runns down a tear,
 Extinguish th' incensed fire.

Then curse I, Freind, the fated sky,
 And from th' altar I fly;
And to my Freinds aloud I cry
 Be happier then I.

WHAT pleasure, God! of like a flame to born,
A virteous fire, that ne'er to vice can turn.
What volupty! when trembling in my arms,
The bosom of my maid my bosom warmeth!
Perpetual kisses of her lips o'erflow,
In holy embrace mighty virtue show.
When I then, rapt, in never felt extase,
My maid! I say, and she, my dearest! says.
When then, my heart, of love and virtue hot,
Cries: come ye angels! Come! See and envy me not.

LE VÉRITABLE AMI

VA te sévrer des baisers de ta belle,
Me dit un jour l'ami; par son air séduisant,
Ses yeux perçans, par son teint éclatant,
Sa taille mince, son langage amusant
Elle te pourroit bien déranger la cervelle;
Fuis de cette beauté le dangereux amour!
Mais pour te faire voir à quel degré je t'aime,
Je veux t'ôter tout espoir du retour
En m'en faisant aimer moi-même.

DIE SCHÖNE NACHT

NUN verlaß ich diese Hütte,
Meiner Liebsten Aufenthalt,
Wandle mit verhülltem Schritte
Durch den öden finstern Wald.
Luna bricht durch Busch und Eichen,
Zephir meldet ihren Lauf,
Und die Birken streun mit Neigen
Ihr den süßten Weihrauch auf.

THE TRUE FRIEND

'COME, wean yourself' (said my friend to me one day) 'from your sweet-
heart's kisses: with her seductive looks, her piercing eyes, her brilliant
complexion, her slender figure, her diverting talk, she may drive you
crazy; flee that fair lady and her dangerous love! But to show you how
fond of you I am, I shall take from you all hope of going back to her by
winning her love myself.'

THE BEAUTIFUL NIGHT

NOW I leave this hut, my sweetheart's dwelling, and walk with stealthy
steps through the dark desolate wood. The Moon breaks through bushes
and oak-trees, the West Wind heralds her course, and the bowing birch-
trees scatter the sweetest incense in her path.

Wie ergötz ich mich im Kühlen
Dieser schönen Sommernacht!
O wie still ist hier zu fühlen,
Was die Seele glücklich macht!
Läßt sich kaum die Wonne fassen!
Und doch wollt ich, Himmel, dir
Tausend solcher Nächte lassen,
Gäb mein Mädchen Eine mir.

MIT EINEM GEMALTEN BAND

Kleine Blumen, kleine Blätter
Streuen mir mit leichter Hand
Gute junge Frühlingsgötter
Tändelnd auf ein luftig Band.

Zephir, nimms auf deine Flügel,
Schlings um meiner Liebsten Kleid;
Und so tritt sie vor den Spiegel
All in ihrer Munterkeit.

How exquisite is the coolness of this beautiful summer night! How the heart fills with happiness in this quiet place! A delight that can scarcely be grasped! – And yet, Heaven, I would forgo a thousand such nights if my darling would only give me one.

TO ACCOMPANY A PAINTED RIBBON

On to this airy ribbon, playfully, lighthandedly, young kindly gods of spring scatter little flowers, little leaves.

Take it, West Wind, on your wings, and wind it round my sweetheart's dress: then she will step in front of the mirror, in all her lively charm.

Sieht mit Rosen sich umgeben,
Selbst wie eine Rose jung.
Einen Blick, geliebtes Leben!
Und ich bin belohnt genung.

Fühle, was dies Herz empfindet,
Reiche frei mir deine Hand,
Und das Band, das uns verbindet,
Sei kein schwaches Rosenband!

MAILIED

WIE herrlich leuchtet
Mir die Natur!
Wie glänzt die Sonne!
Wie lacht die Flur!

Es dringen Blüten
Aus jedem Zweig
Und tausend Stimmen
Aus dem Gesträuch

Und Freud und Wonne
Aus jeder Brust.
O Erd, o Sonne!
O Glück, o Lust!

She will see herself surrounded by roses – she who is herself young like a rose. One look only, my darling! and I am sufficiently rewarded.

Feel what this heart of mine is feeling, freely give me your hand – and may the bond that binds us be no frail ribbon of roses!

MAY SONG

How splendid is the brightness of Nature around me! how the sun shines, how the fields laugh!

Blossoms are bursting from every twig, and a thousand voices from the undergrowth,

and joy and rapture from every heart. Oh earth, oh sun! Oh happiness, oh delight!

7

O Lieb, o Liebe!
So golden schön,
Wie Morgenwolken
Auf jenen Höhn!

Du segnest herrlich
Das frische Feld,
Im Blütendampfe
Die volle Welt.

O Mädchen, Mädchen,
Wie lieb ich dich!
Wie blickt dein Auge!
Wie liebst du mich!

So liebt die Lerche
Gesang und Luft,
Und Morgenblumen
Den Himmelsduft,

Wie ich dich liebe
Mit warmem Blut,
Die du mir Jugend
Und Freud und Mut

Zu neuen Liedern
Und Tänzen gibst.
Sei ewig glücklich,
Wie du mich liebst!

Oh love, oh love! so golden, so beautiful, like the morning clouds on those hills!

Your splendour blesses the fresh fields and the fullness of the world in a mist of blossoms.

Oh sweet, sweet girl, how I love you! How your eyes shine! How you love me!

The lark loves singing and air, and the morning flowers love the scent of the sky,

as I love you, warm-bloodedly, you who give me youth and joy

and hearten me to new songs and new dances. Be happy for ever as in your love for me!

WILLKOMMEN UND ABSCHIED

Es schlug mein Herz, geschwind zu Pferde!
Es war getan fast eh gedacht.
Der Abend wiegte schon die Erde,
Und an den Bergen hing die Nacht;
Schon stand im Nebelkleid die Eiche,
Ein aufgetürmter Riese, da,
Wo Finsternis aus dem Gesträuche
Mit hundert schwarzen Augen sah.

Der Mond von einem Wolkenhügel
Sah kläglich aus dem Duft hervor,
Die Winde schwangen leise Flügel,
Umsausten schauerlich mein Ohr;
Die Nacht schuf tausend Ungeheuer,
Doch frisch und fröhlich war mein Mut:
In meinen Adern welches Feuer!
In meinem Herzen welche Glut!

Dich sah ich, und die milde Freude
Floß von dem süßen Blick auf mich;
Ganz war mein Herz an deiner Seite
Und jeder Atemzug für dich.

WELCOME AND FAREWELL

My heart beat: swiftly to horse! Sooner almost than thought it was done. Already the earth lay cradled in evening's arms, and night hung on the hills; there already the oak-tree stood, mist-cloaked, a towering giant, and a hundred eyes of black darkness looked out of the undergrowth.

The moon, from a cloud-bank, gazed sadly out through the haze; the winds beat their soft wings and whirred round my dread-stricken ears; the night brought forth a thousand monsters, but my spirits were high and glad: what fire in my veins! what warmth in my heart!

I saw you, and your sweet eyes poured upon me a full measure of joy; my heart was with you, undivided, and every breath I drew was drawn for you.

Ein rosenfarbnes Frühlingswetter
Umgab das liebliche Gesicht,
Und Zärtlichkeit für mich – ihr Götter!
Ich hofft es, ich verdient es nicht!

Doch ach, schon mit der Morgensonne
Verengt der Abschied mir das Herz:
In deinen Küssen welche Wonne!
In deinem Auge welcher Schmerz!
Ich ging, du standst und sahst zur Erden
Und sahst mir nach mit nassem Blick:
Und doch, welch Glück, geliebt zu werden!
Und lieben, Götter, welch ein Glück!

HEIDENRÖSLEIN

S AH ein Knab ein Röslein stehn,
Röslein auf der Heiden,
War so jung und morgenschön,
Lief er schnell, es nah zu sehn,
Sahs mit vielen Freuden.
Röslein, Röslein, Röslein rot,
Röslein auf der Heiden.

A rose-red light of spring shone round your lovely face, which looked at me with such tenderness – oh God! I had hoped for this but never deserved it!

But oh, at sunrise already the pain of parting pressed on my heart; what ecstasy there was in your kisses, what sorrow in your eyes! I went, and you stood looking down, looking after me with tear-filled gaze. And yet, what happiness it is to be loved! and to love, oh God! what happiness!

ROSE ON THE HEATH

A BOY saw a rose growing, a little rose on the heath; it was so young and lovely as the morning: quickly he ran to see it from near, and with much delight he saw it. Rose, rose, little red rose, little rose on the heath.

Knabe sprach: Ich breche dich,
Röslein auf der Heiden!
Röslein sprach: Ich steche dich,
Daß du ewig denkst an mich,
Und ich wills nicht leiden.
Röslein, Röslein, Röslein rot,
Röslein auf der Heiden.

Und der wilde Knabe brach
's Röslein auf der Heiden;
Röslein wehrte sich und stach,
Half ihm doch kein Weh und Ach,
Mußt es eben leiden.
Röslein, Röslein, Röslein rot,
Röslein auf der Heiden.

DAS VEILCHEN

Ein Veilchen auf der Wiese stand
Gebückt in sich und unbekannt;
Es war ein herzigs Veilchen.
Da kam eine junge Schäferin
Mit leichtem Schritt und munterm Sinn
Daher, daher,
Die Wiese her, und sang.

Said the boy: I shall pick you, little rose on the heath! Said the rose: I shall prick you, so that you shall never forget me; I won't let you do it! Rose, rose, little red rose, little rose on the heath.

And the rough boy picked the little rose on the heath; the rose defended herself and pricked, but her cries and sighs were in vain, she just had to let it happen. Rose, rose, little red rose, little rose on the heath.

THE VIOLET

A violet stood on the meadow, with bowed head and unnoticed; it was a dear sweet violet. And along came a young shepherdess, light of step and gay of heart, along, along through the meadow, singing.

Ach! denkt das Veilchen, wär ich nur
Die schönste Blume der Natur,
Ach, nur ein kleines Weilchen,
Bis mich das Liebchen abgepflückt
Und an dem Busen matt gedrückt!
Ach nur, ach nur
Ein Viertelstündchen lang!

Ach! aber ach! das Mädchen kam
Und nicht in acht das Veilchen nahm,
Ertrat das arme Veilchen.
Es sank und starb und freut' sich noch:
Und sterb ich denn, so sterb ich doch
Durch sie, durch sie,
Zu ihren Füßen doch.

ZIGEUNERLIED *

IM Nebelgeriesel, im tiefen Schnee,
Im wilden Wald, in der Winternacht,
Ich hörte der Wölfe Hungergeheul,
Ich hörte der Eulen Geschrei.
 Wille wau wau wau!
 Wille wo wo wo!
 Wito hu!

Ah! – thinks the violet – if only I were the loveliest flower in all Nature, oh only for a little while! till my darling had picked me and pressed me to death on her bosom – oh, only, only for a quarter of an hour!

But alas! alas, the girl came, and did not notice the violet, and trampled the poor violet down. It drooped and died, yet still rejoiced: Though I die, nevertheless I am dying by her, by her, at her feet nevertheless.

GIPSY SONG

UNDER cloud and drizzle, in deep snow, in the wild wood, in the wintry night, I heard the wolves' hungry howling, I heard the screech of owls. Willo wow wow wow! Willo wo wo wo! Wito hu!

* From the first version of the play *Götz von Berlichingen.*

Ich schoß einmal eine Katz am Zaun,
Der Anne, der Hex, ihre schwarze liebe Katz.
Da kamen des Nachts sieben Werwölf zu mir,
Waren sieben sieben Weiber vom Dorf.
 Wille wau wau wau!
 Wille wo wo wo!
 Wito hu!

Ich kannte sie all, ich kannte sie wohl,
Die Anne, die Ursel, die Käth,
Die Liese, die Barbe, die Ev, die Beth,
Sie heulten im Kreise mich an.
 Wille wau wau wau!
 Wille wo wo wo!
 Wito hu!

Da nannt ich sie alle bei Namen laut:
Was willst du, Anne? was willst du, Beth?
Da rüttelten sie sich, da schüttelten sie sich,
Und liefen und heulten davon.
 Wille wau wau wau!
 Wille wo wo wo!
 Wito hu!

Once I shot a cat beside the hedge, it was Annie's, the witch, her black pet cat. And at night seven werewolves came to me, they were seven seven women from the village. Willo wow wow wow! Willo wo wo wo! Wito hu!

I knew them well, every one of them: Annie and Sally and Kate and Lizzy and Jenny and Edie and Betty; they made a ring round me and howled at me. Willo wow wow wow! Willo wo wo wo! Wito hu!

So I called them all by their names out loud: What's the matter, Annie? What's the matter, Betty? Then they wobbled and they shook themselves, and ran away howling. Willo wow wow wow! Willo wo wo wo! Wito hu!

13

DER MUSENSOHN *

Durch Feld und Wald zu schweifen,
Mein Liedchen wegzupfeifen,
So gehts von Ort zu Ort!
Und nach dem Takte reget,
Und nach dem Maß beweget
Sich alles an mir fort.

Ich kann sie kaum erwarten,
Die erste Blum im Garten,
Die erst Blüt am Baum.
Sie grüßen meine Lieder,
Und kommt der Winter wieder,
Sing ich noch jenen Traum.

Ich sing ihn in der Weite,
Auf Eises Läng und Breite,
Da blüht der Winter schön!
Auch diese Blüte schwindet,
Und neue Freude findet
Sich auf bebauten Höhn.

THE SON OF THE MUSES

Roaming through fields and woods, whistling out my song, I go from place to place! And they all stir, they all move on in measure with me, keeping time with me.

I can scarcely wait for them to appear, the first flower in the garden, the first blossom on the tree. They greet my songs, and when winter comes again I am still singing my dream of them.

I sing it far and wide, up and down and across the ice, and the winter blossoms in beauty! This blossom also vanishes, and new pleasures are to be found on the fertile hillsides.

* The date of this poem is disputed. It may have been written in the 1770s or in the 1790s.

Denn wie ich bei der Linde
Das junge Völkchen finde,
Sogleich erreg ich sie.
Der stumpfe Bursche bläht sich,
Das steife Mädchen dreht sich
Nach meiner Melodie.

Ihr gebt den Sohlen Flügel
Und treibt durch Tal und Hügel
Den Liebling weit von Haus.
Ihr lieben holden Musen,
Wann ruh ich ihr am Busen
Auch endlich wieder aus?

GANYMED

Wie im Morgenglanze
Du rings mich anglühst,
Frühling, Geliebter!
Mit tausendfacher Liebeswonne
Sich an mein Herz drängt
Deiner ewigen Wärme
Heilig Gefühl,
Unendliche Schöne!

For when, under the linden tree, I find a crowd of young people, I at once stir them to excitement. Dull lads puff themselves up and prim girls pirouette to my melody.

You who give my feet wings, and drive your favourite far from home over hill and dale – you dear sweet Muses, when shall I at last find rest again on her bosom?

GANYMEDE

How you glow upon me, in the brightness of morning, all round me, oh Spring, my lover! With thousandfold rapturous love the holy sense of your everlasting warmth presses against my heart, oh infinite beauty!

Daß ich dich fassen möcht
In diesen Arm!

Ach, an deinem Busen
Lieg ich, schmachte,
Und deine Blumen, dein Gras
Drängen sich an mein Herz.
Du kühlst den brennenden
Durst meines Busens,
Lieblicher Morgenwind!
Ruft drein die Nachtigall
Liebend nach mir aus dem Nebeltal.

Ich komm, ich komme!
Wohin? Ach, wohin?

Hinauf! Hinauf strebts.
Es schweben die Wolken
Abwärts, die Wolken
Neigen sich der sehnenden Liebe.
Mir! Mir!
In euerm Schoße
Aufwärts!
Umfangend umfangen!
Aufwärts an deinen Busen,
Alliebender Vater!

If only I could clasp you in my arms!

Oh, I lie at your breast, I languish, and your flowers and your grass press against my heart. You cool my bosom's burning thirst, dear wind of morning! Out of the misty valley the nightingale calls out to me in love.

I come, I come! Whither, oh whither?

Upwards! upwards I am driven. The clouds float down, the clouds descend to my love and my longing. To me! to me! Aloft, enveloped by you! embraced and embracing! Aloft, to lie at your breast, all-loving father!

PROMETHEUS

BEDECKE deinen Himmel, Zeus,
Mit Wolkendunst
Und übe, dem Knaben gleich,
Der Disteln köpft,
An Eichen dich und Bergeshöhn;
Mußt mir meine Erde
Doch lassen stehn
Und meine Hütte, die du nicht gebaut,
Und meinen Herd,
Um dessen Glut
Du mich beneidest.

Ich kenne nichts Ärmeres
Unter der Sonn als euch, Götter!
Ihr nähret kümmerlich
Von Opfersteuern
Und Gebetshauch
Eure Majestät
Und darbtet, wären
Nicht Kinder und Bettler
Hoffnungsvolle Toren.

PROMETHEUS

COVER your sky, Zeus, with vaporous clouds, and try out, like a boy knocking the heads off thistles, your strength against oak trees and mountain-tops: you still must leave me my earth standing, and my hut which you did not build, and my hearth for whose warm glow you envy me.

I know of no poorer thing under the sun than you gods! Wretchedly you feed your majesty on sacrificial offerings and the breath of prayers, and you would starve if children and beggars were not fools full of hopes.

17

Da ich ein Kind war,
Nicht wußte, wo aus noch ein,
Kehrt ich mein verirrtes Auge
Zur Sonne, als wenn drüber wär
Ein Ohr, zur hören meine Klage,
Ein Herz wie meins,
Sich des Bedrängten zu erbarmen.

Wer half mir
Wider der Titanen Übermut?
Wer rettete vom Tode mich,
Von Sklaverei?
Hast du nicht alles selbst vollendet,
Heilig glühend Herz?
Und glühtest jung und gut,
Betrogen, Rettungsdank
Dem Schlafenden da droben?

Ich dich ehren? Wofür?
Hast du die Schmerzen gelindert
Je des Beladenen?
Hast du die Tränen gestillet
Je des Geängsteten?
Hat nicht mich zum Manne geschmiedet
Die allmächtige Zeit
Und das ewige Schicksal,
Meine Herrn und deine?

When I was a child and did not know which way to turn, I would raise my misguided eyes to the sun, as though up beyond it there were an ear that would hear my complaint, a heart like my own that would have pity on me in my anguish.

Who helped me against the overweening Titans? Who saved me from death, from slavery? Did you not accomplish all this yourself, oh my holy glowing heart? And in your youthful well-meaning error did you not glow with gratitude, for your deliverance, to that Sleeper up there?

I, honour you? Why? Did you ever allay the agony that weighed me down? Did you ever dry my terrified tears? Was I not forged into manhood by almighty Time and everlasting Destiny, my masters and yours?

Wähntest du etwa,
Ich sollte das Leben hassen,
In Wüsten fliehen,
Weil nicht alle
Blütenträume reiften?

Hier sitz ich, forme Menschen
Nach meinem Bilde,
Ein Geschlecht, das mir gleich sei,
Zu leiden, zu weinen,
Zu genießen und zu freuen sich,
Und dein nicht zu achten,
Wie ich!

MAHOMETSGESANG

SEHT den Felsenquell,
Freudehell,
Wie ein Sternenblick;
Über Wolken
Nährten seine Jugend
Gute Geister
Zwischen Klippen im Gebüsch.

Perhaps you thought I should find life hateful, and run away into wildernesses, because not all my dreams blossomed to maturity?

Here I sit, making men in my own image, a race that shall resemble me, a race that shall suffer and weep, and know joy and delight, and be heedless of you, as I am!

A SONG FOR MAHOMMED*

BEHOLD this spring among the rocks, bright with joy, like a gleam of stars: above the clouds its youth was nurtured by good spirits, among cliffs, in the bushes.

* The title (more correctly, though not usually, printed as 'Mahomets-Gesang' or 'Mahometsgesang') does not mean that Mahommed himself is the singer. The poem was originally printed as a dialogue in praise of the Prophet between two of his followers.

Jünglingfrisch
Tanzt er aus der Wolke
Auf die Marmorfelsen nieder,
Jauchzet wieder
Nach dem Himmel.

Durch die Gipfelgänge
Jagt er bunten Kieseln nach,
Und mit frühem Führertritt
Reißt er seine Bruderquellen
Mit sich fort.

Drunten werden in dem Tal
Unter seinem Fußtritt Blumen,
Und die Wiese
Lebt von seinem Hauch.

Doch ihn hält kein Schattental,
Keine Blumen,
Die ihm seine Knie umschlingen,
Ihm mit Liebes-Augen schmeicheln:
Nach der Ebne dringt sein Lauf
Schlangenwandelnd.

Bäche schmiegen
Sich gesellig an. Nun tritt er
In die Ebne silberprangend,

Fresh as a boy it comes dancing out of the cloud, down on to the marble rocks, and rejoices again to the sky.

Along paths through the peaks it runs after many-coloured pebbles, and its step is that of a young leader, carrying his brother springs away with him.

Down in the valley, flowers are born beneath his tread, and his breath gives life to the meadow.

But no shady valley can retain him, no flowers embracing his knees and flattering him with looks of love: he presses on his course towards the plain, snakewise-winding.

Streams come close to his side for company. And now, silver-resplendent, he enters the plain, and the plain is resplendent with him, and the rivers

Und die Ebne prangt mit ihm,
Und die Flüsse von der Ebne
Und die Bäche von den Bergen
Jauchzen ihm und rufen: Bruder!
Bruder, nimm die Brüder mit,
Mit zu deinem alten Vater,
Zu dem ewgen Ozean,
Der mit ausgespannten Armen
Unser wartet,
Die sich, ach! vergebens öffnen,
Seine Sehnenden zu fassen;
Denn uns frißt in öder Wüste
Gierger Sand; die Sonne droben
Saugt an unserm Blut; ein Hügel
Hemmet uns zum Teiche! Bruder,
Nimm die Brüder von der Ebne,
Nimm die Brüder von den Bergen
Mit, zu deinem Vater mit!

Kommt ihr alle! –
Und nun schwillt er
Herrlicher; ein ganz Geschlechte
Trägt den Fürsten hoch empor!
Und im rollenden Triumphe
Gibt er Ländern Namen, Städte
Werden unter seinem Fuß.

of the plain and the streams from the mountains shout to him in exultation:
Brother! Brother, take your brothers with you, with you to your ancient
father, to the everlasting ocean, who awaits us with outstretched arms –
opening them, alas, in vain to embrace his yearning children! For we are
devoured in desolate wastes by greedy sand: the sun up yonder sucks our
blood: a hill hems us in, dams us into a pond! Brother, take your brothers
from the plain, your brothers from the mountains with you, with you to
your father!

Come, all of you! – And now more magnificently he swells: a whole race
raises this prince on high! and in triumph onward rolling he names lands,
stamps cities out of the ground.

Unaufhaltsam rauscht er weiter,
Läßt der Türme Flammengipfel,
Marmorhäuser, eine Schöpfung
Seiner Fülle, hinter sich.

Zedernhäuser trägt der Atlas
Auf den Riesenschultern; sausend
Wehen über seinem Haupte
Tausend Flaggen durch die Lüfte,
Zeugen seiner Herrlichkeit.

Und so trägt er seine Brüder,
Seine Schätze, seine Kinder
Dem erwartenden Erzeuger
Freudebrausend an das Herz.

KÜNSTLERS ABENDLIED

Ach, daß die innre Schöpfungskraft
Durch meinen Sinn erschölle!
Daß eine Bildung voller Saft
Aus meinen Fingern quölle!

Irresistibly he rushes on, leaving behind him flame-topped towers, houses of marble, works of his creative fullness.

Atlas-like, he carries houses of cedar on his giant shoulders; over his head a thousand banners stream noisily through the air, testifying to his magnificence.

And thus he carries his brothers, his treasures, his children, all tumultuous with joy, to their waiting Parent's bosom.

THE ARTIST'S EVENING HYMN

Oh for an inner creative power to thunder through my mind! Oh for a growth full-flowing with sap to spring from my fingers!

Ich zittre nur, ich stottre nur,
Und kann es doch nicht lassen;
Ich fühl, ich kenne dich, Natur,
Und so muß ich dich fassen.

Bedenk ich dann, wie manches Jahr
Sich schon mein Sinn erschließet,
Wie er, wo dürre Heide war,
Nun Freudenquell genießet;

Wie sehn ich mich, Natur, nach dir,
Dich treu und lieb zu fühlen!
Ein lustger Springbrunn wirst du mir
Aus tausend Röhren spielen.

Wirst alle meine Kräfte mir
In meinem Sinn erheitern
Und dieses enge Dasein hier
Zur Ewigkeit erweitern.

I only shudder, I only stutter, and yet I cannot stop; I feel you, I know you, Nature, and so I must grasp you.

When I think then how my mind, these many years, has been opening up, and now tastes a stream of delight where a barren waste used to be –

oh then how I long for you, Nature, and long to feel you with faith and love! You will be for me a leaping fountain of delight, playing from a thousand outlets.

You will enhance and refine all the powers of my mind, and expand this my narrow life to eternity.

LEGENDE

IN der Wüsten ein heiliger Mann
Zu seinem Erstaunen tät treffen an
Einen ziegenfüßigen Faun, der sprach:
«Herr, betet für mich und meine Gefährt,
Daß ich zum Himmel gelassen werd,
Zur seligen Freud; uns dürstet darnach.»
Der heilige Mann dagegen sprach:
«Es sieht mit deiner Bitte gar gefährlich,
Und gewährt wird sie dir schwerlich.
Du kommst nicht zum Englischen Gruß,
Denn du hast einen Ziegenfuß.»
Da sprach hierauf der wilde Mann:
«Was hat euch mein Ziegenfuß getan?
Sah ich doch manche strack und schön
Mit Eselsköpfen gen Himmel gehn.»

KATECHISATION

LEHRER: Bedenk, o Kind! woher sind diese Gaben?
Du kannst nichts von dir selber haben.

A LEGEND

A HOLY man in the wilderness met, to his bewilderment, a goat-footed
faun, who said: 'Sir, pray for me and my companions, that I may be ad-
mitted to heaven and its blessed joys; we thirst after them.' The holy
man replied: 'Your request's a bold one, and I can't see much chance of its being
granted. You don't come to church when they ring the Angelus, for you
have a cloven hoof.' To which the wild man made answer: 'What have you
got against my cloven hoof? After all I've seen many a man go straight
bang up to heaven with an ass's head.'

CATECHIZATION

TEACHER: Consider, child! from whom do these gifts come? You can
have nothing from yourself.

KIND: Ei! Alles hab ich vom Papa.
LEHRER: Und der, woher hats der?
KIND: Vom Großpapa.
LEHRER: Nicht doch! Woher hats denn der Großpapa bekommen?
KIND: Der hats genommen.

[DINER ZU COBLENZ]

ZWISCHEN Lavater und Basedow
Saß ich bei Tisch des Lebens froh.
Herr Helfer, der war gar nicht faul,
Setzt' sich auf einen schwarzen Gaul,
Nahm einen Pfarrer hinter sich
Und auf die Offenbarung strich,
Die uns Johannes der Prophet
Mit Rätseln wohl versiegeln tät;
Eröffnet' die Siegel kurz und gut,
Wie man Theriaksbüchsen öffnen tut,

CHILD: Oh, I get it all from Daddy.
TEACHER: And he? where did he get it from?
CHILD: From Grandpapa.
TEACHER: No, no! How did it all come to Grandpapa then?
CHILD: He took it.

[DINNER AT COBLENZ]

BETWEEN Lavater and Basedow* I sat at table enjoying life. Mr Curate, with unflagging zeal, mounted a black nag, seated a parson behind him, and ran a tilt at Revelation, a book well sealed with riddles for us by the prophet John; he undid the seals in no time, like someone opening jars of venom-

* Two friends of Goethe (a fundamentalist clergyman and an educational theorist) who accompanied him on a trip down the Rhine in 1774.

Und maß mit einem heilgen Rohr
Die Kubusstadt und das Perlentor
Dem hocherstaunten Jünger vor.
Ich war indes nicht weit gereist,
Hatte ein Stück Salmen aufgespeist.

Vater Basedow, unter dieser Zeit,
Packt einen Tanzmeister an seiner Seit
Und zeigt ihm, was die Taufe klar
Bei Christ und seinen Jüngern war;
Und daß sichs gar nicht ziemet jetzt,
Daß man den Kindern die Köpfe netzt.
Drob ärgert sich der andre sehr
Und wollte gar nichts hören mehr
Und sagt: es wüßte ein jedes Kind,
Daß es in der Bibel anders stünd.
Und ich behaglich unterdessen
Hätt einen Hahnen aufgefressen.

Und, wie nach Emmaus, weiter gings
Mit Geist- und Feuerschritten,
Prophete rechts, Prophete links,
Das Weltkind in der Mitten.

cure, and with a holy wand he measured the Cubic City and the Pearly Gates before the amazed eyes of his disciple. I, meanwhile, had made little headway, and had devoured a chunk of salmon.

In the meantime old man Basedow got hold of a dancing-master who was sitting beside him, and was demonstrating to him the plain meaning of baptism for Christ and his disciples, and proving that it is now quite incorrect for children to have their heads wetted. The other was much riled by this, and refused to go on listening. 'Any child' (he declared) 'will tell you that that is not what the Bible says.' And I, during all this, had comfortably tucked away a chicken.

And onward thus we paced, as at Emmaus, our spirit burning within us; a prophet to the right, a prophet to the left, and the child of this world in the middle.

REZENSENT

Da hatt ich einen Kerl zu Gast,
Er war mir eben nicht zur Last;
Ich hatt just mein gewöhnlich Essen,
Hat sich der Kerl pumpsatt gefressen,
Zum Nachtisch, was ich gespeichert hatt.
Und kaum ist mir der Kerl so satt,
Tut ihn der Teufel zum Nachbar führen,
Über mein Essen zu räsonnieren:
«Die Supp hätt können gewürzter sein,
Der Braten brauner, firner der Wein.»
Der Tausendsakerment!
Schlagt ihn tot, den Hund! Es ist ein Rezensent.

NICOLAI AUF WERTHERS GRABE

Ein junger Mensch, ich weiß nicht, wie,
Starb einst an der Hypochondrie
Und ward denn auch begraben.

THE REVIEWER

I had a fellow to dinner – it happened not to be inconvenient; I was just having my usual fare, as it chanced, and this fellow stuffed himself fit to burst and finished all the dessert I had saved up. Well, the fellow has scarcely eaten his fill when devil take it if he doesn't call on my neighbour and discuss my meal: 'The soup might have been richer, the roast better done, the wine more mature.' God's eternal damnation! Knock him dead, the swine: he's a reviewer!

NICOLAI* ON WERTHER'S GRAVE

A young man once, I don't know why,/of melancholy spleen did die/and was duly buried too./Then along came a *bel esprit*, whose belly was running

*A critic who had written *The Joys of Young Werther*, a parody of Goethe's novel.

Da kam ein schöner Geist herbei,
Der hatte seinen Stuhlgang frei,
Wie's denn so Leute haben.
Der setzt' notdürftig sich aufs Grab
Und legte da sein Häuflein ab,
Beschaute freundlich seinen Dreck,
Ging wohl eratmet wieder weg
Und sprach zu sich bedächtiglich:
«Der gute Mensch, er dauert mich,
Wie hat er sich verdorben!
Hätt er geschissen so wie ich,
Er wäre nicht gestorben!»

STOSSGEBET

VOR Werthers Leiden,
Mehr noch vor seinen Freuden
Bewahr uns, lieber Herre Gott!

rather free,/as people's bellies sometimes do./He sat down, as it wouldn't keep,/on the grave, and left his little heap;/benignly his muck he contemplated,/went his ways much alleviated,/and musing to himself did say:/ 'Poor fellow! a life spent amiss!/I'm sorry he has passed away./If he'd only learnt to shit like this,/he'd be alive today!'

EJACULATORY PRAYER

FROM Werther's Sorrows, and still more from his Joys, good Lord deliver us!

HYPOCHONDER

DER Teufel hol das Menschengeschlecht!
Man möchte rasend werden!
Da nehm ich mir so eifrig vor:
Will niemand weiter sehen,
Will all das Volk Gott und sich selbst
Und dem Teufel überlassen!
Und kaum seh ich ein Menschengesicht,
So hab ichs wieder lieb.

NEUE LIEBE NEUES LEBEN

HERZ, mein Herz, was soll das geben?
Was bedränget dich so sehr?
Welch ein fremdes, neues Leben!
Ich erkenne dich nicht mehr.
Weg ist alles, was du liebtest,
Weg, warum du dich betrübtest,
Weg dein Fleiß und deine Ruh –
Ach, wie kamst du nur dazu!

SPLEEN

DEVIL take the human race! It's enough to drive one crazy! I keep making
such firm resolutions to stop seeing people altogether and consign the
whole nation to God and itself and the devil! And then I have only to catch
sight of a human face and I love it again.

NEW LOVE, NEW LIFE

OH, heart, my heart, what does this mean? What is it that so besets you?
What strange new life! I no longer recognize you. Gone is all you used
to love, gone is all that used to grieve you; gone is work and peace of
mind; oh, how can this have come about?

Fesselt dich die Jugendblüte,
Diese liebliche Gestalt,
Dieser Blick voll Treu und Güte
Mit unendlicher Gewalt?
Will ich rasch mich ihr entziehen,
Mich ermannen, ihr entfliehen,
Führet mich im Augenblick,
Ach, mein Weg zu ihr zurück.

Und an diesem Zauberfädchen,
Das sich nicht zerreißen läßt,
Hält das liebe, lose Mädchen
Mich so wider Willen fest:
Muß in ihrem Zauberkreise
Leben nun auf ihre Weise.
Die Verändrung, ach, wie groß!
Liebe! Liebe! laß mich los!

AN BELINDEN

WARUM ziehst du mich unwiderstehlich,
Ach, in jene Pracht?
War ich guter Junge nicht so selig
In der öden Nacht?

Are you ensnared by the bloom of youth, by that lovely figure, those eyes so faithful and kind – ensnared with irresistible force? When I try to run away from her, to pull myself together and quickly escape her – in a moment my way leads me, alas, back to her again.

And thus, by this magic thread that cannot be broken, the dear wanton girl holds me fast against my will; I must live now in her magic circle and in her way. Oh, how great a change this is! Oh love, love, let me go!

TO BELINDA

WHY do you draw me, alas, irresistibly, in among all that finery? Was I not happy – decent simple fellow that I am – in my wilderness and outer darkness?

Heimlich in mein Zimmerchen verschlossen,
Lag im Mondenschein,
Ganz von seinem Schauerlicht umflossen,
Und ich dämmert ein;

Träumte da von vollen goldnen Stunden
Ungemischter Lust,
Hatte schon dein liebes Bild empfunden
Tief in meiner Brust.

Bin ichs noch, den du bei so viel Lichtern
An dem Spieltisch hältst?
Oft so unerträglichen Gesichtern
Gegenüber stellst?

Reizender ist mir des Frühlings Blüte
Nun nicht auf der Flur:
Wo du, Engel, bist, ist Lieb und Güte,
Wo du bist, Natur.

Secret and secluded in my little room, there I lay in the moonlight, its
eerie radiance pouring all over me; and I would doze off
 and dream of crowded golden hours of unmixed delight – your sweet
image had already struck deep into my heart.
 Can this still be myself, whom you hold captive at the card-table among
all these bright lights, often forcing me to look across at such insufferable
faces?
 Not even the blossoming spring in the meadows holds more charm for
me now: darling, where you are, there is love and kindness – where you
are, there Nature is.

AUF DEM SEE

UND frische Nahrung, neues Blut
Saug ich aus freier Welt;
Wie ist Natur so hold und gut,
Die mich am Busen hält!
Die Welle wieget unsern Kahn
Im Rudertakt hinauf,
Und Berge, wolkig himmelan,
Begegnen unserm Lauf.

Aug, mein Aug, was sinkst du nieder?
Goldne Träume, kommt ihr wieder?
Weg, du Traum! so gold du bist;
Hier auch Lieb und Leben ist.

Auf der Welle blinken
Tausend schwebende Sterne,
Weiche Nebel trinken
Rings die türmende Ferne;
Morgenwind umflügelt
Die beschattete Bucht,
Und im See bespiegelt
Sich die reifende Frucht.

ON THE LAKE

AND from these open spaces I suck fresh nourishment and new blood; how sweet and kindly is Nature who holds me to her breast! Our boat rocks up and down on the water in time with the oars, and mountains rise cloudily skywards in our path.

Oh, my eyes, why are you drooping? Are you returning, you golden dreams? Begone, dream, golden as you are! There is love and life here too.

On the water a thousand stars drift and glitter; soft clouds drink up the towering skyline; a breeze of morning speeds round the shadowy bay, and the lake mirrors the ripening fruit.

HERBSTGEFÜHL

FETTER grüne, du Laub,
Am Rebengeländer
Hier mein Fenster herauf!
Gedrängter quellet,
Zwillingsbeeren, und reifet
Schneller und glänzend voller!
Euch brütet der Mutter Sonne
Scheideblick, euch umsäuselt
Des holden Himmels
Fruchtende Fülle;
Euch kühlet des Mondes
Freundlicher Zauberhauch,
Und euch betauen, ach!
Aus diesen Augen
Der ewig belebenden Liebe
Vollschwellende Tränen.

AUTUMN MOOD

MORE lushly green, you leaves on the vine trellis, grow here up my
window! More thickly swell, twin berries, and ripen more quickly to more
lustrous fullness! The parting gleam of your mother the sun broods over
your birth; the sweet sky's fecund bounty suspires around you; the kindly
moon breathes cooling magic upon you, and ah! these eyes bedew you with
the full-flowing tears of love that eternally gives life.

HOLDE Lili, warst so lang
All mein Lust und all mein Sang!
Bist, ach, nun all mein Schmerz, und doch
All mein Sang bist du noch.

NUR Luft und Licht
Und Freundeslieb!
Ermüde nicht,
Wem dies noch blieb.

GENIALISCH TREIBEN

So wälz ich ohne Unterlaß,
Wie Sankt Diogenes, mein Faß.
Bald ist es Ernst, bald ist es Spaß;
Bald ist es Lieb, bald ist es Haß;
Bald ist es dies, bald ist es das;
Es ist ein Nichts und ist ein Was.
So wälz ich ohne Unterlaß,
Wie Sankt Diogenes, mein Faß.

SWEET Lili, for so long you were all my joy and all my song! Now, alas, you are all my sorrow, and yèt you are all my song still.

ONLY air and light and the love of friends! Let no man lose heart who still has these.

THE GENIUS-GAME

AND so, like St Diogenes, I roll my barrel on and on. Sometimes it's serious, sometimes a joke; sometimes love, sometimes hatred; sometimes this, sometimes that; it's a nothing and a something. And so, like St Diogenes, I roll my barrel on and on.

aus FAUST
(Part I, lines 354–97)
[FAUST IM STUDIERZIMMER]

HABE nun, ach! Philosophie,
Juristerei und Medizin
Und leider auch Theologie
Durchaus studiert, mit heißem Bemühn.
Da steh ich nun, ich armer Tor,
Und bin so klug als wie zuvor!
Heiße Magister, heiße Doktor gar,
Und ziehe schon an die zehen Jahr
Herauf, herab und quer und krumm
Meine Schüler an der Nase herum –
Und sehe, daß wir nichts wissen können!
Das will mir schier das Herz verbrennen.
Zwar bin ich gescheiter als alle die Laffen,
Doktoren, Magister, Schreiber und Pfaffen;
Mich plagen keine Skrupel noch Zweifel,
Fürchte mich weder vor Hölle noch Teufel –
Dafür ist mir auch alle Freud entrissen,
Bilde mir nicht ein, was Rechts zu wissen,
Bilde mir nicht ein, ich könnte was lehren,
Die Menschen zu bessern und zu bekehren.

from FAUST
[FAUST IN HIS STUDY]

AH, now I've studied philosophy, jurisprudence and medicine, and alas, theology as well, ardently and painstakingly, from beginning to end. And here I stand, poor fool that I am, as wise as I was before I started. I've the title of Master and even of Doctor, and for about ten years now I've led my pupils by the nose, up and down and around and to and fro – and I realize that we can know nothing! It nearly breaks my heart.

I've more sense, it's true, than all those fools – doctors and masters and clerks and priests; I'm plagued by no scruples or doubts, I fear neither hell nor the devil – but that, too, is why there is no joy left in me; I can't pretend to myself that I know anything worth knowing, can't pretend that I could ever teach anything that would better or edify mankind. What is

Auch hab ich weder Gut noch Geld,
Noch Ehr und Herrlichkeit der Welt:
Es möchte kein Hund so länger leben!
Drum hab ich mich der Magie ergeben,
Ob mir durch Geistes Kraft und Mund
Nicht manch Geheimnis würde kund,
Daß ich nicht mehr mit sauerm Schweiß
Zu sagen brauche, was ich nicht weiß,
Daß ich erkenne, was die Welt
Im Innersten zusammenhält,
Schau alle Wirkenskraft und Samen
Und tu nicht mehr in Worten kramen.

O sähst du, voller Mondenschein,
Zum letztenmal auf meine Pein,
Den ich so manche Mitternacht
An diesem Pult herangewacht:
Dann über Büchern und Papier,
Trübselger Freund, erschienst du mir!
Ach! könnt ich doch auf Bergeshöhn
In deinem lieben Lichte gehn,
Um Bergeshöhle mit Geistern schweben,
Auf Wiesen in deinem Dämmer weben,
Von allem Wissensqualm entladen,
In deinem Tau gesund mich baden!

more, I've neither money nor property nor worldly honour and glory: it's
a life not fit for a dog to go on living! This is why I have devoted myself to
magic, to try if the power and tutelage of spirits will not teach me many
mysteries – so that I may no longer, in the sweat of my brow, have to talk
about things of which I know nothing: that I may understand what holds
the world together in its innermost depths, and see all the Seeds and
the Forces of Life, and stop paddling and peddling in words.

Oh light of the full moon, how I wish you were looking your last on my
anguish! Many a midnight at this desk I have spent wakefully watching for
you, till over my books and papers, sad friend, you rose up before me! Oh,
how I wish I could be walking on mountain heights in your sweet radiance,
hovering with spirits round mountain hollows, floating over meadows in
your half-light, and shed all this burdening fog of knowledge, and bathe
and heal myself in your dew!

(Part I, lines 501–9)

[DER ERDGEIST]

In Lebensfluten, im Tatensturm
Wall ich auf und ab,
Wehe hin und her!
Geburt und Grab,
Ein ewiges Meer,
Ein wechselnd Weben,
Ein glühend Leben:
So schaff ich am sausenden Webstuhl der Zeit
Und wirke der Gottheit lebendiges Kleid.

(Part I, lines 2211–18, 2223–38)

[MEPHISTOS FLOHLIED]

Es war einmal ein König,
Der hatt einen großen Floh,
Den liebt er gar nicht wenig:
Als wie seinen eignen Sohn.
Da rief er seinen Schneider,
Der Schneider kam heran:
«Da, miß dem Junker Kleider
Und miß ihm Hosen an!»

[THE EARTH-SPIRIT]

In waves of living, in the storm of deeds, I float up and down, I blow hither and thither! Birth and the grave, an eternal sea, a weaving of change, a burning life: thus I work at Time's whirring loom, and weave the living garment of the Godhead.

[MEPHISTOPHELES' SONG OF THE FLEA]

There was once a king who had a large flea, which he loved dearly, as if it were his own son. So he called his tailor, and the tailor came: 'Here, measure this young gentleman for clothes, and make him breeches to measure!'

In Sammet und in Seide
War er nun angetan,
Hatte Bänder auf dem Kleide,
Hatt auch ein Kreuz daran,
Und war sogleich Minister
Und hatt einen großen Stern.
Da wurden seine Geschwister
Bei Hof auch große Herrn.

Und Herrn und Fraun am Hofe,
Die waren sehr geplagt,
Die Königin und die Zofe
Gestochen und genagt,
Und durften sie nicht knicken
Und weg sie jucken nicht. –
Wir knicken und ersticken
Doch gleich, wenn einer sticht!

(Part I lines, 2759–82)

[DER KÖNIG IN THULE]

Es war ein König in Thule,
Gar treu bis an das Grab,
Dem sterbend seine Buhle
Einen goldnen Becher gab.

So he was dressed in velvet and silk, and his coat had ribbons on it and a cross too. And at once he was a Minister and wore a big star. So his brothers and sisters became great persons at court as well.

And the court gentlemen and ladies, they were plagued to death; queen and chambermaid were stung and bitten. And they were forbidden to squash them and stop the itching they caused. – But when one of them bites us, we squash it and choke it straight away!

[THE KING IN THULE]

ONCE there was a king in Thule, faithful to the grave, to whom his lady as she died gave a golden wine-cup.

Es ging ihm nichts darüber,
Er leert ihn jeden Schmaus;
Die Augen gingen ihm über,
So oft er trank daraus.

Und als er kam zu sterben,
Zählt er seine Städt im Reich,
Gönnt alles seinem Erben,
Den Becher nicht zugleich.

Er saß beim Königsmahle,
Die Ritter um ihn her,
Auf hohem Vätersaale,
Dort auf dem Schloß am Meer.

Dort stand der alte Zecher,
Trank letzte Lebensglut,
Und warf den heiligen Becher
Hinunter in die Flut.

Er sah ihn stürzen, trinken,
Und sinken tief ins Meer,
Die Augen täten ihm sinken,
Trank nie einen Tropfen mehr.

He valued it above everything, he drained it at every feast, and each time
he drank from it the tears came to his eyes.

And when he came to die he numbered the cities of his kingdom and
withheld nothing from his heir, except only the cup.

He sat at the royal banquet, with his knights all round him, in his high
ancestral hall up there in the castle by the sea.

There the old toper stood, drinking life's last glow, and he threw the
sacred cup down into the waves.

He saw it fall and fill with water and sink right into the sea. Then did his
eyelids droop, and never another drop he drank.

(Part I, lines 3374–413)

[GRETCHEN AM SPINNRAD]

MEINE Ruh ist hin,
Mein Herz ist schwer;
Ich finde sie nimmer
Und nimmermehr.

Wo ich ihn nicht hab,
Ist mir das Grab,
Die ganze Welt
Ist mir vergällt.

Mein armer Kopf
Ist mir verrückt,
Mein armer Sinn
Ist mir zerstückt.

Meine Ruh ist hin,
Mein Herz ist schwer;
Ich finde sie nimmer
Und nimmermehr.

Nach ihm nur schau ich
Zum Fenster hinaus,
Nach ihm nur geh ich
Aus dem Haus.

[GRETCHEN AT THE SPINNING-WHEEL]

MY heart's heavy, I've lost my peace of mind and I'll never never find it
again.

Every place is my grave when he isn't there, my whole world turns
bitter.

My poor head's crazy, my poor mind's all gone to pieces.

My heart's heavy, I've lost my peace of mind and I'll never never find it
again.

It's only for him I look out of the window, it's only to go to him I leave
the house.

Sein hoher Gang,
Sein edle Gestalt,
Seines Mundes Lächeln,
Seiner Augen Gewalt,

Und seiner Rede
Zauberfluß,
Sein Händedruck,
Und ach, sein Kuß!

Meine Ruh ist hin,
Mein Herz ist schwer;
Ich finde sie nimmer
Und nimmermehr.

Mein Busen drängt
Sich nach ihm hin:
Ach, dürft ich fassen
Und halten ihn

Und küssen ihn,
So wie ich wollt,
An seinen Küssen
Vergehen sollt!

His tall step, his proud figure, the smile on his mouth, the power in
his eyes,
 and his words like a stream of magic, the pressure of his hand, and oh,
his kiss!
 My heart's heavy, I've lost my peace of mind and I'll never never find
it again.
 My bosom goes out to him in desire. Oh, if only I could seize him and
hold him,
 and kiss him, the way I want to, so I'd die on his kisses!

(Part I, lines 3426–65)

[FAUST UND GRETCHEN]

GRETCHEN: ... Glaubst du an Gott?

FAUST: Mein Liebchen, wer darf sagen:
 Ich glaub an Gott!
 Magst Priester oder Weise fragen,
 Und ihre Antwort scheint nur Spott
 Über den Frager zu sein.

GRETCHEN: So glaubst du nicht?

FAUST: Mißhör mich nicht, du holdes Angesicht!
 Wer darf ihn nennen
 Und wer bekennen:
 Ich glaub Ihn!
 Wer empfinden
 Und sich unterwinden
 Zu sagen: ich glaub Ihn nicht!
 Der Allumfasser,
 Der Allerhalter,
 Faßt und erhält Er nicht
 Dich, mich, sich selbst?
 Wölbt sich der Himmel nicht dadroben?
 Liegt die Erde nicht hierunten fest?

[FAUST AND GRETCHEN]

GRETCHEN: ... Do you believe in God?

FAUST: My darling, who can really say 'I believe in God'? Ask priests or
wise men, and their answers seem a mere mockery of the questioner.

GRETCHEN: So you don't believe?

FAUST: My sweet beloved, don't misunderstand me! Who can presume to
name him, and to declare 'I believe in him'? and who can feel, and dare
to say 'I do not believe in him'? He who embraces and preserves all
things, does he not hold and uphold you, and me, and himself? Is there
not the vault of heaven above us? and the earth standing fast here below?

Und steigen freundlich blickend
Ewige Sterne nicht herauf?
Schau ich nicht Aug in Auge dir,
Und drängt nicht alles
Nach Haupt und Herzen dir
Und webt in ewigem Geheimnis
Unsichtbar-sichtbar neben dir?
Erfüll davon dein Herz, so groß es ist,
Und wenn du ganz in dem Gefühle selig bist,
Nenn es dann, wie du willst:
Nenns Glück! Herz! Liebe! Gott!
Ich habe keinen Namen
Dafür! Gefühl ist alles;
Name ist Schall und Rauch,
Umnebelnd Himmelsglut.

GRETCHEN: Das ist alles recht schön und gut;
Ungefähr sagt das der Pfarrer auch,
Nur mit ein bißchen andern Worten.

FAUST: Es sagens allerorten
Alle Herzen unter dem himmlischen Tage,
Jedes in seiner Sprache:
Warum nicht ich in der meinen?

and do eternal stars not rise, with their friendly radiance? Do my eyes not look into your eyes, and does it not all besiege your head and your heart and float all around you, seen and unseen, everlasting and mysterious? Fill your heart full of this, big as it is, and when the feeling is all complete delight inside you, then call it what you like – call it happiness! heart! love! God! I have no name for it! Feeling is everything: the name is mere sound and smoke, clouding the light of heaven.

GRETCHEN: That's all very fine and all very well; the parson says much the same thing, though he doesn't use quite the same words.

FAUST: It's what all hearts are saying, everywhere under the heavenly day, each in its own language: why not I in mine?

(Part I, lines 3587–619)

[GRETCHEN VOR DER MATER DOLOROSA]

ACH neige,
Du Schmerzenreiche,
Dein Antlitz gnädig meiner Not!

Das Schwert im Herzen,
Mit tausend Schmerzen
Blickst auf zu deines Sohnes Tod.

Zum Vater blickst du,
Und Seufzer schickst du
Hinauf um sein- und deine Not.

Wer fühlet,
Wie wühlet
Der Schmerz mir im Gebein?
Was mein armes Herz hier banget,
Was es zittert, was verlanget,
Weißt nur du, nur du allein!

[GRETCHEN BEFORE THE MATER DOLOROSA]

OH, thou who art full of sorrow, bow down thy face graciously to my affliction!

With a sword piercing thy heart, and a thousand griefs, thou dost look up at thy dying Son,

and raise thine eyes to His Father, and send up sighs for His affliction and thine.

Who will feel how the pain eats into my very bones? What my poor heart dreads, why it trembles, what it desires, only you, only you can know!

Wohin ich immer gehe,
Wie weh, wie weh, wie wehe
Wird mir im Busen hier!
Ich bin, ach! kaum alleine,
Ich wein, ich wein, ich weine,
Das Herz zerbricht in mir.

Die Scherben vor meinem Fenster
Betaut ich mit Tränen, ach!
Als ich am frühen Morgen
Dir diese Blumen brach.

Schien hell in meine Kammer
Die Sonne früh herauf,
Saß ich in allem Jammer
In meinem Bett schon auf.

Hilf! rette mich von Schmach und Tod!
Ach, neige,
Du Schmerzenreiche,
Dein Antlitz gnädig meiner Not!

Wherever I go, how it hurts, how it hurts, how it hurts here inside me!
Oh, as soon as I am alone I weep, I weep and weep, and my heart inside me
is breaking to pieces.

Oh, my tears fell like dew on the pots by my window early this morning
when I picked these flowers for your shrine.

When the bright sun shone early up into my room, I was sitting up in
bed already in all my misery.

Help! save me from disgrace and death! Oh, thou who art full of sorrow,
bow down thy face graciously to my affliction!

(Part I, lines 3345–65)

[FAUSTS REUE]

WAS ist die Himmelsfreud in ihren Armen?
Laß mich an ihrer Brust erwarmen:
Fühl ich nicht immer ihre Not?
Bin ich der Flüchtling nicht? der Unbehauste?
Der Unmensch ohne Zweck und Ruh,
Der wie ein Wassersturz von Fels zu Felsen brauste,
Begierig wütend, nach dem Abgrund zu?
Und seitwärts sie, mit kindlich-dumpfen Sinnen,
Im Hüttchen auf dem kleinen Alpenfeld,
Und all ihr häusliches Beginnen
Umfangen in der kleinen Welt!
Und ich, der Gottverhaßte,
Hatte nicht genug,
Daß ich die Felsen faßte
Und sie zu Trümmern schlug:
Sie, ihren Frieden mußt ich untergraben!
Du, Hölle, mußtest dieses Opfer haben!
Hilf, Teufel, mir die Zeit der Angst verkürzen!
Was muß geschehn, mags gleich geschehn!
Mag ihr Geschick auf mich zusammenstürzen
Und sie mit mir zugrunde gehn!

[FAUST'S REMORSE]

THE delights of heaven in her arms – what of them? I may grow warm on
her breast, but do I not still feel her anguish? Am I not the fugitive? the
unhoused? the restless, purposeless monster, who has roared like a torrent
from cliff to cliff, greedily raging, down to the abyss? and she, near by,
with her childlike naïve ways, in her little hut on the little mountain
meadow, bounded with all her household tasks in that tiny world! And I,
the God-cursed, was not content to seize the rocks and smash them to
fragments: I had to undermine her, destroy her peace! Oh Hell, you had
to have this victim! – Help me, devil, to shorten the time of suspense! What
must happen, let it happen at once! Let her fate fall down on me, and with
me let her perish!

*FREUDVOLL
Und leidvoll,
Gedankenvoll sein;
Langen
Und bangen
In schwebender Pein;
Himmelhoch jauchzend,
Zum Tode betrübt;
Glücklich allein
Ist die Seele, die liebt.

RASTLOSE LIEBE

DEM Schnee, dem Regen,
Dem Wind entgegen,
Im Dampf der Klüfte,
Durch Nebeldüfte,
Immer zu! Immer zu!
Ohne Rast und Ruh!

Lieber durch Leiden
Möcht ich mich schlagen,
Als so viel Freuden
Des Lebens ertragen.

FULL of joy, full of sorrow, full of thoughts – yearning and trembling in
uncertain anguish – leaping to heaven with joy and cast down to death with
grief: no soul is happy but the soul that loves!

RESTLESS LOVE

INTO the snow and the rain and the wind, in misty hollows, through cloud
and haze, on and on! on and on, without stopping or resting!
 I would rather fight my way through sorrows than endure so many of
life's joys!

* A song from the play *Egmont*.

Alle das Neigen
Von Herzen zu Herzen,
Ach wie so eigen
Schaffet das Schmerzen!

Wie soll ich fliehen?
Wälderwärts ziehen?
Alles vergebens!
Krone des Lebens,
Glück ohne Ruh,
Liebe, bist du!

JÄGERS ABENDLIED

I M Felde schleich ich still und wild,
Gespannt mein Feuerrohr.
Da schwebt so licht dein liebes Bild,
Dein süßes Bild mir vor.

Du wandelst jetzt wohl still und mild
Durch Feld und liebes Tal,
Und ach, mein schnell verrauschend Bild,
Stellt sich dirs nicht einmal?

All this attraction of heart to heart – oh what special anguish it brings!
How shall I escape? shall I flee into the woods? All in vain! Oh love, you
are life's crowning joy, a joy with no rest!

THE HUNTSMAN'S EVENING SONG

T H R O U G H the fields, with my gun cocked, quietly and wildly I creep. And
your dear image, your sweet image hovers so brightly before me.

Now through the fields and the dear valley, no doubt, you are quietly
and mildly walking; and oh, my image, so quickly fleeting, does it not
sometimes come into your view?

Des Menschen, der die Welt durchstreift
Voll Unmut und Verdruß,
Nach Osten und nach Westen schweift,
Weil er dich lassen muß.

Mir ist es, denk ich nur an dich,
Als in den Mond zu sehn;
Ein stiller Friede kommt auf mich,
Weiß nicht, wie mir geschehn.

WANDRERS NACHTLIED I

DER du von dem Himmel bist,
Alles Leid und Schmerzen stillest,
Den, der doppelt elend ist,
Doppelt mit Erquickung füllest,
Ach, ich bin des Treibens müde!
Was soll all der Schmerz und Lust?
Süßer Friede,
Komm, ach komm in meine Brust!

The image of a man roving through the world full of discontentment
and vexation, wandering eastwards and wandering westwards, because he
must leave you.

I have only to think of you and I seem to be looking into the moon; a
quiet peace comes upon me and I cannot tell what has happened to me.

THE WAYFARER'S NIGHT SONG I

THOU which art from heaven, and dost soothe all grief and pain, filling
the doubly wretched doubly with refreshment: oh, I am weary of this rest-
lessness! Why all this pain, all this joy? Come, sweet Peace, oh, come into
my heart!

WANDRERS NACHTLIED II

Über allen Gipfeln
Ist Ruh,
In allen Wipfeln
Spürest du
Kaum einen Hauch;
Die Vögelein schweigen im Walde.
Warte nur, balde
Ruhest du auch.

AN DEN MOND
Erste Fassung

Füllest wieder 's liebe Tal
Still mit Nebelglanz,
Lösest endlich auch einmal
Meine Seele ganz;

THE WAYFARER'S NIGHT SONG II

Over all the hill-tops it is still, in all the tree-tops you can hardly feel a breath stirring. The little birds are silent in the forest. Wait! soon you too will be still.

TO THE MOON
First Version

Silently, once more, you fill the sweet valley with misty radiance, and at last, too, you bring complete peace to my soul;

Breitest über mein Gefild
Lindernd deinen Blick,
Wie der Liebsten Auge mild
Über mein Geschick.

Das du so beweglich kennst,
Dieses Herz in Brand,
Haltet ihr wie ein Gespenst
An den Fluß gebannt,

Wenn in öder Winternacht
Er vom Tode schwillt
Und bei Frühlingslebens Pracht
An den Knospen quillt.

Selig, wer sich vor der Welt
Ohne Haß verschließt,
Einen Mann am Busen hält
Und mit dem genießt,

Was, den Menschen unbewußt
Oder wohl veracht,
Durch das Labyrinth der Brust
Wandelt in der Nacht.

soothingly you spread your bright gaze over the fields around me, like
my beloved watching my destiny with her gentle eyes.

So movable you know this burning heart to be – between you you hold
it spellbound, like a ghost, beside this river,

when in drear winter nights it is swollen deadly still, and when it surges
round buds in the glorious living spring.

Happy are we if without resentment we withdraw from the world and
hold a man to our breast and with him enjoy

that which, unknown or perhaps despised by mankind, wanders through
the heart's labyrinth in darkness.

AN DEN MOND

Letzte Fassung

FÜLLEST wieder Busch und Tal
Still mit Nebelglanz,
Lösest endlich auch einmal
Meine Seele ganz;

Breitest über mein Gefild
Lindernd deinen Blick,
Wie des Freundes Auge mild
Über mein Geschick.

Jeden Nachklang fühlt mein Herz
Froh- und trüber Zeit,
Wandle zwischen Freud und Schmerz
In der Einsamkeit.

Fließe, fließe, lieber Fluß!
Nimmer werd ich froh,
So verrauschte Scherz und Kuß,
Und die Treue so.

TO THE MOON

Final Version

SILENTLY, once more, you fill the bushes and the valley with misty radi-
ance, and at last, too, you bring complete peace to my soul;
soothingly you spread your bright gaze over the fields around me, like
my beloved watching my destiny with his gentle eyes.

All the gladness and sorrows of the past re-echo in my heart, and I walk
between joy and pain, in solitude.

Run on, run on, dear river! Gladness will never come back to me! This
was how they streamed away – laughter, and kisses, and fidelity.

Ich besaß es doch einmal,
Was so köstlich ist!
Daß man doch zu seiner Qual
Nimmer es vergißt!

Rausche, Fluß, das Tal entlang,
Ohne Rast und Ruh,
Rausche, flüstre meinem Sang
Melodien zu,

Wenn du in der Winternacht
Wütend überschwillst,
Oder um die Frühlingspracht
Junger Knospen quillst.

Selig, wer sich der Welt
Ohne Haß verschließt,
Einen Freund am Busen hält
Und mit dem genießt,

Was, von Menschen nicht gewußt
Oder nicht bedacht,
Durch das Labyrinth der Brust
Wandelt in der Nacht.

Yet once I possessed what is so precious! Ah, the torment of never being able to forget it!

Murmur, oh river, along the valley, ceaselessly, restlessly; murmur and whisper melodies for my song,

when on winter nights you rage and overflow, or when you surge round the spring splendour of young buds.

Happy are we if without resentment we withdraw from the world and hold a friend to our breast and with him enjoy

that which, unknown or ignored by mankind, wanders through the heart's labyrinth in darkness.

ALLES geben die Götter, die unendlichen,
Ihren Lieblingen ganz,
Alle Freuden, die unendlichen,
Alle Schmerzen, die unendlichen, ganz.

HARZREISE IM WINTER

DEM Geier gleich,
Der auf schweren Morgenwolken
Mit sanftem Fittich ruhend
Nach Beute schaut,
Schwebe mein Lied.

Denn ein Gott hat
Jedem seine Bahn
Vorgezeichnet,
Die der Glückliche
Rasch zum freudigen
Ziele rennt:
Wem aber Unglück
Das Herz zusammenzog,
Er sträubt vergebens
Sich gegen die Schranken
Des ehernen Fadens,
Den die doch bittre Schere
Nur einmal löst.

To those whom they love, the gods who are infinite give all things wholly: all joys, which are infinite, all sorrows, which are infinite, wholly.

WINTER JOURNEY IN THE HARZ MOUNTAINS

LIKE a hawk poised, with scarce-quivering wings, on lowering morning clouds, watching for prey, let my song hover.

For a god has preordained the path of every man; the fortunate race swiftly along to its joyful end. But he whose heart has been crushed by disaster strives vainly against the bounds of the brazen thread; it is cut once only, by shears which will still be bitter.

In Dickichts-Schauer
Drängt sich das rauhe Wild,
Und mit den Sperlingen
Haben längst die Reichen
In ihre Sümpfe sich gesenkt.

Leicht ists folgen dem Wagen,
Den Fortuna führt,
Wie der gemächliche Troß
Auf gebesserten Wegen
Hinter des Fürsten Einzug.

Aber abseits wer ists?
Ins Gebüsch verliert sich sein Pfad,
Hinter ihm schlagen
Die Sträuche zusammen,
Das Gras steht wieder auf,
Die Öde verschlingt ihn.

Ach, wer heilet die Schmerzen
Des, dem Balsam zu Gift ward?
Der sich Menschenhaß
Aus der Fülle der Liebe trank?
Erst verachtet, nun ein Verächter,
Zehrt er heimlich auf
Seinen eignen Wert
In ungnügender Selbstsucht.

The wild boar plunges into eerie thickets, and long since, like birds, the rich have nested down into their swampy homes.

It is easy to follow the carriage driven by Fortune; as the commodious procession, along improved roads, follows a prince's entry.

But who is this who has turned aside? His path wanders into the undergrowth and is lost, the bushes close and the grass rises again behind him, the wilderness swallows him up.

Ah, who shall heal his pain, whose balm turned to poison, who drank his hatred of mankind from fullness of love? First scorned, now a scorner, he secretly devours, an unsatisfied egoist, all that is good in himself.

Ist auf deinem Psalter,
Vater der Liebe, ein Ton
Seinem Ohre vernehmlich,
So erquicke sein Herz!
Öffne den umwölkten Blick
Über die tausend Quellen
Neben dem Durstenden
In der Wüste.

Der du der Freuden viel schaffst,
Jedem ein überfließend Maß,
Segne die Brüder der Jagd
Auf der Fährte des Wilds
Mit jugendlichem Übermut
Fröhlicher Mordsucht,
Späte Rächer des Unbills,
Dem schon Jahre vergeblich
Wehrt mit Knütteln der Bauer.

Aber den Einsamen hüll
In deine Goldwolken!
Umgib mit Wintergrün,
Bis die Rose wieder heranreift,
Die feuchten Haare,
O Liebe, deines Dichters!

Has your psaltery a note, Father of Love, that his ear can hear? oh, re-
fresh then his heart! Unblind his clouded gaze to the thousand waters that
spring beside him from the desert where he stands thirsting.

Oh Creator of many delights, giver of joy in full measure to each man,
bless my brothers the huntsmen, who are tracking their game with youth-
ful high spirits and gay bloodlust – those late avengers of a mischief that for
years already the farmer's cudgels have vainly fought.

But enclose the solitary in your clouds of gold! With winter-green, till
the rose ripens again, encircle, oh Love, the drenched locks of your poet!

Mit der dämmernden Fackel
Leuchtest du ihm
Durch die Furten bei Nacht,
Über grundlose Wege
Auf öden Gefilden;
Mit dem tausendfarbigen Morgen
Lachst du ins Herz ihm;
Mit dem beizenden Sturm
Trägst du ihn hoch empor;
Winterströme stürzen vom Felsen
In seine Psalmen,
Und Altar des lieblichsten Danks
Wird ihm des gefürchteten Gipfels
Schneebehangner Scheitel,
Den mit Geisterreihen
Kränzten ahnende Völker.

Du stehst mit unerforschtem Busen
Geheimnisvoll offenbar
Über der erstaunten Welt
Und schaust aus Wolken
Auf ihre Reiche und Herrlichkeit,
Die du aus den Adern deiner Brüder
Neben dir wässerst.

With your dim-burning torch you light his feet, across fords in the darkness, along precipitous paths, over desolate wastes; you gladden his heart with the laughter of myriad-hued morning; you raise him aloft on the tingling storm; from the cliff wintry rivers pour into his songs of praise, and for an altar of sweetest thanksgiving he uses the snow-capped brow of that dreaded summit which the imagination of peoples has crowned with dancing spirits.

With unexplored bosom it stands, unknown and unhidden, above the astonished world, whose kingdoms and the glory thereof it beholds from among the clouds, and feeds from the veins of its brother-mountains.

GESANG DER GEISTER
ÜBER DEN WASSERN

DES Menschen Seele
Gleicht dem Wasser:
Vom Himmel kommt es,
Zum Himmel steigt es,
Und wieder nieder
Zur Erde muß es,
Ewig wechselnd.

Strömt von der hohen,
Steilen Felswand
Der reine Strahl,
Dann stäubt er lieblich
In Wolkenwellen
Zum glatten Fels,
Und leicht empfangen
Wallt er verschleiernd,
Leisrauschend
Zur Tiefe nieder.

Ragen Klippen
Dem Sturz entgegen,
Schäumt er unmutig
Stufenweise
Zum Abgrund.

SONG OF THE SPIRITS OVER THE WATERS

MAN'S soul is like water: from heaven it comes, to heaven it rises, and
to earth again it must descend, moving to and fro for ever.

The pure jet leaps from the lofty precipitous rock-face, then rises in
cloud-waves of sweet spray against the smooth rock, and streams, veil-
like, softly murmurous, down to the depths which lightly receive it.

If cliffs project in the path of its fall, then angrily foaming it pours step-
wise into the abyss.

Im flachen Bette
Schleicht er das Wiesental hin,
Und in dem glatten See
Weiden ihr Antlitz
Alle Gestirne.

Wind ist der Welle
Lieblicher Buhler;
Wind mischt vom Grund aus
Schäumende Wogen.

Seele des Menschen,
Wie gleichst du dem Wasser!
Schicksal des Menschen,
Wie gleichst du dem Wind!

GRENZEN DER MENSCHHEIT

Wenn der uralte,
Heilige Vater
Mit gelassener Hand
Aus rollenden Wolken
Segnende Blitze
Über die Erde sät,

In its level bed it meanders down the meadowy vale, and on the lake's smooth surface all the stars gaze at their own faces.

Wind is the water's sweet lover; wind stirs up foaming waves from the deep.

Soul of man, how like water you are! Destiny of man, how like the wind!

HUMAN LIMITATIONS

When the holy Father, the ancient of days, with a calm motion of his hand, from the rolling clouds, scatters beneficent lightnings over the earth,

Küss ich den letzten
Saum seines Kleides,
Kindliche Schauer
Treu in der Brust.

Denn mit Göttern
Soll sich nicht messen
Irgendein Mensch.
Hebt er sich aufwärts
Und berührt
Mit dem Scheitel die Sterne,
Nirgends haften dann
Die unsichern Sohlen,
Und mit ihm spielen
Wolken und Winde.

Steht er mit festen,
Markigen Knochen
Auf der wohlgegründeten
Dauernden Erde,
Reicht er nicht auf,
Nur mit der Eiche
Oder der Rebe
Sich zu vergleichen.

Was unterscheidet
Götter von Menschen?

I kiss the extreme hem of his garment, and my faithful heart is full of child-like awe.

For let no man measure himself against gods. If he rises and reaches upwards till his head touches the stars, there is no hold then anywhere for his unsure feet, and he becomes the plaything of the clouds and winds.

If he stands fast with well-knit bones on the firm-established lasting earth, he cannot attain a height comparable even to the oak-tree or the vine.

What distinguishes gods from mankind? This: that before them many

Daß viele Wellen
Vor jenen wandeln,
Ein ewiger Strom:
Uns hebt die Welle,
Verschlingt die Welle,
Und wir versinken.

Ein kleiner Ring
Begrenzt unser Leben,
Und viele Geschlechter
Reihen sich dauernd
An ihres Daseins
Unendliche Kette.

[DAS LIED DER PARZEN*]

Es fürchte die Götter
Das Menschengeschlecht!
Sie halten die Herrschaft
In ewigen Händen,
Und können sie brauchen,
Wie's ihnen gefällt.

waves move onward, an ever-rolling stream; but as for us, the wave lifts us, the wave swallows us, and we sink.

Our life is bounded in a little ring, and many generations are constantly succeeding each other like links in the endless chain of their existence.

[THE SONG OF THE FATES]

LET human-kind fear the gods! In their hands they hold everlasting over-lordship, and they can use it as they please.

* From the play *Iphigenie auf Tauris*. Iphigenia, a descendant of a family cursed by the gods, describes the song as '*das Lied der Parzen*'.

Der fürchte sie doppelt
Den je sie erheben!
Auf Klippen und Wolken
Sind Stühle bereitet
Um goldene Tische.

Erhebet ein Zwist sich,
So stürzen die Gäste,
Geschmäht und geschändet
In nächtliche Tiefen,
Und harren vergebens,
Im Finstern gebunden,
Gerechten Gerichtes.

Sie aber, sie bleiben
In ewigen Festen
An goldenen Tischen.
Sie schreiten vom Berge
Zu Bergen hinüber:
Aus Schlünden der Tiefe
Dampft ihnen der Atem
Erstickter Titanen,
Gleich Opfergerüchen,
Ein leichtes Gewölke.

Es wenden die Herrscher
Ihr segnendes Auge
Von ganzen Geschlechtern

Let any whom they have exalted fear them doubly! On clouds and preci-
pices thrones stand ready round golden tables.

If discord arises, the guests are hurled down in scorn and disgrace into
nethermost night, and there they wait vainly, in bonds and in darkness, for
justice and judgement.

But the gods remain everlastingly feasting at golden tables. They stride
over mountains from summit to summit: out of deep-down chasms the
breath of suffocated Titans steams up to their nostrils like incense, as deli-
cate vapour.

These lords turn away their eyes and their blessing from whole races,

Und meiden, im Enkel
Die ehmals geliebten,
Still redenden Züge
Des Ahnherrn zu sehn.

So sangen die Parzen;
Es horcht der Verbannte,
In nächtlichen Höhlen
Der Alte die Lieder,
Denkt Kinder und Enkel
Und schüttelt das Haupt.

MEINE GÖTTIN

WELCHER Unsterblichen
Soll der höchste Preis sein?
Mit niemand streit ich,
Aber ich geb ihn
Der ewig beweglichen,
Immer neuen,
Seltsamen Tochter Jovis,
Seinem Schoßkinde,
Der Phantasie.

and shun in descendants the sight, the mute speech of an ancestor's once-loved features.

Thus the Fates sang; the aged exile in his dark caverns listens to their singing, thinks of his children and grandchildren, and shakes his head.

MY GODDESS

To which of the immortal goddesses shall we award highest praise? I seek no dispute, but I myself will give it to the perpetually moving, ever new, strange daughter of Jove, his darling child Imagination.

Denn ihr hat er
Alle Launen,
Die er sonst nur allein
Sich vorbehält,
Zugestanden
Und hat seine Freude
An der Törin.

Sie mag rosenbekränzt
Mit dem Lilienstengel
Blumentäler betreten,
Sommervögeln gebieten
Und leichtnährenden Tau
Mit Bienenlippen
Von Blüten saugen;

Oder sie mag
mit fliegendem Haar
Und düsterm Blicke
Im Winde sausen
Um Felsenwände,
Und tausendfarbig,
Wie Morgen und Abend
Immer wechselnd,
Wie Mondesblicke,
Den Sterblichen scheinen.

For to her he has permitted every fancy, all those which he otherwise reserves to himself alone, and he takes pleasure in her waywardness.

She may come garlanded with roses, holding the lily's stem, treading valleys of flowers, summoning and bidding the birds of summer, and sucking from blossoms with her bee-lips light nourishment of dew;

or with streaming hair and eyes dark-glaring she may roar in the wind round precipices, and myriad-coloured, like morning and evening ever-changing, like gleaming moonlight, shine upon mortals.

Laßt uns alle
Den Vater preisen!
Den alten, hohen,
Der solch eine schöne,
Unverwelkliche Gattin
Dem sterblichen Menschen
Gesellen mögen!

Denn uns allein
Hat er sie verbunden
Mit Himmelsband,
Und ihr geboten,
In Freud und Elend
Als treue Gattin
Nicht zu entweichen.

Alle die andern
Armen Geschlechter
Der kinderreichen,
Lebendigen Erde
Wandeln und weiden
In dunkelm Genuß
Und trüben Schmerzen
Des augenblicklichen
Beschränkten Lebens,
Gebeugt vom Joche
Der Notdurft.

Let us all praise him! the ancient exalted Father, who has vouchsafed to give so beautiful and unfading a bride as companion to mortal men!

For to us alone he bound her with a heavenly bond, and bade her cleave to us, like a true wife, in joy and in sorrow.

All the other poor races that move and feed on the living prolific earth enjoy obscurely, and suffer dimly, a momentary limited life, and are bowed under the yoke of necessity.

Uns aber hat er
Seine gewandteste,
Verzärtelte Tochter,
Freut euch! gegönnt.
Begegnet ihr lieblich
Wie einer Geliebten!
Laßt ihr die Würde
Der Frauen im Haus!

Und daß die alte
Schwiegermutter Weisheit
Das zarte Seelchen
Ja nicht beleidge!

Doch kenn ich ihre Schwester,
Die ältere, gesetztere,
Meine stille Freundin:
O daß die erst
Mit dem Lichte des Lebens
Sich von mir wende,
Die edle Treiberin,
Trösterin Hoffnung!

But to us (oh, rejoice!) he has granted his most gifted, most cherished daughter. Treat her lovingly, like a beloved! Accord to her the dignity of the lady of the house!

And above all let old Wisdom, her mother-in-law, give no offence to the delicate little creature!

But I know too her older, less volatile sister: oh may she, my quiet friend, never leave me till the light of life shall leave me – she who impels and consoles, the noble goddess Hope!

DAS GÖTTLICHE

Edel sei der Mensch,
Hilfreich und gut!
Denn das allein
Unterscheidet ihn
Von allen Wesen,
Die wir kennen.

Heil den unbekannten
Höhern Wesen,
Die wir ahnen!
Ihnen gleiche der Mensch;
Sein Beispiel lehr uns
Jene glauben.

Denn unfühlend
Ist die Natur:
Es leuchtet die Sonne
Über Bös' und Gute,
Und dem Verbrecher
Glänzen wie dem Besten
Der Mond und die Sterne.

DIVINITY

Let man be noble, generous and good! For this alone distinguishes him
from all beings known to us.

Hail to the higher Beings, unknown but surmised by us! Let man be like
them; let his example teach us to believe in them.

For Nature is unfeeling: the sun shines on the evil and on the good, and
the criminal as well as the best of men sees the brightness of the moon and
the stars.

Wind und Ströme,
Donner und Hagel
Rauschen ihren Weg
Und ergreifen
Vorüber eilend
Einen um den andern.

Auch so das Glück
Tappt unter die Menge,
Faßt bald des Knaben
Lockige Unschuld,
Bald auch den kahlen
Schuldigen Scheitel.

Nach ewigen, ehrnen,
Großen Gesetzen
Müssen wir alle
Unseres Daseins
Kreise vollenden.

Nur allein der Mensch
Vermag das Unmögliche:
Er unterscheidet,
Wählet und richtet;
Er kann dem Augenblick
Dauer verleihen.

Wind and streams, thunder and hail, rush and roar on their ways, seizing as they pass first one, then another.

Thus Fortune, too, gropes blindly into the crowd, now clutching a boy's curly-haired innocence, and now a bald guilty pate.

We must all complete the cycles of our existence in accordance with great, eternal, adamantine laws.

Only man can do the impossible: he distinguishes, chooses and judges; he can give permanence to the moment.

Er allein darf
Den Guten lohnen,
Den Bösen strafen,
Heilen und retten,
Alles Irrende, Schweifende
Nützlich verbinden.

Und wir verehren
Die Unsterblichen,
Als wären sie Menschen,
Täten im großen,
Was der Beste im kleinen
Tut oder möchte.

Der edle Mensch
Sei hilfreich und gut!
Unermüdet schaff er
Das Nützliche, Rechte,
Sei uns ein Vorbild
Jener geahneten Wesen!

He alone may reward the good, punish the wicked, heal and save, use-
fully connect all that strays and wanders.

And we reverence the immortals, as if they were men, and could do on
a large scale what on a small scale the best of us does or would like to do.

Let man who is noble be generous and good! Let him untiringly achieve
what is useful and right, that we may model on him those Beings of our
surmise!

[AN CHARLOTTE VON STEIN]

WARUM gabst du uns die tiefen Blicke,
Unsre Zukunft ahndungsvoll zu schaun,
Unsrer Liebe, unserm Erdenglücke
Wähnend selig nimmer hinzutraun?
Warum gabst uns, Schicksal, die Gefühle,
Uns einander in das Herz zu sehn,
Um durch all die seltenen Gewühle
Unser wahr Verhältnis auszuspähn?

Ach, so viele tausend Menschen kennen,
Dumpf sich treibend, kaum ihr eigen Herz,
Schweben zwecklos hin und her und rennen
Hoffnungslos in unversehnem Schmerz;
Jauchzen wieder, wenn der schnellen Freuden
Unerwart'te Morgenröte tagt;
Nur uns armen liebevollen beiden
Ist das wechselseitge Glück versagt,
Uns zu lieben, ohn uns zu verstehen,
In dem andern sehn, was er nie war,
Immer frisch auf Traumglück auszugehen
Und zu schwanken auch in Traumgefahr.

[TO CHARLOTTE VON STEIN]

WHY did you give us deep insight, visions and surmisings of our future, so
that we can never live in trustful abandonment to our love, to our earthly
happiness, in an illusion of joy? Oh Fate, why did you give us these intui-
tions, give us each other's heart to contemplate, and make us see through
all these strange confusions of feeling and discern what we truly are to each
other?

Oh, there are so many thousands of men and women with scarcely any
knowledge of their own hearts, drifting insensitively through life, floating
aimlessly hither and thither, running hopelessly from unforeseen suffering,
and exulting again at the unexpected daybreak of lively joys. Only we, two
poor loving souls, are denied the mutual happiness of loving each other
without understanding each other – of each seeing in the other something
the other never was, of for ever setting out afresh in the pursuit of illusory
happiness and faltering, too, before illusory dangers.

Glücklich, den ein leerer Traum beschäftigt,
Glücklich, dem die Ahndung eitel wär!
Jede Gegenwart und jeder Blick bekräftigt
Traum und Ahndung leider uns noch mehr.
Sag, was will das Schicksal uns bereiten?
Sag, wie band es uns so rein genau?
Ach, du warst in abgelebten Zeiten
Meine Schwester oder meine Frau.

Kanntest jeden Zug in meinem Wesen,
Spähtest, wie die reinste Nerve klingt,
Konntest mich mit Einem Blicke lesen,
Den so schwer ein sterblich Aug durchdringt;
Tropftest Mäßigung dem heißen Blute,
Richtetest den wilden irren Lauf,
Und in deinen Engelsarmen ruhte
Die zerstörte Brust sich wieder auf;
Hieltest zauberleicht ihn angebunden
Und vergaukeltest ihm manchen Tag.
Welche Seligkeit glich jenen Wonnestunden,
Da er dankbar dir zu Füßen lag,

Happy are those whom an empty dream preoccupies! happy are they, whose surmisings would be mere vanity! Our every meeting, alas, and our every look, only confirms the truth of our surmise and our dream. Oh tell me, what does Fate hold in store for us? tell me, how did it fashion between us so pure and strict a bond? Oh, in far bygone times you were my sister or my wife;

you knew my nature then in every detail, you watched for my purest heart-string's music, you could read me at a glance, hard as I am for mortal gaze to penetrate; you would pour the balm of composure into my hot blood, guide my wild wandering footsteps, and in your dear arms I would rest and revive my ravaged soul. With magic ease you held your lover bound to you, and made many a day flit by for him in delight. What blessedness could compare with those hours of rapture when he lay at your

Fühlt' sein Herz an deinem Herzen schwellen,
Fühlte sich in deinem Auge gut,
Alle seine Sinnen sich erhellen
Und beruhigen sein brausend Blut!

Und von allem dem schwebt ein Erinnern
Nur noch um das ungewisse Herz,
Fühlt die alte Wahrheit ewig gleich im Innern,
Und der neue Zustand wird ihm Schmerz.
Und wir scheinen uns nur halb beseelet,
Dämmernd ist um uns der hellste Tag.
Glücklich, daß das Schicksal, das uns quälet,
Uns doch nicht verändern mag!

Du bist mein und bist so zierlich,
Du bist mein und so manierlich,
Aber etwas fehlt dir noch:
Küssest mit so spitzen Lippen,
Wie die Tauben Wasser nippen;
Allzu zierlich bist du doch.

feet in gratitude, felt his heart swelling against your heart, felt himself to be good in your eyes, felt all his senses clarified and his raging blood calmed.

And all that is left of all this now is a memory floating round his uncertain heart; he feels the old truth constant for ever within, and his new state fills him with sorrow. And it seems to us that we are only half alive, and the brightest daylight is twilight around us. Happy are we that Fate can afflict us, yet never alter our love!

You are mine and so dainty, mine and so mannerly – but something you still lack: you kiss with such pointed lips, like a dove sipping water; you really are too dainty.

DER BECHER

EINEN wohlgeschnitzten vollen Becher
Hielt ich drückend in den beiden Händen,
Sog begierig süßen Wein vom Rande,
Gram und Sorg auf einmal zu vertrinken.

Amor trat herein und fand mich sitzen,
Und er lächelte bescheidenweise,
Als den Unverständigen bedauernd:

«Freund, ich kenn ein schöneres Gefäße,
Wert, die ganze Seele drein zu senken;
Was gelobst du, wenn ich dir es gönne,
Es mit anderm Nektar dir erfülle?»

O wie freundlich hat er Wort gehalten!
Da er, Lida, dich mit sanfter Neigung
Mir, dem lange Sehnenden, geeignet.

Wenn ich deinen lieben Leib umfasse
Und von deinen einzig treuen Lippen
Langbewahrter Liebe Balsam koste,
Selig sprech ich dann zu meinem Geiste:

THE CUP

PRESSED between both hands I held a full, beautifully fashioned cup, and greedily sucked sweet wine from its rim, to drink away all my sorrow and care.

Love entered and found me sitting; and with modest wisdom he smiled, as if pitying my folly.

'Friend, I know a fairer vessel, worthy to hold your whole soul plunged in it; what will you vow if I vouchsafe it to you, and fill it for you with a different nectar?'

Oh how kindly he has kept his word! For he has joined you, Lida, to me in gentle affection, after my long desire.

When I hold your dear body in my arms, and from your uniquely faithful lips drink in the balm of long-stored love – then in ecstasy I thus commune with my soul:

Nein, ein solch Gefäß hat, außer Amorn,
Nie ein Gott gebildet noch besessen!
Solche Formen treibet nicht Vulkanus
Mit den sinnbegabten, feinen Hämmern!
Auf belaubten Hügeln mag Lyäus
Durch die ältsten, klügsten seiner Faunen
Ausgesuchte Trauben keltern lassen,
Selbst geheimnisvoller Gärung vorstehn:
Solchen Trank verschafft ihm keine Sorgfalt!

AN LIDA

DEN Einzigen, Lida, welchen du lieben kannst,
Forderst du ganz für dich, und mit Recht.
Auch ist er einzig dein.
Denn seit ich von dir bin,
Scheint mir des schnellsten Lebens
Lärmende Bewegung
Nur ein leichter Flor, durch den ich deine Gestalt
Immerfort wie in Wolken erblicke:
Sie leuchtet mir freundlich und treu,
Wie durch des Nordlichts bewegliche Strahlen
Ewige Sterne schimmern.

'Truly, such a vessel was never moulded or possessed by any god but
Love! Not Vulcan with his subtle hammers, so cunning-gifted, can beat
out such forms! Bacchus on leafy hills may make the oldest and wisest of his
fauns tread the choicest of grapes, and himself preside over their mysterious
fermentation: but not with all his care will he distil a draught like this!'

TO LIDA

THE one man, Lida, whom you can love, you claim wholly for yourself
and rightly so. And he does, indeed, belong only to you. For since I left
you, the loud stir of life at its quickest pace seems no more than a light veil
through which, as if in clouds, I see your shape: it shines kindly and
constantly upon me, like the gleam of eternal stars through the restless
flashing of the Northern Lights.

NACHTGEDANKEN

EUCH bedaur ich, unglückselge Sterne,
Die ihr schön seid und so herrlich scheinet,
Dem bedrängten Schiffer gerne leuchtet,
Unbelohnt von Göttern und von Menschen:
Denn ihr liebt nicht, kanntet nie die Liebe!
Unaufhaltsam führen ewge Stunden
Eure Reihen durch den weiten Himmel.
Welche Reise habt ihr schon vollendet!
Seit ich weilend in dem Arm der Liebsten
Euer und der Mitternacht vergessen.

BIN so in Lieb zu ihr versunken,
Als hätt ich von ihrem Blut getrunken.

NIGHT THOUGHTS

I PITY you, unhappy stars, who are so beautiful and shine so splendidly,
gladly guiding the struggling sailor with your light, and yet have no re-
ward from gods or men: for you do not love, you have never known love!
Ceaselessly by everlasting hours your dance is led across the wide heavens.
How vast a journey you have made already since I, reposing in my sweet-
heart's arms, forgot my thoughts of you and of the midnight!

I AM plunged as deep in love with her as if I had drunk from her blood.

75

EPIPHANIASFEST*

Dɪᴇ heilgen drei König' mit ihrem Stern,
Sie essen, sie trinken, und bezahlen nicht gern;
Sie essen gern, sie trinken gern,
Sie essen, trinken und bezahlen nicht gern.

Die heilgen drei König' sind kommen allhier,
Es sind ihrer drei und sind nicht ihrer vier;
Und wenn zu dreien der vierte wär,
So wär ein heilger drei König mehr.

Ich erster bin der weiß und auch der schön,
Bei Tage solltet ihr erst mich sehn!
Doch ach, mit allen Spezerein
Werd ich sein Tag kein Mädchen mir erfrein.

Ich aber bin der braun und bin der lang,
Bekannt bei Weibern wohl und bei Gesang.
Ich bringe Gold statt Spezerein,
Da werd ich überall willkommen sein.

FEAST OF THE EPIPHANY

Tʜᴇ Three Kings of Orient with their star – they eat, they drink, and don't like to pay; they like eating, they like drinking, they eat and drink and don't like paying.

The Three Kings of Orient, here they come! There are three of them and there aren't four of them. And if you added a fourth one to the three, that would make one more Three-Kings-of-Orient.

'I'm the first, the fair-haired one and the handsome one too; just wait till you see me by daylight! But oh, dear, with all my spices I'll never woo and wed any girl, not all her life long!'

'But I'm the brown-haired one and the tall one, well known to women and well known for song. Instead of spices I've brought gold, so I'll be welcome everywhere.'

* This song (based on an old popular custom) was written for a masked ball at the Weimar court. The first 'king' was played by an actress.

Ich endlich bin der schwarz und bin der klein
Und mag auch wohl einmal recht lustig sein.
Ich esse gern, ich trinke gern,
Ich esse, trinke und bedanke mich gern.

Die heilgen drei König' sind wohlgesinnt,
Sie suchen die Mutter und das Kind;
Der Joseph fromm sitzt auch dabei,
Der Ochs und Esel liegen auf der Streu.

Wir bringen Myrrhen, wir bringen Gold,
Dem Weihrauch sind die Damen hold;
Und haben wir Wein von gutem Gewächs,
So trinken wir drei so gut als ihrer sechs.

Da wir nun hier schöne Herrn und Fraun,
Aber keine Ochsen und Esel schaun,
So sind wir nicht am rechten Ort
Und ziehen unseres Weges weiter fort.

'And finally there's me, the little black one; and I want to have a good time too for once. I like drinking, I like eating and drinking and saying "Thank you!" '

The Three Kings of Orient have the best of intentions; they are looking for the Mother and the Child. Gentle Joseph is sitting there too, and the ox and ass are lying in the straw.

'We've brought myrrh, we've brought gold, and we're sure the ladies will like our frankincense. And when we can get a wine of good vintage, the three of us drink enough for six!

'But since we can see only fine gentlemen and ladies here and no oxen or asses, we conclude we are in the wrong place, and continue on our way.'

VERSUS MEMORIALES

Invocavit wir rufen laut,
Reminiscere o wär ich Braut!
Die *Oculi* gehn hin und her;
Laetare drüber nicht so sehr.
O *Judica* uns nicht so streng!
Palmarum streuen wir die Meng.
Auf Oster-Eier freun sich hie
Viel *Quasi modo geniti.*
Misericordias brauchen wir all,
Jubilate ist ein seltner Fall.
Cantate freut der Menschen Sinn,
Rogate bringt nicht viel Gewinn.
Exaudi uns zu dieser Frist,
Spiritus, der du der letzte bist.

Du bist! du bist! sagt Lavater. Du bist!!
Du bist!!! du bist!!!! du bist Herr Jesus Christ!!!!!
Er wiederholte nicht so heftig Wort und Lehre,
Wenn es ganz just mit dieser Sache wäre.

VERSUS MEMORIALES

Invocavit we loudly pray;/*Reminiscere*, oh for my wedding day!/Our
Oculi rove to and fro;/*Laetare*, it's nothing to sing about so./Oh *Judica* us
not so strictly!/*Palmarum*, these we are scattering thickly./Easter eggs are
expected with pleasure by/many *Quasi modo geniti.*/*Misericordias* we all of
us need;/*Jubilate* is a rare thing indeed./*Cantate* makes for a joyful mood;/
Rogate does us precious little good./*Exaudi* our prayer this time, please,/
Spiritus who art the last of these.

'Thou art! thou art!' says Lavater. 'Thou art!! Thou art!!! thou art!!!!
thou art Lord Jesus Christ!!!!!' He would not protest so much and so often
with the word and the doctrine, if this matter really were beyond doubt.

DER FISCHER

DAS Wasser rauscht', das Wasser schwoll,
Ein Fischer saß daran,
Sah nach dem Angel ruhevoll,
Kühl bis ans Herz hinan.
Und wie er sitzt und wie er lauscht,
Teilt sich die Flut empor;
Aus dem bewegten Wasser rauscht
Ein feuchtes Weib hervor.

Sie sang zu ihm, sie sprach zu ihm:
Was lockst du meine Brut
Mit Menschenwitz und Menschenlist
Hinauf in Todesglut?
Ach wüßtest du, wie's Fischlein ist
So wohlig auf dem Grund,
Du stiegst herunter, wie du bist,
Und würdest erst gesund.

Labt sich die liebe Sonne nicht,
Der Mond sich nicht im Meer?
Kehrt wellenatmend ihr Gesicht
Nicht doppelt schöner her?

THE ANGLER

THE water swirled, the water mounted; an angler sat beside it, watching his
rod calmly, cool to his very heart. And as he sits and as he listens, the
waters divide and surge upwards, and out of their stirring a nymph, all
moist, murmurously rises.

She sang to him, she said to him: 'Why are you enticing my children,
with human wit and human cunning, up into heat and death? Oh, if only
you knew how the little fishes live so snugly down in the depths, you would
come down here yourself, just as you are, and you would know true well-
being then!

'Does not the sweet sun, does not the moon bathe in the sea? and do they
not rise again, breathing the waves' refreshment, with redoubled beauty of

Lockt dich der tiefe Himmel nicht,
Das feuchtverklärte Blau?
Lockt dich dein eigen Angesicht
Nicht her in ewgen Tau?

Das Wasser rauscht', das Wasser schwoll,
Netzt' ihm den nackten Fuß;
Sein Herz wuchs ihm so sehnsuchtsvoll,
Wie bei der Liebsten Gruß.
Sie sprach zu ihm, sie sang zu ihm;
Da wars um ihn geschehn:
Halb zog sie ihn, halb sank er hin,
Und ward nicht mehr gesehn.

ERLKÖNIG

WER reitet so spät durch Nacht und Wind?
Es ist der Vater mit seinem Kind;
Er hat den Knaben wohl in dem Arm,
Er faßt ihn sicher, er hält ihn warm.

countenance? Does not this deep sky, this moist-transfigured blue entice you? does not your own face draw you down into this eternal dew?'

The water swirled, the water mounted, wetting his naked foot, and his heart grew so big with longing, as at the greeting of his beloved. She sang to him, she spoke to him, and soon it was all over with him: she half dragged him, he half sank down, and he never was seen again.

ERLKING

WHO is it riding so late through the windy night? A father with his child; he has his arm well round the boy, holding him safely and keeping him warm.

Mein Sohn, was birgst du so bang dein Gesicht? –
Siehst, Vater, du den Erlkönig nicht?
Den Erlenkönig mit Kron und Schweif? –
Mein Sohn, es ist ein Nebelstreif. –

«Du liebes Kind, komm, geh mit mir!
Gar schöne Spiele spiel ich mit dir;
Manch bunte Blumen sind an dem Strand,
Meine Mutter hat manch gülden Gewand.»

Mein Vater, mein Vater, und hörest du nicht,
Was Erlenkönig mir leise verspricht? –
Sei ruhig, bleibe ruhig, mein Kind;
In dürren Blättern säuselt der Wind. –

«Willst, feiner Knabe, du mit mir gehn?
Meine Töchter sollen dich warten schön;
Meine Töchter führen den nächtlichen Reihn,
Und wiegen und tanzen und singen dich ein.»

Mein Vater, mein Vater, und siehst du nicht dort
Erlkönigs Töchter am düstern Ort? –
Mein Sohn, mein Sohn, ich seh es genau:
Es scheinen die alten Weiden so grau.

'Why do you hide your face so anxiously, son?' 'Don't you see the
Erlking, father? the Erlking with his crown and his long robe?' 'That's a
trail of mist, son.'

'You sweet child, come, come with me! We shall play lovely games to-
gether, there are flowers of many colours by the water's edge, my mother
has many garments of gold.'

'Oh father, father, can't you hear the Erlking's soft voice, promising me
things?' 'Don't fret, don't worry, child; it's the wind rustling in the dry
leaves.'

'Will you come with me, darling boy? My daughters shall be your lovely
attendants; every night my daughters dance a round dance, they will rock
you and dance you and sing you to sleep.'

'Oh father, father, don't you see Erlking's daughters over there, in the
dark place?' 'Son, son, I can see it plain enough; it's the old willow-trees
looking so grey.'

«Ich liebe dich, mich reizt deine schöne Gestalt;
Und bist du nicht willig, so brauch ich Gewalt.»
Mein Vater, mein Vater, jetzt faßt er mich an!
Erlkönig hat mir ein Leids getan! –

Dem Vater grausets, er reitet geschwind,
Er hält in Armen das ächzende Kind,
Erreicht den Hof mit Mühe und Not;
In seinen Armen das Kind war tot.

DER SÄNGER *

Was hör ich draußen vor dem Tor,
Was auf der Brücke schallen?
Laß den Gesang vor unserm Ohr
Im Saale widerhallen!
Der König sprachs, der Page lief;
Der Knabe kam, der König rief:
Laßt mir herein den Alten!

'I love you, I am charmed by your beautiful shape; and if you are not willing, I will use force.' 'Oh father, father, now he's catching hold of me! the Erlking's hurting me!'

The father shudders, he quickens his horse's pace, he holds the moaning child in his arms; with effort and difficulty he reaches the farmhouse: in his arms the child lay dead.

THE MINSTREL

'What sound do I hear out there by the gate and on the bridge? Let the song be performed in our hearing in the hall!' So said the king, and out ran the page; back came the boy, and the king cried: 'Let the old man in!'

* This ballad and the four following poems are from the novel *Wilhelm Meister*. The first two of these five songs are sung by the mad Harp Player, the others by 'Mignon', a pathetic child of mysterious origins.

Gegrüßet seid mir, edle Herrn,
Gegrüßt ihr, schöne Damen!
Welch reicher Himmel! Stern bei Stern!
Wer kennet ihre Namen?
Im Saal voll Pracht und Herrlichkeit
Schließt, Augen, euch; hier ist nicht Zeit,
Sich staunend zu ergetzen.

Der Sänger drückt' die Augen ein
Und schlug in vollen Tönen;
Die Ritter schauten mutig drein,
Und in den Schoß die Schönen.
Der König, dem das Lied gefiel,
Ließ, ihn zu ehren für sein Spiel,
Eine goldne Kette holen.

Die goldne Kette gib mir nicht,
Die Kette gib den Rittern,
Vor deren kühnem Angesicht
Der Feinde Lanzen splittern;
Gib sie dem Kanzler, den du hast,
Und laß ihn noch die goldne Last
Zu andern Lasten tragen.

'Greetings, noble lords, and greetings, fair ladies! How rich are these heavens! star upon star! Who can name them? Close, eyes, in this hall full of splendour and magnificence! this is no time to gaze in delighted amazement.'

The minstrel pressed his eyes shut, and struck up with full voice; the knights looked on boldly, and the fair ladies into their laps. The king, pleased by the song and wishing to honour him for his performance, sent for a golden chain.

'Do not give the golden chain to me! Give it to your knights, before whose valiant countenance your enemies' lances splinter; give it to that Chancellor whom you have by you, and let him carry the golden burden in addition to his other burdens.

Ich singe, wie der Vogel singt,
Der in den Zweigen wohnet;
Das Lied, das aus der Kehle dringt,
Ist Lohn, der reichlich lohnet.
Doch darf ich bitten, bitt ich eins:
Laß mir den besten Becher Weins
In purem Golde reichen.

Er setzt' ihn an, er trank ihn aus:
O Trank voll süßer Labe!
O wohl dem hochbeglückten Haus,
Wo das ist kleine Gabe!
Ergehts euch wohl, so denkt an mich,
Und danket Gott so warm, als ich
Für diesen Trunk euch danke.

WER nie sein Brot mit Tränen aß,
Wer nie die kummervollen Nächte
Auf seinem Bette weinend saß,
Der kennt euch nicht, ihr himmlischen Mächte.

'I sing as the bird sings that lives in the branches; the song that pours from my throat is its own abundant reward. But if I may make a request, I will ask for one thing: let a cup of the best wine be brought to me in pure gold.'

He raised it to his lips and drained it. 'O draught full of sweet refreshment! How blessed is the fortunate house in which this is but a small gift! When you prosper, think of me, and thank God as warmly as I thank you for this cup of wine.'

HE who has never eaten his bread with tears, he who has never, through nights of anguish, sat weeping on his bed – such a man does not know you, you heavenly Powers.

Ihr führt ins Leben uns hinein,
Ihr laßt den Armen schuldig werden,
Dann überläßt ihr ihn der Pein:
Denn alle Schuld rächt sich auf Erden.

KENNST du das Land, wo die Zitronen blühn,
Im dunkeln Laub die Gold-Orangen glühn,
Ein sanfter Wind vom blauen Himmel weht,
Die Myrte still und hoch der Lorbeer steht,
Kennst du es wohl?
 Dahin! Dahin
Möcht ich mit dir, o mein Geliebter, ziehn.

Kennst du das Haus? Auf Säulen ruht sein Dach,
Es glänzt der Saal, es schimmert das Gemach,
Und Marmorbilder stehn und sehn mich an:
Was hat man dir, du armes Kind, getan?
Kennst du es wohl?
 Dahin! Dahin
Möcht ich mit dir, o mein Beschützer, ziehn.

You lead us into life, and by your will, poor wretches, we fall into sin, and then are delivered over to suffering: for on earth there is retribution for every guilt.

Do you know the land where the lemon-trees blossom, where the golden oranges glow in the dark foliage, a soft wind blows from the blue sky, and the myrtle stands silent and the bay-tree is tall? Do you know it perhaps? It is there, there that I would like to go with you, my beloved.

Do you know the house? Its roof rests on columns, the hall gleams, the room glitters, and marble figures stand and look at me: 'What have they done to you, poor child?' Do you know it perhaps? It is there, there that I would like to go with you, my protector.

Kennst du den Berg und seinen Wolkensteg?
Das Maultier sucht im Nebel seinen Weg,
In Höhlen wohnt der Drachen alte Brut,
Es stürzt der Fels und über ihn die Flut;
Kennst du ihn wohl?
 Dahin! Dahin
Geht unser Weg! o Vater, laß uns ziehn!

HEISS mich nicht reden, heiß mich schweigen,
Denn mein Geheimnis ist mir Pflicht;
Ich möchte dir mein ganzes Innre zeigen,
Allein das Schicksal will es nicht.

Zur rechten Zeit vertreibt der Sonne Lauf
Die finstre Nacht, und sie muß sich erhellen;
Der harte Fels schließt seinen Busen auf,
Mißgönnt der Erde nicht die tiefverborgnen Quellen.

Ein jeder sucht im Arm des Freundes Ruh,
Dort kann die Brust in Klagen sich ergießen;
Allein ein Schwur drückt mir die Lippen zu,
Und nur ein Gott vermag sie aufzuschließen.

Do you know the mountain and its cloudy path? The mule picks its way through the mist; in caves the ancient brood of dragons live; the rock-face falls sheer and the stream rushes over it; do you know it perhaps? It is there, there our way leads! Oh, father, let us go!

Do not bid me speak, bid me be silent, for it is my duty to keep my secret. I would like to show you my whole heart, but fate wills otherwise.

The circling sun in due season drives away the dark night and light must take its place; the hard rock opens its bosom and gives its deep-hidden waters ungrudgingly to the earth.

Every man seeks to ease his troubled breast in a friend's arms, where he can pour out his sorrows; but an oath seals my lips, and only a god can open them.

Nur wer die Sehnsucht kennt,
Weiß, was ich leide!
Allein und abgetrennt
Von aller Freude,
Seh ich ans Firmament
Nach jener Seite.
Ach, der mich liebt und kennt,
Ist in der Weite.
Es schwindelt mir, es brennt
Mein Eingeweide.
Nur wer die Sehnsucht kennt,
Weiß, was ich leide!

ZEITMASS

Eros, wie seh ich dich hier! In jeglichem Händchen die
 Sanduhr!
 Wie? Leichtsinniger Gott, missest du doppelt die Zeit?
«Langsam rinnen aus einer die Stunden entfernter Geliebten;
 Gegenwärtigen fließt eilig die zweite herab.»

Only those who know what longing is can know what I suffer! Alone and cut off from all joy, I keep gazing over yonder into the firmament. Alas! he who loves me and knows me is far away. I feel giddy, I am all on fire inside. Only those who know what longing is can know what I suffer!

THE MEASUREMENT OF TIME

Eros, what is this I see? In each of your little hands you have an hourglass! What! frivolous god, are you double-measuring time? 'Slowly through one of them flow the hours of absent lovers; swiftly, for those who are together, the second runs out.'

87

DIE GESCHWISTER

Schlummer und Schlaf, zwei Brüder, zum Dienste der Götter
 berufen,
 Bat sich Prometheus herab, seinem Geschlechte zum Trost;
Aber, den Göttern so leicht, doch schwer zu ertragen den
 Menschen,
 Ward nun ihr Schlummer uns Schlaf, ward nun ihr Schlaf uns
 zum Tod.

ANAKREONS GRAB

Wo die Rose hier blüht, wo Reben um Lorbeer sich schlingen,
 Wo das Turtelchen lockt, wo sich das Grillchen ergetzt,
Welch ein Grab ist hier, das alle Götter mit Leben
 Schön bepflanzt und geziert? Es ist Anakreons Ruh.
Frühling, Sommer und Herbst genoß der glückliche Dichter;
 Vor dem Winter hat ihn endlich der Hügel geschützt.

THE BROTHERS

Slumber and Sleep, two brothers appointed to serve the gods, came down
at Prometheus' request to comfort his race. But what is so easy for gods to
bear was hard for mankind; and their slumber became our sleep, their sleep
our death.

ANACREON'S GRAVE

Here, where the rose blooms, and vines intermingle with laurel, where the
turtle-dove calls to its mate and the cricket sings with delight, what grave
is this, which all the gods have adorned like a garden with the beauty of
life? It is Anacreon's resting-place. Spring, summer, and autumn the happy
poet enjoyed: and at the last this mound has kept winter from him.

II

THE CLASSICAL GOETHE
(1786–1800)

aus den RÖMISCHEN ELEGIEN

I

SAGET, Steine, mir an, o sprecht, ihr hohen Paläste!
 Straßen, redet ein Wort! Genius, regst du dich nicht?
Ja, es ist alles beseelt in deinen heiligen Mauern,
 Ewige Roma; nur mir schweiget noch alles so still.
O wer flüstert mir zu, an welchem Fenster erblick ich
 Einst das holde Geschöpf, das mich versengend erquickt?
Ahn ich die Wege noch nicht, durch die ich immer und immer,
 Zu ihr und von ihr zu gehn, opfre die köstliche Zeit?
Noch betracht ich Kirch und Palast, Ruinen und Säulen,
 Wie ein bedächtiger Mann schicklich die Reise benutzt.
Doch bald ist es vorbei; dann wird ein einziger Tempel,
 Amors Tempel, nur sein, der den Geweihten empfängt.
Eine Welt zwar bist du, o Rom; doch ohne die Liebe
 Wäre die Welt nicht die Welt, wäre denn Rom auch nicht
 Rom.

from ROMAN ELEGIES

I

TELL me, you stones, oh speak, you lofty palaces! Streets, say a word!
Spirit of the place, will you not stir? Yes, everything is alive within your
holy walls, eternal Rome; only for me it is all still so silent. Oh, who shall
whisper it to me, at what window one day shall I see the sweet creature who
will burn me and refresh me? Do I not yet guess the paths I shall always,
always be walking to her and from her, while precious time slips by? Here
I am, still gazing at churches and palaces, ruins and columns, like a serious
man making sensible use of a journey. But this will soon be over, and then
all will be one great temple, the Temple of Love receiving its initiate. Oh,
Rome, though you are a whole world, yet without love the world would
not be the world, nor would Rome be Rome.

2 *Erste Fassung*

FRAGET nun, wen ihr auch wollt, mich werdet ihr nimmer
 erreichen,
 Schöne Damen, und ihr, Herren der feineren Welt!
Ob denn auch Werther gelebt? Ob denn auch alles fein wahr
 sei?
 Welche Stadt sich mit Recht Lottens, der einzigen, rühmt?
Ach, wie hab ich so oft die törichten Blätter verwünschet,
 Die mein jugendlich Leid unter die Menschen gebracht!
Wäre Werther mein Bruder gewesen, ich hätt ihn erschlagen,
 Kaum verfolgte mich so rächend sein trauriger Geist.
So verfolgte das Liedchen *Malbrough* den reisenden Briten
 Erst von Paris nach Livorn, dann von Livorno nach Rom,
Weiter nach Napel hinunter, und wär er nach Madras gesegelt,
 Malbrough empfing ihn auch dort, *Malbrough* im Hafen das
 Lied.
Glücklich bin ich entflohn! Sie kennet Werthern und Lotten,
 Kennet den Namen des Manns, der sie sich eignete, kaum.
Sie erkennet in ihm den freien, rüstigen Fremden,
 Der in Bergen und Schnee hölzerne Häuser bewohnt.

2 *First Version*

ASK whom you will, I am safe from you now, you fair ladies and fine
society gentlemen! 'But did Werther really live? Did it all really happen
like that? Which town has the right to boast the lovely Lotte its citizen?'
Oh, how often I have cursed those foolish pages which made my youthful
sufferings public property! If Werther had been my brother and I had killed
him, I could scarcely have been so persecuted by his avenging sorrowful
ghost. Thus it was that the song '*Malbrouk s'en va-t-en guerre*' pursued the
British traveller, first from Paris to Leghorn, then from Leghorn to Rome,
and then on down to Naples, and if he had sailed to Madras, even there the
ditty, even there '*Malbrouk*' would have greeted him in the harbour. I have
made a lucky escape! *She* has scarcely heard of Werther or Lotte, scarcely
knows the name of the man who now is hers. She sees in him a free, robust
stranger, one of the people who live in wooden houses among mountains
and snow.

2 *Zweite Fassung*

EHRET, wen ihr auch wollt! Nun bin ich endlich geborgen!
 Schöne Damen und ihr, Herren der feineren Welt,
Fraget nach Oheim und Vetter und alten Muhmen und Tanten,
 Und dem gebundnen Gespräch folge das traurige Spiel.
Auch ihr übrigen fahret mir wohl, in großen und kleinen
 Zirkeln, die ihr mich oft nah der Verzweiflung gebracht.
Wiederholet, politisch und zwecklos, jegliche Meinung,
 Die den Wandrer mit Wut über Europa verfolgt.
So verfolgte das Liedchen *Malbrough* den reisenden Briten
 Einst von Paris nach Livorn, dann von Livorno nach Rom,
Weiter nach Napel hinunter, und wär er nach Smyrna gesegelt,
 Malbrough! empfing ihn auch dort! Malbrough! im Hafen das
 Lied.
Und so mußt ich bis jetzt auf allen Tritten und Schritten
 Schelten hören das Volk, schelten der Könige Rat.
Nun entdeckt ihr mich nicht so bald in meinem Asyle,
 Das mir Amor der Fürst, königlich schützend, verlieh.
Hier bedecket er mich mit seinem Fittich; die Liebste
 Fürchtet, römisch gesinnt, wütende Gallier nicht;

2 *Second Version*

HONOUR whom you will! Now at last I have found a safe refuge. Inquire,
fair ladies, and fine society gentlemen, after your uncles and cousins and
elderly aunts, and let your stilted conversation be followed by some dreary
parlour-game! And farewell to the rest of you too, you others in clubs big
and little, who have often driven me to the verge of distraction! Continue
your vain repetition of the clichés of political opinion that so furiously dog
one's steps all over Europe. Thus it was that the song '*Malbrouk s'en va-t-
en guerre*' once pursued the British traveller – from Paris to Leghorn, then
from Leghorn to Rome and then on down to Naples, and if he had sailed to
Smyrna, even there the ditty, even there '*Malbrouk*' would have greeted
him in the harbour. And thus, hitherto, have I been compelled wherever I
went to listen to irate criticisms of the people and irate criticisms of kings
and their councillors. But you'll not track me down so easily now, in this
refuge which Prince Cupid, my royal protector, has granted me! Here he
covers me with his wings; my darling, like a true Roman, is undismayed by

Sie erkundigt sich nie nach neuer Märe; sie spähet
 Sorglich den Wünschen des Manns, dem sie sich eignete,
 nach.
Sie ergetzt sich an ihm, dem freien, rüstigen Fremden,
 Der von Bergen und Schnee, hölzernen Häusern erzählt;
Teilt die Flammen, die sie in seinem Busen entzündet,
 Freut sich, daß er das Gold nicht wie der Römer bedenkt.
Besser ist ihr Tisch nun bestellt; es fehlet an Kleidern,
 Fehlet am Wagen ihr nicht, der nach der Oper sie bringt.
Mutter und Tochter erfreun sich ihres nordischen Gastes,
 Und der Barbare beherrscht römischen Busen und Leib.

3

Lass dich, Geliebte, nicht reun, daß du mir so schnell dich
 ergeben!
 Glaub es, ich denke nicht frech, denke nicht niedrig von dir.
Vielfach wirken die Pfeile des Amor: einige ritzen,
 Und vom schleichenden Gift kranket auf Jahre das Herz.

the storms raging in France. She never asks what the latest news is; she
takes careful thought for the wishes of the man to whom she now belongs.
She is delighted with him, this free, robust stranger who tells her of
mountains and snow and wooden houses; she shares the flames she has
kindled in his breast, and is glad that he is more liberal with gold than the
men of Rome. Her table is better furnished now, and she has no lack of
clothes, or of a carriage to take her to the opera. Both the mother and the
daughter are pleased with their northern guest, and the barbarian has
conquered a Roman bosom and body.

3

Do not regret, beloved, that you gave yourself to me so quickly! Believe
me, I do not think shamelessly or basely of you. The arrows of Cupid are
various in their effects: some graze our skin, and our hearts languish for
years from their creeping poison. But others, stout-feathered and with

Aber mächtig befiedert, mit frisch geschliffener Schärfe
 Dringen die andern ins Mark, zünden behende das Blut.
In der heroischen Zeit, da Götter und Göttinnen liebten,
 Folgte Begierde dem Blick, folgte Genuß der Begier.
Glaubst du, es habe sich lange die Göttin der Liebe besonnen,
 Als im Idäischen Hain einst ihr Anchises gefiel?
Hätte Luna gesäumt, den schönen Schläfer zu küssen,
 Oh, so hätt ihn geschwind, neidend, Aurora geweckt.
Hero erblickte Leandern am lauten Fest, und behende
 Stürzte der Liebende sich heiß in die nächtliche Flut.
Rhea Silvia wandelt, die fürstliche Jungfrau, der Tiber
 Wasser zu schöpfen, hinab, und sie ergreifet der Gott.
So erzeugte die Söhne sich Mars! – Die Zwillinge tränket
 Eine Wölfin, und Rom nennt sich die Fürstin der Welt.

 5

FROH empfind ich mich nun auf klassischem Boden begeistert;
 Vor- und Mitwelt spricht lauter und reizender mir.
Hier befolg ich den Rat, durchblättre die Werke der Alten
 Mit geschäftiger Hand, täglich mit neuem Genuß.

freshly sharpened points, pierce us to the marrow and swiftly kindle the
blood. In the heroic age, when gods and goddesses loved, desire followed
upon a look, and enjoyment followed upon desire. Do you suppose the
goddess of love stopped to think twice when Anchises attracted her in the
grove of Ida? If the Moon had delayed before kissing her beautiful sleeper,
ah then, the Dawn, in envy, would swiftly have waked him. Hero caught
sight of Leander at the noisy feast, and in a trice he plunged, hot with love,
into the nocturnal waves. Rhea Silvia, the royal maiden, walked down to
draw water from the Tiber, and the god seized her. Thus Mars begat his
sons! – A she-wolf suckled the twins, and Rome became queen of the
world.

 5

How glad, how inspired I feel now on classical soil! The world of the past
and the world of the present both speak to me with more voice and more
charm. Here, as I have been counselled, I leaf through the works of the
ancients with busy hand and daily with fresh delight. But throughout the

Aber die Nächte hindurch hält Amor mich anders beschäftigt;
 Werd ich auch halb nur gelehrt, bin ich doch doppelt be-
 glückt.
Und belehr ich mich nicht, indem ich des lieblichen Busens
 Formen spähe, die Hand leite die Hüften hinab?
Dann versteh ich den Marmor erst recht: ich denk und ver-
 gleiche,
 Sehe mit fühlendem Aug, fühle mit sehender Hand.
Raubt die Liebste denn gleich mir einige Stunden des Tages,
 Gibt sie Stunden der Nacht mir zur Entschädigung hin.
Wird doch nicht immer geküßt, es wird vernünftig gesprochen;
 Überfällt sie der Schlaf, lieg ich und denke mir viel.
Oftmals hab ich auch schon in ihren Armen gedichtet
 Und des Hexameters Maß leise mit fingernder Hand
Ihr auf den Rücken gezählt. Sie atmet in lieblichem Schlummer,
 Und es durchglühet ihr Hauch mir bis ins Tiefste die Brust.
Amor schüret die Lamp indes und denket der Zeiten,
 Da er den nämlichen Dienst seinen Triumvirn getan.

nights Cupid keeps me busy in another way; I become only half a scholar, but twice as happy. And is this not learning, to study the forms of her lovely bosom, and slide my hands down over her hips? For I understand marble then all the better: reflecting, comparing, I see with an eye that feels and feel with a hand that sees. What if my darling robs me of some daytime hours? She gives me in compensation hours of the night. After all, we do not spend all the time kissing, but some in sensible conversation; and when sleep overtakes her, I lie and am full of thoughts. I have even many a time composed poetry in her arms, and softly, with fingering hand, counted out on her back the hexameters' measure. Sweetly she sleeps and breathes, and her breath burns right through me, deep down to my heart. Cupid trims the lamp meanwhile, and thinks back to the times when he did the same service for three sovereign poets of Love.

7

O WIE fühl ich in Rom mich so froh! gedenk ich der Zeiten,
 Da mich ein graulicher Tag hinten im Norden umfing,
Trübe der Himmel und schwer auf meine Scheitel sich senkte,
 Farb- und gestaltlos die Welt um den Ermatteten lag,
Und ich über mein Ich, des unbefriedigten Geistes
 Düstre Wege zu spähn, still in Betrachtung versank.
Nun umleuchtet der Glanz des helleren Äthers die Stirne;
 Phöbus rufet, der Gott, Formen und Farben hervor.
Sternhell glänzet die Nacht, sie klingt von weichen Gesängen,
 Und mir leuchtet der Mond heller als nordischer Tag.
Welche Seligkeit ward mir Sterblichem! Träum ich? Empfänget
 Dein ambrosisches Haus, Jupiter Vater, den Gast?
Ach! hier lieg ich und strecke nach deinen Knieen die Hände
 Flehend aus. O vernimm, Jupiter Xenius, mich!
Wie ich hereingekommen, ich kanns nicht sagen; es faßte
 Hebe den Wandrer und zog mich in die Hallen heran.
Hast du ihr einen Heroen heraufzuführen geboten?
 Irrte die Schöne? Vergib! Laß mir des Irrtums Gewinn!

7

OH, how glad I feel to be in Rome, as I remember those times back there in the north, when grey days clung about me and the sky was gloomy and pressed down on my head like a dead weight, and I was surrounded by a colourless, shapeless, dulling, exhausting world, and would sink into contemplation of my ego, trying to spy out the dark paths of my discontented mind. Now, the radiance of a brighter air shines round my brow; Phoebus, the god, calls forms and colours into being. The night is brilliant with stars and resounds softly with singing; and to me the moon shines more brightly than the northern daylight. What blessed happiness has befallen me, mortal that I am! Am I dreaming? Have I been received as a guest, Father Jupiter, into your ambrosial palace? Ah, here I lie, and to your knees I extend my imploring hands. Oh hear me, Jove, lord of guests! I do not know how I got in here. The Goddess of Youth laid hands on me as I wandered, and drew me up into these halls. Did you tell her to go down and fetch a hero? Did the fair maiden make a mistake? Oh pardon it, and let me enjoy the error's advantage! Your daughter Fortune, too, hands out her most splendid gifts

Deine Tochter Fortuna, sie auch! Die herrlichsten Gaben
 Teilt als ein Mädchen sie aus, wie es die Laune gebeut.
Bist du der wirtliche Gott? O Dann so verstoße den Gastfreund
 Nicht von deinem Olymp wieder zur Erde hinab!
«Dichter! wohin versteigest du dich?» – Vergib mir; der hohe
 Kapitolinische Berg ist dir ein zweiter Olymp.
Dulde mich, Jupiter, hier, und Hermes führe mich später,
 Cestius' Mal vorbei, leise zum Orkus hinab.

10

A LEXANDER und Cäsar und Heinrich und Friedrich, die
 Großen,
 Gäben die Hälfte mir gern ihres erworbenen Ruhms,
Könnt ich auf Eine Nacht dies Lager jedem vergönnen;
 Aber die Armen, sie hält strenge des Orkus Gewalt.
Freue dich also, Lebendger, der lieberwärmeten Stätte,
 Ehe den fliehenden Fuß schauerlich Lethe dir netzt.

13

A MOR bleibet ein Schalk, und wer ihm vertraut, ist betrogen!
 Heuchelnd kam er zu mir: «Diesmal nur traue mir noch.

as her girlish fancy dictates. Are you not called 'the hospitable god'? Oh then do not cast your guest down to earth again from your Olympian dwelling! 'Poet, where do you think you are climbing?' Forgive me; the lofty Capitoline Hill is your second Olympus. Let me stay here, Jupiter, and later let Hermes lead me quietly down, past Cestius' pyramid, to the underworld.

10

THE great Alexander, and Caesar, and Henry IV, and Frederick the Great, would gladly all give me half the renown they won, if I could allow them even one night each on this bed; but, poor fellows! they are locked up firmly in Hades. So take your delight, living man, in your warm place of love, ere Lethe's dread waters wet your runaway foot.

13

CUPID remains a rogue; he will let you down if you trust him! He came to me, the hypocrite, and said, 'Trust me again just this once. I mean well by

Redlich mein ichs mit dir: du hast dein Leben und Dichten,
 Dankbar erkenn ich es wohl, meiner Verehrung geweiht.
Siehe, dir bin ich nun gar nach Rom gefolget! ich möchte
 Dir im fremden Gebiet gern was Gefälliges tun.
Jeder Reisende klagt, er finde schlechte Bewirtung;
 Welchen Amor empfiehlt, köstlich bewirtet ist er.
Du betrachtest mit Staunen die Trümmern alter Gebäude
 Und durchwandelst mit Sinn diesen geheiligten Raum.
Du verehrst noch mehr die werten Reste des Bildens
 Einziger Künstler, die stets ich in der Werkstatt besucht.
Diese Gestalten, ich formte sie selbst! Verzeih mir, ich prahle
 Diesmal nicht: du gestehst, was ich dir sage, sei wahr.
Nun du mir lässiger dienst, wo sind die schönen Gestalten,
 Wo die Farben, der Glanz deiner Erfindungen hin?
Denkst du nun wieder zu bilden, o Freund? Die Schule der
 Griechen
 Blieb noch offen, das Tor schlossen die Jahre nicht zu.
Ich, der Lehrer, bin ewig jung, und liebe die Jungen.
 Altklug lieb ich dich nicht! Munter! Begreife mich wohl!
War das Antike doch neu, da jene Glücklichen lebten!
 Lebe glücklich, und so lebe die Vorzeit in dir!

you. You have, as I gratefully acknowledge, devoted your life and your
poetry to doing me honour. Look, I have now even followed you to Rome,
and in these foreign parts I should like to do you some service. Travellers
always complain that they find bad food and lodging; but with a recom-
mendation from Love one gets first-class treatment. Here you are, gazing
in wonder at ruins of ancient buildings, wandering wisely about this sancti-
fied city; and you revere even more the worthy remnants of the handiwork
of great artists, whom I constantly visited in their workshops. It was my-
self who fashioned these figures! Excuse me, this time I am not boasting.
You must admit that what I tell you is true. And now that you have grown
more slack in my service, what has become of the lovely forms, the col-
ours, the brilliance of your inventions? Are you now thinking of being
creative again, my friend? The school of the Greeks has stayed open, the
years have not closed its doors. I, the teacher, am eternally young, and I
love youth. I do not like you to have an old head on young shoulders!
Look lively! Mark my words! After all, antiquity was new in the days of
those happy ancients. Live happily, and so bring the past to life in your-

Stoff zum Liede, wo nimmst du ihn her? Ich muß dir ihn geben,
 Und den höheren Stil lehret die Liebe dich nur.»
Also sprach der Sophist. Wer widerspräch ihm? und leider
 Bin ich zu folgen gewöhnt, wenn der Gebieter befiehlt. –
Nun, verräterisch hält er sein Wort, gibt Stoff zu Gesängen,
 Ach, und raubt mir die Zeit, Kraft und Besinnung zugleich;
Blick und Händedruck, und Küsse, gemütliche Worte,
 Silben köstlichen Sinns wechselt ein liebendes Paar.
Da wird Lispeln Geschwätz, wird Stottern liebliche Rede:
 Solch ein Hymnus verhallt ohne prosodisches Maß.
Dich, Aurora, wie kannt ich dich sonst als Freundin der Musen!
 Hat, Aurora, dich auch Amor, der lose, verführt?
Du erscheinest mir nun als seine Freundin, und weckest
 Mich an seinem Altar wieder zum festlichen Tag.
Find ich die Fülle der Locken an meinem Busen! Das Köpfchen
 Ruhet und drücket den Arm, der sich dem Halse bequemt.
Welch ein freudig Erwachen, erhieltet ihr, ruhige Stunden,
 Mir das Denkmal der Lust, die in den Schlaf uns gewiegt! –
Sie bewegt sich im Schlummer und sinkt auf die Breite des
 Lagers,
 Weggewendet, und doch läßt sie mir Hand noch in Hand.

self! Where will you find matter for your song? It is I who must give it
you, and the higher style you will learn only from Love.'
 So spake the sophist. Who could gainsay him? And, alas, I am accus-
tomed to obey the commands of this lord. Well, he is traitorously keeping
his word, giving me matter for song, and, alas, at the same time depriving
me of time, strength, and senses! A pair of lovers now exchange looks and
pressure of hands, kisses, and words of affection, syllables full of exquisite
meaning. Here lisping becomes conversation, stammering becomes sweet
speech; a hymn like this melts into the air without prosody or numbers. Oh
Goddess of Dawn, how well I once knew you as a friend of the Muses!
Goddess, has wanton Cupid seduced you too? It is as his friend you appear
to me now, and you wake me to festive day again at his altar. On my bosom
I find the abundance of her locks! Her little hand rests and weighs on my
arm that fits snug to her neck. How gladly I waken to find that the quiet
hours have preserved a memorial of the pleasure that lulled us to sleep! She
moves in her slumber, sinks down on the breadth of the bed, turns away
from me, but still leaves her hand in my hand. We are constantly bound to

Herzliche Liebe verbindet uns stets und treues Verlangen,
 Und den Wechsel behielt nur die Begierde sich vor.
Einen Druck der Hand, ich sehe die himmlischen Augen
 Wieder offen. – O nein! laßt auf der Bildung mich ruhn!
Bleibt geschlossen! ihr macht mich verwirrt und trunken, ihr
 raubet
 Mir den stillen Genuß reiner Betrachtung zu früh.
Diese Formen, wie groß! wie edel gewendet die Glieder!
 Schlief Ariadne so schön: Theseus, du konntest entfliehn?
Diesen Lippen ein einziger Kuß! O Theseus, nun scheide!
 Blick ihr ins Auge! Sie wacht! – Ewig nun hält sie dich fest.

14

ZÜNDE mir Licht an, Knabe! – «Noch ist es hell. Ihr verzehret
 Öl und Docht nur umsonst. Schließet die Läden doch nicht!
Hinter die Häuser entwich, nicht hinter den Berg, uns die
 Sonne!
 Ein halb Stündchen noch währts bis zum Geläute der
 Nacht.» –
Unglückseliger! geh und gehorch! Mein Mädchen erwart ich.
 Tröste mich, Lämpchen, indes, lieblicher Bote der Nacht!

each other by heartfelt love and faithful desire, our appetite only reserving
its right to vary. A pressure of my hand – and I shall see these heavenly
eyes open again. Ah, no! Let me rest and still gaze at her shape! Do not
open! For you fill me with drunken confusion, you snatch me too soon
from the quiet delight of pure beholding. How nobly she is formed! Her
limbs, how splendidly fashioned! If Ariadne was so fair in her sleep, how
could Theseus leave her? One kiss on these lips! Oh Theseus, now be gone!
Look in her eyes! She wakes! – She holds you fast now for ever!

14

LIGHT the lamp for me, boy! – 'It's still daylight. You're only wasting oil
and wick. Why, don't close the shutters! The sun has gone down behind
the houses, not under the hill. It'll be half an hour till they sound the bells
for nightfall.' – Wretch! go at once and obey me! My sweetheart is coming.
Till then, little lamp, be my comfort, dear herald of night!

15

Cäsarn wär ich wohl nie zu fernen Britannen gefolget,
　　Florus hätte mich leicht in die Popine geschleppt!
Denn mir bleiben weit mehr die Nebel des traurigen Nordens
　　Als ein geschäftiges Volk südlicher Flöhe verhaßt.
Und noch schöner von heut an seid mir gegrüßet, ihr Schenken,
　　Osterien, wie euch schicklich der Römer benennt;
Denn ihr zeigtet mir heute die Liebste, begleitet vom Oheim,
　　Den die Gute so oft, mich zu besitzen, betriegt.
Hier stand unser Tisch, den Deutsche vertraulich umgaben;
　　Drüben suchte das Kind neben der Mutter den Platz,
Rückte vielmals die Bank und wußt es artig zu machen,
　　Daß ich halb ihr Gesicht, völlig den Nacken gewann.
Lauter sprach sie, als hier die Römerin pfleget, kredenzte,
　　Blickte gewendet nach mir, goß und verfehlte das Glas.

15

I don't suppose I should ever have followed the Emperor to the land of
the distant Britons; Florus would have found it easy to drag me into a
chophouse!* For the mists of the dismal north remain much more hateful
to me than a busy race of southern fleas. And as from today, oh you taverns
– osterie, as the Romans fittingly call you – I shall give you a still fairer
salutation: for today you showed me my darling – she was accompanied by
her uncle, whom the dear creature so often deceives in order to possess me.
　　Here stood our table, with Germans at their ease all round it; over there
the dear girl found a place next to her mother; she shifted the bench several
times and managed to arrange herself prettily so that I gained the sight of
half her face and the whole of her neck. She was talking more loudly than
Roman women usually do here, and pouring out the wine, and as she looked
round at me she poured and missed the glass. Wine flowed over the table,

* An allusion to an anecdote recorded of the Emperor Hadrian and the
poet Florus, in which they exchange versified badinage on their res-
pective occupations.

Wein floß über den Tisch, und sie, mit zierlichem Finger,
 Zog auf dem hölzernen Blatt Kreise der Feuchtigkeit hin.
Meinen Namen verschlang sie dem ihrigen; immer begierig
 Schaut ich dem Fingerchen nach, und sie bemerkte mich wohl.
Endlich zog sie behende das Zeichen der römischen Fünfe
 Und ein Strichlein davor. Schnell, und sobald ichs gesehn,
Schlang sie Kreise durch Kreise, die Lettern und Ziffern zu
 löschen;
 Aber die köstliche *Vier* blieb mir ins Auge geprägt.
Stumm war ich sitzen geblieben und biß die glühende Lippe,
 Halb aus Schalkheit und Lust, halb aus Begierde, mir wund.
Erst noch so lange bis Nacht! dann noch vier Stunden zu warten!
 Hohe Sonne, du weilst, und du beschauest dein Rom!
Größeres sahest du nichts und wirst nichts Größeres sehen,
 Wie es dein Priester Horaz in der Entzückung versprach.
Aber heute verweile mir nicht, und wende die Blicke
 Von dem Siebengebirg früher und williger ab!
Einem Dichter zuliebe verkürze die herrlichen Stunden,
 Die mit begierigem Blick selig der Maler genießt;
Glühend blicke noch schnell zu diesen hohen Fassaden,
 Kuppeln und Säulen zuletzt und Obelisken herauf!

and with a dainty finger she drew liquid circles on the wooden surface. She intertwined my name with hers; eagerly I kept watching the little finger, as well she noticed. At last she nimbly drew the sign of the Roman 'five' with a little stroke in front of it. Quickly, and as soon as I had seen it, she interwove circle upon circle to obliterate the letters and figures; but the precious 'four' remained imprinted on my gaze.

I had sat where I was without a word, biting deep into my burning lip – half from mischievous pleasure and half from desire. Still so long till nightfall! then four more hours to wait! Oh lofty Sun, you are pausing to contemplate Rome – your Rome! You have never seen anything greater, and nothing greater shall you ever see – as Horace, your priest, once prophesied in his rapture. Yet today do not tarry, and turn your gaze sooner and more willingly away from the Seven Hills! For a poet's sake, shorten these splendid hours on which the greedy eyes of a painter blessedly feasts; cast one more swift burning glance up at these lofty façades and domes and obelisks; plunge quickly into the sea, all the sooner to behold tomorrow

Stürze dich eilig ins Meer, um morgen früher zu sehen,
 Was Jahrhunderte schon göttliche Lust dir gewährt:
Diese feuchten, mit Rohr so lange bewachsnen Gestade,
 Diese mit Bäumen und Busch düster beschatteten Höhn.
Wenig Hütten zeigten sie erst; dann sahst du auf einmal
 Sie vom wimmelnden Volk glücklicher Räuber belebt.
Alles schleppten sie drauf an diese Stätte zusammen:
 Kaum war das übrige Rund deiner Betrachtung noch wert.
Sahst eine Welt hier entstehn, sahst dann eine Welt hier in
 Trümmern,
 Aus den Trümmern aufs neu fast eine größere Welt!
Daß ich diese noch lange von dir beleuchtet erblicke,
 Spinne die Parze mir klug langsam den Faden herab!
Aber sie eile herbei, die schön bezeichnete Stunde! —
 Glücklich! hör ich sie schon? Nein; doch ich höre schon
 Drei.
So, ihr lieben Musen, betrogt ihr wieder die Länge
 Dieser Weile, die mich von der Geliebten getrennt.
Lebet wohl! Nun eil ich und fürcht euch nicht zu beleidgen:
 Denn ihr Stolzen, ihr gebt Amorn doch immer den Rang.

what you have already beheld for centuries with divine delight — these moist shores so long overgrown with reeds, these heights darkly overshadowed with trees and bushes. At first there were only a few huts to be seen there; then all at once you saw them come alive and swarm with a nation of successful marauders. They collected everything and dragged it to this place; scarcely anything worthy of your notice was left in the surrounding district. Here you saw a world come into being, and later a world in ruins, and then again out of the ruins an almost greater world rising! May I long have the sight of this last, with your light shining over it — may the Fates be prudent and slow in unwinding my thread!

But the hour she appointed so sweetly, may it come soon! — Oh joy! is that it, already striking? No; but three strokes already. Thus once more, dear Muses, you have beguiled this long interval that divided me from my beloved. Farewell! I now hasten away, without fear of offending you; for proud as you are, you give precedence always to Love.

17

MANCHE Töne sind mir Verdruß, doch bleibet am meisten
 Hundegebell mir verhaßt; kläffend zerreißt es mein Ohr.
Einen Hund nur hör ich sehr oft mit frohem Behagen
 Bellend kläffen: den Hund, den sich der Nachbar erzog.
Denn er bellte mir einst mein Mädchen an, da sie sich heimlich
 Zu mir stahl, und verriet unser Geheimnis beinah.
Jetzo, hör ich ihn bellen, so denk ich mir immer: sie kommt
 wohl!
 Oder ich denke der Zeit, da die Erwartete kam.

18

EINES ist mir verdrießlich vor allen Dingen, ein andres
 Bleibt mir abscheulich, empört jegliche Faser in mir,
Nur der bloße Gedanke. Ich will es euch, Freunde, gestehen:
 Gar verdrießlich ist mir einsam das Lager zu Nacht.
Aber ganz abscheulich ists, auf dem Wege der Liebe
 Schlangen zu fürchten und Gift unter den Rosen der Lust,

17

MANY noises annoy me, but barking of dogs I detest above all; my ears are
split by their yelping. There is one dog only whose high-pitched bark often
fills me with gladness, and that is the dog my neighbour has reared. For he
once barked at my sweetheart when she was stealing to me on the sly, and
nearly betrayed our secret. And now, when I hear him bark, I think always:
she must be coming! Or I remember a time when I waited for her, and she
came.

18

THERE is one thing that vexes me more than anything else, and another
thing that I find abominable and revolting; my hair stands on end at the
very thought of it. I will confess to you, my friends, that the thing I find
very vexatious is having to sleep alone at night. But the quite abominable
thing is when one must fear serpents on the pathway of love and poison
under the roses of pleasure; when at the sweetest moment of self-abandon-

Wenn im schönsten Moment der hin sich gebenden Freude
 Deinem sinkenden Haupt lispelnde Sorge sich naht.
Darum macht Faustine mein Glück; sie teilet das Lager
 Gerne mit mir, und bewahrt Treue dem Treuen genau!
Reizendes Hindernis will die rasche Jugend; ich liebe,
 Mich des versicherten Guts lange bequem zu erfreun.
Welche Seligkeit ists! wir wechseln sichere Küsse,
 Atem und Leben getrost saugen und flößen wir ein.
So erfreuen wir uns der langen Nächte, wir lauschen,
 Busen an Busen gedrängt, Stürmen und Regen und Guß.
Und so dämmert der Morgen heran; es bringen die Stunden
 Neue Blumen herbei, schmücken uns festlich den Tag.
Gönnet mir, o Quiriten! das Glück, und jedem gewähre
 Aller Güter der Welt erstes und letztes der Gott!

20

ZIERET Stärke den Mann und freies, mutiges Wesen,
 Oh! so ziemet ihm fast tiefes Geheimnis noch mehr.
Städtebezwingerin du, Verschwiegenheit, Fürstin der Völker,
 Teure Göttin, die mich sicher durchs Leben geführt,

ment and delight, whispering Care draws near one's drooping head. That is why Faustina gives me such happiness: she shares my bed gladly and keeps careful faith to me, as I to her. Impetuous youth finds hindrance an added charm, but I love the long, commodious enjoyment of secure possession. What sweet contentment! There is no danger in our kisses; we exchange life and breath, indrawn and outpoured with confidence. Thus we enjoy the long nights, lying and listening, heart pressed on heart, to storms and the streaming rain. And thus dawn breaks and the hours bring fresh garlands with them, adorning our festive day. Oh Romans, do not begrudge me this bliss – and may the god grant to all men this first and last of the world's good things.

20

STRENGTH and liberality and courage are qualities that adorn a man, but oh, the deepest secrecy becomes him perhaps even more! You conqueror of cities and ruler of peoples, Discretion, beloved goddess, who have led me safely through life, what a fate is now mine! The jesting Muse and roguish

Welches Schicksal erfahr ich! Es löset scherzend die Muse,
 Amor löset, der Schalk, mir den verschlossenen Mund.
Ach, schon wird es so schwer, der Könige Schande verbergen!
 Weder die Krone bedeckt, weder ein phrygischer Bund
Midas' verlängertes Ohr: der nächste Diener entdeckt es,
 Und ihm ängstet und drückt gleich das Geheimnis die Brust.
In die Erde vergrüb er es gern, um sich zu erleichtern:
 Doch die Erde verwahrt solche Geheimnisse nicht;
Rohre sprießen hervor und rauschen und lispeln im Winde:
 Midas! Midas, der Fürst, trägt ein verlängertes Ohr!
Schwerer wird es nun mir, ein schönes Geheimnis zu wahren;
 Ach, den Lippen entquillt Fülle des Herzens so leicht!
Keiner Freundin darf ichs vertraun: sie möchte mich schelten;
 Keinem Freunde: vielleicht brächte der Freund mir Gefahr.
Mein Entzücken dem Hain, dem schallenden Felsen zu sagen,
 Bin ich endlich nicht jung, bin ich nicht einsam genug.
Dir, Hexameter, dir, Pentameter, sei es vertrauet,
 Wie sie des Tags mich erfreut, wie sie des Nachts mich
 beglückt.
Sie, von vielen Männern gesucht, vermeidet die Schlingen,
 Die ihr der Kühnere frech, heimlich der Listige legt;

Love are unlocking my closed mouth; alas, already the shame of kings is getting so hard to hide! Neither the crown nor a Phrygian cap can cover Midas's lengthened ears: his closest servant discovers it, and at once the secret presses and weighs on his breast. He would gladly bury it in the earth to get relief; but the earth will not guard such secrets. Reeds spring forth and rustle and lisp in the wind: 'Midas, Midas the monarch, has overgrown ears!' And now I too am finding it harder to keep a sweet secret; ah, how easily the heart's fullness spills from the lips! I can confide it to no friend — neither woman, for she might chide me, nor man, for he might become a dangerous rival. And I am not young enough or solitary enough to tell my rapture to the grove or the echoing rock. To you, hexameter, and to you, pentameter, I will confide how she gladdens me by day and enchants me by night. Much sought after by men, she avoids the snares that her bolder admirers lay for her insolently, and the cunning ones secretly; deftly and

Klug und zierlich schlüpft sie vorbei und kennet die Wege,
 Wo sie der Liebste gewiß lauschend begierig empfängt.
Zaudre, Luna, sie kommt! damit sie der Nachbar nicht sehe;
 Rausche, Lüftchen, im Laub! niemand vernehme den Tritt.
Und ihr, wachset und blüht, geliebte Lieder, und wieget
 Euch im leisesten Hauch lauer und liebender Luft,
Und entdeckt den Quiriten, wie jene Rohre geschwätzig,
 Eines glücklichen Paars schönes Geheimnis zuletzt.

CUPIDO, loser, eigensinniger Knabe!
Du batst mich um Quartier auf einige Stunden.
Wie viele Tag und Nächte bist du geblieben!
Und bist nun herrisch und Meister im Hause geworden!

Von meinem breiten Lager bin ich vertrieben;
Nun sitz ich an der Erde, Nächte gequälet;
Dein Mutwill schüret Flamm auf Flamme des Herdes,
Verbrennet den Vorrat des Winters und senget mich Armen.

daintily she slips by, knowing the roads, knowing where her sweetheart will surely be waiting and listening with impatient ardour to receive her. Oh moon, do not move, she is coming! Do not let the neighbours see her! Oh rustle the leaves, little breeze, so that no one shall hear her step! And you, my beloved songs, grow tall and flourish, and sway in the gentlest breath of warm loving air, and like those chattering reeds, reveal at last to the citizens of Rome the sweet secret of two happy lovers.

CUPID, you wanton, self-willed boy! You asked me to give you lodging for a few hours. How many days and nights you have stayed! And now you have made yourself master and are lording it in the house!

 I have been turned out of my wide bed; I sit on the ground now, passing wretched nights. In your wicked caprice you are fanning a hotter and hotter fire in my hearth, burning up my stocks of winter fuel and scorching poor me.

Du hast mir mein Geräte verstellt und verschoben;
Ich such und bin wie blind und irre geworden.
Du lärmst so ungeschickt; ich fürchte, das Seelchen
Entflieht, um dir zu entfliehn, und räumet die Hütte.

FRECH UND FROH

LIEBESQUAL verschmäht mein Herz,
Sanften Jammer, süßen Schmerz;
Nur vom Tüchtgen will ich wissen,
Heißem Äugeln, derben Küssen.
Sei ein armer Hund erfrischt
Von der Lust, mit Pein gemischt!
Mädchen, gib der frischen Brust
Nichts von Pein, und alle Lust!

*SINGET nicht in Trauertönen
Von der Einsamkeit der Nacht;
Nein, sie ist, o holde Schönen,
Zur Geselligkeit gemacht.

You have moved my things from their places and pushed them about;
I keep searching, and think I must have gone blind or crazy. You make such
a noise that I fear my poor little soul will be frightened away, and move out
of the hut altogether.

GAY INSOLENCE

MY heart despises the torment of lovers, sweet sorrow and soft moan: tell me
of none but the vigorous kind – bold burning glances and smacking kisses.
Let poor dull dogs find refreshment in pleasure that is mingled with pain!
I am fresh of heart, my girl: give me no pain, give me nothing but pleasure!

Do not sing, in tones of sorrow, of the solitude of night! No, sweet ladies!
night is made for company.

* Philina's song, written for the later version of *Wilhelm Meister.*

Wie das Weib dem Mann gegeben
Als die schönste Hälfte war,
Ist die Nacht das halbe Leben,
Und die schönste Hälfte zwar.

Könnt ihr euch des Tages freuen,
Der nur Freuden unterbricht?
Er ist gut, sich zu zerstreuen,
Zu was anderm taugt er nicht.

Aber wenn in nächtger Stunde
Süßer Lampe Dämmrung fließt,
Und vom Mund zum nahen Munde
Scherz und Liebe sich ergießt;

Wenn der rasche lose Knabe,
Der sonst wild und feurig eilt,
Oft bei einer kleinen Gabe
Unter leichten Spielen weilt;

Wenn die Nachtigall Verliebten
Liebevoll ein Liedchen singt,
Das Gefangnen und Betrübten
Nur wie Ach und Wehe klingt:

Woman was given to man as his better half, and likewise night is half of life, and the better half too.

Can you take pleasure in the day, which only interrupts pleasure? It is good for distractions, and good for nothing else.

But when in the hours of darkness the sweet lamp sheds its faint radiance, and from lips to close lips a stream of love and gaiety pours;

when impulsive wanton boys, used to wild and fiery haste, often remain content with a small favour and trifling dalliance;

when the nightingale, full of love, sings a song for lovers, which to the captive and the melancholy seems to tell only of grief and pain –

Mit wie leichtem Herzensregen
Horchet ihr der Glocke nicht,
Die mit zwölf bedächtgen Schlägen
Ruh und Sicherheit verspricht!

Darum an dem langen Tage
Merke dir es, liebe Brust:
Jeder Tag hat seine Plage,
Und die Nacht hat ihre Lust.

NÄHE DES GELIEBTEN

Ich denke dein, wenn mir der Sonne Schimmer
 Vom Meere strahlt;
Ich denke dein, wenn sich des Mondes Flimmer
 In Quellen malt.

Ich sehe dich, wenn auf dem fernen Wege
 Der Staub sich hebt;
In tiefer Nacht, wenn auf dem schmalen Stege
 Der Wandrer bebt.

Ich höre dich, wenn dort mit dumpfem Rauschen
 Die Welle steigt.
Im stillen Haine geh ich oft zu lauschen,
 Wenn alles schweigt.

how lightly then your hearts stir as you listen to the bell, with its twelve solemn strokes which promise repose and security!

Therefore, during the long day, dear heart, remember: every day has its troubles, and the night has its joys.

THE NEARNESS OF THE BELOVED

I THINK of you when I watch the sunlight glitter on the sea; I think of you when streams mirror the shimmering moon.

I see you when dust rises on a distant road, and in deep night, when the wayfarer trembles on the narrow footbridge.

I hear you in that dull roaring of rising waves. In the still grove I often walk and listen, when all is silent.

Ich bin bei dir, du seist auch noch so ferne,
 Du bist mir nah!
Die Sonne sinkt, bald leuchten mir die Sterne.
 O wärst du da!

DER CHINESE IN ROM

Einen Chinesen sah ich in Rom; die gesamten Gebäude
 Alter und neuerer Zeit schienen ihm lästig und schwer.
Ach! so seufzt' er, die Armen! ich hoffe, sie sollen begreifen,
 Wie erst Säulchen von Holz tragen des Daches Gezelt,
Daß an Latten und Pappen, Geschnitz und bunter Vergoldung
 Sich des gebildeten Augs feinerer Sinn nur erfreut. –
Siehe, da glaubt ich, im Bilde so manchen Schwärmer zu
 schauen,
 Der sein luftig Gespinst mit der soliden Natur
Ewigem Teppich vergleicht, den echten, reinen Gesunden
 Krank nennt, daß ja nur *er* heiße, der Kranke, gesund.

I am beside you, however far away you may be, you are near me! The
sun sinks, soon the stars will shine above me: would you were here!

THE CHINAMAN IN ROME

I saw a Chinaman in Rome; he thought the entire architecture of ancient
and modern times burdensome and cumbrous. 'Alas, poor people!' he
sighed. 'Let us hope they will learn how a tented roof should really be sup-
ported, on slender wooden columns; and that only laths and pasteboard,
carving and gay gold-lacquering can delight the subtler sense of the cul-
tivated eye.' – That, I thought, was a parable of many a foolish fanatic who
compares his brain's airy nothings to the eternal tapestry of solid Nature,
and calls pure genuine health sickness, merely in order that *his* sickness may
be called health.

aus den VENEZIANISCHEN EPIGRAMMEN

I

SARKOPHAGEN und Urnen verzierte der Heide mit Leben:
 Faunen tanzen umher, mit der Bacchantinnen Chor
Machen sie bunte Reihe; der ziegengefüßete Pausback
 Zwingt den heiseren Ton wild aus dem schmetternden Horn.
Zimbeln, Trommeln erklingen; wir sehen und hören den
 Marmor.
 Flatternde Vögel, wie schmeckt herrlich dem Schnabel die
 Frucht!
Euch verscheuchet kein Lärm, noch weniger scheucht er den
 Amor,
 Der in dem bunten Gewühl erst sich der Fackel erfreut.
So überwältiget Fülle den Tod; und die Asche da drinnen
 Scheint, im stillen Bezirk, noch sich des Lebens zu freun.
So umgebe denn spät den Sarkophagen des Dichters
 Diese Rolle, von ihm reichlich mit Leben geschmückt.

from VENETIAN EPIGRAMS

I

PAGAN sarcophagi and urns were adorned with images of life: fauns dancing about, arranged in pairs with the chorus of Bacchic women; goat-footed creatures puffing their cheeks and forcing wild raucous notes out of blaring horns. Cymbals clash, drums beat; we both see and hear the marble. Fluttering birds! how exquisite the fruit tastes in your beaks! No din can scare you away, still less scare away Cupid, who swings his torch all the more gladly in this gay throng. Thus death is conquered by fullness; and the ashes inside seem still, in their silent home, to be feeling the joy of living. May my tomb likewise one day be adorned with this book which I, the poet, have filled with life's beauty.

4

DAS ist Italien, das ich verließ. Noch stäuben die Wege,
 Noch ist der Fremde geprellt, stell er sich, wie er auch will.
Deutsche Redlichkeit suchst du in allen Winkeln vergebens:
 Leben und Weben ist hier, aber nicht Ordnung und Zucht;
Jeder sorgt nur für sich, mißtrauet dem andern, ist eitel,
 Und die Meister des Staats sorgen nur wieder für sich.
Schön ist das Land; doch, ach! Faustinen find ich nicht wieder.
 Das ist Italien nicht mehr, das ich mit Schmerzen verließ.

8

DIESE Gondel vergleich ich der sanft einschaukelnden Wiege,
 Und das Kästchen darauf scheint ein geräumiger Sarg.
Recht so! Zwischen der Wieg und dem Sarg wir schwanken
 und schweben
 Auf dem großen Kanal sorglos durchs Leben dahin.

4

THIS is the Italy I left! Still clouds of dust on the roads, and the foreigner still swindled no matter what he does. One looks vainly in every corner for German honesty; there is life and movement here, but no order or discipline; everyone cares only for himself, suspects everyone else, and is full of vanity; and the rulers of the state, in their turn, care only for themselves. It is a beautiful country; but alas! there is no Faustina here now. This is no longer the Italy it so hurt me to leave.

8

I WOULD compare this gondola to the cradle that gently rocks one to sleep; and the box on top of it is like a spacious coffin. Just so! Between cradle and coffin we sway and float, carefree, along the Grand Canal of life.

27

OFT sind alle Neune gekommen, ich meine die Musen;
 Doch ich achtet es nicht, hatte das Mädchen im Schoß.
Nun verließ ich mein Liebchen; mich haben die Musen verlassen,
 Und ich schielte verwirrt, suchte nach Messer und Strick.
Aber der Himmel ist voll von Göttern; du kamst mir zu Hülfe,
 Langeweile! du bist Mutter der Musen gegrüßt.

29

VIELES hab ich versucht, gezeichnet, in Kupfer gestochen,
 Öl gemalt, in Ton hab ich auch manches gedruckt,
Unbeständig jedoch, und nichts gelernt noch geleistet;
 Nur ein einzig Talent bracht ich der Meisterschaft nah.
Deutsch zu schreiben. Und so verderb ich unglücklicher Dichter
 In dem schlechtesten Stoff leider nun Leben und Kunst.

34b

KLEIN ist unter den Fürsten Germaniens freilich der meine;
 Kurz und schmal ist sein Land, mäßig nur, was er vermag.

27

ALL nine of them – the Muses, I mean – often used to visit me; but
I paid no attention, having my sweetheart in my arms. Now I have left my
darling; and the Muses have deserted me, and I have been rolling my eyes
in confusion, looking for a knife or a rope. But heaven is full of deities;
you have come to my rescue, oh Boredom! I salute you, mother of the
Muses.

29

I HAVE tried many things; I have drawn, engraved in copper, painted in
oils, even moulded a number of things in clay; but sporadically, and with-
out learning or achieving anything. Only one talent I have brought near to
mastery: the writing of German. And thus, a poor poet, alas! in this most
miserable medium I now waste my life and my art.

34b

MY prince, it is true, is small among the princes of Germany; his territory
is short and narrow, his scope limited. But if every prince were to make

Aber so wende nach innen, so wende nach außen die Kräfte
 Jeder, da wär es ein Fest, Deutscher mit Deutschen zu sein.
Doch was priesest du ihn, den Taten und Werke verkünden?
 Und bestochen erschien' deine Verehrung vielleicht;
Denn mir hat er gegeben, was Große selten gewähren,
 Neigung, Muße, Vertraun, Felder und Garten und Haus.
Niemand braucht ich zu danken als Ihm, und manches bedurft
 ich,
 Der ich mich auf den Erwerb schlecht, als ein Dichter,
 verstand.
Hat mich Europa gelobt, was hat mir Europa gegeben?
 Nichts! Ich habe, wie schwer! meine Gedichte bezahlt.
Deutschland ahmte mich nach, und Frankreich mochte mich
 lesen.
 England! freundlich empfingst du den zerrütteten Gast.
Doch was fördert es mich, daß auch sogar der Chinese
 Malet, mit ängstlicher Hand, Werthern und Lotten auf Glas?
Niemals frug ein Kaiser nach mir, es hat sich kein König
 Um mich bekümmert, und Er war mir August und Mäcen.

such good use of his powers, both inside and outside his territory, then in-
deed it would be a delight to be a German among Germans. Yet why
should one sing his praises, when deeds and achievements proclaim him?
And one's homage might well not seem disinterested; for to me he has given
things that great ones seldom bestow: affection and trust, and leisure, and a
house and garden and fields. I have never been indebted to anyone but him,
and I have needed many things, for as a poet I have never been good at
earning my living. Though Europe has praised me, what has Europe given
me? Nothing! I have paid for my poems, they have cost me dear! Germany
has imitated me, France has read me with pleasure; and you, England, have
given a distraught visitor kindly welcome. But what good does it do me,
though even the Chinese, with hesitant hands, have painted Werther and
Lotte on glass? No emperor ever asked after me, no king ever gave me a
thought – and *he* was my Augustus and my Maecenas.

37

WIE, von der künstlichsten Hand geschnitzt, das liebe
 Figürchen,
Weich und ohne Gebein, wie die Molluska nur schwimmt!
Alles ist Glied, und alles Gelenk, und alles gefällig,
 Alles nach Maßen gebaut, alles nach Willkür bewegt.
Menschen hab ich gekannt und Tiere, so Vögel als Fische,
 Manches besondre Gewürm, Wunder der großen Natur;
Und doch staun ich dich an, Bettine, liebliches Wunder,
 Die du alles zugleich bist, und ein Engel dazu.

48

BÖCKE, zur Linken mit euch! so ordnet künftig der Richter:
 Und ihr Schäfchen, ihr sollt ruhig zur Rechten mir stehn!
Wohl! Doch eines ist noch von ihm zu hoffen; dann sagt er:
 Seid, Vernünftige, mir grad gegenüber gestellt!

37

HOW soft this dear little image, carved with exquisite art, how boneless she
is, for all the world like a floating mollusc! She is all limbs, and all joints,
and all accommodating; all constructed to measure, and all in capricious
motion. I have known human beings and animals, both birds and fish, and
many peculiar creeping things, great Nature's miracles; but you, Bettina, I
watch in amazement, you charming miracle! for you are all these things at
once, and an angel as well.

48

'GOATS, to the left with you!' the Judge one day will ordain. 'And you,
little sheep, stand quietly here on my right!' – Fair enough; but it is to be
hoped he will say one thing more, namely: 'As for you, stand right
opposite me, you men of sense!'

50

ALLE Freiheitsapostel, sie waren mir immer zuwider;
　　Willkür suchte doch nur jeder am Ende für sich.
Willst du viele befrein, so wag es, vielen zu dienen.
　　Wie gefährlich das sei, willst du es wissen? Versuchs!

53

FRANKREICHS traurig Geschick, die Großen mögens bedenken;
　　Aber bedenken fürwahr sollen es Kleine noch mehr.
Große gingen zugrunde: doch wer beschützte die Menge
　　Gegen die Menge? Da war Menge der Menge Tyrann.

—

WIE der Mensch das Pfuschen so liebt! Fast glaub ich dem
　　Mythus,
　　Der mir erzählet, ich sei selbst ein verpfuschtes Geschöpf.*

50

I ALWAYS disliked them, all those apostles of freedom; in the last resort
each of them was merely seeking licence for himself. If you want to liberate
many, then have the courage to be a servant of many; and if you want to
know how dangerous that is, just try it.

53

LET the great of this world reflect upon France's sad fate; but indeed, let
lesser men reflect on it even more. The great perished; but who protected
the mob from the mob? It was then that the mob turned tyrant to itself.

—

How mankind loves bungling! I almost believe the myth that tells me that
I myself am a bungled creature.

* Epigrams headed by a dash are from those which Goethe withheld
from publication.

—

DAS Gemeine lockt jeden: siehst du in Kürze von vielen
 Etwas geschehen, sogleich denke nur: dies ist gemein.

65

ISTS denn so großes Geheimnis, was Gott und der Mensch
 und die Welt sei?
 Nein! Doch keiner mags gern hören; da bleibt es geheim.

66

VIELES kann ich ertragen. Die meisten beschwerlichen Dinge
 Duld ich mit ruhigem Mut, wie es ein Gott mir gebeut.
Wenige sind mir jedoch wie Gift und Schlange zuwider;
 Viere: Rauch des Tabaks, Wanzen und Knoblauch und +.

—

BASENESS attracts everyone; if you see something being done quickly
by a number of people, you may at once conclude that it is something base.

65

Is it really so great a mystery what God is, and man is, and the world is?
No! But we all prefer not to hear it; and so it remains mysterious.

66

I CAN stand a good deal. I put up with most objectionable things calmly, as
a god commands me. There are a few, however, that I really hate like
adder's fangs — four things: tobacco-smoke, bugs, and garlic, and (a
Christian*).

* Goethe's manuscript reads *Christ*, for which a cross+ has always been
substituted in the editions. *Christ* may here be rhetorical singular for
Christen ('Christians') but it could also mean 'Christ'.

Juden und Heiden hinaus! so duldet der christliche Schwärmer.
 Christ und Heide verflucht! murmelt ein jüdischer Bart.
Mit den Christen an Spieß und mit den Juden ins Feuer!
 Singet ein türkisches Kind Christen und Juden zum Spott.
Welcher ist der Klügste? Entscheide! Aber sind diese
 Narren in deinem Palast, Gottheit, so geh ich vorbei.

Was vom Christentum gilt, gilt von den Stoikern; freien
 Menschen geziemet es nicht, Christ oder Stoiker sein.

Was auch Helden getan, was Kluge gelehrt, es verachtets
 Wähnender christlicher Stolz neben den Wundern des Herrn.
Und doch schmückt er sich selbst und seinen nackten Erlöser
 Mit dem Besten heraus, was uns der Heide verließ.
So versammelt der Pfaffe die edlen leuchtenden Kerzen
 Um das gestempelte Brot, das er zum Gott sich geweiht.

'Out with all Jews and heathen!' – so much for the perfervid Christian's
tolerance. 'A curse on Christians and heathen!' mutters a Jew in his beard
'All Christians to be impaled, all Jews to be burnt!' sings a Turkish child,
mocking Christians and Jews. – Which is the wisest? Take your choice!
But if you have these fools in your palace, Deity, I shall pass it by.

What applies to Christianity applies to the Stoics as well. To be a Christian or a Stoic is unfitting for a free human being.

All that heroes have done, all that wise men have taught, to the Christian's
deluded pride it is all nothing beside the miracles of his Lord. And nevertheless he decks himself and his naked Saviour out with all that is best in
the pagan tradition. Thus a priest places noble shining candles all round the
piece of printed bread which he has consecrated as his God.

—

«Warum willst du den Christen des Glaubens selige Wonne
 Grausam rauben?» Nicht ich, niemand vermag es zu tun.
Steht doch deutlich geschrieben: die Heiden toben vergeblich.
 Seht, ich erfülle die Schrift, lest und erbaut euch an mir.

67

Lange schon hätt ich euch gern von jenen Tierchen
 gesprochen,
 Die so zierlich und schnell fahren dahin und daher.
Schlängelchen scheinen sie gleich, doch viergefüßet; sie laufen,
 Kriechen und schleichen, und leicht schleppen die Schwänz-
 chen sie nach.
Seht, hier sind sie! und hier! Nun sind sie verschwunden! Wo
 sind sie?
 Welche Ritze, welch Kraut nahm die Entfliehenden auf?
Wollt ihr mirs künftig erlauben, so nenn ich die Tierchen
 Lazerten;
 Denn ich brauche sie noch oft als gefälliges Bild.

—

'Why do you try so cruelly to deprive Christians of the blessed joy of
faith?' Not I; no one can do such a thing. Why, it is written plain enough:
'The heathen rage vainly.' You see: I fulfil the scriptures. Read them, and
be edified by me.

67

I have wanted for some time to tell you about those little animals that dart
to and fro so prettily and quickly. They look like tiny snakes, but with four
feet; they run, creep, and crawl, and whisk their little tails behind them.
Look! here they are, and there! Now they've vanished! Where are they?
What cranny, what greenery have they escaped into? From now on, if you
will permit me, I shall call these little beasts *lacertae* [lizards]; for I shall
often be needing them as a convenient image.

68

WER Lazerten gesehn, der kann sich die zierlichen Mädchen
 Denken, die über den Platz fahren dahin und daher.
Schnell und beweglich sind sie und gleiten, stehen und
 schwatzen,
 Und es rauscht das Gewand hinter den Eilenden drein.
Sieh! hier ist sie! und hier! Verlierst du sie einmal, so suchst du
 Sie vergebens; so bald kommt sie nicht wieder hervor.
Wenn du aber die Winkel nicht scheust, nicht Gäßchen und
 Treppchen,
 Folg ihr, wie sie dich lockt, in die Spelunke hinein!

69

WAS Spelunke nun sei, verlangt ihr zu wissen? Da wird ja
 Fast zum Lexikon dies epigrammatische Buch.
Dunkele Häuser sinds in engen Gäßchen; zum Kaffee
 Führt dich die Schöne, und sie zeigt sich geschäftig, nicht du.

68

ANYONE who has seen lizards can imagine those pretty girls who dart to
and fro across the *piazza*. They are quick and nimble, and skim about or
stand about chattering, and their skirts flutter behind them as they hasten
past. Look! here she is, and there! If you once let her slip, you will look for
her in vain; she will not emerge again in a hurry. But if you don't mind
holes and corners, little alleys and stairways, then follow her when she
entices you, into her *spelunca* [den].

69

SO now you want to know what a *spelunca* is? Well, this book of epigrams
is getting rather like a dictionary. They are dark houses in narrow little
streets; the pretty creature takes you in for 'coffee', and it is she, not you,
who does the work.

WUNDERN kann es mich nicht, daß unser Herr Christus mit...*
Gern und mit Sündern gelebt, gehts mir doch eben auch so.

KNABEN liebt ich wohl auch, doch lieber sind mir die Mädchen;
Hab ich als Mädchen sie satt, dient sie als Knabe mir noch.

IN dem engsten der Gäßchen – es drängte sich kaum durch die
 Mauern –
Saß mir ein Mädchen im Weg, als ich Venedig durchlief.
Sie war reizend, der Ort, ich ließ mich Fremder verführen;
 Ach, ein weiter Kanal tat sich dem Forschenden auf.
Hättest du Mädchen wie deine Kanäle, Venedig, und Fotzen
 Wie die Gäßchen in dir, wärst du die herrlichste Stadt.

I'M not surprised that our Lord Christ liked to live with (?harlots*) and
sinners; that's just how it is with me too.

WELL, I might have loved boys too; but girls are what I prefer. If I tire of
one as a girl, I can still use her as a boy.

IN the narrowest of little side-streets – one could hardly get through be-
tween the walls – I once found a girl sitting in my path, as I was walking
through Venice. She was charming; a charming place; and I, the foreigner,
let myself be seduced. Alas! my explorations took me into a wide canal. If
only, Venice, you had girls like your canals, and cunts like your side-
streets, you would be the world's finest town.

* The last word (probably *Dirnen*) is illegible in the manuscript.

72

WÄR ich ein häusliches Weib und hätte, was ich bedürfte,
 Treu sein wollt ich und froh, herzen und küssen den Mann.
So sang, unter andern, gemeinen Liedern, ein Dirnchen
 Mir in Venedig, und nie hört ich ein frömmer Gebet.

73

WUNDERN kann es mich nicht, daß Menschen die Hunde so
 lieben:
Denn ein erbärmlicher Schuft ist, wie der Mensch, so der
 Hund.

77

MIT Botanik gibst du dich ab? mit Optik? Was tust du?
 Ist es nicht schönrer Gewinn, rühren ein zärtliches Herz?
Ach, die zärtlichen Herzen! Ein Pfuscher vermag sie zu rühren;
 Sei es mein einziges Glück, dich zu berühren, Natur!

72

'IF I were a married woman, and had what I need, I'd be faithful and happy
and hug my husband and kiss him.' A little whore in Venice sang me this,
among other dirtier songs; and I have never heard a devouter prayer.

73

I AM not surprised that men are so fond of dogs; for they are both con-
temptible scoundrels – like dog, like man.

77

'YOU devote your time to botany? to optics? What are you thinking of!
Is it not more pleasant and profitable to touch a tender heart?' Oh, those
tender hearts! An amateur can touch them. Let it be my sole delight to
make contact with you, oh Nature!

83

WILLST du mit reinem Gefühl der Liebe Freuden genießen,
 O laß Frechheit und Ernst ferne vom Herzen dir sein.
Jener will Amorn verjagen, und dieser denkt ihn zu fesseln;
 Beiden das Gegenteil lächelt der schelmische Gott.

90

WELCH ein lustiges Spiel! Es windet am Faden die Scheibe,
 Die von der Hand entfloh, eilig sich wieder herauf!
Seht, so schein ich mein Herz bald dieser Schönen, bald jener
 Zuzuwerfen; doch gleich kehrt es im Fluge zurück.

–

LANGE sucht ich ein Weib mir, ich suchte, da fand ich nur
 Dirnen,
 Endlich erhascht ich dich mir, Dirnchen, da fand ich ein Weib.

83

IF you wish to enjoy the pleasure of love single-heartedly, then banish both shamelessness and solemnity far from your heart! The former tries to drive Love away, and the latter thinks it can tie him down; the roguish god smiles a denial to them both.

90

WHAT an amusing game! the disk leaps from my hand and quickly winds itself back again on its string. You see: this is how I seem to be throwing my heart now to one lovely girl and now to another – but at once it flies back to me again.

–

FOR a long time I looked for a wife; I looked, and found only whores. In the end I picked you up, little whore, and discovered a wife.

91

O WIE achtet ich sonst auf alle Zeiten des Jahres,
 Grüßte den kommenden Lenz, sehnte dem Herbste mich
 nach!
Aber nun ist nicht Sommer noch Winter, seit mich Beglückten
 Amors Fittich bedeckt, ewiger Frühling umschwebt.

 –

HAT dich Hymen geflohn? Hast du ihn gemieden? – Was sag
 ich?
 Hymen! köstlich ist er, aber zu ernsthaft für mich.
Aus dem Ehbett darf man nicht schwätzen, und Dichter sind
 schwatzhaft.
 Freie Liebe, sie läßt frei uns die Zunge, den Mut.

91

OH, how I used to notice all the seasons of the year, and greet the coming
of spring, and long for the autumn! But now there is neither summer nor
winter since I found happiness in the shelter of Love's wings, and there
hovers about me a perpetual springtime.

 –

'DID the god of Marriage run away from you? or did you shun him?'
What shall I say? The pleasures of wedlock are exquisite, but too solemn
for me. One must not tell tales about the marriage bed; and poets are great
tellers of tales. Free love gives free rein to our minds and tongues.

96

GLÄNZEN sah ich das Meer, und blinken die liebliche Welle;
 Frisch mit günstigem Wind zogen die Segel dahin.
Keine Sehnsucht fühlte mein Herz; es wendete rückwärts
 Nach dem Schnee des Gebirgs bald sich der schmachtende
 Blick.
Südwärts liegen der Schätze wie viel! Doch einer im Norden
 Zieht, ein großer Magnet, unwiderstehlich zurück.

100

TRAURIG, Midas, war dein Geschick: in bebenden Händen
 Fühltest du, hungriger Greis, schwere verwandelte Kost.
Lustiger geht mirs auf ähnliche Weise; denn, was ich berühre,
 Wird mir unter der Hand gleich ein behendes Gedicht.
Holde Musen, ich sträube mich nicht; nur daß ihr mein
 Liebchen,
 Drück ich es fest an die Brust, nicht mir zum Märchen
 verkehrt!

96

I SAW the sea glitter and the sweet waves sparkle, and sails speeding over
it before favourable winds. My heart felt no desire; my languishing gaze
soon turned back, to the snowy mountains. How many treasures there are
in the south! Yet one in the north, like a great magnet, draws me back
irresistibly.

100

A SAD fate, Midas, was yours: a hungry old man, and the transformed food
lying heavy in your hands. I am in similar but happier case; for everything
I touch turns in my hand into a lively poem. Sweet Muses, I do not pro-
test – if only you will not change my darling into a fairy-tale when I hug
her in my arms.

102

Wonniglich ists, die Geliebte verlangend im Arme zu
 halten,
 Wenn ihr klopfendes Herz Liebe zuerst dir gesteht.
Wonniglicher, das Pochen des Neulebendigen fühlen,
 Das in dem lieblichen Schoß immer sich nährend bewegt.
Schon versucht es die Sprünge der raschen Jugend; es klopfet
 Ungeduldig schon an, sehnt sich nach himmlischem Licht.
Harre noch wenige Tage! Auf allen Pfaden des Lebens
 Führen die Horen dich streng, wie es das Schicksal gebeut.
Widerfahre dir, was dir auch will, du wachsender Liebling –
 Liebe bildete dich; werde dir Liebe zuteil!

103

Und so tändelt ich mir, von allen Freuden geschieden,
 In der Neptunischen Stadt Tage wie Stunden hinweg.
Alles, was ich erfuhr, ich würzt es mit süßer Erinnrung,
 Würzt es mit Hoffnung; sie sind lieblichste Würzen der Welt.

102

It is wonderful to hold one's beloved in one's eager arms as her beating
heart first tells you of her love; still more wonderful to feel the throbbing
of the new living thing that constantly stirs in the sweet womb which
nourishes it. Already it is trying youth's lively leaps; already it is knocking
impatiently, longing for the light of heaven. Wait for a few days yet! Along
life's paths the Hours must strictly conduct you, as Fate decrees. But let
your fortune be what it will, you growing darling – love made you, and
may you meet with your share of love!

103

And thus, parted from all joys, I trifled away my days and hours in this
city of Neptune. All that I experienced I made savoury with delightful
memories, savoury with hope; they are the world's sweetest savours.

aus den VIER JAHRESZEITEN

KENNST du das herrliche Gift der unbefriedigten Liebe?
Es versengt und erquickt, zehret am Mark und erneuts.

KENNST du die herrliche Wirkung der endlich befriedigten
 Liebe?
Körper verbindet sie schön, wenn sie die Geister befreit.

DAS ist die wahre Liebe, die immer und immer sich gleich-
 bleibt,
Wenn man ihr alles gewährt, wenn man ihr alles versagt.

ALLES wünscht ich zu haben, um mit ihr alles zu teilen;
Alles gäb ich dahin, wär sie, die Einzige, mein.

WARUM bin ich vergänglich, o Zeus? so fragte die Schönheit.
Macht ich doch, sagte der Gott, nur das Vergängliche schön.

IMMER strebe zum Ganzen, und kannst du selber kein Ganzes
Werden, als dienendes Glied schließ an ein Ganzes dich an.

from THE FOUR SEASONS

DO you know the splendid poison of unsatisfied love? It burns and re-
freshes, devours the marrow and renews it.

DO you know the splendid effects of love at last satisfied? It ties bodies
with a beautiful bond, and sets spirits free.

TRUE love is that which remains for ever the same whether all that it asks
is granted or all refused.

I SHOULD like to have everything, that I might share everything with her;
I would surrender everything if she, who is all I love, were mine.

BEAUTY asked: 'Why must I perish, oh Zeus?' 'Why, I gave beauty',
answered the god, 'only to perishable things.'

AIM always at what is whole; and if you cannot become a whole yourself,
then attach yourself to a whole as a member in its service.

WEM zu glauben ist, redlicher Freund, das kann ich dir sagen:
 Glaube dem Leben; es lehrt besser als Redner und Buch.

ALLE Blüten müssen vergehn, daß Früchte beglücken;
 Blüten und Frucht zugleich gebet ihr Musen allein.

SCHÄDLICHE Wahrheit, ich ziehe sie vor dem nützlichen
 Irrtum.
 Wahrheit heilet den Schmerz, den sie vielleicht uns erregt.

GLEICH sei keiner dem andern; doch gleich sei jeder dem
 Höchsten.
 Wie das zu machen? Es sei jeder vollendet in sich.

SELBST erfinden ist schön, doch glücklich von andern
 Gefundnes
 Fröhlich erkannt und geschätzt, nennst du das weniger dein?

WER ist der glücklichste Mensch? Der fremdes Verdienst zu
 empfinden
 Weiß und an fremdem Genuß sich wie an eignem zu freun.

WHOM must one believe? My honest friend, let me tell you: believe life! it is a better teacher than orator or book.

ALL blossoms must perish, that fruit may satisfy; only you Muses can give blossom and fruit both at once.

I PREFER an injurious truth to a useful error. Truth heals any pain it may inflict on us.

LET none be like any other; but let each be like that which is highest. How is this to be achieved? By each achieving perfection within himself.

TO invent something of your own is fine; but when others have luckily lighted on something which you gladly appreciate and value, is it the less yours for that?

WHO is the happiest of men? He who can appreciate another's merit, and can enjoy another's pleasure as if it were his own.

ALEXIS UND DORA

Aᴄʜ, unaufhaltsam strebet das Schiff mit jedem Momente
 Durch die schäumende Flut weiter und weiter hinaus!
Lange Furchen hinter sich ziehend, worin die Delphine
 Springend folgen, als flöh ihnen die Beute davon.
Alles deutet die glücklichste Fahrt: der ruhige Bootsmann
 Ruckt am Segel gelind, das sich statt seiner bemüht;
Alle Gedanken sind vorwärts gerichtet, wie Flaggen und
 Wimpel;
 Nur ein Trauriger steht rückwärts gewendet am Mast,
Sieht die Berge schon blau, die scheidenden, sieht in das Meer sie
Niedersinken, es sinkt jegliche Freude vor ihm.
Auch dir ist es verschwunden, das Schiff, das deinen Alexis,
 Dir, o Dora, den Freund, dir, ach! den Bräutigam raubt.
Auch du blickest vergebens nach mir. Noch schlagen die Herzen
 Füreinander, doch ach! nun aneinander nicht mehr.
Nur Ein Augenblick wars, in dem ich lebte, der wieget
 Alle Tage, die sonst kalt mir verschwindenden, auf.
Nur Ein Augenblick wars, der letzte, da stieg mir ein Leben
 Unvermutet in dir, wie von den Göttern, herab.

ALEXIS AND DORA

Aʜ! relentlessly further and further with every moment the ship moves
onward and outward through the foaming waves! In its wake it leaves long
furrows, in which leaping dolphins follow, as if some prey were escaping
them. All bids fair for the voyage; the calm sailsman tugs gently at the
sheet that is doing the work in his stead; the voyagers' spirits are carried
ahead of them like the flags and pennants. Only one of them stands by
the mast looking sadly backwards; he sees the vanishing mountains,
blue already, sink into the sea, and all joy sinks away as he watches.

'Oh Dora, you too have lost sight of it, this ship that is carrying your
Alexis, your betrothed lover, away from you! You too are gazing vainly
after me. Our hearts still beat each for the other, but alas! each on the other
no longer. Only one moment of life have I had, but it has outweighed all
my other cold unremembered days! Only in one last moment an unfore-
seen life came down upon me, as if god-given. Oh Sungod, all in vain your

Nur umsonst verklärst du mit deinem Lichte den Äther,
 Phöbus, mir ist er verhaßt, dieser alleuchtende Tag.
In mich selber kehr ich zurück; da will ich im stillen
 Wiederholen die Zeit, als sie mir täglich erschien.
War es möglich, die Schönheit zu sehen und nicht zu empfinden?
 Wirkte der himmlische Reiz nicht auf dein stumpfes Gemüt?
Klage dich, Armer, nicht an! – So legt der Dichter ein Rätsel,
 Künstlich mit Worten verschränkt, oft der Versammlung ins
 Ohr:
Jeden freuet die seltne Verknüpfung der zierlichen Bilder,
 Aber noch fehlet das Wort, das die Bedeutung verwahrt;
Ist es endlich gefunden, dann heitert sich jedes Gemüt auf
 Und erblickt im Gedicht doppelt erfreulichen Sinn.
Ach, warum so spät, o Amor, nahmst du die Binde,
 Die du ums Aug mir geknüpft, nahmst sie zu spät mir
 hinweg!
Lange harrte befrachtet das Schiff auf günstige Lüfte;
 Endlich strebte der Wind glücklich vom Ufer ins Meer.
Leere Zeiten der Jugend! und leere Träume der Zukunft!
 Ihr verschwindet, es bleibt einzig die Stunde mir nur.
Ja, sie bleibt, es bleibt mir das Glück! ich halte dich, Dora!
 Und die Hoffnung zeigt, Dora, dein Bild mir allein.

light makes the ether brilliant; this all-overshining day is hateful to me.
I will withdraw into myself; there in silence let me think back again to the
time when I saw her daily.
 'Was it possible to see beauty and remain insensible to it? Did not one's
dull soul respond to such heavenly charm? Poor wretch, do not blame
yourself! – It is thus that poets often recite to their audience an artful riddle
of words interwoven; every hearer enjoys the strange combination of
attractive images, but the word is still missing in which the meaning lies
locked. When finally it is revealed, every mind is gladdened, and all discern
a doubly pleasing sense in the poem. Alas, Love, why so late, having
bound my eyes, why did you unbind them too late? Already the ship, with
its cargo loaded, had long been waiting for favourable breezes; at last a fair
wind blew from the shore out to sea. Oh empty years of youth! and empty
dreams of the future! you vanish away – only that hour remains in my
mind. Yes, I still have it; I still have that happiness! I hold you fast, Dora!
and your image alone, Dora, lives in my hopes.

Öfter sah ich dich gehn zum Tempel, geschmückt und gesittet,
 Und das Mütterchen ging feierlich neben dir her.
Eilig warst du und frisch, zu Markte die Früchte zu tragen,
 Und vom Brunnen, wie kühn! wiegte dein Haupt das Gefäß.
Da erschien dein Hals, erschien dein Nacken vor allen,
 Und vor allen erschien deiner Bewegungen Maß.
Oftmals hab ich gesorgt, es möchte der Krug dir entstürzen,
 Doch er hielte sich stet auf dem geringelten Tuch.
Schöne Nachbarin, ja, so war ich gewohnt dich zu sehen,
 Wie man die Sterne sieht, wie man den Mond sich beschaut,
Sich an ihnen erfreut, und innen im ruhigen Busen
 Nicht der entfernteste Wunsch, sie zu besitzen, sich regt.
Jahre, so gingt ihr dahin! Nur zwanzig Schritte getrennet
 Waren die Häuser, und nie hab ich die Schwelle berührt.
Und nun trennt uns die gräßliche Flut! Du lügst nur den
 Himmel,
 Welle! dein herrliches Blau ist mir die Farbe der Nacht.
Alles rührte sich schon; da kam ein Knabe gelaufen
 An mein väterlich Haus, rief mich zum Strande hinab:

'Often I would see you on your way to the temple, adorned and modest,
with your mother walking solemnly along beside you. You were so nimble
and lively as you carried the fruit to market, and how boldly you balanced
the pitcher on your head as you came from the well! I could tell your neck
then, in front or behind, from everyone else's, and the symmetry of your
movements stood out among all the others. I often used to be afraid the jug
might fall off, but it held steady on your tight-rolled head-cloth. Ah,
yes, my lovely neighbour, that is how I was accustomed to see you – as one
sees the stars, as one looks at the moon, and is gladdened by the sight of
them, and not the remotest wish to possess them stirs in the calmness of
one's heart. Thus the years passed by! Our houses were only twenty paces
apart, and I never crossed her threshold. And now this hideous sea divides
us! Oh waves, your reflection of the sky is false! in my eyes your splendid
blue is the colour of night.
 'They were all stirring already; then a boy came running to my father's
house and called me down to the shore: "The sail is up already (he said)

Schon erhebt sich das Segel, so sprach er, es flattert im Winde,
 Und gelichtet, mit Kraft, trennt sich der Anker vom Sand;
Komm, Alexis, o komm! Da drückte der wackere Vater,
 Segnend die würdige Hand mir auf das lockige Haupt;
Sorglich reichte die Mutter ein nachbereitetes Bündel:
 Glücklich kehre zurück! riefen sie, glücklich und reich!
Und so sprang ich hinweg, das Bündelchen unter dem Arme,
 An der Mauer hinab, fand an der Türe dich stehn
Deines Gartens. Du lächeltest mir und sagtest: Alexis!
 Sind die Lärmenden dort deine Gesellen der Fahrt?
Fremde Gegenden wirst du besuchen, und köstliche Waren
 Wiederbringen und Schmuck reichen Matronen der Stadt.
Aber bringe mir auch ein leichtes Kettchen; ich will es
 Dankbar bezahlen, schon oft hab ich die Zierde gewünscht!
Stehen war ich geblieben und fragte, nach Weise des Kaufmanns,
 Erst nach Form und Gewicht deiner Bestellung genau.
Gar bescheiden erwogst du den Preis! da blickt ich indessen
 Nach dem Halse, des Schmucks unserer Königin wert.
Immerfort tönte das Rufen der Schiffer; da sagtest du freundlich:
 Nimm aus dem Garten noch einige Früchte mit dir!

and flapping in the breeze; their strong hands are weighing the anchor and
pulling it out of the sand; oh, come, Alexis, come along!" Then with dig-
nity my worthy father laid his hand in blessing on my curly head; my
mother in her solicitude handed me an extra bundle prepared at the last
moment. "A happy return!" they cried, "happy and rich!" And off I
dashed, with the little bundle under my arm, down along the wall, and
found you standing at the door of your garden. You smiled at me and said:
"Alexis! does that shouting come from your travelling companions? You
will be visiting foreign shores now, and bringing back expensive goods,
and jewellery for the rich married ladies of the town. But bring back a little
necklace for me, too! I will gratefully pay for it – I have so often wanted
such an ornament!" I had stopped, and like a good merchant I inquired
first exactly what you wanted me to get, what shape, what weight. Very
modestly you pondered the price! and meanwhile I gazed at your neck,
worthy of the jewels of our queen. I could still hear the cries of my ship-
mates; then kindly you said: "Take some fruit from the garden with you

Nimm die reifsten Orangen, die weißen Feigen; das Meer bringt
　　Keine Früchte, sie bringt jegliches Land nicht hervor.
Und so trat ich herein. Du brachst nun die Früchte geschäftig,
　　Und die goldene Last zog das geschürzte Gewand.
Öfters bat ich: es sei nun genug! und immer noch eine
　　Schönere Frucht fiel dir, leise berührt, in die Hand.
Endlich warst du zur Laube gekommen, da fandst du ein
　　Körbchen,
　　Und die Myrte bog blühend sich über uns hin.
Schweigend begannest du nun geschickt die Früchte zu ordnen:
　　Erst die Orange, die schwer ruht, als ein goldener Ball,
Dann die weichliche Feige, die jeder Druck schon entstellet;
　　Und mit Myrte bedeckt ward und geziert das Geschenk.
Aber ich hob es nicht auf; ich ging nicht. Wir sahen einander
　　In die Augen, und mir ward vor dem Auge so trüb.
Deinen Busen fühlt ich an meinem! Den herrlichen Nacken,
　　Ihn umschlang nun mein Arm, tausendmal küßt ich den Hals;
Mir war dein Haupt auf die Schulter gesunken; nun knüpften
　　auch deine
　　Lieblichen Arme das Band um den Beglückten herum.

as well! Take the ripest oranges and the softest figs; fruit does not grow
in the sea, and not in every land."

'So in I went. And you set about picking the fruit, holding out your
dress like an apron, and the golden burden weighed it down. Several times
I begged you: "Let that suffice!" And every time a still finer fruit dropped
into your hand at the gentlest touch. At last you came to the arbour; there
was a little basket there, and the blossoming myrtle was arching above us.
In silence now you skilfully began to arrange the fruit: first the oranges,
each heavy and still like a ball of gold, then the yielding figs which every
touch disfigures; and the gift was covered and decorated with myrtle. But I
did not pick it up; I did not go. We looked into each other's eyes, and
before mine everything turned so dim. I felt your breast against my own!
Your wonderful neck, my arm was round it now, and I covered it with a
thousand kisses; your head had sunk down on my shoulder, and now your
sweet arms too encircled me with a bond of happiness. I felt Love seize me:

Amors Hände fühlt ich: er drückt' uns gewaltig zusammen,
 Und aus heiterer Luft donnert' es dreimal; da floß
Häufig die Träne vom Aug mir herab, du weintest, ich weinte,
 Und vor Jammer und Glück schien uns die Welt zu vergehn.
Immer heftiger riefen die Schiffer; da wollten die Füße
 Mich nicht tragen, ich rief: Dora! und bist du nicht mein?
Ewig! sagtest du leise. Da schienen unsere Tränen,
 Wie durch göttliche Luft, leise vom Auge gehaucht.
Stärker riefs in dem Gäßchen: Alexis! Da sah mich der Knabe
 Durch die Türe und kam. Wie er das Körbchen empfing!
Wie er mich trieb! Wie ich dir die Hand noch drückte! – Zu
 Schiffe
Wie ich gekommen? Ich weiß, daß ich ein Trunkener schien.
Und so hielten mich auch die Gesellen, sie schonten den Kranken;
 Und schon deckte der Hauch trüber Entfernung die Stadt.
Ewig! lispeltest du, o Dora; mir schallt es im Ohre
 Mit dem Donner des Zeus! Ja, sie stand neben dem Thron,
Seine Tochter, die Göttin der Liebe; die Grazien standen
 Ihr zur Seiten! Er ist götterbekräftigt, der Bund!

he pressed us powerfully together, and out of the clear sky came three claps of thunder. Then tear upon tear poured down from my eyes, you wept, and I wept, and in our grief and happiness the whole world seemed to dissolve around us.

'Louder and louder the sailors shouted; and scarcely able to stand, I cried: "Dora! do you not belong to me?" and softly you answered: "*For ever!*" Then our tears, as if by some gentle breath of divine wind, seemed to dry from our eyes. Then came a louder call from the street: "Alexis!" And the boy looked through the door and saw me and came in. How he snatched up the basket! How he hurried me! How I pressed your hand a last time! – How did I get on board the ship? I know I must have seemed like a drunken man, and that indeed is how my comrades treated me, sparing my indisposition; and already the town was hidden in the haze of dim distance. Oh, Dora! you murmured "for ever"! It resounds in my ear with Zeus's thunder! And indeed, his daughter the Goddess of Love was standing by his throne, and the Graces were standing beside her! The gods have confirmed our betrothal!

O so eile denn, Schiff, mit allen günstigen Winden!
 Strebe, mächtiger Kiel, trenne die schäumende Flut!
Bringe dem fremden Hafen mich zu, damit mir der Goldschmied
 Aus der Werkstatt sogleich reiche das himmlische Pfand.
Wahrlich! es soll zur Kette werden das Kettchen, o Dora!
 Neunmal umgebe sie dir, locker gewunden, den Hals!
Außerdem schaff ich noch Schmuck, den mannigfaltigsten; goldne
 Spangen sollen dir auch reichlich verzieren die Hand.
Da wetteifre Rubin und Smaragd, der liebliche Saphir
 Stelle dem Hyazinth sich gegenüber, und Gold
Halte die herrlichsten Steine in schöner Verbindung zusammen.
 O, wie den Bräutigam freut, einzig zu schmücken die Braut!
Seh ich Perlen, so denk ich an dich; bei jeglichem Ringe
 Kommt mir der länglichen Hand schönes Gebild in den Sinn.
Tauschen will ich und kaufen; du sollst das Schönste von allem
 Wählen; ich widmete gern alle die Ladung nur dir.
Doch nicht Schmuck und Juwelen allein verschafft dein
 Geliebter:
 Was ein häusliches Weib freuet, das bringt er dir auch.
Feine wollene Decken mit Purpursäumen, ein Lager
 Zu bereiten, das uns traulich und weichlich empfängt;

'Oh, hasten onward, then, ship, before every favouring wind! Surge for-
ward, strong keel, and divide the foaming water! Take me to the foreign
port, that the goldsmith may at once, from his workshop, deliver the
precious keepsake. Truly, that necklace, Dora, shall grow into a chain!
Nine times, loosely wound, it shall encircle your neck! And I shall get
jewels as well, of many kinds, and your hands shall be richly adorned with
golden rings: there the ruby shall vie with the emerald, and the lovely
sapphire confront the hyacinth, and gold shall hold the most splendid stones
together in beautiful combinations. Oh, what joy it is for a future husband
to find unique ornaments for his bride! When I see pearls, I think of you,
and every ring I see reminds me of the beautiful shape of your long slender
hands. I will barter and buy, and you shall choose what is finest of all;
gladly I would devote the whole cargo to you.
 'But your beloved will acquire other things besides ornaments and jewel-
lery: he will bring you things to delight a housewife as well. Fine woollen
blankets with purple hems, to prepare a friendly soft bed to receive us;

Stücke köstlicher Leinwand. Du sitzest und nähest und kleidest
 Mich und dich und auch wohl noch ein Drittes darein.
Bilder der Hoffnung, o täuschet mein Herz! O mäßiget, Götter,
 Diesen gewaltigen Brand, der mir den Busen durchtobt!
Aber auch sie verlang ich zurück, die schmerzliche Freude,
 Wenn die Sorge sich kalt, gräßlich gelassen, mir naht.
Nicht der Erinnyen Fackel, das Bellen der höllischen Hunde
 Schreckt den Verbrecher so in der Verzweiflung Gefild,
Als das gelaßne Gespenst mich, das mir die Schöne von ferne
 Zeiget: die Türe steht wirklich des Gartens noch auf!
Und ein anderer kommt! Für ihn auch fallen die Früchte!
 Und die Feige gewährt stärkenden Honig auch ihm!
Lockt sie auch ihn nach der Laube? und folgt er? O macht
 mich, ihr Götter,
 Blind, verwischet das Bild jeder Erinnrung in mir!
Ja, ein Mädchen ist sie! und die sich geschwinde dem einen
 Gibt, sie kehret sich auch schnell zu dem andern herum.
Lache nicht diesmal, o Zeus, der frech gebrochenen Schwüre!
 Donnere schrecklicher! Triff! – Halte die Blitze zurück!
Sende die schwankenden Wolken mir nach! Im nächtlichen
 Dunkel
 Treffe dein leuchtender Blitz diesen unglücklichen Mast!

costly pieces of linen. You will be sitting and sewing them, to clothe me and
yourself and perhaps another little one too. Oh images of hope, delude my
heart! Oh you gods, moderate this mighty fire that rages in my bosom!
 'Yet even it I wish back, even this joy that hurts, when I begin to be
touched by the deliberate, hideous chill of anxious care. Not the brands of
the Furies, not the barking of hell-hounds so terrify the criminal in the
domain of despair as does this heartless spectre when from far away it shows
me my fair one: the garden door is indeed still open! and another man
comes! And for him too the fruit drops from the trees! the fig gives its sus-
taining honey to him as well! Is she luring him too to the arbour? and does
he follow her? Oh, blind me, you gods, wipe away from my mind every
memory's image! Why, yes, she is a girl! and if she can give herself quickly
to one man, she can also turn away quickly to another! Do not laugh this
time, Zeus, at vows so wantonly broken! Thunder more terribly! Strike
her! – No, withhold your lightning! Send the hesitant clouds in pursuit of

Streue die Planken umher und gib der tobenden Welle
 Diese Waren, und mich gib den Delphinen zum Raub! –
Nun, ihr Musen, genug! Vergebens strebt ihr zu schildern,
 Wie sich Jammer und Glück wechseln in liebender Brust.
Heilen könnet ihr nicht die Wunden, die Amor geschlagen;
 Aber Linderung kommt einzig, ihr Guten, von euch.

EUPHROSYNE

Auch von des höchsten Gebirgs beeisten zackigen Gipfeln
 Schwindet Purpur und Glanz scheidender Sonne hinweg.
Lange verhüllt schon Nacht das Tal und die Pfade des Wandrers,
 Der, am tosenden Strom, auf zu der Hütte sich sehnt,
Zu dem Ziele des Tags, der stillen hirtlichen Wohnung;
 Und der göttliche Schlaf eilet gefällig voraus,
Dieser holde Geselle des Reisenden. Daß er auch heute
 Segnend kränze das Haupt mir mit dem heiligen Mohn!

me! In night and darkness let your glittering lightning strike this unhappy mast! Scatter the planks, and let this cargo be a prey to the raging waves, and myself to the dolphins!'

But enough, oh Muses! In vain you attempt to portray how misery and happiness succeed one another in a lover's heart. When Love has inflicted its wounds, you cannot heal them; but they can be soothed, dear Muses, only by you.

EUPHROSYNE*

Now even from the craggy peaks of the highest mountains the sunset's purple glow is ebbing away. Night has long since hidden the valley and the paths of the wayfarer, who climbs beside the raging stream and longs for the hut higher up, his day's objective, a quiet pastoral dwelling. Divine sleep, that sweet companion of travellers, hastens helpfully ahead; may he tonight, too, bless me and crown my head with the sacred poppy!

* An elegy for the young Weimar actress Christiane Neumann (1778–97). Goethe received the news of her death while travelling in Switzerland; he had last seen her appear in the part of Euphrosyne (one of the three Graces).

Aber was leuchtet mir dort vom Felsen glänzend herüber
 Und erhellet den Duft schäumender Ströme so hold?
Strahlt die Sonne vielleicht durch heimliche Spalten und Klüfte?
 Denn kein irdischer Glanz ist es, der wandelnde, dort.
Näher wälzt sich die Wolke, sie glüht. Ich staune dem Wunder!
 Wird der rosige Strahl nicht ein bewegtes Gebild?
Welche Göttin nahet sich mir? und welche der Musen
 Suchet den treuen Freund selbst in dem grausen Geklüft?
Schöne Göttin! enthülle dich mir, und täusche, verschwindend,
 Nicht den begeisterten Sinn, nicht das gerührte Gemüt.
Nenne, wenn du es darfst vor einem Sterblichen, deinen
 Göttlichen Namen; wo nicht: rege bedeutend mich auf,
Daß ich fühle, welche du seist von den ewigen Töchtern
 Zeus', und der Dichter sogleich preise dich würdig im Lied.
«Kennst du mich, Guter, nicht mehr? Und käme diese Gestalt
 dir,
 Die du doch sonst geliebt, schon als ein fremdes Gebild?
Zwar der Erde gehör ich nicht mehr, und trauernd entschwang
 sich
 Schon der schaudernde Geist jugendlich frohem Genuß;
Aber ich hoffte mein Bild noch fest in des Freundes Erinnrung
 Eingeschrieben und noch schön durch die Liebe verklärt.

But what light shines towards me from yonder rock, filling the haze from the foaming streams so sweetly with brightness? Can the sun be gleaming through hidden clefts and crannies? For that wandering radiance is not earthly. Nearer the cloud rolls, glowing. I stand wondering at this miracle! Is the rose-red ray not becoming a moving shape? What goddess is approaching me? and which of the Muses is seeking her faithful friend, even in these terrible chasms? Fair goddess! reveal yourself to me, and do not, by vanishing, disappoint my mind which you have inspired, my heart which you have moved. Utter, if you may do so before a mortal, your divine name; if not, then stir my apprehension significantly, that I may feel which of the eternal daughters of Zeus you are, and that a poet's song may at once worthily praise you. 'Dear friend, do you no longer know me? And is it possible that my form, for you used to love it, already appears to you as a shape of strangeness? To the earth, indeed, I belong no longer, and sadly already my shud-

Ja, schon sagt mir gerührt dein Blick, mir sagt es die Träne:
 Euphrosyne, sie ist noch von dem Freunde gekannt.
Sieh, die Scheidende zieht durch Wälder und grause Gebirge,
 Sucht den wandernden Mann, ach! in der Ferne noch auf;
Sucht den Lehrer, den Freund, den Vater und blicket noch einmal
 Nach dem leichten Gerüst irdischer Freuden zurück.
Laß mich der Tage gedenken, da mich, das Kind, du dem Spiele,
 Jener täuschenden Kunst reizender Musen geweiht.
Laß mich der Stunde gedenken und jedes kleineren Umstands;
 Ach, wer ruft nicht so gern Unwiederbringliches an!
Jenes süße Gedränge der leichtesten irdischen Tage,
 Ach, wer schätzt ihn genug, diesen vereilenden Wert!
Klein erscheinet es nun, doch ach! nicht kleinlich dem Herzen;
 Macht die Liebe, die Kunst jegliches Kleine doch groß.
Denkst du der Stunde noch wohl, wie auf dem Brettergerüste
 Du mich der höheren Kunst ernstere Stufen geführt?
Knabe schien ich, ein rührendes Kind, du nanntest mich Arthur
 Und belebtest in mir britisches Dichter-Gebild,
Drohtest mit grimmiger Glut den armen Augen und wandtest
 Selbst den tränenden Blick, innig getäuschet, hinweg.

dering spirit has outsoared the joys and pleasures of youth; but I hoped that in a friend's memory my image might still be fast-inscribed, and still sweetly transfigured by love. Yes! I can tell by your emotion, your eyes, your tears: Euphrosyne is still no stranger to her friend. See, through forests and terrible mountains her departing spirit comes, ah! still seeking out the far-off wanderer; seeking her teacher, her friend, her father, and once more looking back at the fragile stage of earthly joys. Let me remember the days when, as a child, you dedicated me to the player's art, that make-believe of the enchanting Muses. Let me remember the hour and each little detail: oh, who does not love to recall what can never come back! Those lightest of earthly days, with their sweet urgency – oh, which of us sets enough store by this fleeting treasure! To my heart it seems small now, but oh, not of small account! For love and art can make all little things great. Do you perhaps still remember that time when you guided me, on the stage, through the sterner steps of the higher art? I had the semblance of a boy, a pathetic child; you called me 'Arthur', and brought to life in me the creature of an English poet's imagination; you threatened my poor eyes

Ach! da warst du so hold und schütztest ein trauriges Leben,
 Das die verwegene Flucht endlich dem Knaben entriß.
Freundlich faßtest du mich, den Zerschmetterten, trugst mich
 von dannen,
 Und ich heuchelte lang, dir an dem Busen, den Tod.
Endlich schlug die Augen ich auf und sah dich, in ernste,
 Stille Betrachtung versenkt, über den Liebling geneigt.
Kindlich strebt ich empor und küßte dir dankbar die Hände,
 Reichte zum reinen Kuß dir den gefälligen Mund,
Fragte: Warum, mein Vater, so ernst? und hab ich gefehlet,
 O so zeige mir an, wie mir das Beßre gelingt.
Keine Mühe verdrießt mich bei dir, und alles und jedes
 Wiederhol ich so gern, wenn du mich leitest und lehrst.
Aber du faßtest mich stark und drücktest mich fester im Arme,
 Und es schauderte mir tief in dem Busen das Herz.
Nein! mein liebliches Kind, so riefst du, alles und jedes,
 Wie du es heute gezeigt, zeig es auch morgen der Stadt.
Rühre sie alle, wie mich du gerührt, und es fließen zum Beifall
 Dir von dem trockensten Aug herrliche Tränen herab.

with fierce red heat and had to turn away your own tear-filled gaze, so deep
was the illusion. Oh, and then you were so gentle and protected that sad
little life, which the boy finally lost in his reckless flight. There I lay shat-
tered, and kindly you took me in your arms and carried me from the spot,
and for long, at your breast, I simulated death. At last I opened my eyes and
saw you, immersed in grave silent meditation, looking down at your be-
loved pupil. I reached up like a child and kissed your hands in gratitude,
and held out my willing lips to you for a chaste kiss, asking: "Why so
serious, my father? and if I have made a mistake, oh, then show me how
to do better. With you as a teacher I find no effort irksome, and gladly re-
peat every single thing under your guidance."

'But you held me tight and pressed me closer in your arms, and my heart
shuddered deep in my breast. "No, my sweet child!" you exclaimed. "Do
all this before the town tomorrow, every single thing you have done before
me today. Move them all as you have moved me, and fine tears will drop
from the driest of eyes to applaud you. But me you have stricken most

Aber am tiefsten trafst du doch mich, den Freund, der im Arm
dich
Hält, den selber der Schein früherer Leiche geschreckt.
Ach, Natur, wie sicher und groß in allem erscheinst du!
Himmel und Erde befolgt ewiges, festes Gesetz:
Jahre folgen auf Jahre, dem Frühlinge reichet der Sommer,
Und dem reichlichen Herbst traulich der Winter die Hand.
Felsen stehen gegründet, es stürzt sich das ewige Wasser
Aus der bewölkten Kluft schäumend und brausend hinab.
Fichten grünen so fort, und selbst die entlaubten Gebüsche
Hegen, im Winter schon, heimliche Knospen am Zweig.
Alles entsteht und vergeht nach Gesetz; doch über des Menschen
Leben, dem köstlichen Schatz, herrschet ein schwankendes Los.
Nicht dem blühenden nickt der willig scheidende Vater,
Seinem trefflichen Sohn, freundlich vom Rande der Gruft;
Nicht der Jüngere schließt dem Älteren immer das Auge,
Das sich willig gesenkt, kräftig dem Schwächeren zu.
Öfter, ach! verkehrt das Geschick die Ordnung der Tage:
Hilflos klaget ein Greis Kinder und Enkel umsonst,
Steht, ein beschädigter Stamm, dem rings zerschmetterte Zweige
Um die Seiten umher strömende Schloßen gestreckt.

deeply of all, your friend who holds you in his arms, and who was startled
even before by your seemingly inanimate body. Ah, Nature, all things show
you so sure and great! Heaven and earth obey firm everlasting laws: year
follows year, the summer clasps hands with the spring and the kindly winter
with the abundant autumn. Cliffs stand firm-founded, eternal waters pour
foaming and roaring down out of cloudy clefts. Pines are perpetually green,
and even the leafless bushes, in winter already, bear secret buds on their
branches. There is law in the making and in the unmaking of all things: but
human life, that treasure of great price, is ruled by a dubious destiny. Not
always does a father, from the grave's edge, nod a kindly-willing farewell
to his fine son in the bloom of youth; not always the young and strong
close the willingly drooping eyelids of their weak elders. Alas! Fate often
inverts the order of days: an old man helplessly, vainly laments his children
and grandchildren, and stands like a torn tree-trunk with its shattered

Und so, liebliches Kind, durchdrang mich die tiefe Betrachtung,
 Als du, zur Leiche verstellt, über die Arme mir hingst;
Aber freudig seh ich dich mir in dem Glanze der Jugend,
 Vielgeliebtes Geschöpf, wieder am Herzen belebt.
Springe fröhlich dahin, verstellter Knabe! Das Mädchen
 Wächst zur Freude der Welt, mir zum Entzücken heran.
Immer strebe so fort, und deine natürlichen Gaben
 Bilde, bei jeglichem Schritt steigenden Lebens, die Kunst.
Sei mir lange zur Lust, und eh mein Auge sich schließet,
 Wünsch ich dein schönes Talent glücklich vollendet zu sehn.–
Also sprachst du, und nie vergaß ich der wichtigen Stunde!
 Deutend entwickelt ich mich an dem erhabenen Wort.
O wie sprach ich so gerne zum Volk die rührenden Reden,
 Die du, voller Gehalt, kindlichen Lippen vertraut!
O wie bildet ich mich an deinen Augen und suchte
 Dich im tiefen Gedräng staunender Hörer heraus!
Doch dort wirst du nun sein, und stehn, und nimmer bewegt
 sich
 Euphrosyne hervor, dir zu erheitern den Blick.

branches all round it, which showers of hail have laid low. And this, dear child, was the deep meditation that pierced me as you hung, in simulated lifelessness, across my arms. But with joy, my darling, I see you revive on my bosom in your young splendour. Jump away light of heart, my make-believe boy! As a girl you will grow to rejoice the world and enchant my eyes. Never cease from these endeavours, and may your natural gifts, at each upward step of your life, be nurtured by art. Live long for my delight! and before my eyes close I hope to see your fine talent reach happy perfection."

'Thus you spoke, and that significant hour I have never forgotten! and your memorable words explained themselves as I developed. Oh, how I loved to recite in public those moving speeches, so full of meaning, which you entrusted to my childish lips! Oh, how I took shape as I watched your eyes, as I looked for you in the dense throng of amazed spectators! But now there you will be, standing there, and never again shall Euphrosyne appear

Du vernimmst sie nicht mehr, die Töne des wachsenden
 Zöglings,
 Die du zu liebendem Schmerz frühe, so frühe! gestimmt.
Andere kommen und gehn; es werden dir andre gefallen,
 Selbst dem großen Talent drängt sich ein größeres nach.
Aber du, vergesse mich nicht! Wenn eine dir jemals
 Sich im verworrnen Geschäft heiter entgegen bewegt,
Deinem Winke sich fügt, an deinem Lächeln sich freuet
 Und am Platze sich nur, den du bestimmtest, gefällt,
Wenn sie Mühe nicht spart noch Fleiß, wenn tätig der Kräfte,
 Selbst bis zur Pforte des Grabs, freudiges Opfer sie bringt –
Dann gedenkest du mein, du Guter! und rufest auch spät noch:
 Euphrosyne, sie ist wieder erstanden vor mir!
Vieles sagt ich noch gern; doch ach! die Scheidende weilt nicht,
 Wie sie wollte; mich führt streng ein gebietender Gott.
Lebe wohl! schon zieht michs dahin in schwankendem Eilen.
 Einen Wunsch nur vernimm, freundlich gewähre mir ihn:
Laß nicht ungerühmt mich zu den Schatten hinabgehn!
 Nur die Muse gewährt einiges Leben dem Tod.
Denn gestaltlos schweben umher in Persephoneias
 Reiche, massenweis, Schatten vom Namen getrennt;

and unsadden your gaze. You will never again hear the voice of your grow-
ing pupil, those tones that you tuned so early, so early! to love and pain.
Others will come and go, and others will please you; even great talent must
make way for greater which follows. But you, you must not forget me!
If ever another should come, and in the confusion of work be drawn gladly
towards you, and obey your every gesture, and be pleased by your smile,
and be content to stand only where you have placed her – if she spares no
trouble and pains, if she gladly, even to death's door, offers up all her
powers in work – oh, then, my dear, you shall think of me, and exclaim
even after so long: "She, Euphrosyne, has come to life again before me!"
 'There is much I should still like to say; but alas! I cannot delay my de-
parture as I would – for a god who is my master strictly conducts me. Fare-
well! I am drawn away already in hesitant haste. Hear but one wish, and
grant it to me as a friend: do not let me go down unsung to the shades!
Only the Muse can give the dead a little life. For shapeless they throng and
hover around in Persephone's kingdom, shadows who have lost their

Wen der Dichter aber gerühmt, der wandelt, gestaltet,
 Einzeln, gesellet dem Chor aller Heroen sich zu.
Freudig tret ich einher, von deinem Liede verkündet,
 Und der Göttin Blick weilet gefällig auf mir.
Mild empfängt sie mich dann und nennt mich; es winken die
 hohen
 Göttlichen Frauen mich an, immer die nächsten am Thron.
Penelopeia redet mir zu, die treuste der Weiber,
 Auch Euadne, gelehnt auf den geliebten Gemahl.
Jüngere nahen sich dann, zu früh herunter gesandte,
 Und beklagen mit mir unser gemeines Geschick.
Wenn Antigone kommt, die schwesterlichste der Seelen,
 Und Polyxena, trüb noch von dem bräutlichen Tod,
Seh ich als Schwestern sie an und trete würdig zu ihnen;
 Denn der tragischen Kunst holde Geschöpfe sind sie.
Bildete doch ein Dichter auch mich; und seine Gesänge,
 Ja, sie vollenden an mir, was mir das Leben versagt.» –
Also sprach sie, und noch bewegte der liebliche Mund sich,
 Weiter zu reden; allein schwirrend versagte der Ton.

names; but one whom a poet has sung takes shape and walks singly, and
joins the chorus of all the heroes. Heralded by your song, I shall come
with joy in my step, and the eyes of the goddess will rest upon me with
favour. Then she will graciously receive me, and call me by name; divine
noble women who stand always nearest her throne will beckon to me in
greeting. Penelope, faithfullest of wives, will speak to me, and Evadne
too, leaning against her beloved husband. Then younger ones will
approach, who have been sent down here too early, and together we shall
lament our common fate. When Antigone comes, that greatest soul of all
sisters, and Polyxena, still mournful with bridal death, they will seem like
sisters to me, and I shall be worthy to approach them; for they are the
graceful creations of tragic art, and I too am a poet's handiwork! a poet
indeed whose songs will give me the fulfilment which life withheld.'
 Thus she spoke, and her sweet lips were still moving to say more; but
her voice faded into a gasp of air. For out of the hovering ever-moving

Denn aus dem Purpurgewölk, dem schwebenden, immer
 bewegten,
 Trat der herrliche Gott, Hermes, gelassen hervor;
Mild erhob er den Stab und deutete; wallend verschlangen
 Wachsende Wolken, im Zug, beide Gestalten vor mir.
Tiefer liegt die Nacht um mich her; die stürzenden Wasser
 Brausen gewaltiger nun neben dem schlüpfrigen Pfad.
Unbezwingliche Trauer befällt mich, entkräftender Jammer,
 Und ein moosiger Fels stützet den Sinkenden nur.
Wehmut reißt durch die Saiten der Brust, die nächtlichen
 Tränen
 Fließen; und über dem Wald kündet der Morgen sich an.

DIE METAMORPHOSE DER PFLANZEN

DICH verwirret, Geliebte, die tausendfältige Mischung
 Dieses Blumengewühls über dem Garten umher;
Viele Namen hörest du an, und immer verdränget
 Mit barbarischem Klang einer den andern im Ohr.
Alle Gestalten sind ähnlich, und keine gleichet der andern;
 Und so deutet das Chor auf ein geheimes Gesetz,

purple cloud the noble god Hermes calmly stepped, gently raising his staff
and pointing: and a drifting procession of billowing clouds swallowed up
both figures before my eyes. Night deepens around me; more loudly the
waterfalls roar by my slippery path. I am seized by an uncontrollable sad-
ness, by a crippling grief; I sink, and lean on a mossy rock for my only sup-
port. Sorrow tears at the strings of my heart, I weep in the darkness; and
above the forest the sky heralds the morning.

THE METAMORPHOSIS OF PLANTS

YOU are confused, beloved, by the thousandfold mingled multitude of
flowers all over the garden. You listen to their many names which are for
ever, one after another, ringing outlandishly in your ears. All their shapes
are similar, yet none is the same as the next; and thus the whole chorus of

Auf ein heiliges Rätsel. O könnt ich dir, liebliche Freundın,
 Überliefern sogleich glücklich das lösende Wort! –
Werdend betrachte sie nun, wie nach und nach sich die Pflanze,
 Stufenweise geführt, bildet zu Blüten und Frucht.
Aus dem Samen entwickelt sie sich, sobald ihn der Erde
 Stille befruchtender Schoß hold in das Leben entläßt
Und dem Reize des Lichts, des heiligen, ewig bewegten,
 Gleich den zärtesten Bau keimender Blätter empfiehlt.
Einfach schlief in dem Samen die Kraft; ein beginnendes Vorbild
 Lag, verschlossen in sich, unter die Hülle gebeugt,
Blatt und Wurzel und Keim, nur halb geformet und farblos;
 Trocken erhält so der Kern ruhiges Leben bewahrt,
Quillet strebend empor, sich milder Feuchte vertrauend,
 Und erhebt sich sogleich aus der umgebenden Nacht.
Aber einfach bleibt die Gestalt der ersten Erscheinung,
 Und so bezeichnet sich auch unter den Pflanzen das Kind.
Gleich darauf ein folgender Trieb, sich erhebend, erneuet,
 Knoten auf Knoten getürmt, immer das erste Gebild.
Zwar nicht immer das gleiche; denn mannigfaltig erzeugt sich,
 Ausgebildet, du siehsts, immer das folgende Blatt,

them suggests a secret law, a sacred riddle. Sweet lady, could I but at once convey to you in a word the happy solution!

 Consider them now as they grow: how the plant gradually, through stage after stage, fashions itself into blossom and fruit. From the seed it develops, as soon as the sweet earth's quietly fruitful womb releases it into life, at once delivering over to the action of the holy ever-moving light this most delicate structure of germinating leaves. The simple force slept in the seed; an incipient prototype lay, self-enclosed, curved under the husk, leaf and root and germ, only half-formed and colourless; thus the kernel preserves and guards in dryness an unstirring life, and sprouts eagerly forth, entrusting itself to gentle moisture, and at once rises out of the surrounding darkness.

 But the shape of the first manifestation remains simple, and thus we recognize childhood among plants too. At once then a further impulse always arises, which renews the first formation, adding joint upon joint. It does not, indeed, always renew it alike; for the leaf that follows, as you see,

Ausgedehnter, gekerbter, getrennter in Spitzen und Teile,
 Die verwachsen vorher ruhten im untern Organ.
Und so erreicht es zuerst die höchst bestimmte Vollendung,
 Die bei manchem Geschlecht dich zum Erstaunen bewegt.
Viel gerippt und gezackt, auf mastig strotzender Fläche,
 Scheinet die Fülle des Triebs frei und unendlich zu sein.
Doch hier hält die Natur, mit mächtigen Händen, die Bildung
 An und lenket sie sanft in das Vollkommnere hin.
Mäßiger leitet sie nun den Saft, verengt die Gefäße,
 Und gleich zeigt die Gestalt zärtere Wirkungen an.
Stille zieht sich der Trieb der strebenden Ränder zurücke,
 Und die Rippe des Stiels bildet sich völliger aus.
Blattlos aber und schnell erhebt sich der zärtere Stengel,
 Und ein Wundergebild zieht den Betrachtenden an.
Rings im Kreise stellet sich nun, gezählet und ohne
 Zahl, das kleinere Blatt neben dem ähnlichen hin.
Um die Achse gedrängt, entscheidet der bergende Kelch sich,
 Der zur höchsten Gestalt farbige Kronen entläßt.
Also prangt die Natur in hoher, voller Erscheinung,
 Und sie zeiget, gereiht, Glieder an Glieder gestuft.

always reproduces itself in a manifold and complex shape – more extended, more serrated, with more widely separated extremities which were formerly ingrown and unmoving in the lower organ. And thus it first achieves that clearly defined perfection which in many species moves you to wonder. Many-ribbed, much-indented, with thick swelling surface – the richness of the impulse seems limitless and endless.

Yet here Nature, with her powerful hands, restrains the formative process and gently guides it towards something still more perfect. She now moderates the flow of the sap, narrows the ducts, and at once more delicate effects begin to show themselves in the shape. Quietly the outward impulse of the striving extremities is retracted, and the rib of the stem develops more fully. But leafless and swift the more delicate stalk ascends, and a marvellous formation delights the beholder. In a circle, numbered and numberless, the smaller leaves now take their place next to those they resemble. Concentrated round its axis, the enclosing calyx unsheathes itself, from which the supreme shapes, the corollae of many colours, issue.

Thus does Nature manifest her splendour in lofty fullness, and displays

Immer staunst du aufs neue, sobald sich am Stengel die Blume
 Über dem schlanken Gerüst wechselnder Blätter bewegt.
Aber die Herrlichkeit wird des neuen Schaffens Verkündung.
 Ja, das farbige Blatt fühlet die göttliche Hand;
Und zusammen zieht es sich schnell; die zärtesten Formen,
 Zwiefach streben sie vor, sich zu vereinen bestimmt.
Traulich stehen sie nun, die holden Paare, beisammen,
 Zahlreich ordnen sie sich um den geweihten Altar.
Hymen schwebet herbei, und herrliche Düfte, gewaltig,
 Strömen süßen Geruch, alles belebend, umher.
Nun vereinzelt schwellen sogleich unzählige Keime,
 Hold in den Mutterschoß schwellender Früchte gehüllt.
Und hier schließt die Natur den Ring der ewigen Kräfte;
 Doch ein neuer sogleich fasset den vorigen an,
Daß die Kette sich fort durch alle Zeiten verlänge,
 Und das Ganze belebt, so wie das Einzelne, sei.
Wende nun, o Geliebte, den Blick zum bunten Gewimmel,
 Das verwirrend nicht mehr sich vor dem Geiste bewegt.
Jede Pflanze verkündet dir nun die ewgen Gesetze,
 Jede Blume, sie spricht lauter und lauter mit dir.

limb upon limb in graded series. You are filled at once with ever-fresh wonder as the flower moves on its stalk above the slender framework of changing leaves. But this glory heralds a new creation. Yes, the coloured petal feels the divine touch, and quickly contracts; and twofold shapes of the utmost delicacy thrust themselves forwards, destined to unite. Lovingly now they stand side by side, the sweet couples, crowding round the consecrated altar. The nuptial god approaches, hovering, and splendid sweet powerful life-giving fragrance fills the surrounding air. And now at once each one of countless seeds begins to swell, sweetly enclosed in the wombs of swelling fruit. And here Nature closes the ring of eternal forces; but at once a new cycle links itself to the preceding one, that the chain may be prolonged from age to age, and that the whole may be, like each of its parts, a living thing.

Turn now your gaze, beloved, to the many-coloured throng, which no longer moves confusingly before your mind's eye. Now every plant proclaims to you the eternal laws, every flower speaks to you with ever clearer voice. But having once learnt here to decipher the sacred characters of the

Aber entzifferst du hier der Göttin heilige Lettern,
 Überall siehst du sie dann, auch in verändertem Zug.
Kriechend zaudre die Raupe, der Schmetterling eile geschäftig,
 Bildsam ändre der Mensch selbst die bestimmte Gestalt.
O gedenke denn auch, wie aus dem Keim der Bekanntschaft
 Nach und nach in uns holde Gewohnheit entsproß,
Freundschaft sich mit Macht aus unserm Innern enthüllte
 Und wie Amor zuletzt Blüten und Früchte gezeugt.
Denke, wie mannigfach bald die, bald jene Gestalten,
 Still entfaltend, Natur unsern Gefühlen geliehn!
Freue dich auch des heutigen Tags! Die heilige Liebe
 Strebt zu der höchsten Frucht gleicher Gesinnungen auf,
Gleicher Ansicht der Dinge, damit in harmonischem Anschaun
 Sich verbinde das Paar, finde die höhere Welt.

METAMORPHOSE DER TIERE

WAGT ihr, also bereitet, die letzte Stufe zu steigen
Dieses Gipfels, so reicht mir die Hand und öffnet den freien
Blick ins weite Feld der Natur. Sie spendet die reichen
Lebensgaben umher, die Göttin; aber empfindet

goddess, you can read them everywhere, though the writing may vary. The grub's slow crawl must become the butterfly's busy haste; man himself shall reshape his determinate shape. Oh, remember then, too, how in us, out of acquaintanceship's seed, sweet habit has gradually grown, how friendship has powerfully unfolded from our hearts and how at last Love has engendered blossom and fruit. Think what manifold forms – now this, now that, in silent disclosure – Nature has lent to our feelings! Rejoice, too, in the present day! Holy love strives upwards towards its supreme fruit: kinship of spirits, a likeminded view of all things – that the lovers may unite in harmonious contemplation, and enter the higher world.

METAMORPHOSIS OF ANIMALS

IF, thus prepared, you will venture to climb the final ascent to this summit, then give me your hand, open your eyes and gaze freely into the wide field of Nature. She, the goddess, lavishes about her the rich gifts of life, but

Keine Sorge wie sterbliche Fraun um ihrer Gebornen
Sichere Nahrung; ihr ziemet es nicht: denn zwiefach bestimmte
Sie das höchste Gesetz, beschränkte jegliches Leben,
Gab ihm gemeßnes Bedürfnis, und ungemessene Gaben,
Leicht zu finden, streute sie aus, und ruhig begünstigt
Sie das muntre Bemühn der vielfach bedürftigen Kinder;
Unerzogen schwärmen sie fort nach ihrer Bestimmung.

Zweck sein selbst ist jegliches Tier, vollkommen entspringt es
Aus dem Schoß der Natur und zeugt vollkommene Kinder.
Alle Glieder bilden sich aus nach ewgen Gesetzen,
Und die seltenste Form bewahrt im Geheimen das Urbild.
So ist jeglicher Mund geschickt, die Speise zu fassen,
Welche dem Körper gebührt; es sei nun schwächlich und
 zahnlos
Oder mächtig der Kiefer gezahnt, in jeglichem Falle
Fördert ein schicklich Organ den übrigen Gliedern die Nahrung.
Auch bewegt sich jeglicher Fuß, der lange, der kurze,
Ganz harmonisch zum Sinne des Tiers und seinem Bedürfnis.
So ist jedem der Kinder die volle, reine Gesundheit
Von der Mutter bestimmt: denn alle lebendigen Glieder
Widersprechen sich nie und wirken alle zum Leben.

feels none of the solicitude of mortal women for the secure nourishment of
her offspring – such cares do not befit her. For she has ordained the
supreme law in twofold wise: she has set bounds to each life, giving it limited
needs; and she has scattered unlimited gifts, easy to find. Calmly she favours
the lively toil of her children, so various in their requirements; untaught,
they wander on according to their preordained function.
 Every animal is an end in itself, it comes forth perfect from Nature's
womb and begets young that are perfect. All limbs develop according to
eternal laws, and even the rarest of forms mysteriously preserves the arche-
type. Thus every mouth is skilled to grasp the kind of food that suits the
body; whether the jaw be feeble and toothless, or strongly toothed, in
every case a suitable organ conveys the food to the rest of the limbs. Every
foot, too, whether long or short, moves in complete harmony with the
animal's intentions and needs. Thus for each of her children the Mother
ordains pure and entire health; for no living limbs ever function in con-

Also bestimmt die Gestalt die Lebensweise des Tieres,
Und die Weise, zu leben, sie wirkt auf alle Gestalten
Mächtig zurück. So zeiget sich fest die geordnete Bildung,
Welche zum Wechsel sich neigt durch äußerlich wirkende
 Wesen.
Doch im Innern befindet die Kraft der edlern Geschöpfe
Sich im heiligen Kreise lebendiger Bildung beschlossen.
Diese Grenzen erweitert kein Gott, es ehrt die Natur sie:
Denn nur also beschränkt war je das Vollkommene möglich.

Doch im Inneren scheint ein Geist gewaltig zu ringen,
Wie er durchbräche den Kreis, Willkür zu schaffen den Formen
Wie dem Wollen; doch was er beginnt, beginnt er vergebens.
Denn zwar drängt er sich vor zu diesen Gliedern, zu jenen,
Stattet mächtig sie aus, jedoch schon darben dagegen
Andere Glieder, die Last des Übergewichtes vernichtet
Alle Schöne der Form und alle reine Bewegung.
Siehst du also dem einen Geschöpf besonderen Vorzug
Irgend gegönnt, so frage nur gleich: wo leidet es etwa
Mangel anderswo? und suche mit forschendem Geiste;
Finden wirst du sogleich zu aller Bildung den Schlüssel.

tradiction to each other, and all act in the interests of life. In this way the
animal's shape is determined by its way of life, and the way of life, in its
turn, exerts in all cases a powerful influence upon the shape. Thus ordered
development displays both constancy and a tendency to change because of
external forces. The internal energy, however, of the nobler sort of
creatures finds itself bounded by the sacred circle of living development.
These are bounds which no god can extend, and Nature honours them: for
only within such limitations has perfection ever been possible.

Nevertheless, a spirit within seems to struggle mightily to break through
this circle, to introduce caprice into the forms and the instincts; yet its
enterprise is a vain one. It may, indeed, penetrate to these limbs or those,
and develop them impressively; but other limbs at once become stunted in
compensation, and the burden of preponderance destroys all beauty of
form and purity of movement. If, therefore, you see any creature endowed
with some special advantage, then ask at once: in what other respect can it
be deficient? and let your mind seek and investigate; you will immediately
discover the key to all development. For no animal, for example, whose

Denn so hat kein Tier, dem sämtliche Zähne den obern
Kiefer umzäunen, ein Horn auf seiner Stirne getragen,
Und daher ist den Löwen gehörnt der ewigen Mutter
Ganz unmöglich zu bilden, und böte sie alle Gewalt auf;
Denn sie hat nicht Masse genug, die Reihen der Zähne
Völlig zu pflanzen und auch Geweih und Hörner zu treiben.

Dieser schöne Begriff von Macht und Schranken, von Willkür
Und Gesetz, von Freiheit und Maß, von beweglicher Ordnung,
Vorzug und Mangel erfreue dich hoch; die heilige Muse
Bringt harmonisch ihn dir, mit sanftem Zwange belehrend.
Keinen höhern Begriff erringt der sittliche Denker,
Keinen der tätige Mann, der dichtende Künstler; der Herrscher,
Der verdient, es zu sein, erfreut nur durch ihn sich der Krone.
Freue dich, höchstes Geschöpf der Natur, du fühlest dich fähig,
Ihr den höchsten Gedanken, zu dem sie schaffend sich auf-
 schwang,
Nachzudenken. Hier stehe nun still und wende die Blicke
Rückwärts, prüfe, vergleiche, und nimm vom Munde der Muse,
Daß du schauest, nicht schwärmst, die liebliche volle Gewißheit.

upper jaw is hedged by a complete set of teeth has ever carried a horn on its
forehead, and it would therefore be quite impossible for the eternal Mother
to fashion a lion with horns, whatever efforts she might make; for she has
not material enough to plant the rows of teeth complete and to sprout
antlers and horns as well.

 May your mind dwell with delight upon this noble concept of power and
constraint, of caprice and law, freedom and moderation, movement within
order, pre-eminence and deficiency. The sacred Muse brings it to you in
harmonious numbers, instructing you with gentle compulsion. No higher
concept than this is achieved by the moral philosopher, none by the man of
action, or the imaginative artist; by it alone the ruler, if he deserves to rule,
enjoys possession of his crown. Rejoice, supreme product of Nature, in
your ability to re-think her supreme thought, the highest to which, in her
creativeness, she has risen. Pause here now and look back, consider and
compare, and receive from the lips of the Muse the sweet complete certainty
that your vision is fact and not fancy.

aus HERMANN UND DOROTHEA

(Vierter Gesang, 1–70)

ALSO sprachen die Männer, sich unterhaltend. Die Mutter
Ging indessen, den Sohn erst vor dem Hause zu suchen,
Auf der steinernen Bank, wo sein gewöhnlicher Sitz war.
Als sie daselbst ihn nicht fand, so ging sie, im Stalle zu schauen,
Ob er die herrlichen Pferde, die Hengste, selber besorgte,
Die er als Fohlen gekauft und die er niemand vertraute.
Und es sagte der Knecht: Er ist in den Garten gegangen.
Da durchschritt sie behende die langen doppelten Höfe,
Ließ die Ställe zurück und die wohlgezimmerten Scheunen,
Trat in den Garten, der weit bis an die Mauern des Städtchens
Reichte, schritt ihn hindurch, und freute sich jeglichen Wachs-
 tums,
Stellte die Stützen zurecht, auf denen beladen die Äste
Ruhten des Apfelbaums, wie des Birnbaums lastende Zweige,
Nahm gleich einige Raupen vom kräftig strotzenden Kohl weg;
Denn ein geschäftiges Weib tut keine Schritte vergebens.

from HERMANN AND DOROTHEA

(Fourth Canto, lines 1–70)

THUS the men spoke and conversed. The mother, meanwhile, went to
look for her son, first in front of the house, on the stone bench where he
usually sat. Not finding him there, she went to the stable to see whether he
was looking after the horses himself, the fine stallions which he had bought
as foals and which he entrusted to no one else. And the stable-boy said:
'He went into the garden.' Then quickly she crossed the long double
courtyards, leaving the stables and the well-constructed barns behind her,
and entered the garden, which extended right out to the walls of the little
town; she walked through it, noticing with pleasure all the growing things,
straightening the props that held up the loaded limbs of the apple-tree and
the pear-tree's burdening branches, and removing as she passed a few grubs
from the strong rich cabbage-leaves – for a busy wife never wastes a step.

Also war sie ans Ende des langen Gartens gekommen,
Bis zur Laube, mit Geisblatt bedeckt: nicht fand sie den Sohn da,
Ebensowenig, als sie bis jetzt ihn im Garten erblickte.
Aber nur angelehnt war das Pförtchen, das aus der Laube,
Aus besonderer Gunst, durch die Mauer des Städtchens
 gebrochen
Hatte der Ahnherr einst, der würdige Burgemeister.
Und so ging sie bequem den trocknen Graben hinüber,
Wo an der Straße sogleich der wohlumzäunete Weinberg
Aufstieg steileren Pfads, die Fläche zur Sonne gekehret.
Auch den schritt sie hinauf und freute der Fülle der Trauben
Sich im Steigen, die kaum sich unter den Blättern verbargen.
Schattig war und bedeckt der hohe mittlere Laubgang,
Den man auf Stufen erstieg von unbehauenen Platten.
Und es hingen herein Gutedel und Muskateller,
Rötlich blaue daneben von ganz besonderer Größe,
Alle mit Fleiße gepflanzt, der Gäste Nachtisch zu zieren.
Aber den übrigen Berg bedeckten einzelne Stöcke,
Kleinere Trauben tragend, von denen der köstliche Wein
 kommt.

Thus she came to the bottom of the long garden, to the arbour that was covered with honeysuckle: she did not find her son there, nor had she yet seen him anywhere else in the garden; but the little door out of the arbour, which Hermann's forebear, the worthy burgomaster, had made in the town wall by special permission, was not quite closed. And so she could conveniently cross the dry ditch, where just by the roadside the well-hedged vineyard rose, steep-pathed, full-facing the sun. Up through it, too, she walked, taking pleasure as she climbed in the abundance of the grapes which could scarcely hide themselves under the leaves. The high middle path through the vines was covered and shady; one mounted it by steps made of rough-hewn stone. And over it chasselas and museadels hung, and beside them purple grapes of extra large size, all carefully grown as an after-dinner delicacy for guests. But the rest of the vineyard was planted with single vines bearing the smaller grapes which yield the exquisite wine. Thus uphill she walked, already enjoying in anticipation the

Also schritt sie hinauf, sich schon des Herbstes erfreuend
Und des festlichen Tags, an dem die Gegend im Jubel
Trauben lieset und tritt, und den Most in die Fässer versammelt,
Feuerwerke des Abends von allen Orten und Enden
Leuchten und knallen, und so der Ernten schönste geehrt wird.
Doch unruhiger ging sie, nachdem sie dem Sohne gerufen
Zwei-, auch dreimal, und nur das Echo vielfach zurückkam,
Das von den Türmen der Stadt, ein sehr geschwätziges,
 herklang.
Ihn zu suchen, war ihr so fremd; er entfernte sich niemals
Weit, er sagt' es ihr denn, um zu verhüten die Sorge
Seiner liebenden Mutter und ihre Furcht vor dem Unfall.
Aber sie hoffte noch stets, ihn auf dem Wege zu finden;
Denn die Türen, die untre, sowie die obre, des Weinbergs
Standen gleichfalls offen. Und so nun trat sie ins Feld ein,
Das mit weiter Fläche den Rücken des Hügels bedeckte.
Immer noch wandelte sie auf eigenem Boden, und freute
Sich der eigenen Saat und des herrlich nickenden Kornes,
Das mit goldener Kraft sich im ganzen Felde bewegte.
Zwischen den Äckern schritt sie hindurch, auf dem Raine, den
 Fußpfad,

autumn and the festive day on which the people from the whole district
come rejoicing to gather and tread the grapes and collect the new wine in
the vats, and in the evening fireworks blaze and explode from far and near,
and thus honour is done to the finest of harvests. But she walked more un-
easily after she had called her son two or three times and heard no reply but
the many-voiced echo that chattered back as usual from the towers of the
town. It was so strange to her to have to look for him: he never went any
distance without telling her, to forestall his doting mother's anxiety and her
apprehension of accidents. But she still kept hoping she would meet him on
her way; for the doors, at the foot and at the top of the vineyard, were both
standing open. And so she now entered the wide field which covered the
whole of the back of the hill. She was still walking on her own land, enjoy-
ing the sight of her own crops and the fine nodding corn that rippled, lush
and golden, all over the field. Between the plots she passed, by the foot-
path along the ridge, with her eye on the pear-tree, the big tree on the hill,

Hatte den Birnbaum im Auge, den großen, der auf dem Hügel
Stand, die Grenze der Felder, die ihrem Hause gehörten.
Wer ihn gepflanzt, man konnt es nicht wissen. Er war in der
 Gegend
Weit und breit gesehn, und berühmt die Früchte des Baumes.
Unter ihm pflegten die Schnitter des Mahls sich zu freuen am
 Mittag,
Und die Hirten des Viehs in seinem Schatten zu warten;
Bänke fanden sie da von rohen Steinen und Rasen.
Und sie irrete nicht; dort saß ihr Hermann und ruhte,
Saß mit dem Arme gestützt und schien in die Gegend zu schauen
Jenseits nach dem Gebirg, er kehrte der Mutter den Rücken.
Sachte schlich sie hinan und rührt' ihm leise die Schulter.
Und er wandte sich schnell; da sah sie ihm Tränen im Auge.

Mutter, sagt' er betroffen, ihr überrascht mich! Und eilig
Trocknet' er ab die Träne, der Jüngling edlen Gefühles.
Wie? du weinest, mein Sohn? versetzte die Mutter betroffen:
Daran kenn ich dich nicht! ich habe das niemals erfahren!
Sag, was beklemmt dir das Herz? was treibt dich, einsam zu
 sitzen
Unter dem Birnbaum hier? was bringt dir Tränen ins Auge?

which marked the boundary of the fields that belonged to her house. No
one knew who had planted it. It could be seen far and wide in the district,
and its fruit was famous. Under it the mowers used to enjoy their midday
meal, and the herdsmen used to wait in its shade: there they found simple
stone benches and soft grass. And sure enough, there was her Hermann
sitting and resting; he sat leaning on his arm and seemed to be looking out
over the countryside, towards the mountains beyond it, and his back was
turned to his mother. Softly she crept up and touched him gently on the
shoulder. He turned round quickly; and she saw that he had tears in
his eyes.
 'Mother!' he said in some confusion. 'You have taken me unawares!'
And quickly he wiped his tears away, like a well-bred sensitive boy. 'What!
Are you crying, my son?' replied his mother in astonishment. 'That is not
like you; I have never known you do it! Tell me! what is on your mind?
what has driven you here to sit by yourself under the pear-tree? what has
brought these tears to your eyes?'

DIE BRAUT VON KORINTH

NACH Korinthus von Athen gezogen
Kam ein Jüngling, dort noch unbekannt.
Einen Bürger hofft' er sich gewogen;
Beide Väter waren gastverwandt,
Hatten frühe schon
Töchterchen und Sohn
Braut und Bräutigam voraus genannt.

Aber wird er auch willkommen scheinen,
Wenn er teuer nicht die Gunst erkauft?
Er ist noch ein Heide mit den Seinen,
Und sie sind schon Christen und getauft.
Keimt ein Glaube neu,
Wird oft Lieb und Treu
Wie ein böses Unkraut ausgerauft.

Und schon lag das ganze Haus im stillen,
Vater, Töchter, nur die Mutter wacht;
Sie empfängt den Gast mit bestem Willen,
Gleich ins Prunkgemach wird er gebracht.

THE BRIDE OF CORINTH

To Corinth, journeying from Athens, came a young man, still a stranger
in the town. He had expectations of friendship from one of the citizens;
the two fathers were bound by ties of hospitality, and had long ago or-
dained that the young daughter and the son should be bride and bride-
groom.

But will he indeed be welcome, unless he pays dearly for the favour? He,
with his family, is still a pagan, and these are already Christians and bap-
tized. When a new faith is germinating, affection and loyalty are often
uprooted like dangerous weeds.

And already the whole household lay at rest, the father and the daugh-
ters – only the mother was still awake. Full of good will she receives the

Wein und Essen prangt,
Eh er es verlangt:
So versorgend wünscht sie gute Nacht.

Aber bei dem wohlbestellten Essen
Wird die Lust der Speise nicht erregt;
Müdigkeit läßt Speis und Trank vergessen,
Daß er angekleidet sich aufs Bette legt,
Und er schlummert fast,
Als ein seltner Gast
Sich zur offnen Tür herein bewegt.

Denn er sieht, bei seiner Lampe Schimmer
Tritt, mit weißem Schleier und Gewand,
Sittsam still ein Mädchen in das Zimmer,
Um die Stirn ein schwarz- und goldnes Band.
Wie sie ihn erblickt,
Hebt sie, die erschrickt,
Mit Erstaunen eine weiße Hand.

Bin ich, rief sie aus, so fremd im Hause,
Daß ich von dem Gaste nichts vernahm?
Ach, so hält man mich in meiner Klause!
Und nun überfällt mich hier die Scham.

guest, he is taken at once to the finest bedroom, a magnificent array of wine and food appears before he asks for it; and thus providing for him, she wishes him good night.

Nevertheless, this well-prepared meal fails to stir his appetite; he is so weary that he forgets food and drink, and lies down fully dressed on the bed; and he is almost asleep when a strange guest enters by the open door.

For by the light of his lamp he sees a girl come quietly and modestly into the room, veiled and robed in white, with a black and golden fillet round her brow. Startled at the sight of him, she raises a white hand in astonishment.

'Am I', she exclaimed, 'such a stranger in the house that I have heard nothing of our guest? Alas, that is how they treat me in my cell! And now

Ruhe nur so fort
Auf dem Lager dort,
Und ich gehe schnell, so wie ich kam.

Bleibe, schönes Mädchen! ruft der Knabe,
Rafft von seinem Lager sich geschwind:
Hier ist Ceres', hier ist Bacchus' Gabe,
Und du bringst den Amor, liebes Kind!
Bist vor Schrecken blaß!
Liebe, komm und laß,
Laß uns sehn, wie froh die Götter sind.

Ferne bleib, o Jüngling, bleibe stehen!
Ich gehöre nicht den Freuden an.
Schon der letzte Schritt ist, ach! geschehen
Durch der guten Mutter kranken Wahn,
Die genesend schwur:
Jugend und Natur
Sei dem Himmel künftig untertan.

Und der alten Götter bunt Gewimmel
Hat sogleich das stille Haus geleert.
Unsichtbar wird Einer nur im Himmel,
Und ein Heiland wird am Kreuz verehrt;

I am overcome with shame in this place. Rest on, then, on that bed, and I
will go away quickly as I came.'
 'Stay, lovely maiden!' cries the boy, rising at once from his bed. 'Here
are the gifts of Ceres and of Bacchus, and you, sweet child, bring Cupid
with you! You are pale with alarm! Dearest, come, and let us try the good
cheer of the gods!'
 'Stop, youth, do not approach me! I am no partaker in pleasures. The
final step, alas, has already been taken, through the sick delusion of my
poor mother, who vowed on her recovery that from then on youth and
nature should be in bondage to Heaven.
 'And immediately the gay throng of the ancient gods departed from this
silent house. One only is worshipped, an invisible One in Heaven, and a

Opfer fallen hier,
Weder Lamm noch Stier,
Aber Menschenopfer unerhört.

Und er fragt und wäget alle Worte,
Deren keines seinem Geist entgeht.
Ist es möglich, daß am stillen Orte
Die geliebte Braut hier vor mir steht?
Sei die Meine nur!
Unsrer Väter Schwur
Hat vom Himmel Segen uns erfleht.

Mich erhältst du nicht, du gute Seele!
Meiner zweiten Schwester gönnt man dich.
Wenn ich mich in stiller Klause quäle,
Ach! in ihren Armen denk an mich,
Die an dich nur denkt,
Die sich liebend kränkt;
In die Erde bald verbirgt sie sich.

Nein! bei dieser Flamme seis geschworen,
Gütig zeigt sie Hymen uns voraus;
Bist der Freude nicht und mir verloren,
Kommst mit mir in meines Vaters Haus.

Saviour on the cross. Here no lambs or bulls are killed as offerings, but
human beings are monstrously sacrificed.'

And he questions her and ponders all her words, not one escaping his
mind. 'Is it possible that here, standing before me in this silent place, is my
beloved bride? Why, then, be mine! The vow exchanged by our fathers
has brought the blessing of heaven down upon us.'

'Poor soul, you cannot have me! They are giving you to my younger
sister. When I am back suffering in my silent cell, and you are in her arms,
oh! think of me, who will be thinking only of you, and wasting away with
love, and will soon be hidden in the earth.'

'No! I swear by this kindly flame, which prophesies our wedding torches,
that you are not lost to happiness and to me, and you shall come with me

Liebchen, bleibe hier!
Feire gleich mit mir
Unerwartet unsern Hochzeitschmaus.

Und schon wechseln sie der Treue Zeichen;
Golden reicht sie ihm die Kette dar,
Und er will ihr eine Schale reichen,
Silbern, künstlich, wie nicht eine war.
Die ist nicht für mich;
Doch, ich bitte dich,
Eine Locke gib von deinem Haar.

Eben schlug die dumpfe Geisterstunde,
Und nun schien es ihr erst wohl zu sein.
Gierig schlürfte sie mit blassem Munde
Nun den dunkel blutgefärbten Wein;
Doch vom Weizenbrot,
Das er freundlich bot,
Nahm sie nicht den kleinsten Bissen ein.

Und dem Jüngling reichte sie die Schale,
Der, wie sie, nun hastig lüstern trank.
Liebe fordert er beim stillen Mahle;
Ach, sein armes Herz war liebekrank.

to my father's house. Sweetheart, stay here! and celebrate at once with me
our unexpected nuptial feast.'

And already they exchange tokens of plighted troth: she hands him her
golden chain, and he offers her a cup of silver, artfully and rarely wrought.
'This cup is not for me. But give me, I pray you, a lock of your hair.'

Just then the hollow witching hour struck, and now for the first time she
seemed at her ease. Greedily, with pale mouth, she swallowed the dark
blood-red wine; but of the wheaten bread which he tenderly offered she
consumed not the smallest morsel.

And she gave the cup to the boy, and he, like her, now drank with avid
haste. During this silent feast he demands her love – alas, his poor heart was

Doch sie widersteht,
Wie er immer fleht,
Bis er weinend auf das Bette sank.

Und sie kommt und wirft sich zu ihm nieder:
Ach, wie ungern seh ich dich gequält!
Aber, ach! berührst du meine Glieder,
Fühlst du schaudernd, was ich dir verhehlt.
Wie der Schnee so weiß,
Aber kalt wie Eis
Ist das Liebchen, das du dir erwählt.

Heftig faßt er sie mit starken Armen,
Von der Liebe Jugendkraft durchmannt:
Hoffe doch, bei mir noch zu erwarmen,
Wärst du selbst mir aus dem Grab gesandt!
Wechselhauch und Kuß!
Liebesüberfluß!
Brennst du nicht und fühlest mich entbrannt?

Liebe schließet fester sie zusammen,
Tränen mischen sich in ihre Lust;
Gierig saugt sie seines Mundes Flammen,
Eins ist nur im andern sich bewußt.

sick with love. But she resisted, plead as he might, until he sank down on the bed weeping.

And she comes and throws herself down beside him: 'Oh, how I hate to see you suffer! But alas! if you touch my limbs you will feel with horror what I have concealed from you: the sweetheart you have chosen is white as snow, but cold as ice.'

Eagerly he seizes her in his strong arms, nerved to manhood by love's youthful energy: 'Have hope, nevertheless, that I can still make you warm, even if you were sent to me out of the grave!' They exchange breaths and kisses and overflowing love. 'Are you not burning, feeling me all in flames?'

Love binds them closer together, and tears mingle with their delight; greedily she sucks the fire out of his mouth, and they are conscious of

Seine Liebeswut
Wärmt ihr starres Blut,
Doch es schlägt kein Herz in ihrer Brust.

Unterdessen schleichet auf dem Gange
Häuslich spät die Mutter noch vorbei,
Horchet an der Tür und horchet lange,
Welch ein sonderbarer Ton es sei:
Klag- und Wonnelaut
Bräutigams und Braut,
Und des Liebestammelns Raserei.

Unbeweglich bleibt sie an der Türe,
Weil sie erst sich überzeugen muß,
Und sie hört die höchsten Liebesschwüre,
Lieb- und Schmeichelworte, mit Verdruß –
Still! der Hahn erwacht! –
Aber morgen nacht
Bist du wieder da? – und Kuß auf Kuß.

Länger hält die Mutter nicht das Zürnen,
Öffnet das bekannte Schloß geschwind: –
Gibt es hier im Hause solche Dirnen,
Die dem Fremden gleich zu Willen sind? –

themselves only in each other. The frenzy of his love warms her sluggish
blood – but no heart beats in her breast.

Meanwhile her mother, still belated by domestic duties, creeps past along
the passage, stops to listen at the door and goes on listening, wondering at
these strange sounds – sighs and exclamations of delight as of a bride-
groom and bride, and the mad stammering speech of lovers.

She stands by the door motionless, for she must first make quite sure;
and full of indignation she hears supreme avowals of love, amorous and
caressing words: 'Hush! the cock is waking!' 'But you will come again to-
morrow night?' – followed by repeated kisses.

The mother can restrain her anger no longer, and quickly unlocks the
familiar door: 'Are there such harlots in this house, who will do a stranger's

So zur Tür hinein.
Bei der Lampe Schein
Sieht sie – Gott! sie sieht ihr eigen Kind.

Und der Jüngling will im ersten Schrecken
Mit des Mädchens eignem Schleierflor,
Mit dem Teppich die Geliebte decken;
Doch sie windet gleich sich selbst hervor.
Wie mit Geists Gewalt
Hebet die Gestalt
Lang und langsam sich im Bett empor.

Mutter! Mutter! spricht sie hohle Worte,
So mißgönnt Ihr mir die schöne Nacht!
Ihr vertreibt mich von dem warmen Orte.
Bin ich zur Verzweiflung nur erwacht?
Ists Euch nicht genug,
Daß ins Leichentuch,
Daß Ihr früh mich in das Grab gebracht?

Aber aus der schwerbedeckten Enge
Treibet mich ein eigenes Gericht.
Eurer Priester summende Gesänge
Und ihr Segen haben kein Gewicht;

pleasure straight away?' And with these words she enters. By the lamplight she sees – oh, God! she sees her own child.

And the young man, in his first alarm, tries to cover the girl with her own veil, to hide his beloved with the counterpane; but she frees herself immediately. As if impelled by a spirit, her tall figure raises itself slowly on the bed.

'Mother! Mother!' she says, in hollow tones. 'So you begrudge me my night of joy! You drive me away from this warm place. Did I awaken only to despair? Are you not satisfied with having put me too soon into my shroud, too soon into my grave?

'But out of that heavily-covered narrow place a strange doom drives me. The droning chants of your priests and their blessing are powerless;

Salz und Wasser kühlt
Nicht, wo Jugend fühlt;
Ach! die Erde kühlt die Liebe nicht.

Dieser Jüngling war mir erst versprochen,
Als noch Venus' heitrer Tempel stand.
Mutter, habt Ihr doch das Wort gebrochen,
Weil ein fremd, ein falsch Gelübd Euch band!
Doch kein Gott erhört,
Wenn die Mutter schwört,
Zu versagen ihrer Tochter Hand.

Aus dem Grabe werd ich ausgetrieben,
Noch zu suchen das vermißte Gut,
Noch den schon verlornen Mann zu lieben
Und zu saugen seines Herzens Blut.
Ists um den geschehn,
Muß nach andern gehn,
Und das junge Volk erliegt der Wut.

Schöner Jüngling! kannst nicht länger leben;
Du versiechest nun an diesem Ort.
Meine Kette hab ich dir gegeben;
Deine Locke nehm ich mit mir fort.

sprinklings of salted water do not cool the passions of youth; alas! the earth cannot cool love.

'This youth was already promised to me when the glad temple of Venus was still standing. Mother, you broke your word because an alien and false oath bound you! But no god gives ear to a mother's vow to refuse her daughter in marriage.

'I am driven forth out of my grave to go on seeking that which is mine and which I miss – to go on loving the man I have already lost, and to suck his heart's blood. When he has perished I must seek out others, and the nation's youth must be destroyed by my frenzy.

'Beautiful boy! your days are numbered; here you now will waste away. I have given you my chain; your lock of hair I shall take with me. Look at

Sieh sie an genau!
Morgen bist du grau,
Und nur braun erscheinst du wieder dort.

Höre, Mutter, nun die letzte Bitte:
Einen Scheiterhaufen schichte du;
Öffne meine bange, kleine Hütte,
Bring in Flammen Liebende zur Ruh!
Wenn der Funke sprüht,
Wenn die Asche glüht,
Eilen wir den alten Göttern zu.

DER GOTT UND DIE BAJADERE
Indische Legende

Mahadöh, der Herr der Erde,
Kommt herab zum sechsten Mal,
Daß er unsersgleichen werde,
Mit zu fühlen Freud und Qual.
Er bequemt sich, hier zu wohnen,
Läßt sich alles selbst geschehn.

it closely! Tomorrow you will be grey, and you will only appear brown again in that other place.

'Mother, hear now my last request: make a funeral pyre, open my unquiet little house, and in flames consign a pair of lovers to their rest! When the sparks leap and the embers glow, we shall swiftly depart to our ancient gods.'

THE GOD AND THE DANCING-GIRL

Mahadeva,* Lord of the Earth, came down from heaven a sixth time, to become one of us, and feel our joys and sorrows. He deigned to make his dwelling here, and to undergo all things himself. For if he is to punish

* i.e. the 'great god'.

Soll er strafen oder schonen,
Muß er Menschen menschlich sehn.
Und hat er die Stadt sich als Wandrer betrachtet,
Die Großen belauert, auf Kleine geachtet,
Verläßt er sie abends, um weiter zu gehn.

Als er nun hinausgegangen,
Wo die letzten Häuser sind,
Sieht er, mit gemalten Wangen,
Ein verlornes schönes Kind.
Grüß dich, Jungfrau! – Dank der Ehre!
Wart, ich komme gleich hinaus –
Und wer bist du? – Bajadere,
Und dies ist der Liebe Haus.
Sie rührt sich, die Zimbeln zum Tanze zu schlagen,
Sie weiß sich so lieblich im Kreise zu tragen,
Sie neigt sich und biegt sich und reicht ihm den Strauß.

Schmeichelnd zieht sie ihn zur Schwelle,
Lebhaft ihn ins Haus hinein.
Schöner Fremdling, lampenhelle
Soll sogleich die Hütte sein.

or pardon, he must look at mankind with human eyes. In the form of a wayfarer he would view a city, watching the great and noticing the humble; then in the evening he would leave it and continue his journey.

Having thus walked out to where the houses end, he saw a pretty fallen girl with painted cheeks. 'Greetings to you, lady!' 'I thank you for the honour you do me! Wait, I will come straight out.' 'And who are you?' 'A dancing-girl, and this is the house of love.' And she hastens to begin a dance, striking the cymbals, moving round in a circle with such skilful charm, stooping and twisting and offering him the garland of flowers.

With flattering animated gestures she draws him to the door and into the house. 'In a moment, handsome stranger, the hut shall be bright with lamp-

Bist du müd, ich will dich laben,
Lindern deiner Füße Schmerz.
Was du willst, das sollst du haben:
Ruhe, Freuden oder Scherz.
Sie lindert geschäftig geheuchelte Leiden.
Der Göttliche lächelt; er siehet mit Freuden
Durch tiefes Verderben ein menschliches Herz.

Und er fordert Sklavendienste;
Immer heitrer wird sie nur,
Und des Mädchens frühe Künste
Werden nach und nach Natur.
Und so stellet auf die Blüte
Bald und bald die Frucht sich ein;
Ist Gehorsam im Gemüte,
Wird nicht fern die Liebe sein.
Aber, sie schärfer und schärfer zu prüfen,
Wählet der Kenner der Höhen und Tiefen
Lust und Entsetzen und grimmige Pein.

Und er küßt die bunten Wangen,
Und sie fühlt der Liebe Qual,
Und das Mädchen steht gefangen,
Und sie weint zum erstenmal,

light. If you are tired, I will refresh you, and soothe your sore feet. You shall have whatever you want: rest, or pleasure, or play.' Busily she provides relief for his feigned ailments; the god smiles, rejoicing to discern, through depths of corruption, a human heart.

And he demands services such as are performed by slaves, but it only makes her all the happier; and the girl's arts, so early learnt, gradually become nature. Thus fruit follows quickly upon blossom; if there is obedience in the soul, love will not be far off. But in order to put her more and more closely to the test, he prescribes (for he knows both the heights and the depths) terror and fierce pain as well as pleasure.

And he kisses her gaily-daubed cheeks, and the girl feels the anguish of love, and she stands captive, and she weeps for the first time; she sinks

Sinkt zu seinen Füßen nieder,
Nicht um Wollust noch Gewinst,
Ach! und die gelenken Glieder,
Sie versagen allen Dienst.
Und so zu des Lagers vergnüglicher Feier
Bereiten den dunklen, behaglichen Schleier
Die nächtlichen Stunden, das schöne Gespinst.

Spät entschlummert unter Scherzen,
Früh erwacht nach kurzer Rast,
Findet sie an ihrem Herzen
Tot den vielgeliebten Gast.
Schreiend stürzt sie auf ihn nieder,
Aber nicht erweckt sie ihn;
Und man trägt die starren Glieder
Bald zur Flammengrube hin.
Sie höret die Priester, die Totengesänge,
Sie raset und rennet und teilet die Menge.
Wer bist du? Was drängt zu der Grube dich hin?

Bei der Bahre stürzt sie nieder,
Ihr Geschrei durchdringt die Luft:
Meinen Gatten will ich wieder!
Und ich such ihn in der Gruft.

down at his feet, seeking neither pleasure nor gain, and alas! her supple limbs deny her their service entirely. And thus, over the bed's pleasant ceremonial, the night hours weave from their fair tissue a dark commodious veil.

Falling asleep late amid sportful play, and waking early after brief repose, she finds the well-loved guest dead by her side. Screaming, she falls upon him, but cannot revive him; and soon the rigid limbs are carried away to a fiery grave. She hears the priests, she hears the dirge; in frenzy she runs and forces a way through the crowd. 'Who are you? What drives you to this graveside?'

By the bier she falls down, and her wild cry pierces the air: 'Give me back my husband! I seek him in the tomb. Shall these divine wonderful

Soll zu Asche mir zerfallen
Dieser Glieder Götterpracht?
Mein! er war es, mein vor allen!
Ach, nur Eine süße Nacht!
Es singen die Priester: Wir tragen die Alten,
Nach langem Ermatten und spätem Erkalten,
Wir tragen die Jugend, noch eh sies gedacht.

Höre deiner Priester Lehre:
Dieser war dein Gatte nicht.
Lebst du doch als Bajadere,
Und so hast du keine Pflicht.
Nur dem Körper folgt der Schatten
In das stille Totenreich;
Nur die Gattin folgt dem Gatten:
Das ist Pflicht und Ruhm zugleich.
Ertöne, Drommete, zu heiliger Klage!
O nehmet, ihr Götter, die Zierde der Tage,
O nehmet den Jüngling in Flammen zu euch!

So das Chor, das ohn Erbarmen
Mehret ihres Herzens Not;
Und mit ausgestreckten Armen
Springt sie in den heißen Tod.

limbs fall to ashes before my eyes? Mine! he was mine and no one else's –
alas, for only one sweet night!' The priests chant: 'We carry away the aged,
the slowly-exhausted, the late-grown-cold; and we carry away the young
sooner than they expect.

'Hear the teaching of your priests: this man was not your husband. For
you live as a dancing-girl; duty therefore does not bind you. Only the
body's shadow follows it into death's silent kingdom; only the wife follows
the husband – such is her duty and also her renown. Sound, trumpet, the
sacred lament! Receive, oh gods, the flower of his days, this youth – receive
him to yourselves in flames!'

Thus sang the choir, pitilessly increasing her heart's anguish; and with
outstretched arms she leapt into the burning death. But the divine Youth

Doch der Götter-Jüngling hebet
Aus der Flamme sich empor,
Und in seinen Armen schwebet
Die Geliebte mit hervor.
Es freut sich die Gottheit der reuigen Sünder;
Unsterbliche heben verlorene Kinder
Mit feurigen Armen zum Himmel empor.

DER ZAUBERLEHRLING

H AT der alte Hexenmeister
Sich doch einmal wegbegeben!
Und nun sollen seine Geister
Auch nach meinem Willen leben.
Seine Wort' und Werke
Merkt ich und den Brauch,
Und mit Geistesstärke
Tu ich Wunder auch.

Walle! walle
Manche Strecke,
Daß zum Zwecke
Wasser fließe
Und mit reichem, vollem Schwalle
Zu dem Bade sich ergieße.

rose from the pyre, and in his arms his beloved soared forth with him. The Godhead rejoices in penitent sinners; lost children are raised up to heaven by Immortals with arms of fire.

THE SORCERER'S APPRENTICE

WELL, for once he has taken himself off, the old witch-master! and now my will too shall bring his spirits to life. I have noted his words and operations and the method, and now, with the strength of spirits, I shall work wonders as well.

Wander, wander, hither and yonder! that water so in full flood may flow, and the bath be filled as I have willed.

Und nun komm, du alter Besen!
Nimm die schlechten Lumpenhüllen;
Bist schon lange Knecht gewesen:
Nun erfülle meinen Willen!
Auf zwei Beinen stehe,
Oben sei ein Kopf,
Eile nun und gehe
Mit dem Wassertopf!

Walle! walle
Manche Strecke
Daß zum Zwecke
Wasser fließe
Und mit reichem, vollem Schwalle
Zu dem Bade sich ergieße.

Seht, er läuft zum Ufer nieder!
Wahrlich! ist schon an dem Flusse,
Und mit Blitzesschnelle wieder
Ist er hier mit raschem Gusse.
Schon zum zweiten Male!
Wie das Becken schwillt!
Wie sich jede Schale
Voll mit Wasser füllt!

So come along, old broomstick! Put on your rotten rags; you have
been a long time in service – obey my orders now! Stand up on two legs;
let us have a head at the top; and now look sharp and walk with the
water-jug!

*Wander, wander, hither and yonder! that water so in full flood may flow,
and the bath be filled as I have willed.*

Look, down he hurries to the bank – he's at the river already and no
mistake! Back he comes quick as lightning, and pours it out in a trice. Here
he is already for the second time! Just look how the water mounts in the
tub, and every basin fills to overflowing!

Stehe! stehe!
Denn wir haben
Deiner Gaben
Vollgemessen! –
Ach, ich merk es! Wehe! wehe!
Hab ich doch das Wort vergessen!

Ach, das Wort, worauf am Ende
Er das wird, was er gewesen.
Ach, er läuft und bringt behende!
Wärst du doch der alte Besen!
Immer neue Güsse
Bringt er schnell herein,
Ach, und hundert Flüsse
Stürzen auf mich ein.

Nein, nicht länger
Kann ichs lassen;
Will ihn fassen.
Das ist Tücke!
Ach, nun wird mir immer bänger!
Welche Miene! welche Blicke!

Stand still, stand still! We have had our fill of your gifts – oh dear! oh
dear! I realize now, I've forgotten the words!
Oh dear, the words, that would make him turn back again into what he
was! Oh, how he hurries and carries! I wish you were the old broomstick
again! He keeps rushing in with tubful after tubful, and oh, dear! rivers by
the score are flooding in on me.
No! I can stand by no longer: I will seize it. – Oh! the spiteful thing!
Now I really am getting scared! What a face, what eyes it has!

O, du Ausgeburt der Hölle!
Soll das ganze Haus ersaufen?
Seh ich über jede Schwelle
Doch schon Wasserströme laufen.
Ein verruchter Besen,
Der nicht hören will!
Stock, der du gewesen,
Steh doch wieder still!

Willsts am Ende
Gar nicht lassen?
Will dich fassen,
Will dich halten
Und das alte Holz behende
Mit dem scharfen Beile spalten.

Seht, da kommt er schleppend wieder!
Wie ich mich nur auf dich werfe,
Gleich, o Kobold, liegst du nieder;
Krachend trifft die glatte Schärfe.
Wahrlich! brav getroffen!
Seht, er ist entzwei!
Und nun kann ich hoffen,
Und ich atme frei!

Oh, you offspring of hell! Is the whole house to be drowned? Why,
look! there are streams of water pouring through every door already.
Damned broom, why won't it listen! Stick, will you be what you were and
stand still!

Will you never stop, then? I'll catch you, I'll hold you. I'll split this old
piece of wood double quick with the sharp hatchet.

Look, here it comes trundling back again! Wait till I get to grips with
you, you hobgoblin, I'll knock you flat: smack goes the smooth sharp
blade! Hurrah! well hit, sir! Look, I've cut him in two! And now there's
hope, now I can breathe freely!

Wehe! wehe!
Beide Teile
Stehn in Eile
Schon als Knechte
Völlig fertig in die Höhe!
Helft mir, ach! ihr hohen Mächte!

Und sie laufen! Naß und nässer
Wirds im Saal und auf den Stufen.
Welch entsetzliches Gewässer!
Herr und Meister! hör mich rufen! –
Ach, da kommt der Meister!
Herr, die Not ist groß!
Die ich rief, die Geister
Werd ich nun nicht los.

«In die Ecke,
Besen! Besen!
Seids gewesen!
Denn als Geister
Ruft euch nur, zu diesem Zwecke,
Erst hervor der alte Meister.»

Oh! oh! both the pieces stand up at once, a couple of ready-made servants! Oh, help me, you powers on high!

And away they go! The hall and the steps get wetter and wetter. What a ghastly inundation! Lord and master, hear me calling! – Ah, here comes my master! Sir, I'm in a terrible mess! The spirits I summoned, I can't get rid of them!

'*Be done with you, broom and broom! To the corner of the room!* For to this end you shall not be called out as spirits by anyone except your old Master.'

aus FAUST

ZUEIGNUNG*

IHR naht euch wieder, schwankende Gestalten,
Die früh sich einst dem trüben Blick gezeigt.
Versuch ich wohl, euch diesmal festzuhalten?
Fühl ich mein Herz noch jenem Wahn geneigt?
Ihr drängt euch zu! Nun gut, so mögt ihr walten,
Wie ihr aus Dunst und Nebel um mich steigt;
Mein Busen fühlt sich jugendlich erschüttert
Vom Zauberhauch, der euren Zug umwittert.

Ihr bringt mit euch die Bilder froher Tage,
Und manche liebe Schatten steigen auf;
Gleich einer alten, halbverklungnen Sage
Kommt erste Lieb und Freundschaft mit herauf;
Der Schmerz wird neu, es wiederholt die Klage
Des Lebens labyrinthisch irren Lauf
Und nennt die Guten, die, um schöne Stunden
Vom Glück getäuscht, vor mir hinweggeschwunden.

from FAUST

DEDICATORY POEM

ONCE again you draw near, you uncertain shapes that long ago appeared before my clouded vision. Shall I try this time to take possession of you? Does that folly still move me to longing? You throng about me: so be it! have your will, you who rise round me out of mist and haze. My heart is stirred, touched as in youth by the breath of enchantment that plays about you as you pass by.

You bring with you the images of happy days, and many a well-loved shade comes back to life: first love and friendship rise again with them, like an old half-forgotten legend; pain is renewed, and grief once more retraces life's labyrinthine erring course, and names those dear ones whom Fortune has cheated of hours of joy and who have vanished from sight before me.

* This poem expresses Goethe's feelings on resuming work, in 1797, on his *Faust* manuscript, most of which had been written more than twenty years earlier.

Sie hören nicht die folgenden Gesänge,
Die Seelen, denen ich die ersten sang;
Zerstoben ist das freundliche Gedränge,
Verklungen, ach! der erst Widerklang.
Mein Leid ertönt der unbekannten Menge,
Ihr Beifall selbst macht meinem Herzen bang,
Und was sich sonst an meinem Lied erfreuet,
Wenn es noch lebt, irrt in der Welt zerstreuet.

Und mich ergreift ein längst entwöhntes Sehnen
Nach jenem stillen, ernsten Geisterreich,
Es schwebet nun in unbestimmten Tönen
Mein lispelnd Lied, der Äolsharfe gleich,
Ein Schauer faßt mich, Träne folgt den Tränen,
Das strenge Herz, es fühlt sich mild und weich;
Was ich besitze, seh ich wie im Weiten,
Und was verschwand, wird mir zu Wirklichkeiten.

They cannot hear the songs that follow, those souls to whom I sang the first of them; their sympathetic concourse is scattered, that first response re-echoes, alas, no longer. The unknown multitude hears my sorrow's music, and even its applause dismays my heart; and if there are any others still alive who once took pleasure in my singing, they are wandering dispersed about the world.

And I am seized by a long-unwonted yearning for that silent solemn realm of spirits; my lisping song floats now in indeterminate tones, like an Aeolian harp; a tremor comes upon me, tear follows upon tear, my austere heart is softened to gentleness; what I possess now seems remote, and what has disappeared becomes reality.

(Prologue in Heaven, lines 243–70)

[GESANG DER ERZENGEL]

RAPHAEL: Die Sonne tönt nach alter Weise
In Brudersphären Wettgesang,
Und ihre vorgeschriebne Reise
Vollendet sie mit Donnergang.
Ihr Anblick gibt den Engeln Stärke,
Wenn keiner sie ergründen mag;
Die unbegreiflich hohen Werke
Sind herrlich wie am ersten Tag.

GABRIEL: Und schnell und unbegreiflich schnelle
Dreht sich umher der Erde Pracht;
Es wechselt Paradieseshelle
Mit tiefer, schauervoller Nacht;
Es schäumt das Meer in breiten Flüssen
Am tiefen Grund der Felsen auf,
Und Fels und Meer wird fortgerissen
In ewig-schnellem Sphärenlauf.

MICHAEL: Und Stürme brausen um die Wette
Vom Meer aufs Land, vom Land aufs Meer,
Und bilden wütend eine Kette
Der tiefsten Wirkung ringsumher.

[SONG OF THE ARCHANGELS]

RAPHAEL: The Sun's singing, as of old, rivals the music of his brother
spheres, and with thunderous course he completes his predestined cir-
cuit. The sight of him gives strength to the angels, though none of them
can fathom his nature; the inconceivably lofty works of Creation are as
splendid as on the first day.

GABRIEL: And swiftly, inconceivably swiftly, the magnificent Earth ro-
tates; the brightness of paradise alternates with deep and dreadful night;
the wide-flooding ocean foams against the cliff's deep base, and the cliffs
and the ocean are carried onwards in the spheres' perpetual swift journey.

MICHAEL: And storms in rivalry roar from the sea over the land, and from
the land over the sea, and form in their rage a chain of profoundest in-
fluence all about them. There the destructive lightning flames, precursor

Da flammt ein blitzendes Verheeren
Dem Pfade vor des Donnerschlags;
Doch deine Boten, Herr, verehren
Das sanfte Wandeln deines Tags.
ZU DREI: Der Anblick gibt den Engeln Stärke,
Da keiner dich ergründen mag,
Und alle deine hohen Werke
Sind herrlich wie am ersten Tag.

(Part I, lines 903–40)
[FAUST AM OSTERMORGEN]

VOM Eise befreit sind Strom und Bäche
Durch des Frühlings holden, belebenden Blick,
Im Tale grünet Hoffnungsglück;
Der alte Winter, in seiner Schwäche,
Zog sich in rauhe Berge zurück.
Von dorther sendet er, fliehend, nur
Ohnmächtige Schauer körnigen Eises
In Streifen über die grünende Flur;
Aber die Sonne duldet kein Weißes:

of the thunder's path; but thy Messengers, Lord, revere the gentle
motion of thy day.
THE THREE IN CHORUS: This sight gives strength to the angels, for
none can fathom thy nature; and all thy lofty works are as splendid as on
the first day.

[FAUST ON EASTER MORNING]

RIVER and streams have got rid of their ice in the sweet reviving gleam of
spring: the valley is green with hope and happiness; old winter in his weak-
ness has retreated into wild mountains, and from there he can only send
impotent showers of hail to make incursions across the verdant fields. But
the sun will not tolerate anything white: there are impulses of growth and

Überall regt sich Bildung und Streben,
Alles will sie mit Farben beleben;
Doch an Blumen fehlts im Revier:
Sie nimmt geputzte Menschen dafür.
Kehre dich um, von diesen Höhen
Nach der Stadt zurückzusehen!
Aus dem hohlen, finstern Tor
Dringt ein buntes Gewimmel hervor.
Jeder sonnt sich heute so gern.
Sie feiern die Auferstehung des Herrn;
Denn sie sind selber auferstanden:
Aus niedriger Häuser dumpfen Gemächern,
Aus Handwerks- und Gewerbesbanden,
Aus dem Druck von Giebeln und Dächern,
Aus der Straßen quetschender Enge,
Aus der Kirchen ehrwürdiger Nacht
Sind sie alle ans Licht gebracht.
Sieh nur, sieh! wie behend sich die Menge
Durch die Gärten und Felder zerschlägt,
Wie der Fluß in Breit und Länge
So manchen lustigen Nachen bewegt,
Und, bis zum Sinken überladen,
Entfernt sich dieser letzte Kahn.
Selbst von des Berges fernen Pfaden

formation astir everywhere, and the sun is trying to enliven everything with colour; there are not enough flowers in the countryside, so it uses gaily-dressed people instead. Look round, from the high ground look back at the town! Out of the hollow gloomy gate a colourful crowd is pouring. Everyone loves to take the sun today. They are celebrating the risen Lord – because they themselves have risen: out of stuffy rooms in small houses, out of the bondage of handiwork and trade, out of the oppression of gables and roofs, out of the narrow strangling streets, out of the churches' reverend gloom they have all been brought out into the light. Look, just look! how quickly the crowd scatters all over the gardens and fields, how right across and down the river all these gay boats are moving, and this last one leaving loaded to sinking-point! Even from paths on the distant hillside we

Blinken uns farbige Kleider an.
Ich höre schon des Dorfs Getümmel,
Hier ist des Volkes wahrer Himmel,
Zufrieden jauchzet groß und klein:
«Hier bin ich Mensch, hier darf ichs sein!»

(Part I, lines 1070–99)

[FAUST BETRACHTET DEN SONNENUNTERGANG]

BETRACHTE, wie in Abendsonneglut
Die grünumgebnen Hütten schimmern!
Sie rückt und weicht, der Tag ist überlebt,
Dort eilt sie hin und fördert neues Leben.
O daß kein Flügel mich vom Boden hebt,
Ihr nach und immer nach zu streben!
Ich säh im ewigen Abendstrahl
Die stille Welt zu meinen Füßen,
Entzündet alle Höhen, beruhigt jedes Tal,
Den Silberbach in goldne Ströme fließen.
Nicht hemmte dann den göttergleichen Lauf

can see a gleam of colourful attire. I can hear the noise from the village already. Here is the people's true heaven – great and small are contented and shouting with delight: 'Here I am human, here I *can* be human!'

[FAUST CONTEMPLATES THE SUNSET]

LOOK how those little houses, surrounded with green, are gleaming in the fire of the evening sun! The day is spent, the sun is retreating and moving away; there it goes, there it hastens, to give new life elsewhere. Oh, why does no wing raise me from the ground, that I might follow it farther and farther! I should see the silent world at my feet, in an unceasing glow of sunset, all the hills burning, all the valleys at rest, the silver brook running

Der wilde Berg mit allen seinen Schluchten;
Schon tut das Meer sich mit erwärmten Buchten
Vor den erstaunten Augen auf.
Doch scheint die Göttin endlich wegzusinken;
Allein der neue Trieb erwacht:
Ich eile fort, ihr ewges Licht zu trinken,
Vor mir den Tag und hinter mir die Nacht,
Den Himmel über mir und unter mir die Wellen.
Ein schöner Traum, indessen sie entweicht.
Ach, zu des Geistes Flügeln wird so leicht
Kein körperlicher Flügel sich gesellen!
Doch ist es jedem eingeboren,
Daß sein Gefühl hinauf- und vorwärtsdringt,
Wenn über uns, im blauen Raum verloren,
Ihr schmetternd Lied die Lerche singt,
Wenn über schroffen Fichtenhöhen
Der Adler ausgebreitet schwebt
Und über Flächen, über Seen
Der Kranich nach der Heimat strebt.

into streams of gold. Not the wild mountain then with all its gorges should check my god-like course: already before my astonished eyes the sea lies open, with its gulfs warmed by the rays of the divine sun, which now at last seems to be sinking out of sight – but a new impulse wakens and I hasten on to drink its eternal brightness, with the day in front of me and the night behind me, the sky above me, and beneath me the sea.

A beautiful dream! and meanwhile the sun disappears. Alas, no bodily wing is likely to match the wings of the mind! And yet in each of us there is born an impulse of feeling that carries him upwards and onwards, when we hear above us the lark, lost in blue space, singing its brilliant song, or when the eagle hovers outspread over rugged pine-clad heights, and over plains and lakes the eager crane flies homewards.

(Part I, lines 1224–37)

[FAUST ÜBERSETZT DAS EVANGELIUM]

GESCHRIEBEN steht: «Im Anfang war das *Wort*!»
Hier stock ich schon! Wer hilft mir weiter fort?
Ich kann das *Wort* so hoch unmöglich schätzen,
Ich muß es anders übersetzen,
Wenn ich vom Geiste recht erleuchtet bin.
Geschrieben steht: Im Anfang war der *Sinn*.
Bedenke wohl die erste Zeile,
Daß deine Feder sich nicht übereile!
Ist es der *Sinn*, der alles wirkt und schafft?
Es sollte stehn: Im Anfang war die *Kraft*!
Doch auch indem ich dieses niederschreibe,
Schon warnt mich was, daß ich dabei nicht bleibe.
Mir hilft der Geist! auf einmal seh ich Rat
Und schreibe getrost: Im Anfang war die *Tat*! –

[FAUST TRANSLATES THE GOSPEL]

IT is written: 'In the beginning was the *Word*.' Here I am stuck already!
Who will help me on? To set so high a value on a 'word' is impossible: I
must translate it some other way, if the spirit is giving me real enlighten-
ment. It is written: 'In the beginning was *Mind*.' Consider the first line
well, let your pen not move on too fast! Is it by *Mind* that all things are
done and made? It should read: 'In the beginning was *Energy*.' And yet, at
the very moment of writing it down, something warns me not to leave it at
that. The spirit moves me! I suddenly see the answer, and boldly write: 'In
the beginning was the *Deed*.'

(Part I, lines 1446–1505)

[GEISTERCHOR]

Schwindet, ihr dunkeln
Wölbungen droben!
Reizender schaue
Freundlich der blaue
Äther herein!
Wären die dunkeln
Wolken zerronnen!
Sternelein funkeln,
Mildere Sonnen
Scheinen darein.
Himmlischer Söhne
Geistige Schöne,
Schwankende Beugung
Schwebet vorüber;
Sehnende Neigung

Folget hinüber.
Und der Gewänder
Flatternde Bänder
Decken die Länder,
Decken die Laube,
Wo sich fürs Leben,
Tief in Gedanken,
Liebende geben.
Laube bei Laube!
Sprossende Ranken!
Lastende Traube
Stürzt ins Behälter
Drängender Kelter;
Stürzen in Bächen
Schäumende Weine,

[SPIRIT CHORUS]

Vanish, you dark vaulted ceilings above him! Let the lovelier ethereal blue gaze in kindly upon him! Would that the dark clouds were dissolved! Little stars glitter, milder suns shine. The spiritual beauty of sons of heaven hovers past, swaying, inclining; passionate longing follows them onwards. And the wind-blown ribbons of garments cover the landscape, cover the bower where lovers, deep in thought, give themselves to each other for ever. Bower by bower! Lush vegetation! The vine lets fall its abundant burden into its vessel, the thronging winepress; foaming wines

Rieseln durch reine
Edle Gesteine,
Lassen die Höhen
Hinter sich liegen,
Breiten zu Seen
Sich ums Genügen
Grünender Hügel.
Und das Geflügel
Schlürfet sich Wonne,
Flieget der Sonne,
Flieget den hellen
Inseln entgegen,
Die sich auf Wellen
Gauklend bewegen,
Wo wir in Chören

Jauchzende hören,
Über den Auen
Tanzende schauen,
Die sich im Freien
Alle zerstreuen.
Einige klimmen
Über die Höhen,
Andere schwimmen
Über die Seen,
Andere schweben:
Alle zum Leben,
Alle zur Ferne
Liebender Sterne,
Seliger Huld.

pour down in rivulets, ripple through pure precious stones, leave the heights behind them and spread into lakes round placid verdant hills. And the birds drink rapture, they soar towards the sun, towards the bright islands that dazzlingly dance on the waves, and there we hear voices exulting in chorus, there we see dancers crossing the meadows, who scatter far and wide under the open sky. Some climb over the mountains, some swim across the lakes, others hover in the air: all towards life, all into the distance, to stars of love, to ecstasy and grace.

(Part II, lines 8488–515)
[HELENAS AUFTRITT]

BEWUNDERT viel und viel gescholten, Helena,
Vom Strande komm ich, wo wir erst gelandet sind,
Noch immer trunken von des Gewoges regsamem
Geschaukel, das vom phrygischen Blachgefild uns her
Auf sträubig-hohem Rücken durch Poseidons Gunst
Und Euros' Kraft in vaterländische Buchten trug.
Dort unten freuet nun der König Menelas
Der Rückkehr samt den tapfersten seiner Krieger sich.
Du aber heiße mich willkommen, hohes Haus,
Das Tyndareos, mein Vater, nah dem Hange sich
Von Pallas' Hügel wiederkehrend aufgebaut
Und, als ich hier mit Klytämnestren schwesterlich,
Mit Kastor auch und Pollux fröhlich spielend wuchs,
Vor allen Häusern Spartas herrlich ausgeschmückt.
Gegrüßt seid mir, der ehrnen Pforte Flügel ihr!
Durch euer gastlich ladendes Weit-Eröffnen einst
Geschahs, daß mir, erwählt aus vielen, Menelas
In Bräutigamsgestalt entgegenleuchtete.
Eröffnet mir sie wieder, daß ich ein Eilgebot
Des Königs treu erfülle, wie der Gattin ziemt!

[OPENING SPEECH OF HELEN]

I, HELEN, the much-admired and much-reviled, have come from the shore where we have just landed, still drunk from the lively rocking of the waves, on whose high-tossing back we have ridden, by Poseidon's favour and the East Wind's force, from the plains of Troy to the harbours of our homeland. Down there King Menelaus, with the bravest of his warriors, is now celebrating his return. But I ask a welcome from you, oh lofty house which my father Tyndareus, on his homecoming, built near the slope of Pallas Athene's hill, and furnished more magnificently than all the other houses in Sparta, at the time when I was growing up here with my sister Clytemnestra and happily playing with Castor and Pollux. I salute you, great brazen double doors! It was through you, invitingly flung wide open, that Menelaus once approached me as a bridegroom, radiant to see, chosen among many. Open them to me again, that I may loyally, as befits a wife, fulfil an urgent behest of the King! Let me enter! and may I leave behind

Laßt mich hinein! und alles bleibe hinter mir,
Was mich umstürmte bis hierher, verhängnisvoll!
Denn seit ich diese Schwelle sorgenlos verließ,
Cytherens Tempel besuchend, heiliger Pflicht gemäß,
Mich aber dort ein Räuber griff, der phrygische,
Ist viel geschehen, was die Menschen weit und breit
So gern erzählen, aber der nicht gerne hört,
Von dem die Sage wachsend sich zum Märchen spann.

(Part II, lines 11424–94)

[FAUST UND SORGE]

SORGE: Würde mich kein Ohr vernehmen,
 Müßt es doch im Herzen dröhnen;
 In verwandelter Gestalt
 Üb ich grimmige Gewalt:
 Auf den Pfaden, auf der Welle,
 Ewig ängstlicher Geselle,
 Stets gefunden, nie gesucht,
 So geschmeichelt wie verflucht! –
 Hast du die Sorge nie gekannt?

all the fateful strife that has raged around me till now! For since I last
crossed this threshold, light of heart, to visit Aphrodite's temple as sacred
duty bade me, but there was seized by a Trojan robber – since then many
things have befallen, which men far and wide so love to tell, though those
of whom they tell it do not love to hear this story, for it has grown into
a fable.

[FAUST AND CARE]

CARE: Even though no ear should hear me, my murmuring must re-echo
in the heart; in transformed form I wield a dreadful power: on highways
and byways and on the sea I am a perpetual uneasy companion, always
found and never looked for, flattered and cursed alike! – Have you
never known Care?

FAUST: Ich bin nur durch die Welt gerannt!
Ein jed Gelüst ergriff ich bei den Haaren,
Was nicht genügte, ließ ich fahren,
Was mir entwischte, ließ ich ziehn.
Ich habe nur begehrt und nur vollbracht
Und abermals gewünscht und so mit Macht
Mein Leben durchgestürmt: erst groß und mächtig,
Nun aber geht es weise, geht bedächtig.
Der Erdenkreis ist mir genug bekannt.
Nach drüben ist die Aussicht uns verrannt;
Tor, wer dorthin die Augen blinzelnd richtet,
Sich über Wolken seinesgleichen dichtet!
Er stehe fest und sehe hier sich um:
Dem Tüchtigen ist diese Welt nicht stumm!
Was braucht er in die Ewigkeit zu schweifen?
Was er erkennt, läßt sich ergreifen.
Er wandle so den Erdentag entlang;
Wenn Geister spuken, geh er seinen Gang,
Im Weiterschreiten find er Qual und Glück,
Er, unbefriedigt jeden Augenblick!

FAUST: I have merely raced through the world! I have seized every appetite by the hair; what did not satisfy me, I abandoned; what slipped through my grasp, I let go. I have merely craved and achieved and then desired again, and thus I have rushed through my life like a strong storm: great and mighty at first, but now I am wise, now I look before I leap. The world is well enough known to me now. Our view beyond it is blocked; only idiots turn their blinking eyes up yonder, and dream of beings in our own image above the clouds! Let us stand firm down here and look about us: to the sound and sane this earth has much to say! Why should one stray into eternity? Our hands can seize what our minds can grasp. Let man pursue thus his earth-and-daylight path; spirits may spook, but let him walk on; let him find his pain and his joy in advancing farther, this man whom no moment can ever satisfy!

SORGE: Wen ich einmal mir besitze,
 Dem ist alle Welt nichts nütze:
 Ewiges Düstre steigt herunter,
 Sonne geht nicht auf noch unter,
 Bei vollkommen äußern Sinnen
 Wohnen Finsternisse drinnen,
 Und er weiß von allen Schätzen
 Sich nicht in Besitz zu setzen.
 Glück und Unglück wird zur Grille,
 Er verhungert in der Fülle,
 Sei es Wonne, sei es Plage,
 Schiebt ers zu dem andern Tage,
 Ist der Zukunft nur gewärtig,
 Und so wird er niemals fertig.
FAUST: Hör auf! so kommst du mir nicht bei!
 Ich mag nicht solchen Unsinn hören.
 Fahr hin! Die schlechte Litanei,
 Sie könnte selbst den klügsten Mann betören.
SORGE: Soll er gehen? soll er kommen?
 Der Entschluß ist ihm genommen;
 Auf gebahnten Weges Mitte
 Wankt er tastend halbe Schritte.

CARE: When once I have taken possession of a man, the whole world is
 of no avail to him: down on him comes perpetual darkness, the sun
 never rises and never sets; his outward senses are unimpaired, but night
 has nested in his soul, and though he may be surrounded by treasures
 he can make none of them his own. His happiness and unhappiness hang
 on whims, he starves amid abundance, he procrastinates pleasure and
 procrastinates toil; he looks to nothing but the future, and thus he can
 never have done with anything.
FAUST: Stop! You'll not get me like this. I refuse to listen to such rubbish.
 Get away from me. Your wretched litany is enough to drive the wisest
 of men crazy.
CARE: Shall he come or shall he go? He has lost the power to decide; in
 the middle of an open road he gropes with hesitant half-steps. He

Er verliert sich immer tiefer,
Siehet alle Dinge schiefer,
Sich und andre lästig drückend,
Atem holend und erstickend,
Nicht erstickt und ohne Leben,
Nicht verzweifelnd, nicht ergeben.
So ein unaufhaltsam Rollen,
Schmerzlich Lassen, widrig Sollen,
Bald Befreien, bald Erdrücken,
Halber Schlaf und schlecht Erquicken
Heftet ihn an seine Stelle
Und bereitet ihn zur Hölle.

FAUST: Unselige Gespenster! so behandelt ihr
Das menschliche Geschlecht zu tausend Malen;
Gleichgültige Tage selbst verwandelt ihr
In garstigen Wirrwarr netzumstrickter Qualen.
Dämonen, weiß ich, wird man schwerlich los,
Das geistig-strenge Band ist nicht zu trennen;
Doch deine Macht, o Sorge, schleichend-groß,
Ich werde sie nicht anerkennen!

wanders ever deeper into the maze, sees all things more and more distortedly, is a burden to himself and to others; he chokes as he draws breath, and though not choked to death he is lifeless; though not despairing, he does not accept. This helpless rolling to and fro, the painful letting-go, the irksome must-do-so, this state that now frees and now smothers, this half-sleep, this unrefreshing repose, all this rivets him fast to where he is, and makes him ready for hell.

FAUST: Miserable phantoms! these are the thousand plagues you visit on the race of men. Even our indifferent days you transform into a disgusting chaos and entangling net of torment. Demons, I know, are hard to banish; these spirit-bonds are strict and will not break; but I will not acknowledge you, great creeping power of Care!

III

MIDDLE AGE AND OLD AGE

(1800–32)

DAUER IM WECHSEL

HIELTE diesen frühen Segen,
Ach, nur Eine Stunde fest!
Aber vollen Blütenregen
Schüttelt schon der laue West.
Soll ich mich des Grünen freuen,
Dem ich Schatten erst verdankt?
Bald wird Sturm auch das zerstreuen
Wenn es falb im Herbst geschwankt.

Willst du nach den Früchten greifen,
Eilig nimm dein Teil davon!
Diese fangen an zu reifen,
Und die andern keimen schon;
Gleich mit jedem Regengusse,
Ändert sich dein holdes Tal,
Ach, und in demselben Flusse
Schwimmst du nicht zum zweitenmal.

Du nun selbst! Was felsenfeste
Sich vor dir hervorgetan,
Mauern siehst du, siehst Paläste
Stets mit andern Augen an.

PERMANENCE IN CHANGE

AH, if this early bounty of blossoms could but last one hour! But the warm west wind already shakes them and they rain down abundantly. Shall I take pleasure in the green leaves in whose shade but lately I stood? Soon they will tremble sere in autumn and a storm will scatter them too.

If you wish to grasp the fruit, make haste to take your share of it! for some of it is beginning to ripen, and some is already germinating. Swiftly, with every shower of rain, your sweet valley changes: and alas, in one and the same river you cannot swim a second time.

And you yourself! At all those things that seemed to stand forth before you firm as rock, at those walls and palaces, you look with ever-changing eyes. That lip has wasted away whose pain was once healed by kisses, that

Weggeschwunden ist die Lippe,
Die im Kusse sonst genas,
Jener Fuß, der an der Klippe
Sich mit Gemsenfreche maß.

Jene Hand, die gern und milde
Sich bewegte wohlzutun,
Das gegliederte Gebilde,
Alles ist ein andres nun.
Und was sich an jener Stelle
Nun mit deinem Namen nennt,
Kam herbei wie eine Welle,
Und so eilts zum Element.

Laß den Anfang mit dem Ende
Sich in Eins zusammenziehn!
Schneller als die Gegenstände
Selber dich vorüberfliehn!
Danke, daß die Gunst der Musen
Unvergängliches verheißt,
Den Gehalt in deinem Busen
Und die Form in deinem Geist.

foot which once boldly leapt like a mountain goat to the precipice's challenge.

That hand, that articulated structure, once so gladly and generously extended to give happiness – all these things are different now. And that which in their place now calls itself by your name came hither like a wave, and is hastening likewise to mingle with the elements.

Then let the beginning and the end contract into a single point, and let yourself speed by even more swiftly than these objects! Give thanks that the favour of the Muses promises an imperishable thing: the meaning in your heart, and the form in your mind.

NATUR UND KUNST

Natur und Kunst, sie scheinen sich zu fliehen,
Und haben sich, eh man es denkt, gefunden;
Der Widerwille ist auch mir verschwunden,
Und beide scheinen gleich mich anzuziehen.

Es gilt wohl nur ein redliches Bemühen!
Und wenn wir erst in abgemeßnen Stunden
Mit Geist und Fleiß uns an die Kunst gebunden,
Mag frei Natur im Herzen wieder glühen.

So ists mit aller Bildung auch beschaffen:
Vergebens werden ungebundne Geister
Nach der Vollendung reiner Höhe streben.

Wer Großes will, muß sich zusammenraffen;
In der Beschränkung zeigt sich erst der Meister,
Und das Gesetz nur kann uns Freiheit geben.

NATURE AND ART

Nature and Art: no sooner do they seem to flee each other, than they come together. In me, too, the antagonism has disappeared, and they seem to attract me both equally.

Honest toil, I suppose, is the whole secret! And after we have devoted to Art regular hours of intelligent hard work, we may again allow Nature to glow freely in our hearts.

And it is thus with all culture: unfettered spirits will aspire in vain to the pure heights of perfection.

He who wills great things must gird up his loins; only in limitation is mastery revealed, and law alone can give us freedom.

197

DAS SONETT

S ICH in erneutem Kungstgebrauch zu üben,
Ist heilge Pflicht, die wir dir auferlegen.
Du kannst dich auch, wie wir, bestimmt bewegen
Nach Tritt und Schritt, wie es dir vorgeschrieben.

Denn eben die Beschränkung läßt sich lieben,
Wenn sich die Geister gar gewaltig regen;
Und wie sie sich denn auch gebärden mögen,
Das Werk zuletzt ist doch vollendet blieben.

So möcht ich selbst in künstlichen Sonetten,
In sprachgewandter Maße kühnem Stolze,
Das Beste, was Gefühl mir gäbe, reimen;

Nur weiß ich hier mich nicht bequem zu betten,
Ich schneide sonst so gern aus ganzem Holze
Und müßte nun doch auch mitunter leimen.

THE SONNET

'To practise a revived usage of art is a sacred duty which we impose upon you. You too can move, as we do, in a well-defined motion and with the prescribed measured tread.

'For it is precisely such limitation that becomes attractive when the vital spirits are mightily astir; so that however these may disport themselves, the work in the end will have achieved perfection.'

I too should like to mould the best inspiration of my feelings into the rhymes of artful sonnets, the bold pride of numbers in skilled language;

but I do not find this a comfortable bed; normally I like to carve out of a whole block of wood, and here, from time to time, I should have to be using glue.

MÄCHTIGES ÜBERRASCHEN

Ein Strom entrauscht umwölktem Felsensaale,
Dem Ozean sich eilig zu verbinden;
Was auch sich spiegeln mag von Grund zu Gründen,
Er wandelt unaufhaltsam fort zu Tale.

Dämonisch aber stürzt mit einem Male –
Ihr folgen Berg und Wald in Wirbelwinden –
Sich Oreas, Behagen dort zu finden,
Und hemmt den Lauf, begrenzt die weite Schale.

Die Welle sprüht und staunt zurück und weichet
Und schwillt bergan, sich immer selbst zu trinken;
Gehemmt ist nun zum Vater hin das Streben.

Sie schwankt und ruht, zum See zurückgedeichet;
Gestirne, spiegelnd sich, beschaun das Blinken
Des Wellenschlags am Fels, ein neues Leben.

SURPRISED BY MIGHT

Out of a cloud-surrounded hall of rocks a stream gushes, eager to mingle
with the ocean; he cares not what may be mirrored in his downward course,
but sweeps on irresistibly to the valley.

Yet suddenly the goddess of the mountain, with demonic swiftness –
hillside and forest following her in whirlwinds – slides down and settles
there, checking his course, and setting bounds to the wide basin.

The astonished flood recoils foaming, yields and swells back summit-
ward, drinking himself up and up; his striving to join his father is now
checked.

Shuddering, he comes to rest, dammed back into a lake: stars, mirrored,
gaze down at the glittering water which laps against the rock – down at a
new life.

WACHSTUM

ALS kleines artges Kind nach Feld und Auen
Sprangst du mit mir so manchen Frühlingsmorgen.
«Für solch ein Töchterchen, mit holden Sorgen,
Möcht ich als Vater segnend Häuser bauen!»

Und als du anfingst, in die Welt zu schauen,
War deine Freude häusliches Besorgen.
«Solch eine Schwester! und ich wär geborgen:
Wie könnt ich ihr, ach! wie sie mir vertrauen!»

Nun kann den schönen Wachstum nichts beschränken;
Ich fühl im Herzen heißes Liebetoben.
Umfass ich sie, die Schmerzen zu beschwichtgen?

Doch ach! nun muß ich dich als Fürstin denken:
Du stehst so schroff vor mir emporgehoben;
Ich beuge mich vor deinem Blick, dem flüchtgen.

GROWTH

As a little dear child, on many a spring morning, you would jump along beside me to the fields and meadows. 'For a little daughter like this I would suffer a father's sweet cares; I would build, with blessings, many a house!'

And when you began to open your eyes to the world, you took delight in household duties. 'A sister like this, and I should be well provided for! Oh, how much I could entrust to her, and she to me!'

And now nothing can stay the lovely growth; I feel the hot madness of love in my heart. Shall I embrace her, to ease my pain?

Ah, but now I can see you only as a princess – you stand towering above me so high! I bow before your glance, so fleeting.

REISEZEHRUNG

ENTWÖHNEN sollt ich mich vom Glanz der Blicke,
Mein Leben sollten sie nicht mehr verschönen.
Was man Geschick nennt, läßt sich nicht versöhnen,
Ich weiß es wohl, und trat bestürzt zurücke.

Nun wußt ich auch von keinem weitern Glücke;
Gleich fing ich an von diesen und von jenen
Notwendgen Dingen sonst mich zu entwöhnen:
Notwendig schien mir nichts als ihre Blicke.

Des Weines Glut, den Vielgenuß der Speisen,
Bequemlichkeit und Schlaf und sonstge Gaben,
Gesellschaft wies ich weg, daß wenig bliebe.

So kann ich ruhig durch die Welt nun reisen:
Was ich bedarf, ist überall zu haben,
Und Unentbehrlichs bring ich mit – die Liebe.

PROVISION FOR THE JOURNEY

I WAS to learn to forgo her shining eyes – they were to beautify my life
no longer. There is a thing called fate which is inexorable – I know it
well! – and I stepped back in dismay.

And now I knew of no other happiness either. I began at once to un-
earn this and that other necessity as well: for to me nothing but her looks
seemed necessary.

The glow of wine, much food's enjoyment, comfort and sleep and other
gifts, and all company, I abjured, that little might be left.

Thus I can now travel lighthearted through the world; what I need is to
be had anywhere, and I take with me that which alone is indispensable –
love.

DAS TAGEBUCH

— aliam tenui, sed iam quum gaudia adirem,
Admonuit dominae deseruitque Venus.

WIR hörens oft und glaubens wohl am Ende:
Das Menschenherz sei ewig unergründlich,
Und wie man auch sich hin und wieder wende,
So sei der Christe wie der Heide sündlich.
Das Beste bleibt, wir geben uns die Hände
Und nehmens mit der Lehre nicht empfindlich;
Denn zeigt sich auch ein Dämon, uns versuchend,
So waltet was, gerettet ist die Tugend.

Von meiner Trauten lange Zeit entfernet,
Wie's öfters geht, nach irdischem Gewinne,
Und was ich auch gewonnen und gelernet,
So hatt ich doch nur immer Sie im Sinne;
Und wie zu Nacht der Himmel erst sich sternet,
Erinnrung uns umleuchtet ferner Minne:
So ward im Federzug des Tags Ereignis
Mit süßen Worten ihr ein freundlich Gleichnis.

THE DIARY

I had another woman in my arms, but as I was about to take
my pleasure, Venus reminded me of my lady, and deserted me.
— TIBULLUS I, 5

WE often hear it said — and in the end no doubt we believe it — that the
human heart is for ever unfathomable, and that twist and turn as we will,
both Christian and pagan are sinners. In the end we had better shake hands
on it and not take the doctrine too much to heart; for though some demon
may approach and tempt us, something else prevails, and virtue is saved.

Once when, as sometimes happens, I was a long time away from my lady,
seeking earthly gain, I always, whatever I had profited and learnt, thought
only of her: and as it is at nightfall that the stars cover the sky and the
memory of far-off love shines round us, so I, with my pen, would make in
sweet words a kindly image for her of the day's events.

Ich eilte nun zurück. Zerbrochen sollte
Mein Wagen mich noch eine Nacht verspäten;
Schon dacht ich mich, wie ich zu Hause rollte,
Allein da war Geduld und Werk vonnöten.
Und wie ich auch mit Schmied und Wagner tollte,
Sie hämmerten, verschmähten, viel zu reden.
Ein jedes Handwerk hat nun seine Schnurren.
Was blieb mir nun? Zu weilen und zu murren.

So stand ich nun. Der Stern des nächsten Schildes
Berief mich hin, die Wohnung schien erträglich.
Ein Mädchen kam, des seltensten Gebildes,
Das Licht erleuchtend. Mir ward gleich behäglich.
Hausflur und Treppe sah ich als ein Mildes,
Die Zimmerchen erfreuten mich unsäglich.
Den sündigen Menschen, der im Freien schwebet –
Die Schönheit spinnt, sie ists, die ihn umwebet.

Nun setzt ich mich zu meiner Tasch und Briefen
Und meines Tagebuchs Genauigkeiten,
Und so wie sonst, wenn alle Menschen schliefen,
Mir und der Trauten Freude zu bereiten;

And now I was hastening back to her. My carriage, as it proved, was to delay me yet another night, with a broken axle: already I had fancied myself rolling homewards, but there was need of patience and labour; and storm though I would at the smith and the wheelwright, they just hammered away and wasted few words. Every handicraft has its mysteries. What could I do? Merely grumble and wait.

So there I stood. The '*Star*' on the nearest inn-sign spoke its summons. The lodging seemed decent enough. A girl came with the light; she was most rarely shaped, and at once I felt at ease. I found the hall and staircase very pleasing, and the little bedrooms absolutely delightful. When a sinful man is wandering abroad, it is beauty that spins a web to ensnare him.

I now sat down to my portfolio and letters and careful diary-entries, intending as usual to give, while everyone else was asleep, a pleasure to myself and my beloved; but somehow the inky words did not spread them-

Doch weiß ich nicht, die Tintenworte liefen
Nicht so wie sonst in alle Kleinigkeiten:
Das Mädchen kam, des Abendessens Bürde
Verteilte sie gewandt mit Gruß und Würde.

Sie geht und kommt; ich spreche, sie erwidert;
Mit jedem Wort erscheint sie mir geschmückter.
Und wie sie leicht mir nun das Huhn zergliedert,
Bewegend Hand und Arm, geschickt, geschickter –
Was auch das tolle Zeug in uns befiedert –
Genug, ich bin verworrner, bin verrückter,
Den Stuhl umwerfend, spring ich auf und fasse
Das schöne Kind; sie lispelt: «Lasse, lasse!

Die Muhme drunten lauscht, ein alter Drache,
Sie zählt bedächtig des Geschäfts Minute;
Sie denkt sich unten, was ich oben mache,
Bei jedem Zögern schwenkt sie frisch die Rute.
Doch schließe deine Türe nicht und wache,
So kommt die Mitternacht uns wohl zugute.»
Rasch meinem Arm entwindet sie die Glieder,
Und eilet fort und kommt nur dienend wieder;

selves as usual into every detail. The girl came, loaded with supper which,
with a dignified greeting, she skilfully set out before me.

She comes and goes, I speak, she answers: she looks prettier with every
word she says. And now, as she dissects the chicken for me with easy, neat,
deft movements of her hands and arms – just the thing to make one's
mad feathers sprout – in a word, I grow more and more confused, I grow
crazy. I leap to my feet, knocking the chair over, and seize the dear charmer
– she whispers: 'Hush, let me go!

'My aunt is listening downstairs, the old dragon; she counts every minute
I take over my work; when she is down there she thinks about what I am
doing up here, and brandishes the rod at every delay. But leave your door
open, and stay awake; and perhaps midnight will stand us in good stead.'
Quickly she wriggles out of my embrace and hurries off, and then comes
back to serve me:

Doch blickend auch! So daß aus jedem Blicke
Sich himmlisches Versprechen mir entfaltet.
Den stillen Seufzer drängt sie nicht zurücke,
Der ihren Busen herrlicher gestaltet.
Ich sehe, daß am Ohr, um Hals und Gnicke
Der flüchtigen Röte Liebesblüte waltet,
Und da sie nichts zu leisten wieder findet,
Geht sie und zögert, sieht sich um, verschwindet.

Der Mitternacht gehören Haus und Straßen,
Mir ist ein weites Lager aufgebreitet,
Wovon den kleinsten Teil mir anzumaßen
Die Liebe rät, die alles wohl bereitet;
Ich zaudre noch, die Kerzen auszublasen,
Nun hör ich sie, wie leise sie auch gleitet,
Mit gierigem Blick die Hochgestalt umschweif ich,
Sie senkt sich her, die Wohlgestalt ergreif ich.

Sie macht sich los: «Vergönne, daß ich rede,
Damit ich dir nicht völlig fremd gehöre.
Der Schein ist wider mich; sonst war ich blöde,
Stets gegen Männer setzt ich mich zur Wehre.

but to look at me too! And a heavenly promise blossoms from every
glance. Nor does she suppress soft little sighs, which finely round out her
bosom. I can see on her ears and round her neck and shoulders the love-
bloom of fleeting blushes; and then, finding nothing further to do, she
goes, hesitates, looks round and disappears.

Midnight has fallen upon house and streets; a wide bed has been made
up for me, of which I appropriate only a small part, as Love counsels, who
prepares all things well; I have not yet blown out the candles, and now I
hear her, softly though she glides; my passionate gaze roves over her form,
she sinks down at my side, I take the fair creature into my arms.

She frees herself: 'Let me speak – for I do not want you to take me know-
ing nothing at all about me. Appearances are against me; I used to be timid,
and always resisted the advances of men. I have a reputation for coldness in

Mich nennt die Stadt, mich nennt die Gegend spröde;
Nun aber weiß ich, wie das Herz sich kehre:
Du bist mein Sieger, laß dichs nicht verdrießen,
Ich sah, ich liebte, schwur dich zu genießen.

Du hast mich rein, und wenn ichs besser wüßte,
So gäb ichs dir; ich tue, was ich sage.»
So schließt sie mich an ihre süßen Brüste,
Als ob ihr nun an meiner Brust behage.
Und wie ich Mund und Aug und Stirne küßte,
So war ich doch in wunderbarer Lage:
Denn der so hitzig sonst den Meister spielet,
Weicht schülerhaft zurück und abgekühlet.

Ihr scheint ein süßes Wort, ein Kuß zu gnügen,
Als wär es alles, was ihr Herz begehrte.
Wie keusch sie mir, mit liebevollem Fügen,
Des süßen Körpers Fülleform gewährte!
Entzückt und froh in allen ihren Zügen
Und ruhig dann, als wenn sie nichts entbehrte.
So ruht ich auch, gefällig sie beschauend,
Noch auf den Meister hoffend und vertrauend.

this town and district, but I know now how hearts are turned! You have
won me – do not begrudge yourself! I saw you and loved you, and vowed
I would have you.

'You are the first to have me, and if I knew of anything more I could
give you, it should be yours.' So saying, she clasped me to her sweet
breasts, as if she now felt quite at ease in my arms. And yet, as I kissed her
mouth and eyes and forehead, I was in a wondrous situation: for that
which at other times plays the master so hotly, shrank back like a school-
boy, its ardour cooled!

She seems satisfied with sweet words and kisses, as if that were all her
heart desired. How chastely, with loving consent, she made me free of her
sweet body's shapely fullness! She showed rapture and delight in every
feature – and then was still as if she felt no lack. So I too rested, gazing
contentedly at her, still relying hopefully on my master-performer.

Doch als ich länger mein Geschick bedachte,
Von tausend Flüchen mir die Seele kochte,
Mich selbst verwünschend, grinsend mich belachte,
Nichts besser ward, wie ich auch zaudern mochte,
Da lag sie schlafend, schöner als sie wachte;
Die Lichter dämmerten mit langem Dochte.
Der Tages-Arbeit, jugendlicher Mühe
Gesellt sich gern der Schlaf und nie zu frühe.

So lag sie himmlisch an bequemer Stelle,
Als wenn das Lager ihr allein gehörte,
Und an die Wand gedrückt, gequetscht zur Hölle,
Ohnmächtig jener, dem sie nichts verwehrte.
Vom Schlangenbisse fällt zunächst der Quelle
Ein Wandrer so, den schon der Durst verzehrte.
Sie atmet lieblich holdem Traum entgegen;
Er hält den Atem, sie nicht aufzuregen.

Gefaßt bei dem, was ihm noch nie begegnet,
Spricht er zu sich: So mußt du doch erfahren,
Warum der Bräutigam sich kreuzt und segnet,
Vor Nestelknüpfen scheu sich zu bewahren.

But the longer I thought of what had befallen me, and though my soul
seethed with a thousand maledictions, and though I cursed and sardonic-
ally mocked myself, things got no better, wait as I might; and there she
lay, asleep, more beautiful than when she was awake; and the candles with
their long wicks burned low. To the young who toil after a day's labour,
sleep comes quickly and never too soon.

So thus the heavenly creature lay, making herself comfortable as if the
bed were all hers; and pushed against the wall, squashed like the very
devil, he to whom she permitted everything lay and could do nothing.
Thus a wayfarer, already parched with thirst, falls dead of snakebite at the
very edge of the spring. She breathed sweetly, dreaming a fair dream; and
he held his breath lest he should disturb her.

Putting a good face on what had never happened to him before, he said
to himself: 'Well! Now you have discovered after all why bridegrooms
cross and bless themselves in dread, to guard against magic knots! Far

Weit lieber da, wos Hellebarden regnet,
Als hier im Schimpf! So war es nicht vor Jahren,
Als deine Herrin dir zum ersten Male
Vors Auge trat im prachterhellten Saale.

Da quoll dein Herz, da quollen deine Sinnen,
So daß der ganze Mensch entzückt sich regte,
Zum raschen Tanze trugst du sie von hinnen,
Die kaum der Arm und schon der Busen hegte,
Als wolltest du dir selbst sie abgewinnen;
Vervielfacht war, was sich für sie bewegte:
Verstand und Witz und alle Lebensgeister
Und rascher als die andern jener Meister.

So immerfort wuchs Neigung und Begierde,
Brautleute wurden wir im frühen Jahre,
Sie selbst des Maien schönste Blum und Zierde;
Wie wuchs die Kraft zur Lust im jungen Paare!
Und als ich endlich sie zur Kirche führte,
Gesteh ichs nur, vor Priester und Altare,
Vor deinem Jammerkreuz, blutrünstiger Christe,
Verzeih mirs Gott, es regte sich der Iste.

better to be standing in the thick of battle, than lying here in such disgrace!
Things were very different years ago, when first you caught sight of your
true love, in that bright splendid room.

'At that moment your heart and all your senses leapt up, the whole man
was moved to ecstasy: you swept her off into a quick dance, and although
only half in your arms, she was already wholly in your heart; it was as
though you were rivalling yourself to win her; everything in you was
quickened and multiplied for her sake – intelligence and wit and all your
faculties, and that same master-performer was quicker than them all.

'Thus affection and desire continued to grow; we were betrothed in
spring time, and she herself was May's fairest flower and ornament; how
swiftly the young pair grew in strength of appetite! And when at last I
took her to church – let me confess it – in front of the priest and the altar,
in front of your cross of sorrow, poor bleeding Christ! may God forgive
me, but John Thomas was stirring.

Und ihr, der Brautnacht reiche Bettgehänge,
Ihr Pfühle, die ihr euch so breit erstrecktet,
Ihr Teppiche, die Lieb und Lustgedränge
Mit euren seidnen Fittichen bedecktet!
Ihr Käfigvögel, deren Zwitscher-Sänge
Zu neuer Lust und nie zu früh uns wecktet!
Ihr kanntet uns, von euerm Schutz umfriedet,
Teilnehmend sie, mich immer unermüdet.

Und wie wir oft sodann im Raub genossen
Nach Buhlenart des Ehstands heilge Rechte,
Von reifer Saat umwogt, vom Rohr umschlossen,
An manchem Unort, wo ichs mich erfrechte,
Wir waren augenblicklich, unverdrossen
Und wiederholt bedient vom braven Knechte!
Verfluchter Knecht, wie unerwecklich liegst du!
Und deinen Herrn ums schönste Glück betriegst du.

Doch Meister Iste hat nun seine Grillen
Und läßt sich nicht befehlen, noch verachten,
Auf einmal ist er da, und ganz im stillen
Erhebt er sich zu allen seinen Prachten;

'And you, oh rich bed-hangings of the bridal night, you pillows spread so broad, you tapestries that hid beneath your silken wings the urgency of love and desire! You cage-birds, whose twittering song woke us, never too early, to new delights! You all, who so peacefully protected us, knew us well! You knew how lovingly she took my part, and how untiring was my affection.

'And then, many a time, when like secret lovers, on the sly, we enjoyed the sacred rights of matrimony, with ripe corn waving round us, or reeds enclosing us, and at many an unsuitable place where I thought I dared try it – we were instantly, indefatigably, and repeatedly obliged by that excellent servant. Oh, cursed slave, how fast asleep you lie now, cheating your lord of his sweetest happiness!'

But there it is: Master John Thomas has his moods, and may neither be commanded nor ignored; all at once he presents himself and quietly he rises to his full magnificence; and thus the wayfarer is no longer under the

So steht es nun dem Wandrer ganz zu Willen,
Nicht lechzend mehr am Quell zu übernachten.
Er neigt sich hin, er will die Schläferin küssen,
Allein er stockt, er fühlt sich weggerissen.

Wer hat zur Kraft ihn wieder aufgestählet,
Als jenes Bild, das ihm auf ewig teuer,
Mit dem er sich in Jugendlust vermählet?
Dort leuchtet her ein frisch erquicklich Feuer,
Und wie er erst in Ohnmacht sich gequälet,
So wird nun hier dem Starken nicht geheuer;
Er schaudert weg, vorsichtig, leise, leise
Entzieht er sich dem holden Zauberkreise,

Sitzt, schreibt: «Ich nahte mich der heimischen Pforte,
Entfernen wollten mich die letzten Stunden,
Da hab ich nun, am sonderbarsten Orte,
Mein treues Herz aufs neue dir verbunden.
Zum Schlusse findest du geheime Worte:
Die Krankheit erst bewähret den Gesunden.
Dies Büchlein soll dir manches Gute zeigen,
Das Beste nur muß ich zuletzt verschweigen.»

necessity of spending a thirsty night at the water's edge. He leans towards
the sleeping beauty and is about to kiss her – but stops and feels something
drawing him back.

Who has steeled him again to renewed vigour? What else but that image
ever dear to him, to which in youthful delight he wedded himself? It is
from thence it glows, this fresh life-giving fire! And even as in his in-
capacity he fretted, so now in his strength he feels strangely ill at ease: he
moves fearfully away, carefully, gently, gently he withdraws himself from
the sweet place of enchantment,

seats himself and writes: 'I was nearing the gates of home, and the last
few hours seemed about to take me far away again: but now, in the strangest
of situations, I have plighted my faithful heart to you once more. I will end
with some secret words: *Illness is the truest test of health.* This little book
has tried to tell you many good things, but at the last I must pass over the
best of them all in silence.'

Da kräht der Hahn. Das Mädchen schnell entwindet
Der Decke sich und wirft sich rasch ins Mieder.
Und da sie sich so seltsam wiederfindet,
So stutzt sie, blickt und schlägt die Augen nieder;
Und da sie ihm zum letztenmal verschwindet,
Im Auge bleiben ihm die schönen Glieder.
Das Posthorn tönt, er wirft sich in den Wagen
Und läßt getrost sich zu der Liebsten tragen.

Und weil zuletzt bei jeder Dichtungsweise
Moralien uns ernstlich fördern sollen,
So will auch ich in so beliebtem Gleise
Euch gern bekennen, was die Verse wollen:
Wir stolpern wohl auf unsrer Lebensreise,
Und doch vermögen in der Welt, der tollen,
Zwei Hebel viel aufs irdische Getriebe:
Sehr viel die Pflicht, unendlich mehr die Liebe!

At that the cock crew. In a trice the girl had thrown off the bedclothes and thrown on her bodice, and finding herself so strangely situated, she faltered, looked and cast down her eyes: and as she slipped out of his sight for the last time, her lovely limbs remain impressed on his mind's eye. The post-horn sounds, he leaps into the carriage full of good cheer, and lets himself be carried home to his dear one.

And since, in every style of poetry, the end demands a moral to improve our minds, I too will tread so popular a path and willingly confess to you the meaning of these verses: On our journey through life we may stumble, yet in this mad world there are two forces mightily active in human affairs: the compelling power of Duty, and the infinitely greater power of Love!

FRÜHZEITIGER FRÜHLING

TAGE der Wonne,
Kommt ihr so bald?
Schenkt mir die Sonne,
Hügel und Wald?

Reichlicher fließen
Bächlein zumal.
Sind es die Wiesen?
Ist es das Tal?

Blauliche Frische!
Himmel und Höh!
Goldene Fische
Wimmeln im See.

Buntes Gefieder
Rauschet im Hain;
Himmlische Lieder
Schallen darein.

THE SPRING BEFORE SPRINGTIME

ARE you coming so soon, oh days of enchantment? Are you giving me the sun, the hills and the woods?

And the brooks, too, are flowing fuller! Are these the meadows? Is this the valley?

How blue and fresh! Oh, the sky and the heights! Golden fishes are swarming in the lake.

There is a murmur of many-coloured plumage in the grove, and heavenly songs fall upon my ear.

Unter des Grünen
Blühender Kraft
Naschen die Bienen
Summend am Saft.

Leise Bewegung
Bebt in der Luft,
Reizende Regung,
Schläfernder Duft.

Mächtiger rühret
Bald sich ein Hauch,
Doch er verlieret
Gleich sich im Strauch.

Aber zum Busen
Kehrt er zurück.
Helfet, ihr Musen,
Tragen das Glück!

Saget, seit gestern
Wie mir geschah?
Liebliche Schwestern,
Liebchen ist da!

Amid the blossoming strength of the greenery, the bees hum and suck the sweet relish.

There is a soft tremulous motion in the air, a stirring that charms, a fragrance that lulls.

From time to time there is a breath of stronger wind, lost at once in the undergrowth.

But to the heart it returns. Oh Muses, help me to endure this happiness!

Tell me, since yesterday, how is it with me? Oh sweet sisters, my sweetheart is here!

NACHTGESANG

O GIB, vom weichen Pfühle,
Träumend, ein halb Gehör!
Bei meinem Saitenspiele
Schlafe! was willst du mehr?

Bei meinem Saitenspiele
Segnet der Sterne Heer
Die ewigen Gefühle;
Schlafe! was willst du mehr?

Die ewigen Gefühle
Heben mich, hoch und hehr,
Aus irdischem Gewühle;
Schlafe! was willst du mehr?

Vom irdischen Gewühle
Trennst du mich nur zu sehr,
Bannst mich in diese Kühle;
Schlafe! was willst du mehr?

Bannst mich in diese Kühle,
Gibst nur im Traum Gehör.
Ach, auf dem weichen Pfühle
Schlafe! was willst du mehr?

NIGHT SONG

As you lie on your soft pillow, oh, listen, half-listen in dreams! As I play on these strings, sleep, what more do you desire?

As I play on these strings, the starry host blesses the eternal affections; sleep, what more do you desire?

The eternal affections lift me sublimely aloft, out of earthly turmoil. Sleep, what more do you desire?

Out of earthly turmoil you take me, ah, too far, and hold me ravished in this cool place. Sleep, what more do you desire?

In this cool place holding me ravished, you listen only in dreams. Ah, on your soft pillow, sleep, what more do you desire?

[FLIEGENTOD]

SIE saugt mit Gier verrätrisches Getränke
Unabgesetzt, vom ersten Zug verführt;
Sie fühlt sich wohl, und längst sind die Gelenke
Der zarten Beinchen schon paralysiert,
Nicht mehr gewandt, die Flügelchen zu putzen,
Nicht mehr geschickt, das Köpfchen aufzustutzen –
Das Leben so sich im Genuß verliert.
Zum Stehen kaum wird noch das Füßchen taugen;
So schlürft sie fort, und mitten unterm Saugen
Umnebelt ihr der Tod die tausend Augen.

[THE DEATH OF A FLY]

GREEDILY, without stopping, he sucks the treacherous brew, seduced by the first draught; he feels full of well-being, though already the joints of his delicate legs are quite paralysed and no longer skilled to polish his little wings or deftly preen his head – thus, in pleasure, his life ebbs away. His tiny feet will scarcely support him now; and so he drinks on, and even as he sucks, death darkens his thousand eyes.

MAILIED

ZWISCHEN Weizen und Korn,
Zwischen Hecken und Dorn,
Zwischen Bäumen und Gras,
Wo gehts Liebchen?
Sag mir das!

Fand mein Holdchen
Nicht daheim;
Muß das Goldchen
Draußen sein.

Grünt und blühet
Schön der Mai,
Liebchen ziehet
Froh und frei.

An dem Felsen beim Fluß,
Wo sie reichte den Kuß,
Jenen ersten im Gras,
Seh ich etwas!
Ist sie das?

MAY SONG

AMID the corn and the rye, amid the hedgerows and thorn blossoms, amid the trees and the grass, where is my darling walking? Oh tell me!

I did not find the sweet creature at home; she must be out here, the precious treasure.

May is green and blossoming fair, and my darling wanders free and happy.

There under the rock by the river, where she kissed me that first time, in the grass, I see something! Is it she?

GEGENWART

ALLES kündet dich an!
Erscheinet die herrliche Sonne,
Folgst du, so hoff ich es, bald.

Trittst du im Garten hervor,
So bist du die Rose der Rosen,
Lilie der Lilien zugleich.

Wenn du im Tanze dich regst,
So regen sich alle Gestirne
Mit dir und um dich umher.

Nacht! und so wär es denn Nacht!
Nun überscheinst du des Mondes
Lieblichen, ladenden Glanz.

Ladend und lieblich bist du,
Und Blumen, Mond und Gestirne
Huldigen, Sonne, nur dir.

Sonne! so sei du auch mir
Die Schöpferin herrlicher Tage;
Leben und Ewigkeit ists.

PRESENCE

EVERYTHING heralds you! When the splendid sun appears, I am filled
with hope that you soon will follow it.

When you walk in the garden, you are both the rose of roses and the lily
of lilies.

When you move in a dance, all the stars move with you and round you.

Night! And so it is night! And now you outshine the moon's lovely, in-
viting radiance.

You are inviting and lovely, and the flowers, the moon and the stars pay
homage, oh sun, only to you.

Oh sun, be to me also the creator of splendid days! This is life ever-
lasting.

GEFUNDEN

Ich ging im Walde
So für mich hin,
Und nichts zu suchen,
Das war mein Sinn.

Im Schatten sah ich
Ein Blümchen stehn,
Wie Sterne leuchtend,
Wie Äuglein schön.

Ich wollt es brechen,
Da sagt' es fein:
Soll ich zum Welken
Gebrochen sein?

Ich grubs mit allen
Den Würzlein aus,
Zum Garten trug ichs
Am hübschen Haus.

Und pflanzt es wieder
Am stillen Ort;
Nun zweigt es immer
Und blüht so fort.

A FIND

I was just walking along in the wood by myself, without any idea of looking for anything.

I saw a little flower, growing in the shade, bright as the stars, lovely as a sweet pair of eyes.

I was just going to pick it, when it said, in a tiny voice: 'Am I to be picked, and wither?'

I dug it out with all its little roots, I carried it to the garden of my lovely house,

and planted it again in this quiet corner; and now it continues to branch out and blossom.

DIE WANDELNDE GLOCKE

Es war ein Kind, das wollte nie
Zur Kirche sich bequemen,
Und Sonntags fand es stets ein Wie,
Den Weg ins Feld zu nehmen.

Die Mutter sprach: Die Glocke tönt,
Und so ist dirs befohlen,
Und hast du dich nicht hingewöhnt,
Sie kommt und wird dich holen.

Das Kind, es denkt: Die Glocke hängt
Da droben auf dem Stuhle.
Schon hats den Weg ins Feld gelenkt,
Als lief' es aus der Schule.

Die Glocke Glocke tönt nicht mehr,
Die Mutter hat gefackelt.
Doch welch ein Schrecken! hinterher
Die Glocke kommt gewackelt.

Sie wackelt schnell, man glaubt es kaum;
Das arme Kind im Schrecken,
Es lauft, es kommt als wie im Traum;
Die Glocke wird es decken.

THE WALKING BELL

ONCE upon a time there was a child who would never consent to go to church, and on Sundays he always found an excuse to run out into the fields.

His mother said: 'The bell rings, and that means you are to go, and if you don't make a habit of going, it will come and fetch you.'

The child thinks: the bell is hanging up there in the belfry. And already he is away off towards the fields, as if he were running out of school.

The bell, the bell, it has stopped ringing. Mother was talking nonsense. But, oh, my goodness! The bell is coming waddling along behind him!

How quickly it waddles, the thing is unbelievable! The poor child runs and runs in terror, as if in a dream – the bell will smother him.

Doch nimmt es richtig seinen Husch,
Und mit gewandter Schnelle
Eilt es durch Anger, Feld und Busch
Zur Kirche, zur Kapelle.

Und jeden Sonn- und Feiertag
Gedenkt es an den Schaden,
Läßt durch den ersten Glockenschlag,
Nicht in Person sich laden.

DER TOTENTANZ

DER Türmer, der schaut zumitten der Nacht
Hinab auf die Gräber in Lage;
Der Mond, der hat alles ins Helle gebracht,
Der Kirchhof, er liegt wie am Tage.
Da regt sich ein Grab und ein anderes dann:
Sie kommen hervor, ein Weib da, ein Mann,
In weißen und schleppenden Hemden.

But he heads in the right direction, and as fast as his clever legs will carry him he rushes across the common and over the fields and through the bushes towards the church, towards the chapel.

And every Sunday and feast day he remembers this misadventure, and, at the very first stroke of the bell, he does not wait to be invited in person.

THE DANCE OF THE DEAD

THE watchman in the clock tower, at the dead of night, looks down at the level grave-stones; everything is bright in the moonlight, the churchyard is as clear as day. And now one grave stirs and then another: out they come, here a woman, there a man, in trailing white shrouds.

Das reckt nun, es will sich ergetzen sogleich,
Die Knöchel zur Runde, zum Kranze,
So arm und so jung, und so alt und so reich;
Doch hindern die Schleppen am Tanze.
Und weil hier die Scham nun nicht weiter gebeut,
Sie schütteln sich alle, da liegen zerstreut
Die Hemdelein über den Hügeln.

Nun hebt sich der Schenkel, nun wackelt das Bein,
Gebärden da gibt es vertrackte;
Dann klipperts und klapperts mitunter hinein,
Als schlüg man die Hölzlein zum Takte.
Das kommt nun dem Türmer so lächerlich vor;
Da raunt ihm der Schalk, der Versucher, ins Ohr:
Geh! hole dir einen der Laken.

Getan wie gedacht! und er flüchtet sich schnell
Nun hinter geheiligte Türen.
Der Mond, und noch immer er scheinet so hell
Zum Tanz, den sie schauderlich führen.
Doch endlich verlieret sich dieser und der,
Schleicht eins nach dem andern gekleidet einher,
Und husch! ist es unter dem Rasen.

Eager for immediate pleasure, they stretch their bones and begin a round
dance, both poor and young and old and rich. But their trains are a hind-
rance to dancing, and since the laws of decency no longer apply here, they
all shake themselves and their shrouds lie scattered over the grave-mounds.
And now they caper with their thighs and wag their legs in mad antics,
and from time to time there is a clicking and clacking as if someone were
keeping time with castanets. To the watchman it all looks so ridiculous;
and the tempter, that rogue, murmurs in his ear: Go and take away one of
the sheets!
No sooner thought than done! and then quickly he retreats behind hal-
lowed doors. And still the moon glitters so brightly on the horrible dance
they are dancing. But at length this one and that one disappears and one
after another they creep back with their shrouds on and are underground
again in a trice.

Nur einer, der trippelt und stolpert zuletzt
Und tappet und grapst an den Grüften;
Doch hat kein Geselle so schwer ihn verletzt,
Er wittert das Tuch in den Lüften.
Er rüttelt die Turmtür, sie schlägt ihn zurück,
Geziert und gesegnet, dem Türmer zum Glück,
Sie blinkt von metallenen Kreuzen.

Das Hemd muß er haben, da rastet er nicht,
Da gilt auch kein langes Besinnen;
Den gotischen Zierat ergreift nun der Wicht
Und klettert von Zinne zu Zinnen.
Nun ists um den armen, den Türmer getan!
Es ruckt sich von Schnörkel zu Schnörkel hinan,
Langbeinigen Spinnen vergleichbar.

Der Türmer erbleichet, der Türmer erbebt,
Gern gäb er ihn wieder, den Laken.
Da häkelt – jetzt hat er am längsten gelebt –
Den Zipfel ein eiserner Zacken.
Schon trübet der Mond sich verschwindenden Scheins,
Die Glocke, sie donnert ein mächtiges Eins,
Und unten zerschellt das Gerippe.

Only one of them is left, tripping and stumbling along, and groping and snatching at the graves; but none of his comrades has done him this grave injury; he sniffs the smell of the sheet in the air. He rattles the gate of the tower; it repels him; fortunately for the keeper, it has been decorated and blessed and is covered with shining metal crosses.

But he must get the shroud back, and he loses no time, he does not stop to think twice: seizing the Gothic ornamentations, the creature begins to climb from coping to coping. Poor watchman, he is done for now! Up it comes, from pinnacle to pinnacle, for all the world like a long-legged spider.

The watchman turns pale, the watchman trembles. He tries to give the sheet back, but a corner of it – now his minutes are numbered – catches on an iron spike! Already the moon is clouding over, its light is fading: then, like a mighty thunderclap, the clock strikes one – and the skeleton is dashed to pieces below.

DER NEUE KOPERNIKUS

ARTGES Häuschen hab ich klein,
Und, darin verstecket,
Bin ich vor der Sonne Schein
Gar bequem bedecket.

Denn da gibt es Schalterlein,
Federchen und Lädchen,
Finde mich so wohl allein
Als mit hübschen Mädchen.

Denn, o Wunder! mir zur Lust
Regen sich die Wälder,
Näher kommen meiner Brust
Die entfernten Felder.

Und so tanzen auch vorbei
Die bewachsnen Berge;
Fehlet nur das Lustgeschrei
Aufgeregter Zwerge.

Doch so gänzlich still und stumm
Rennt es mir vorüber,
Meistens grad und oft auch krumm,
Und so ists mir lieber.

THE MODERN COPERNICUS

I HAVE a dainty small house, and hidden inside it I am very comfortably screened from the sun's rays,
 for in it there are little windows, springs and shutters, and in there I enjoy myself as much alone as with pretty girls.
 For, strange to relate, the forests move for my pleasure, and the distant fields come nearer to my breast;
 likewise the wooded hills dance past; only the merry shouting of excited dwarfs is missing.
 But it rushes past me in complete silence, sometimes straight and often round bends as well, and this is what I prefer.

Wenn ichs recht betrachten will
Und es ernst gewahre,
Steht vielleicht das alles still –
Und ich selber fahre.

GLEICH UND GLEICH

Eɪɴ Blumenglöckchen
Vom Boden hervor
War früh gesprosset
In lieblichem Flor;
Da kam ein Bienchen
Und naschte fein: –
Die müssen wohl beide
Für einander sein.

FRÜHLING ÜBERS JAHR

Dᴀs Beet, schon lockert
Sichs in die Höh,
Da wanken Glöckchen
So weiß wie Schnee;
Safran entfaltet
Gewaltge Glut,

If I choose to look closely and consider the thing seriously, I daresay all these things are standing still – and it is I myself who am travelling.

LIKE TO LIKE

Aʟɪᴛᴛʟᴇ early flower, with a lovely bloom like a bell, had sprung up from the ground; along came a little bee and sipped delicately: I suppose the two must have been made for one another.

PERENNIAL SPRING

Aʟʀᴇᴀᴅʏ the flowers' upward thrust is breaking the soil of their bed: here are trembling snowdrops white as snow, crocuses blaze with intense

Smaragden keimt es
Und keimt wie Blut.
Primeln stolzieren
So naseweis,
Schalkhafte Veilchen,
Versteckt mit Fleiß;
Was auch noch alles
Da regt und webt,
Genug, der Frühling,
Er wirkt und lebt.

Doch was im Garten
Am reichsten blüht,
Das ist des Liebchens
Lieblich Gemüt.
Da glühen Blicke
Mir immerfort,
Erregend Liedchen,
Erheiternd Wort;
Ein immer offen,
Ein Blütenherz,
Im Ernste freundlich
Und rein im Scherz.
Wenn Ros und Lilie
Der Sommer bringt,
Er doch vergebens
Mit Liebchen ringt.

colour, there are buds green as emerald or red as blood. Primroses proudly and so knowingly disport themselves, and there are mischievous violets cunningly hidden; and a great deal else, too, stirring and moving: in a word, the spring is here, active and alive!

But a richer blossom than anything else in the garden is my darling's sweet soul. She gives me looks for ever radiant, moving me to song, gladdening me to speech. Her heart is for ever open like a flower, kind in its emotion and clear in its laughter. Summer may bring the rose and the lily, but vies in vain with my darling.

IMMER UND ÜBERALL

DRINGE tief zu Berges Grüften,
Wolken folge hoch zu Lüften;
Muse ruft zu Bach und Tale
Tausend, aber tausendmale.

Sobald ein frisches Kelchlein blüht,
Es fordert neue Lieder;
Und wenn die Zeit verrauschend flieht,
Jahrszeiten kommen wieder.

MÄRZ

Es ist ein Schnee gefallen,
Denn es ist noch nicht Zeit,
Daß von den Blümlein allen,
Daß von den Blümlein allen,
Wir werden hoch erfreut.

Der Sonnenblick betrüget
Mit mildem, falschem Schein,
Die Schwalbe selber lüget,
Die Schwalbe selber lüget,
Warum? Sie kommt allein!

FOR EVER AND EVERYWHERE

EXPLORE deep mountain chasms, soar high in the air in the wake of clouds; to brook and valley the Muse calls – a thousand and a thousand times.

When a fresh calyx newly blooms, it calls for new songs; and though streaming Time flees from us, the seasons come again.

MARCH

THERE has been a fall of snow, for it is still too soon for all the flowers, for all the flowers to gladden our hearts.

The sunlight cheats us with its mild, false lustre: even the swallow lies, even the swallow lies: why? – he comes alone!

Sollt ich mich einzeln freuen,
Wenn auch der Frühling nah?
Doch kommen wir zu zweien,
Doch kommen wir zu zweien,
Gleich ist der Sommer da.

APRIL

AUGEN, sagt mir, sagt, was sagt ihr?
Denn ihr sagt was gar zu Schönes,
Gar des lieblichsten Getönes;
Und in gleichem Sinne fragt ihr.

Doch ich glaub euch zu erfassen:
Hinter dieser Augen Klarheit
Ruht ein Herz in Lieb und Wahrheit
Jetzt sich selber überlassen,

Dem es wohl behagen müßte,
Unter so viel stumpfen, blinden
Endlich einen Blick zu finden,
Der es auch zu schätzen wüßte.

Could I take pleasure by myself, even on the verge of spring? But if there are two of us, if there are two of us, all at once it is summer!

APRIL

TELL me, eyes, tell me, what do you tell me? For you are telling something all too lovely, making a music all too sweet; and asking a question of the same kind.

Yet I think I read your message: behind the brightness of these eyes dwells a heart full of love and truth which now, thrown back upon itself,

would surely be happy to encounter – among so many dull, blind, looks – one look that could see its true value.

Und indem ich diese Chiffern
Mich versenke zu studieren,
Laßt euch ebenfalls verführen,
Meine Blicke zu entziffern!

MAI

LEICHTE Silberwolken schweben
Durch die erst erwärmten Lüfte,
Mild, von Schimmer sanft umgeben,
Blickt die Sonne durch die Düfte.
Leise wallt und drängt die Welle
Sich am reichen Ufer hin;
Und wie reingewaschen helle,
Schwankend hin und her und hin,
Spiegelt sich das junge Grün.

Still ist Luft und Lüftchen stille;
Was bewegt mir das Gezweige?
Schwüle Liebe dieser Fülle,
Von den Bäumen durchs Gesträuche.

And as I am absorbed in the study of this secret writing, may you too,
oh eyes, be enticed to decipher my looks!

MAY

LIGHT silvery clouds are drifting through the air, which now is warmer;
the sun gleams softly through the haze, surrounded by a gentle radiance.
The quietly moving water surges past the richly covered bank, and sway-
ing, swaying to and fro, bright as if it had been washed clean, the young
greenery is mirrored on the surface.

The air is motionless, the little breezes still; what is stirring those
branches? It is this fullness, heavy with warm love, that breathes through
the undergrowth from the trees. And now a sudden bright gleam; see a

Nun der Blick auf einmal helle,
Sieh! der Bübchen Flatterschar,
Das bewegt und regt so schnelle,
Wie der Morgen sie gebar,
Flügelhaft sich Paar und Paar.

Fangen an, das Dach zu flechten –
Wer bedürfte dieser Hütte? –
Und wie Zimmrer, die gerechten,
Bank und Tischchen in der Mitte!
Und so bin ich noch verwundert,
Sonne sinkt, ich fühl es kaum;
Und nun führen aberhundert
Mir das Liebchen in den Raum,
Tag und Abend, welch ein Traum!

ST NEPOMUKS VORABEND

Lichtlein schwimmen auf dem Strome,
Kinder singen auf der Brücken,
Glocke, Glöckchen fügt vom Dome
Sich der Andacht, dem Entzücken.

host of little fluttering boys! In wingèd pairs they move and stir as swiftly as the morning gave them birth.

They begin to thatch the roof (who can need this hut?) and to make, like real carpenters, a bench and table in the middle of it. And thus I still marvel, and scarcely notice the sun going down; and now a hundred or more of them bring my darling into the room. Oh day, oh evening, how sweet a dream!

ST NEPOMUK'S EVE

Little lights are floating on the river, children singing on the bridges; bells great and small from the cathedral chime fittingly for these devotions, for this rapture.

229

Lichtlein schwinden, Sterne schwinden;
Also löste sich die Seele
Unsres Heilgen, nicht verkünden
Durft er anvertraute Fehle.

Lichtlein, schwimmet! Spielt, ihr Kinder!
Kinder-Chor, o! singe, singe!
Und verkündiget nicht minder,
Was den Stern zu Sternen bringe.

aus dem WEST-ÖSTLICHEN DIVAN

HEGIRE

Nord und West und Süd zersplittern,
Throne bersten, Reiche zittern,
Flüchte du, im reinen Osten
Patriarchenluft zu kosten!
Unter Lieben, Trinken, Singen
Soll dich Chisers Quell verjüngen.

The lights disappear, the stars disappear; thus our saint's soul melted away; he could not divulge the transgression that had been entrusted to his ears.

Float, little lights! children, play on! Sing, choir of children, oh sing! no less proclaiming what brings a star among the stars.

from the WEST-EASTERN DIVAN

HEJIRA

The North, the West and the South are disintegrating, thrones are bursting, empires are trembling: make your escape, and in the pure Orient taste the air of the Patriarchs! Amid loving and drinking and singing, let Khiser's fountain renew your youth.

Dort, im Reinen und im Rechten
Will ich menschlichen Geschlechten
In des Ursprungs Tiefe dringen,
Wo sie noch von Gott empfingen
Himmelslehr in Erdesprachen
Und sich nicht den Kopf zerbrachen;

Wo sie Väter hoch verehrten,
Jeden fremden Dienst verwehrten.
Will mich freun der Jugendschranke:
Glaube weit, eng der Gedanke,
Wie das Wort so wichtig dort war,
Weil es ein gesprochen Wort war.

Will mich unter Hirten mischen,
An Oasen mich erfrischen,
Wenn mit Karawanen wandle,
Shawl, Kaffee und Moschus handle;
Jeden Pfad will ich betreten
Von der Wüste zu den Städten.

There, where life is pure and good, I will go back to the deep origins of the races of men, to the time when God still taught them heavenly wisdom in earthly tongues and they did not have to rack their brains;

when they paid high honour to their fathers and resisted all foreign bondage. I will enjoy the limitations of that youthful age, when belief was wide and thought was narrow – those lands where the word carried such weight, because it was a spoken word.

I will mingle with herdsmen and refresh myself at oases, as I travel with caravans and trade in shawls and coffee and musk; I will tread all the paths between the wilderness and the cities.

Bösen Felsweg auf und nieder
Trösten, Hafis, deine Lieder,
Wenn der Führer mit Entzücken
Von des Maultiers hohem Rücken
Singt, die Sterne zu erwecken
Und die Räuber zu erschrecken.

Will in Bädern und in Schenken,
Heilger Hafis, dein gedenken,
Wenn den Schleier Liebchen lüftet,
Schüttelnd Ambralocken düftet.
Ja, des Dichters Liebeflüstern
Mache selbst die Huris lüstern.

Wolltet ihr ihm dies beneiden
Oder etwa gar verleiden,
Wisset nur, daß Dichterworte
Um des Paradieses Pforte
Immer leise klopfend schweben,
Sich erbittend ewges Leben.

Up and down rough mountain tracks your songs, Háfiz, give consolation, when the train leader, high on his mule, rapturously sings to wake
the stars and scare the robbers.

I will remember you, holy Háfiz, in bath-houses and taverns, when
my sweetheart lifts her veil and shakes the sandalwood-scent from her hair.
Yes, the poet's whisperings of love shall fill the very Houris with desire.

And if you should envy him this, or even try to spoil his pleasure, let
me tell you that the words of poets are for ever hovering round the gate
of paradise, softly knocking on it, begging and winning everlasting life.

TALISMANE

G OTTES ist der Orient!
Gottes ist der Okzident!
Nord- und südliches Gelände
Ruht im Frieden seiner Hände.

*

Er, der einzige Gerechte,
Will für jedermann das Rechte.
Sei von seinen hundert Namen
Dieser hochgelobet! Amen.

*

Mich verwirren will das Irren;
Doch du weißt mich zu entwirren.
Wenn ich handle, wenn ich dichte,
Gib du meinem Weg die Richte.

*

Ob ich Irdsches denk und sinne,
Das gereicht zu höherem Gewinne.
Mit dem Staube nicht der Geist zerstoben,
Dringet, in sich selbst gedrängt, nach oben.

*

TALISMANS

THE East is God's, the West is God's! Northern and southern lands rest in
the peace of His hands.

*

He, who alone is just, wills what is right for every man. Of his hundred
names let this one be high-extolled. Amen.

*

My wandering leads me into confusion; but you can straighten me out.
When I act and when I write, may you be the guide of my ways.

*

Though my thoughts and meditations are of earthly matters, yet this stands
me in higher stead. The spirit is not scattered with the dust, but is forced
back into itself and rises aloft.

*

Im Atemholen sind zweierlei Gnaden:
Die Luft einziehn, sich ihrer entladen;
Jenes bedrängt, dieses erfrischt;
So wunderbar ist das Leben gemischt.
Du danke Gott, wenn er dich preßt,
Und dank ihm, wenn er dich wieder entläßt.

PHÄNOMEN

WENN zu der Regenwand
Phöbus sich gattet,
Gleich steht ein Bogenrand
Farbig beschattet.

Im Nebel gleichen Kreis
Seh ich gezogen,
Zwar ist der Bogen weiß,
Doch Himmelsbogen.

So sollst du, muntrer Greis,
Dich nicht betrüben;
Sind gleich die Haare weiß,
Doch wirst du lieben.

There are two graces in breathing: drawing in air and discharging it. The former constrains, the latter refreshes: so marvellously is life mixed. Thank God then when he presses you, and thank him again when he lets you go.

PHENOMENON

WHEN the Sun-god mates with a curtain of rain, an arching rim shaded with colours at once appears.

I see this same circle drawn in the mist: it is a white bow, yet it is a bow of heaven.

So be lively, old man, do not lose heart: your hair may be white, yet you will love.

IM GEGENWÄRTIGEN VERGANGNES

Ros und Lilie morgentaulich
Blüht im Garten meiner Nähe;
Hintenan, bebuscht und traulich,
Steigt der Felsen in die Höhe;
Und mit hohem Wald umzogen
Und mit Ritterschloß gekrönet,
Lenkt sich hin des Gipfels Bogen,
Bis er sich dem Tal versöhnet.

Und da duftets wie vor alters,
Da wir noch von Liebe litten
Und die Saiten meines Psalters
Mit dem Morgenstrahl sich stritten;
Wo das Jagdlied aus den Büschen
Fülle runden Tons enthauchte,
Anzufeuern, zu erfrischen,
Wie's der Busen wollt und brauchte.

Nun die Wälder ewig sprossen,
So ermutigt euch mit diesen;
Was ihr sonst für euch genossen,
Läßt in andern sich genießen.

THE PAST IN THE PRESENT

Roses and lilies full of morning dew blossom in the garden near me; and behind and beyond it the friendly bush-covered rocky slope rises. And girdled with tall forest, crowned by a feudal castle, the mountain curves upward and downward until it is at one again with the valley.

And there the same fragrance lingers as it did long ago, in the days when we still suffered love, and the strings of my psalter vied with the rays of morning; when from the thicket the hunting-song poured forth a rounded fullness of sound to fire us, to refresh us, at the heart's desire and need.

Take courage then from the eternal burgeoning forests: the joy you experienced for yourselves long ago may now be experienced in others. We

Niemand wird uns dann beschreien,
Daß wirs uns alleine gönnen;
Nun in allen Lebensreihen
Müsset ihr genießen können.

Und mit diesem Lied und Wendung
Sind wir wieder bei Hafisen;
Denn es ziemt, des Tags Vollendung
Mit Genießern zu genießen.

LIED UND GEBILDE

MAG der Grieche seinen Ton
Zu Gestalten drücken,
An der eignen Hände Sohn
Steigern sein Entzücken;

Aber uns ist wonnereich,
In den Euphrat greifen
Und im flüßgen Element
Hin und wider schweifen.

Löscht ich so der Seele Brand,
Lied, es wird erschallen;
Schöpft des Dichters reine Hand,
Wasser wird sich ballen.

cannot then be accused of begrudging it to anyone else! You must be capable now of tasting the joy of every stage of life.

And at this point in our song we come back to Háfiz; for it is fitting to share the joy of the day's completeness with masters of experience.

SONG AND FORM

LET the Greek mould his clay into shapes and take ever-increasing delight in the child of his own hands.

But to us it is an exquisite pleasure to plunge our fingers into the Euphrates and to drift to and fro in the liquid element.

When I have thus quenched my burning soul, I shall utter my song; when the poet's pure hand draws water, the water will become a crystal ball.

UNBEGRENZT

Dass du nicht enden kannst, das macht dich groß,
Und daß du nie beginnst, das ist dein Los.
Dein Lied ist drehend wie das Sterngewölbe,
Anfang und Ende immerfort dasselbe,
Und was die Mitte bringt, ist offenbar
Das, was zu Ende bleibt und anfangs war.

Du bist der Freuden echte Dichterquelle,
Und ungezählt entfließt dir Well auf Welle.
Zum Küssen stets bereiter Mund,
Ein Brustgesang, der lieblich fließet,
Zum Trinken stets gereizter Schlund,
Ein gutes Herz, das sich ergießet.

Und mag die ganze Welt versinken,
Hafis, mit dir, mit dir allein
Will ich wetteifern! Lust und Pein
Sei uns, den Zwillingen, gemein!
Wie du zu lieben und zu trinken,
Das soll mein Stolz, mein Leben sein.

Nun töne, Lied, mit eignem Feuer!
Denn du bist älter, du bist neuer.

UNCIRCUMSCRIBED

That you cannot end is what makes you great, and it is your destiny never to begin. Your song moves round like the vault of the stars, its beginning and ending for ever the same, and what is in the middle but what remains at the end and was there at the beginning?

You are the true poetic fountainhead of delights; and waters unnumbered flow from you. A mouth for ever shaped to kiss, a deep-voiced sweetly-flowing song, a gullet ever-thirsty, a heart of self-outpouring kindness.

And though the whole world sink to ruin, I will emulate you, Háfiz, you alone! Let us, who are twin spirits, share pleasure and sorrow! To love like you, and drink like you, shall be my pride and my life-long occupation.

Now, oh my song, speak forth with fire of your own! For you are both older and younger than his.

VERSUNKEN

VOLL Locken kraus ein Haupt so rund! –
Und darf ich dann in solchen reichen Haaren
Mit vollen Händen hin und wider fahren,
Da fühl ich mich von Herzensgrund gesund.
Und küss ich Stirne, Bogen, Auge, Mund,
Dann bin ich frisch und immer wieder wund.
Der fünfgezackte Kamm, wo sollt er stocken?
Er kehrt schon wieder zu den Locken.
Das Ohr versagt sich nicht dem Spiel,
Hier ist nicht Fleisch, hier ist nicht Haut,
So zart zum Scherz, so liebeviel!
Doch wie man auf dem Köpfchen kraut,
Man wird in solchen reichen Haaren
Für ewig auf und nieder fahren.
So hast du, Hafis, auch getan,
Wir fangen es von vornen an.

IMMERSED

A HEAD so round and full of curly locks! – And when she lets me fill my hands with this abundance of hair and run them to and fro in it, I am filled with well-being, from the bottom of my heart. And when I kiss her forehead, her eyebrows, her eyes, and her mouth, I am stricken afresh and ever again. The five-pronged comb, where should it come to rest? Back it goes to her hair already, her ear joins in the game too; this is no flesh, this is no skin, so delicate to the playful touch, so rich with love! He who strokes this little head will be moving up and down in its abundance of hair for ever. All this, Háfiz, you also did, and here we are, doing it all over again.

GEHEIMES

Uber meines Liebchens Äugeln
Stehn verwundert alle Leute;
Ich, der Wissende, dagegen
Weiß recht gut, was das bedeute.

Denn es heißt: ich liebe diesen,
Und nicht etwa den und jenen.
Lasset nur, ihr guten Leute,
Euer Wundern, euer Sehnen!

Ja, mit ungeheuren Mächten
Blicket sie wohl in die Runde;
Doch sie sucht nur zu verkünden
Ihm die nächste süße Stunde.

SULEIKA SPRICHT

Der Spiegel sagt mir: ich bin schön!
Ihr sagt: zu altern sei auch mein Geschick.
Vor Gott muß alles ewig stehn,
In mir liebt ihn, für diesen Augenblick.

A SECRET

Everyone wonders at the way my darling makes eyes; but I, the initiate, know very well what it means.

For she is saying: 'It is this man I love, and not that one or the other one, as you might suppose.' So stop your wondering, good people, and your longing!

She does indeed, I dare say, cast a most mighty eye about her; but she is only trying to give him a forecast of our next sweet hour.

SULEIKA SPEAKS

The mirror tells me: I am beautiful! You all say: I am also destined to grow old. Before God all things must stand still for ever: love him in me, for this moment.

239

SELIGE SEHNSUCHT

Sagt es niemand, nur den Weisen,
Weil die Menge gleich verhöhnet:
Das Lebendge will ich preisen,
Das nach Flammentod sich sehnet.

In der Liebesnächte Kühlung,
Die dich zeugte, wo du zeugtest,
Überfällt dich fremde Fühlung,
Wenn die stille Kerze leuchtet.

Nicht mehr bleibest du umfangen
In der Finsternis Beschattung,
Und dich reißet neu Verlangen
Auf zu höherer Begattung.

Keine Ferne macht dich schwierig,
Kommst geflogen und gebannt,
Und zuletzt, des Lichts begierig,
Bist du, Schmetterling, verbrannt.

Und solang du das nicht hast,
Dieses: Stirb und werde!
Bist du nur ein trüber Gast
Auf der dunklen Erde.

ECSTASY AND DESIRE

Tell it to no one, tell it only to the wise, for the mob will only mock: I would praise the living thing that longs for death by fire.

In those nights of love, when your ardour has been slaked and cooled, begetting you as you begat, the gleam of the silent candle fills you with a strange emotion.

You remain a prisoner no longer in the shadowing darkness, and a new desire snatches you upwards to a higher union.

No distance can weigh you down, you come flying, fascinated, and at last, lusting for the light, poor moth, you perish in the flame.

And until you possess it, this commandment: Die and become! you will be but a dismal guest on the dark earth.

SULEIKA: ALS ich auf dem Euphrat schiffte,
Streifte sich der goldne Ring
Fingerab in Wasserklufte,
Den ich jüngst von dir empfing.

Also träumt ich. Morgenröte
Blitzt' ins Auge durch den Baum.
Sag, Poete, sag, Prophete!
Was bedeutet dieser Traum?

HATEM: DIES zu deuten bin erbötig!
Hab ich dir nicht oft erzählt,
Wie der Doge von Venedig
Mit dem Meere sich vermählt?

So von deinen Fingergliedern
Fiel der Ring dem Euphrat zu.
Ach, zu tausend Himmelsliedern,
Süßer Traum, begeisterst du!

Mich, der von den Indostanen
Streifte bis Damaskus hin,
Um mit neuen Karawanen
Bis ans rote Meer zu ziehn,

SULEIKA: As I was sailing on the Euphrates, the gold ring that lately you gave me slipped down from my finger into watery chasms.

Thus I dreamed. Dawn flashed into my eyes through the branches of the tree. Tell me, oh poet, tell me, oh prophet! what does this dream mean?

HATEM: I will gladly interpret this. Have I not often told you how the Doge of Venice weds himself to the sea?

Thus it was that the ring from the joints of your finger fell into the Euphrates. Oh, to a thousand heavenly songs this sweet dream inspires me!

I, who have wandered from the Indies to Damascus and come with fresh caravans as far as the Red Sea –

Mich vermählst du deinem Flusse,
Der Terrasse, diesem Hain;
Hier soll bis zum letzten Kusse
Dir mein Geist gewidmet sein.

KOMM, Liebchen, komm! umwinde mir die Mütze!
Aus deiner Hand nur ist der Tulbend schön.
Hat Abbas doch, auf Irans höchstem Sitze,
Sein Haupt nicht zierlicher umwinden sehn!

Ein Tulbend war das Band, das Alexandern
In Schleifen schön vom Haupte fiel
Und allen Folgeherrschern, jenen andern,
Als Königszierde wohlgefiel.

Ein Tulbend ists, der unsern Kaiser schmücket;
Sie nennens Krone. Name geht wohl hin!
Juwel und Perle! sei das Aug entzücket!
Der schönste Schmuck ist stets der Musselin.

Und diesen hier, ganz rein und silberstreifig,
Umwinde, Liebchen, um die Stirn umher.
Was ist denn Hoheit? Mir ist sie geläufig!
Du schaust mich an, ich bin so groß als Er.

I, by you, am wedded to your river, to the terrace, to this grove; and
here, until the last kiss, my spirit shall be dedicated to you.

COME, sweetheart, come and wind this bonnet round my head! Only the
turban from your hand is beautiful. Even Abbas the Great on Iran's
highest throne did not have his head more exquisitely bound.

A turban was the circlet that fell in fine loops from the head of Alexander
and was acceptable to those others, all the rulers who succeeded him, as a
royal ornament.

It is a turban that adorns our Emperor; they call it a crown. What's in a
name! Let jewels and pearls delight the eye! The fairest adornment still is
muslin.

So wind this muslin here, so pure and silver-threaded, wind it round my
brow. Why, what is highness? A familiar thing to me! One look from you
and I am as great as an Emperor.

Nur wenig ists, was ich verlange,
Weil eben alles mir gefällt,
Und dieses wenige wie lange
Gibt mir gefällig schon die Welt!

Oft sitz ich heiter in der Schenke
Und heiter im beschränkten Haus;
Allein sobald ich dein gedenke,
Dehnt sich mein Geist erobernd aus.

Dir sollten Timurs Reiche dienen,
Gehorchen sein gebietend Heer,
Badakschan zollte dir Rubinen,
Türkise das Hyrkansche Meer.

Getrocknet honigsüße Früchte
Von Bochara, dem Sonnenland,
Und tausend liebliche Gedichte
Auf Seidenblatt von Samarkand.

Da solltest du mit Freude lesen,
Was ich von Ormus dir verschrieb,
Und wie das ganze Handelswesen
Sich nur bewegte dir zulieb;

I ASK for but little – that, you see, is because I like everything; and already
the world has obligingly been giving me that little for some time now.

I have often sat happily in a tavern, and contentedly in a small house.
But as soon as I think of you, my spirit expands like that of a conqueror.

The kingdoms of Tamburlaine should serve you, his all-mastering army
obey you; from Badakshan you would receive a tribute of rubies, and of
turquoises from the Caspian Sea.

You would have dried fruits sweet as honey from Bokhara, the land of
the sun; and a thousand sweet poems from Samarkand, written on pages of
silk.

Therein you should read with delight of the things I had ordered to be
sent to you from Ormuz, and of how the entire trade of the Empire was
being set in motion for your sake alone.

Wie in dem Lande der Brahmanen
Viel tausend Finger sich bemüht,
Daß alle Pracht der Indostanen
Für dich auf Woll und Seide blüht;

Ja, zu Verherrlichung der Lieben,
Gießbäche Soumelpours durchwühlt,
Aus Erde, Grus, Gerill, Geschieben
Dir Diamanten ausgespült;

Wie Taucherschar verwegner Männer
Der Perle Schatz dem Golf entriß,
Darauf ein Divan scharfer Kenner
Sie dir zu reihen sich befliß.

Wenn nun Bassora noch das Letzte,
Gewürz und Weihrauch, beigetan,
Bringt alles, was die Welt ergetzte,
Die Karawane dir heran.

Doch alle diese Kaisergüter
Verwirrten doch zuletzt den Blick;
Und wahrhaft liebende Gemüter
Eins nur im andern fühlt sein Glück.

You should read how in the land of the Brahmans a myriad fingers toiled to make all the splendour of the Indies blossom for you on wool and silk;

how, to adorn my darling, the streams of Soumelpour had been dredged, and diamonds washed up for you out of soil and dust and rocks and crevices;

how a host of bold divers snatched from the gulf a treasure of pearls, which were then diligently arranged for you by a council of subtle connoisseurs.

And then, when Basra at the last had yielded its spices and incense, the caravan should bring you everything that has enchanted the world.

And yet, all these imperial riches would nevertheless in the end confuse the beholder; and truly loving souls find their happiness in one another alone.

LIEB um Liebe, Stund um Stunde,
Wort um Wort und Blick um Blick;
Kuß um Kuß vom treusten Munde,
Hauch um Hauch und Glück um Glück
So am Abend, so am Morgen!
Doch du fühlst an meinen Liedern
Immer noch geheime Sorgen;
Jussuphs Reize möcht ich borgen,
Deine Schönheit zu erwidern.

HATEM: LOCKEN, haltet mich gefangen
In dem Kreise des Gesichts!
Euch geliebten braunen Schlangen
Zu erwidern hab ich nichts.

Nur dies Herz, es ist von Dauer,
Schwillt in jugendlichstem Flor;
Unter Schnee und Nebelschauer
Rast ein Ätna dir hervor.

Du beschämst wie Morgenröte
Jener Gipfel ernste Wand,
Und noch einmal fühlet Hatem*
Frühlingshauch und Sommerbrand.

LOVE for love, hour for hour, word for word and look for look; kiss for kiss from faithfullest lips; breath for breath and joy for joy. Thus in the evening, and thus in the morning! Yet still a secret anxiety speaks to you from my songs; I would fain borrow the charms of Joseph, that I might requite you beauty for beauty.

HATEM: Locks of her hair, hold me prisoner in the circle of her face! You sweet dark serpents, I have nothing that can requite you.

Only this heart is permanent and rich in youthful blossom; from under snow and drifting mist an Etna of passion pours out towards her.

Like the dawn she puts to shame these stern cliffs and peaks, and once again Hatem feels the breath of spring, and the fire of summer.

* Goethe intends the rhyme-scheme here to suggest the substitution of his own name for 'Hatem'.

Schenke her! Noch eine Flasche!
Diesen Becher bring ich ihr!
Findet sie ein Häufchen Asche,
Sagt sie: Der verbrannte mir.

SULEIKA: NIMMER will ich dich verlieren!
Liebe gibt der Liebe Kraft.
Magst du meine Jugend zieren
Mit gewaltger Leidenschaft.

Ach! wie schmeichelts meinem Triebe,
Wenn man meinen Dichter preist:
Denn das Leben ist die Liebe,
Und des Lebens Leben Geist.

AN vollen Büschelzweigen,
Geliebte, sieh nur hin!
Laß dir die Früchte zeigen,
Umschalet stachlig grün.

Sie hängen längst geballet,
Still, unbekannt mit sich;
Ein Ast, der schaukelnd wallet,
Wiegt sie geduldiglich.

Come, boy! Another bottle! I raise this glass to her! When she finds a little heap of ashes she can say: 'He burnt to death for my sake!'

SULEIKA: May I never lose you! Love gives strength to love. May you adorn my youth with powerful passion.

Ah, how they flatter my heart's desire when they praise my poet! For life is love, and the life of life is intellect.

LOOK, on these branches full of clustering leaves, beloved, let me show you this fruit with its prickly green shell.

For a long time it has been hanging, round and dense and silent, and has not discovered itself; a bough with swaying motion rocks it patiently.

Doch immer reift von innen
Und schwillt der braune Kern,
Er möchte Luft gewinnen
Und säh die Sonne gern.

Die Schale platzt, und nieder
Macht er sich freudig los;
So fallen meine Lieder
Gehäuft in deinen Schoß.

SULEIKA: AN des lustgen Brunnens Rand,
Der in Wasserfäden spielt,
Wußt ich nicht, was fest mich hielt;
Doch da war von deiner Hand
Meine Chiffer leis gezogen,
Niederblickt ich, dir gewogen.

Hier, am Ende des Kanals
Der gereihten Hauptallee,
Blick ich wieder in die Höh,
Und da seh ich abermals
Meine Lettern fein gezogen:
Bleibe! bleibe mir gewogen!

But from within the brown kernel steadily ripens and swells, longing to breathe the air and see the sun.

The shell splits, and joyfully it breaks free and falls; thus the abundance of my songs falls into your lap.

SULEIKA: At the rim of the gay fountain where threads of water play, I tarried without knowing why; but there, by your hand, the cypher of my name had been softly traced, and I gazed down in affection for you.

Here, at the end of the tree-lined main avenue's canal, I gaze up again, and there once more I see my letters delicately traced: remain, remain affectionate to me!

HATEM: Möge Wasser springend, wallend
Die Zypressen dir gestehn:
Von Suleika zu Suleika
Ist mein Kommen und mein Gehn.

BEHRAMGUR, sagt man, hat den Reim erfunden,
Er sprach entzückt aus reiner Seele Drang;
Dilaram schell, die Freundin seiner Stunden,
Erwiderte mit gleichem Wort und Klang.

Und so, Geliebte, warst du mir beschieden,
Des Reims zu finden holden Lustgebrauch,
Daß auch Behramgur ich, den Sassaniden,
Nicht mehr beneiden darf: mir ward es auch.

Hast mir dies Buch geweckt, du hasts gegeben;
Denn was ich froh, aus vollem Herzen sprach,
Das klang zurück aus deinem holden Leben,
Wie Blick dem Blick, so Reim dem Reime nach.

Nun tön es fort zu dir, auch aus der Ferne;
Das Wort erreicht, und schwände Ton und Schall.
Ists nicht der Mantel noch gesäter Sterne?
Ists nicht der Liebe hochverklärtes All?

HATEM: Let the leaping moving water and the cypresses confess to you:
from Suleika to Suleika is my coming and my going.

KING BEHRAMGUR, they say, invented rhyme; ecstatically he spoke,
from his pure soul's impulse; and Dilaram, the darling of his hours, swiftly
replied with matching word and sound.

Likewise, beloved, you were destined to be mine, that we too might
discover rhyme's sweet delightful use; and thus I need no longer envy
Behramgur, the Sassanid King, for it has fallen to me as well.

You wakened this book in my mind, you gave it to me; for the words
I spoke in delight and from a full heart were echoed back from your
sweet life, rhyme answering rhyme as look answered look.

And may you now still hear them, even from afar; words reach their goal,
though voice and sound may have died away. Are they not still the mantle
sown with stars? Are they not the high-transfigured universe of love?

GINGO BILOBA

Dieses Baums Blatt, der von Osten
Meinem Garten anvertraut,
Gibt geheimen Sinn zu kosten,
Wie's den Wissenden erbaut.

Ist es Ein lebendig Wesen,
Das sich in sich selbst getrennt?
Sind es zwei, die sich erlesen,
Daß man sie als Eines kennt?

Solche Frage zu erwidern
Fand ich wohl den rechten Sinn:
Fühlst du nicht an meinen Liedern,
Daß ich Eins und doppelt bin?

* SULEIKA: Was bedeutet die Bewegung?
Bringt der Ost mir frohe Kunde?
Seiner Schwingen frische Regung
Kühlt des Herzens tiefe Wunde.

GINGO BILOBA

The leaf of this Eastern tree which has been entrusted to my garden offers a feast of secret significance, for the edification of the initiate.

Is it one living thing that has become divided within itself? Are these two who have chosen each other, so that we know them as one?

I think I have found the right answer to these questions; do my songs not make you feel that I am both one and twain?

SULEIKA: What does this stirring portend? Is the East Wind bringing me good tidings? The refreshing motion of its wings brings coolness to my heart's deep wound.

* This and the following poem were in fact written by Marianne von Willemer and adopted by Goethe, with slight alterations which are not always improvements. In the case of the first of these two poems I have here given Marianne's original text.

Kosend spielt er mit dem Staube,
Jagt ihn auf in leichten Wölkchen,
Treibt zur sichern Rebenlaube
Der Insekten frohes Völkchen.

Lindert sanft der Sonne Glühen,
Kühlt auch mir die heißen Wangen,
Küßt die Reben noch im Fliehen,
Die auf Feld und Hügel prangen.

Und mich soll sein leises Flüstern
Von dem Freunde lieblich grüßen,
Eh noch diese Hügel düstern,
Sitz ich still zu seinen Füßen.

Und du magst nun weiter ziehen,
Diene Frohen und Betrübten,
Dort wo hohe Mauern glühen,
Finde ich den Vielgeliebten.

Ach, die wahre Herzenskunde,
Liebeshauch, erfrischtes Leben
Wird mir nur aus seinem Munde,
Kann mir nur sein Atem geben.

It plays caressingly with the dust, raises it in light little clouds, drives
the little happy insect people in among the sheltered vine-leaves.

It gently allays the burning of the sun, cools my hot cheeks also and
kisses, even as it flies, the vines that glisten on the fields and hillsides.

And its gentle whispering is sent as a dear message from my lover: even
before these hills darken, I shall be sitting quietly at his feet.

So now, fly on and serve the joyful and the sad; yonder, where high
walls are glowing, I shall find my well-beloved.

Ah, the true message of the heart, the breath of love and refreshment of
life, comes to me from his mouth alone, and his breath alone can give it to
me.

SULEIKA: ACH, um deine feuchten Schwingen,
West, wie sehr ich dich beneide:
Denn du kannst ihm Kunde bringen,
Was ich in der Trennung leide!

Die Bewegung deiner Flügel
Weckt im Busen stilles Sehnen;
Blumen, Augen, Wald und Hügel
Stehn bei deinem Hauch in Tränen.

Doch dein mildes, sanftes Wehen
Kühlt die wunden Augenlider;
Ach, für Leid müßt ich vergehen,
Hofft ich nicht zu sehn ihn wieder.

Eile denn zu meinem Lieben,
Spreche sanft zu seinem Herzen;
Doch vermeid, ihn zu betrüben,
Und verbirg ihm meine Schmerzen.

Sag ihm, aber sags bescheiden:
Seine Liebe sei mein Leben;
Freudiges Gefühl von beiden
Wird mir seine Nähe geben.

SULEIKA: Ah, how I envy you, West Wind, your moist pinions: for you can bring him word of what I suffer in separation from him!

The movement of your wings wakens a silent longing in the heart; flowers, eyes, forest and hillside stand in tears at your breath.

Yet your mild, gentle breeze cools my sore eyelids; oh, I should surely die of grief if I did not hope to see him again.

Hasten then to my dear one and speak gently to his heart; but take care not to sadden him, and hide my anguish from him.

Tell him – but tell him delicately – that his love is my life; and his nearness will fill me with the joy of both.

WIEDERFINDEN

Ist es möglich! Stern der Sterne,
Drück ich wieder dich ans Herz!
Ach, was ist die Nacht der Ferne
Für ein Abgrund, für ein Schmerz!
Ja, du bist es, meiner Freuden
Süßer, lieber Widerpart;
Eingedenk vergangner Leiden,
Schaudr ich vor der Gegenwart.

Als die Welt im tiefsten Grunde
Lag an Gottes ewger Brust,
Ordnet' er die erste Stunde
Mit erhabner Schöpfungslust,
Und er sprach das Wort: Es werde!
Da erklang ein schmerzlich Ach!
Als das All mit Machtgebärde
In die Wirklichkeiten brach.

Auf tat sich das Licht: so trennte
Scheu sich Finsternis von ihm,
Und sogleich die Elemente
Scheidend auseinanderfliehn.

REUNION

Is it possible! most radiant of stars, do I press you again to my heart? Ah, the darkness of separation! what an abyss, what anguish! Yes, it is you, dear sweet sharer of my joys; I remember past suffering, and the present fills me with dread.

When the world, in its uttermost depths, lay on the eternal breast of God, he ordained the first hour with sublime creative joy, and uttered the words: 'Let there be!' And a cry of anguish was heard, as the universe, with a mighty gesture, burst and divided into separate realities.

The light opened – thus the darkness recoiled from it, and immediately the elements parted and fled from each other. Swiftly, in wild, chaotic

Rasch, in wilden, wüsten Träumen
Jedes nach der Weite rang,
Starr, in ungemeßnen Räumen,
Ohne Sehnsucht, ohne Klang.

Stumm war alles, still und öde,
Einsam Gott zum erstenmal!
Da erschuf er Morgenröte,
Die erbarmte sich der Qual;
Sie entwickelte dem Trüben
Ein erklingend Farbenspiel,
Und nun konnte wieder lieben,
Was erst auseinander fiel.

Und mit eiligem Bestreben
Sucht sich, was sich angehört;
Und zu ungemeßnem Leben
Ist Gefühl und Blick gekehrt.
Seis Ergreifen, sei es Raffen,
Wenn es nur sich faßt und hält!
Allah braucht nicht mehr zu schaffen,
Wir erschaffen seine Welt.

dreams, they all strove outwards to distant places, and became numb and rigid in measureless space, empty of longing and of music.

All was dumb, silent and desolate – and God, for the first time, was lonely. And now he created the dawn, who took pity on the pain of division; glowing through opacity, she brought a symphony of colours into being, and now those elements that first had fallen apart could fall together again in love.

And with swift aspiration destined partners seek each other out, and the heart and the eyes have turned towards life immeasurable. Let lovers seize or snatch one another, if they will but hold each other fast! Allah now need create no longer, for we are bringing his world into being.

So, mit morgenroten Flügeln,
Riß es mich an deinen Mund,
Und die Nacht mit tausend Siegeln
Kräftigt sternenhell den Bund.
Beide sind wir auf der Erde
Musterhaft in Freud und Qual,
Und ein zweites Wort: Es werde!
Trennt uns nicht zum zweitenmal.

VOLLMONDNACHT

Herrin, sag, was heißt das Flüstern?
Was bewegt dir leis die Lippen?
Lispelst immer vor dich hin,
Lieblicher als Weines Nippen!
Denkst du, deinen Mundgeschwistern
Noch ein Pärchen herzuziehn?
　　«Ich will küssen! Küssen! sagt ich.»

Schau! Im zweifelhaften Dunkel
Glühen blühend alle Zweige,
Nieder spielet Stern auf Stern;

It was thus, with wings of the dawn, that a power drew me to your mouth, and the star-radiant night confirms our bond with a million seals. In joy and pain we are both paragons on earth, and no second 'Let there be!' shall divide us again.

THE NIGHT OF THE FULL MOON

Lady, say, what do you whisper? What is it that softly moves your lips? You murmur constantly to yourself, sweeter than sipping of wine! Would you summon, for your mouth's twins, another pair to keep them company?

'I would kiss! would kiss, I said.'

See! In the uncertain gloaming all the branches glow and blossom, starlight plays down upon star, and through the thicket a myriad

Und smaragden durchs Gesträuche
Tausendfältiger Karfunkel:
Doch dein Geist ist allem fern.
　«Ich will küssen! Küssen! sagt ich.»

Dein Geliebter, fern, erprobet
Gleicherweis im Sauersüßen,
Fühlt ein unglückselges Glück.
Euch im Vollmond zu begrüßen,
Habt ihr heilig angelobet;
Dieses ist der Augenblick.
　«Ich will küssen! Küssen! sag ich.»

[ALLGEGENWÄRTIGE]

IN tausend Formen magst du dich verstecken,
Doch, Allerliebste, gleich erkenn ich dich;
Du magst mit Zauberschleiern dich bedecken,
Allgegenwärtge, gleich erkenn ich dich.

An der Zypresse reinstem, jungem Streben,
Allschöngewachsne, gleich erkenn ich dich;
In des Kanales reinem Wellenleben,
Allschmeichelhafte, wohl erkenn ich dich.

gems seem to glitter like emerald: but from all this your mind is absent.
　'I would kiss! would kiss, I said.'
　Your lover far away, no less experienced in bitterness and sweetness, is full of unhappy happiness. You both took a sacred vow to greet each other at every full moon: this is the hour.
　'I would kiss! would kiss, I say.'

[HER OMNIPRESENCE]

THOUGH you may hide yourself in a thousand shapes, yet, All-Beloved! at once I recognize you. You may cover yourself with magic veils: at once, All-Present One, I recognize you.

　In the young cypress-tree's purest upward growth, All-Shapeliest One, at once I recognize you; in the pure living moving water of the canal, All-Flattering One, how well I recognize you.

Wenn steigend sich der Wasserstrahl entfaltet,
Allspielende, wie froh erkenn ich dich;
Wenn Wolke sich gestaltend umgestaltet,
Allmannigfaltge, dort erkenn ich dich.

An des geblümten Schleiers Wiesenteppich,
Allbuntbesternte, schön erkenn ich dich;
Und greift umher ein tausendarmger Eppich,
O Allumklammernde, da kenn ich dich.

Wenn am Gebirg der Morgen sich entzündet,
Gleich, Allerheiternde, begrüß ich dich;
Dann über mir der Himmel rein sich ründet,
Allherzerweiternde, dann atm ich dich.

Was ich mit äußerm Sinn, mit innerm kenne,
Du Allbelehrende, kenn ich durch dich;
Und wenn ich Allahs Namenhundert nenne,
Mit jedem klingt ein Name nach für dich.

When the leaping fountain-jet unfolds, All-Playful One, joyfully I recognize you; when clouds form and re-form themselves, there too, All-Manifold One, I recognize you.

In the flowery veil, the tapestry of fields, All-Starry-Many-Coloured One, in your beauty I recognize you; and when ivy stretches forth its thousand arms, there, All-Embracing One, I know you.

When morning catches fire on the mountains, at once, All-Gladdening One, I salute you; then the sky grows pure and round above me, and then, Lifter of All Hearts, I draw breath in you.

All that I know by outward and inward sense, Teacher of All Men, I have learnt from you; and when I name the Hundred Names of Allah, each of them is echoed by a name for you.

WANDRERS GEMÜTSRUHE

ÜBERS Niederträchtige
Niemand sich beklage;
Denn es ist das Mächtige,
Was man dir auch sage.

In dem Schlechten waltet es
Sich zu Hochgewinne,
Und mit Rechtem schaltet es
Ganz nach seinem Sinne.

Wandrer! – Gegen solche Not
Wolltest du dich sträuben?
Wirbelwind und trocknen Kot,
Laß sie drehn und stäuben.

TRUNKEN müssen wir alle sein!
Jugend ist Trunkenheit ohne Wein;
Trinkt sich das Alter wieder zu Jugend,
So ist es wundervolle Tugend.
Für Sorgen sorgt das liebe Leben,
Und Sorgenbrecher sind die Reben.

THE WAYFARER'S EQUANIMITY

LET no one complain about infamy; for say what you like, it is the most powerful of forces.

It rules amid rottenness with great profit to itself, and manipulates righteousness exactly as it pleases.

Wayfarer! why struggle against such an evil? Let the whirlwind whirl, and the dry dirt be stirred.

WE must all be drunk! Youth is wineless drunkenness, and old age that drinks itself young again is marvellous virtue. Life, bless it, takes care to supply us with cares; and the caster-out of cares is the vine.

Solang man nüchtern ist,
Gefällt das Schlechte;
Wie man getrunken hat,
Weiß man das Rechte;
Nur ist das Übermaß
Auch gleich zu Handen:
Hafis, o lehre mich,
Wie dus verstanden!

Denn meine Meinung ist
Nicht übertrieben:
Wenn man nicht trinken kann,
Soll man nicht lieben;
Doch sollt ihr Trinker euch
Nicht besser dünken:
Wenn man nicht lieben kann,
Soll man nicht trinken.

DEM KELLNER

Setze mir nicht, du Grobian,
Mir den Krug so derb vor die Nase!
Wer mir Wein bringt, sehe mich freundlich an,
Sonst trübt sich der Eilfer im Glase.

As long as we are sober, we like what is inferior; but when we have drunk, we know what is what. Yet excess, too, lurks near at hand; oh teach me, Háfiz, what your wisdom taught you!

For I hold, not unjustly, that if a man cannot drink, neither should he love. But do not you drinkers be giving yourselves airs: if a man cannot love, neither let him drink.

TO THE WAITER

Don't slam the jug down in front of my nose like that, you curmudgeon! I want friendly looks from anyone who brings me wine; otherwise the 1811 vintage goes bad in the glass.

DEM SCHENKEN

Du zierlicher Knabe, du komm herein,
Was stehst du denn da auf der Schwelle?
Du sollst mir künftig der Schenke sein,
Jeder Wein ist schmackhaft und helle.

SCHENKE: Welch ein Zustand! Herr, so späte
Schleichst du heut aus deiner Kammer;
Perser nennens Bidamag buden,
Deutsche sagen Katzenjammer.

DICHTER: Laß mich jetzt, geliebter Knabe!
Mir will nicht die Welt gefallen,
Nicht der Schein, der Duft der Rose,
Nicht der Sang der Nachtigallen.

SCHENKE: Eben das will ich behandeln,
Und ich denk, es soll mir klecken;
Hier! genieß die frischen Mandeln,
Und der Wein wird wieder schmecken.

TO THE CUPBEARER

Come along in, pretty boy; why are you standing there in the doorway? You shall be my cupbearer from now on, and every wine will taste delicious and clear.

CUPBEARER: What a state of things! Sir, how late you come creeping out of your room this morning! The Persians call it 'bidamag buden'; the English say 'a hangover'.

POET: Let me alone now, dearest boy! I can take no pleasure in the world, neither in the brightness or the fragrance of the rose, nor in the song of the nightingales.

CUPBEARER: That is just what I intend to set to rights, and I think I can manage it. Here! eat these fresh almonds, and wine will taste good again.

Dann will ich auf der Terrasse
Dich mit frischen Lüften tränken;
Wie ich dich ins Auge fasse,
Gibst du einen Kuß dem Schenken.

Schau! die Welt ist keine Höhle,
Immer reich an Brut und Nestern,
Rosenduft und Rosenöle;
Bulbul auch, sie singt wie gestern.

SCHENKE: Nennen dich den großen Dichter,
Wenn dich auf dem Markte zeigest;
Gerne hör ich, wenn du singest,
Und ich horche, wenn du schweigest.

Doch ich liebe dich noch lieber,
Wenn du küssest zum Erinnern;
Denn die Worte gehn vorüber,
Und der Kuß, der bleibt im Innern.

Reim auf Reim will was bedeuten,
Besser ist es, viel zu denken.
Singe du den andern Leuten
Und verstumme mit dem Schenken.

Then I shall make you drink fresh breezes on the terrace; and when I look you in the eye, you will give the cupbearer a kiss.

See, the world is no gloomy cavern, it is as full as ever of bird-brood and nests, and the scent and the attar of roses! And Bulbul, too, is singing as she sang yesterday.

CUPBEARER: YOU are 'the great poet' to them when you walk about the market; I am glad to hear your singing, and I listen to your silence.

But I love you still more dearly when you give a kiss as keepsake. For the sound of words is transient, but a kiss lives on within me.

Making rhymes is an achievement; thinking deeply is still better. But let others hear your singing: with the cupbearer be silent.

DICHTER: Schenke, komm! Noch einen Becher!

SCHENKE: Herr, du hast genug getrunken;
 Nennen dich den wilden Zecher!

DICHTER: Sahst du je, daß ich gesunken?

SCHENKE: Mahomet verbietets.

DICHTER: Liebchen!
 Hört es niemand, will dirs sagen.

SCHENKE: Wenn du einmal gerne redest,
 Brauch ich gar nicht viel zu fragen.

DICHTER: Horch! wir andren Musulmanen,
 Nüchtern sollen wir gebückt sein,
 Er, in seinem heilgen Eifer,
 Möchte gern allein verrückt sein.

.

POET: Come, boy! Another glass!

CUPBEARER: Sir, you have drunk enough; people call you 'the wine-bibber'.

POET: Have you ever seen me overcome by drink?

CUPBEARER: Wine is forbidden by Mahomed!

POET: My dear! If no one is listening I will tell you something.

CUPBEARER: Well, if you are in the talking mood, I shan't need to ask many questions.

POET: Listen! He wants us other Moslems to knuckle under and go sober; for he, in his holy zeal, would like to be the only crazy one.

SOMMERNACHT

DICHTER: Niedergangen ist die Sonne,
Doch im Westen glänzt es immer;
Wissen möcht ich wohl, wie lange
Dauert noch der goldne Schimmer?

SCHENKE: Willst du, Herr, so will ich bleiben,
Warten außer diesen Zelten;
Ist die Nacht des Schimmers Herrin,
Komm ich gleich, es dir zu melden.

Denn ich weiß, du liebst, das Droben,
Das Unendliche zu schauen,
Wenn sie sich einander loben,
Jene Feuer in dem Blauen.

Und das hellste will nur sagen:
«Jetzo glänz ich meiner Stelle;
Wollte Gott euch mehr betagen,
Glänztet ihr wie ich so helle.»

Denn vor Gott ist alles herrlich,
Eben weil er ist der Beste;
Und so schläft nun aller Vogel
In dem groß- und kleinen Neste.

SUMMER NIGHT

POET: The sun is down, but the Western sky is still shining. I wonder how long this golden brightness will last.

CUPBEARER: If you like, sir, I'll stay and watch outside these tents, and when the night gets the better of the brightness, I'll come at once and tell you.

For I know you love to gaze at what's up there, at endless space, when they're singing hymns to each other, those fires in the blue sky.

And the brightest of them is only trying to tell us: 'Here I am, shining away where I belong; if only God would give you more light, you'd all be shining as brightly as me.'

For in God's eyes everything is wonderful, just because he is better than anyone; so now all the birds are sleeping, in their big nests and little nests.

Einer sitzt auch wohl gestängelt
Auf den Ästen der Zypresse,
Wo der laue Wind ihn gängelt,
Bis zu Taues luftger Nässe.

Solches hast du mich gelehret,
Oder etwas auch dergleichen;
Was ich je dir abgehöret,
Wird dem Herzen nicht entweichen.

Eule will ich deinetwegen
Kauzen hier auf der Terrasse,
Bis ich erst des Nordgestirnes
Zwillings-Wendung wohl erpasse.

Und da wird es Mitternacht sein,
Wo du oft zu früh ermunterst,
Und dann wird es eine Pracht sein,
Wenn das All mit mir bewunderst.

DICHTER: Zwar in diesem Duft und Garten
Tönet Bulbul ganze Nächte;
Doch du könntest lange warten,
Bis die Nacht so viel vermöchte.

And one of them is probably perching in the branches of that cypress,
where the mild wind will rock him till dew moistens the air.

That's what you've taught me – or something like that, anyhow; my
heart will always remember whatever I have heard you say.

I'll be an owl and squat here for you on the terrace, till I can make sure
the northerly sun has reached the turning-point of his two-sided course.

And at that moment it will be midnight, the time when you often wake
up too soon, and then the two of us will have a wonderful time looking at
the universe together.

POET: I know that in this sweet-smelling garden the nightingale sings
all night long; but you might have a long time to wait if you wait for so
powerful a night as that.

Denn in dieser Zeit der Flora,
Wie das Griechenvolk sie nennet,
Die Strohwitwe, die Aurora,
Ist in Hesperus entbrennet.

Sieh dich um! sie kommt! wie schnelle!
Über Blumenfelds Gelänge! –
Hüben hell und drüben helle;
Ja, die Nacht kommt ins Gedränge.

Und auf roten leichten Sohlen
Ihn, der mit der Sonn entlaufen,
Eilt sie irrig einzuholen;
Fühlst du nicht ein Liebe-Schnaufen?

Geh nur, lieblichster der Söhne,
Tief ins Innre, schließ die Türen;
Denn sie möchte deine Schöne
Als den Hesperus entführen.

DER SCHENKE (schläfrig): So hab ich endlich von dir erharrt:
In allen Elementen Gottes Gegenwart.
Wie du mir das so lieblich gibst!
Am lieblichsten aber, daß du liebst.

For at this season of Flora, as the Greek people call it, that grass-widow,
the goddess of Dawn, burns with love for Hesperus, the evening star.

Look about you, how quickly she comes over the length of the flowering
meadow! It is bright this side and bright that side: yes, indeed, the night is
having a narrow time.

The Star ran away beside the setting sun, and now Dawn, on her red
soft feet, is running crazily to catch him up; can't you hear her panting
with love?

Go then, loveliest of boys, and shut yourself right up indoors; for she
might mistake your beauty for the evening Star, and carry you away.

CUPBEARER (sleepily): So I have got it from you, at last: God's presence
is in all the elements. How dear you are when you show me this! But your
love is dearest of all.

HATEM: Der schläft recht süß und hat ein Recht zu schlafen.
Du guter Knabe, hast mir eingeschenkt,
Vom Freund und Lehrer, ohne Zwang und Strafen,
So jung vernommen, wie der Alte denkt.
Nun aber kommt Gesundheit holder Fülle
Dir in die Glieder, daß du dich erneust.
Ich trinke noch, bin aber stille, stille,
Damit du mich, erwachend nicht, erfreust.

VOM Himmel sank in wilder Meere Schauer
Ein Tropfe bangend, gräßlich schlug die Flut;
Doch lohnte Gott bescheidnen Glaubensmut
Und gab dem Tropfen Kraft und Dauer.
Ihn schloß die stille Muschel ein.
Und nun, zu ewgem Ruhm und Lohne,
Die Perle glänzt an unsers Kaisers Krone
Mit holdem Blick und mildem Schein.

HATEM: His sleep is very sweet, and he has a right to it. Dear boy! You have been pouring out wine for me, and listening to your friend and teacher, and without any forcing or punishing you have learnt so young how an old man thinks. But now fair health is filling your limbs and you are renewing your life. And I am still drinking, but I will not make a sound, because I want you to delight my eyes, not waking up.

FROM heaven, into wild tempestuous seas, sank a terrified raindrop. The waves raged hideously; but God rewarded modest courage and faith, and gave the drop strength and durability. The quiet oyster-shell enclosed it. And now, to its eternal renown and reward, the pearl gleams in our emperor's crown with a mild and gentle radiance.

ES IST GUT

Bei Mondeschein im Paradeis
Fand Jehovah im Schlafe tief
Adam versunken, legte leis
Zur Seit ein Evchen, das auch entschlief.
Da lagen nun, in Erdeschranken,
Gottes zwei lieblichste Gedanken. –
Gut!!! rief er sich zum Meisterlohn;
Er ging sogar nicht gern davon.

Kein Wunder, daß es uns berückt,
Wenn Auge frisch in Auge blickt,
Als hätten wirs so weit gebracht,
Bei dem zu sein, der uns gedacht.
Und ruft er uns, wohlan, es sei!
Nur, das beding ich, alle zwei.
Dich halten dieser Arme Schranken,
Liebster von allen Gottes-Gedanken.

IT IS GOOD

By the light of the moon in Paradise, Jehovah found Adam deep in slumber, and softly laid at his side a little Eve, who also fell asleep. So there in earthly bonds they lay, God's two loveliest thoughts. 'Good!' exclaimed the Master, rewarding himself with praise; he even went away rather reluctantly.

No wonder it enchants us, when eyes gaze boldly into eyes; it feels as if we had succeeded in reaching the presence of him who thought us. And if he should call us to himself, well, so be it! But, by his leave, it must be both of us together! In the bonds of these arms I hold you, dearest of all the thoughts of God.

BEGÜNSTIGTE TIERE

VIER Tieren auch verheißen war,
Ins Paradies zu kommen,
Dort leben sie das ewge Jahr
Mit Heiligen und Frommen.

Den Vortritt hier ein Esel hat,
Er kommt mit muntern Schritten:
Denn Jesus zur Propheten-Stadt
Auf ihm ist eingeritten.

Halb schüchtern kommt ein Wolf sodann,
Dem Mahomet befohlen:
Laß dieses Schaf dem armen Mann,
Dem Reichen magst dus holen.

Nun, immer wedelnd, munter, brav,
Mit seinem Herrn, dem braven,
Das Hündlein, das den Siebenschlaf
So treulich mitgeschlafen.

Abuherriras Katze hier
Knurrt um den Herrn und schmeichelt:
Denn immer ists ein heilig Tier,
Das der Prophet gestreichelt.

PRIVILEGED ANIMALS

FOUR animals have also been promised admission to Paradise; they will
live out the Eternal Year there with the saints and the devout.

An ass here has precedence, he comes trundling cheerfully along; for
Jesus rode on him into the Prophet's City.

Then, rather timidly, comes a wolf, to whom Mahommed once gave the
order: 'Leave the poor man that sheep; you can take one from the rich
man.'

Next, still cheerfully wagging his tail, with his good master comes the
good little dog, who slept the Seven Sleeps so faithfully.

And here is Abuherrira's cat, purring around her master and rubbing
against him; for after all, an animal is sacred if the Prophet has stroked it.

HÖHERES UND HÖCHSTES

Dass wir solche Dinge lehren,
Möge man uns nicht bestrafen:
Wie das alles zu erklären,
Dürft ihr euer Tiefstes fragen.

Und so werdet ihr vernehmen,
Daß der Mensch, mit sich zufrieden,
Gern sein Ich gerettet sähe,
So da droben wie hienieden.

Und mein liebes Ich bedürfte
Mancherlei Bequemlichkeiten;
Freuden, wie ich hier sie schlürfte,
Wünscht ich auch für ewge Zeiten.

So gefallen schöne Gärten,
Blum und Frucht und hübsche Kinder,
Die uns allen hier gefielen,
Auch verjüngtem Geist nicht minder.

Und so möcht ich alle Freunde,
Jung und alt, in eins versammeln,
Gar zu gern in deutscher Sprache
Paradieses-Worte stammeln.

HIGHER AND HIGHEST THINGS

To expound these things will not, I hope, be looked upon as reprehensible. The explanation of it all may be sought deep down within each one of you.

And this is how you will learn that man, in his contentment with himself, desires to have his identity preserved, in heaven as on earth.

And as for my own dear self, it needs certain comforts; I would wish the delights I have tasted here to be mine for eternity too.

Thus it is that beautiful gardens, flowers and fruit and lovely girls, which we have all enjoyed down here, are equally pleasing to the rejuvenated spirit.

And likewise I would wish to gather all my friends, young and old, together, and should dearly like to lisp Paradise-words in my native tongue.

Doch man horcht nun Dialekten,
Wie sich Mensch und Engel kosen,
Der Grammatik, der versteckten,
Deklinierend Mohn und Rosen.

Mag man ferner auch in Blicken
Sich rhetorisch gern ergehen
Und zu himmlischem Entzücken
Ohne Klang und Ton erhöhen.

Ton und Klang jedoch entwindet
Sich dem Worte selbstverständlich,
Und entschiedener empfindet
Der Verklärte sich unendlich.

Ist somit dem Fünf der Sinne
Vorgesehn im Paradiese,
Sicher ist es, ich gewinne
Einen Sinn für alle diese.

Und nun dring ich aller Orten
Leichter durch die ewgen Kreise,
Die durchdrungen sind vom Worte
Gottes rein-lebendger Weise.

Up here, however, as men and angels make intimate acquaintance, we shall listen to new dialects, to the hidden grammar, the declensions of poppies and roses.

We shall gladly indulge also in the rhetoric of looks, and rise to heavenly rapture that has no sound or voice.

Yet voice and sound will disengage themselves naturally from words, and the transfigured spirit will pass more decisively into a consciousness of its own infinity.

And thus, the five senses being provided for in Paradise, it is very sure that I shall acquire a single sense embracing all of them.

And I shall then everywhere penetrate more easily through the eternal spheres, which are permeated by the pure living speech of God.

Ungehemmt mit heißem Triebe
Läßt sich da kein Ende finden,
Bis im Anschaun ewger Liebe
Wir verschweben, wir verschwinden.

PROOEMION

Im Namen dessen, der sich Selbst erschuf!
Von Ewigkeit in schaffendem Beruf;
In Seinem Namen, der den Glauben schafft,
Vertrauen, Liebe, Tätigkeit und Kraft;
In Jenes Namen, der, so oft genannt,
Dem Wesen nach blieb immer unbekannt:

Soweit das Ohr, soweit das Auge reicht,
Du findest nur Bekanntes, das Ihm gleicht,
Und deines Geistes höchster Feuerflug
Hat schon am Gleichnis, hat am Bild genug;

Untrammelled, and burning with desire, there will be no end to the search,
until in the contemplation of eternal Love we soar out of sight and disappear.

PRELUDE

In the name of Him who created Himself and whose work of creativity is
eternal; in His name who creates faith, trust, love, activity, and strength;
in the name of that Being who is named so often but whose nature has
remained for ever unknown:

so far as ear and eye can reach you will find nothing but known things
which resemble Him, and even in its highest empyrean flight your mind
is satisfied with the likeness, satisfied with the image. They fascinate you,

Es zieht dich an, es reißt dich heiter fort,
Und wo du wandelst, schmückt sich Weg und Ort;
Du zählst nicht mehr, berechnest keine Zeit,
Und jeder Schritt ist Unermeßlichkeit.

*

Was wär ein Gott, der nur von außen stieße,
Im Kreis das All am Finger laufen ließe!
Ihm ziemts, die Welt im Innern zu bewegen,
Natur in Sich, Sich in Natur zu hegen,
So daß, was in Ihm lebt und webt und ist,
Nie Seine Kraft, nie Seinen Geist vermißt.

*

Im Innern ist ein Universum auch;
Daher der Völker löblicher Gebrauch,
Daß jeglicher das Beste, was er kennt,
Er Gott, ja seinen Gott benennt,
Ihm Himmel und Erden übergibt,
Ihn fürchtet, und womöglich liebt.

they draw you joyfully on, and beauty adorns every path you tread and every place you reach. You cease to count or calculate time, and every step is measureless.

*

What sort of God would it be who merely gave the universe a push from outside and rotated it with his finger! It befits Him to impart motion to the world from within, to cherish Nature in Himself and Himself in Nature, so that all that lives and moves and has its being in Him is never without His power and His spirit.

*

Within us, too, there is a universe; hence the praiseworthy custom of peoples, by which each man gives the name of God to the best thing he knows, and calls it, indeed, his God – consigning heaven and earth to His care, fearing Him and seeking to love Him.

PARABASE

*

F<small>REUDIG</small> war, vor vielen Jahren,
Eifrig so der Geist bestrebt,
Zu erforschen, zu erfahren,
Wie Natur im Schaffen lebt.
Und es ist das ewig Eine,
Das sich vielfach offenbart:
Klein das Große, groß das Kleine,
Alles nach der eignen Art;
Immer wechselnd, fest sich haltend,
Nah und fern und fern und nah,
So gestaltend, umgestaltend –
Zum Erstaunen bin ich da.

*

DIE METAMORPHOSE DER PFLANZEN
(see page 147)

*

PARABASIS

*

M<small>ANY</small> years ago, as now, my mind strove with eager delight to study and discover the creative life of Nature. It is eternal Unity in manifold manifestation: the great is little, the little is great, and everything after its kind; ever changing and yet preserving itself, near and far and far and near, and so shaping and re-shaping itself – I am here to wonder at it.

*

THE METAMORPHOSIS OF PLANTS
(see page 147)

*

EPIRRHEMA

Müsset im Naturbetrachten
Immer eins wie alles achten:
Nichts ist drinnen, nichts ist draußen;
Denn was innen, das ist außen.
So ergreifet ohne Säumnis
Heilig öffentlich Geheimnis.

Freuet euch des wahren Scheins,
Euch des ernsten Spieles:
Kein Lebendiges ist ein Eins,
Immer ists ein Vieles.

*

METAMORPHOSE DER TIERE
(see page 151)

*

EPIRRHEMA

You must, in studying Nature, always consider both each single thing and the whole: nothing is inside and nothing is outside, for what is within is without. Make haste, then, to grasp this holy mystery which is public knowledge.

Rejoice in the true illusion, in the serious game: no living thing is a unity, it is always manifold.

*

METAMORPHOSIS OF ANIMALS
(see page 151)

*

ANTEPIRRHEMA

So schauet mit bescheidnem Blick
Der ewigen Weberin Meisterstück,
Wie *ein* Tritt tausend Fäden regt,
Die Schifflein hinüber herüber schießen,
Die Fäden sich begegnend fließen,
Ein Schlag tausend Verbindungen schlägt!
Das hat sie nicht zusammengebettelt;
Sie hats von Ewigkeit angezettelt,
Damit der ewige Meistermann
Getrost den Einschlag werfen kann.

EINS UND ALLES

Im Grenzenlosen sich zu finden,
Wird gern der einzelne verschwinden,
Da löst sich aller Überdruß;
Statt heißem Wünschen, wildem Wollen,
Statt lästgem Fordern, strengem Sollen
Sich aufzugeben ist Genuß.

ANTEPIRRHEMA

Look, then, with reverent gaze, upon the eternal Weaver's masterpiece:
see how one pressure of her foot sets a thousand threads in motion – how
the shuttles dart to and fro, the flowing strands intertwine and a thousand
connexions are made at one stroke! This is no rag-and-bone collection:
from all eternity she has been spreading out this warp, that the weft may
be boldly and easily cast by the eternal Master.

ONE AND ALL

The individual will gladly perish if he can find himself again in boundless
infinity, where all vexations dissolve; where instead of passionate wishes
and wild desires, irksome demands and stern obligations, the self will
delight in self-surrender.

Weltseele, komm, uns zu durchdringen!
Dann mit dem Weltgeist selbst zu ringen,
Wird unsrer Kräfte Hochberuf.
Teilnehmend führen gute Geister,
Gelinde leitend höchste Meister
Zu dem, der alles schafft und schuf.

Und umzuschaffen das Geschaffne,
Damit sichs nicht zum Starren waffne,
Wirkt ewiges, lebendiges Tun.
Und was nicht war, nun will es werden
Zu reinen Sonnen, farbigen Erden;
In keinem Falle darf es ruhn.

Es soll sich regen, schaffend handeln,
Erst sich gestalten, dann verwandeln;
Nur scheinbar stehts Momente still.
Das Ewige regt sich fort in allen:
Denn alles muß in Nichts zerfallen,
Wenn es im Sein beharren will.

Come, Soul of the world, and flood through us! To vie then with the
very Spirit of the world will be the supreme task of our strength. Good
spirits shall sympathetically guide us, great master minds gently conduct
us towards him who is creating and has created all things.

And an eternal, living Activity works to create anew what has been
created, lest it entrench itself in rigidity. And that which has not yet been
seeks now to come into being, as pure suns and many-coloured earths:
none of it may remain at rest.

It is intended to move, to act and create – first to form and then to trans-
form itself; its moments of immobility are only apparent. In all that lives
the Eternal Force works on: for everything must dissolve into nothingness,
if it is to remain in Being.

VERMÄCHTNIS

KEIN Wesen kann zu Nichts zerfallen!
Das Ewge regt sich fort in allen,
Am Sein erhalte dich beglückt!
Das Sein ist ewig: denn Gesetze
Bewahren die lebendgen Schätze,
Aus welchen sich das All geschmückt.

Das Wahre war schon längst gefunden,
Hat edle Geisterschaft verbunden;
Das alte Wahre, fass es an!
Verdank es, Erdensohn, dem Weisen,
Der ihr, die Sonne zu umkreisen,
Und dem Geschwister wies die Bahn.

Sofort nun wende dich nach innen:
Das Zentrum findest du da drinnen,
Woran kein Edler zweifeln mag.
Wirst keine Regel da vermissen:
Denn das selbständige Gewissen
Ist Sonne deinem Sittentag.

LEGACY

NOTHING that is can dissolve into nothingness! In all that lives the
Eternal Force works on: remain, rejoicing, in Being! Being is eternal; for
laws preserve the living treasures with which the universe has adorned
itself.

The truth has long since been known, and has become a bond between
noble intelligences; grasp it, the age-old truth! Acknowledge, oh son of
the earth, that you owe it to that wise thinker who taught her and her
brothers and sisters their paths round the sun.

And then at once turn your gaze inward: you will find the Centre there
within, and this no noble mind can doubt. There you will feel no lack of
governance, for conscience, relying upon itself, is the sun of your moral
day.

Den Sinnen hast du dann zu trauen,
Kein Falsches lassen sie dich schauen,
Wenn dein Verstand dich wach erhält.
Mit frischem Blick bemerke freudig
Und wandle, sicher wie geschmeidig
Durch Auen reichbegabter Welt.

Genieße mäßig Füll und Segen;
Vernunft sei überall zugegen,
Wo Leben sich des Lebens freut.
Dann ist Vergangenheit beständig,
Das Künftige voraus lebendig,
Der Augenblick ist Ewigkeit.

Und war es endlich dir gelungen,
Und bist du vom Gefühl durchdrungen:
Was fruchtbar ist, allein ist wahr –
Du prüfst das allgemeine Walten,
Es wird nach seiner Weise schalten,
Geselle dich zur kleinsten Schar.

Next, you must trust your senses: they will show you nothing false if your intelligence keeps you awake. Keep your eyes fresh and open and joyful, and move with sure steps, yet flexibly, through the fields of a world so richly endowed.

Enjoy with moderation its fullness and blessing; let reason be ever present where life takes delight in life. At such times the past lives on, and the future lives in advance, and the moment is eternity.

And if in the end you have achieved this, and have come to feel thoroughly convinced that only what bears fruit is true – consider the conduct of the majority, leave them to arrange things as they please, and choose your company among the élite.

Und wie von alters her, im stillen
Ein Liebewerk nach eignem Willen
Der Philosoph, der Dichter schuf,
So wirst du schönste Gunst erzielen:
Denn edlen Seelen vorzufühlen
Ist wünschenswertester Beruf.

[VERMISCHTE EPIGRAMME]

WILL Licht einem Körper sich vermählen,
Es wird den ganz durchsichtgen wählen.

Du aber halte dich mit Liebe
An das Durchscheinende, das Trübe.

Denn steht das Trübste vor der Sonne,
Da siehst die herrlichste Purpur-Wonne.

Und will das Licht sich dem Trübsten entwinden,
So wird es glühend Rot entzünden.

From of old the philosopher or poet has brought forth his work of love in tranquillity, and as he wills it to be; in this way, too, you will win fairest favour; for to devise patterns of feeling for noble souls is the most desirable of all callings.

[MISCELLANEOUS EPIGRAMS]

WHEN light seeks union with a body, it will choose one which is completely transparent.

But you must attach yourself lovingly to that which is translucent and opaque.

For when that which is most opaque of all stands between you and the sun, you will see a splendid rapture of purple.

And when light seeks to break free of what is most opaque, it will kindle a glowing red.

Und wie das Trübste verdunstet und weicht,
Das Rote zum hellsten Gelb erbleicht.

Ist endlich der Äther rein und klar,
Ist das Licht weiß, wie es anfangs war.

Steht vor dem Finstern milchig Grau,
Die Sonne bescheints, da wird es Blau.

Auf Bergen, in der reinsten Höhe,
Tief Rötlichblau ist Himmelsnähe.

Du staunest über die Königspracht,
Und gleich ist sammetschwarz die Nacht.

Und so bleibt auch, in ewigem Frieden,
Die Finsternis vom Licht geschieden.

Daß sie miteinander streiten können,
Das ist eine bare Torheit zu nennen.

Sie streiten mit der Körperwelt,
Die sie ewig auseinanderhält.

And as the opacity evaporates and vanishes, the red pales to the brightest yellow.

When at last the air is pure and clear, the light is white, as it was at the beginning.

When a milky grey stands in front of the darkness, and the sun illuminates it, it becomes blue.

On mountains, in the purest heights, deep reddish-blue is nearness to heaven.

You look in amazement at this royal splendour, and at once the night is black as velvet.

And thus, in perpetual peace, darkness remains separated from light.

To say that they can conflict with each other is sheer foolishness.

They conflict with the world of bodies, which holds them perpetually apart.

WER Wissenschaft und Kunst besitzt,
Hat auch Religion;
Wer jene beiden nicht besitzt,
Der habe Religion.

WAS hieße wohl die Natur ergründen?
Gott ebenso außen als innen zu finden.

WILLST du ins Unendliche schreiten,
Geh nur im Endlichen nach allen Seiten.

WILLST du dich am Ganzen erquicken,
So mußt du das Ganze im Kleinsten erblicken.

WENN im Unendlichen dasselbe
Sich wiederholend ewig fließt,
Das tausendfältige Gewölbe
Sich kräftig ineinander schließt,
Strömt Lebenslust aus allen Dingen,
Dem kleinsten wie dem größten Stern,
Und alles Drängen, alles Ringen
Ist ewige Ruh in Gott dem Herrn.

ANYONE who possesses science and art has religion as well; anyone who possesses neither of these had better have religion.

WHAT should the solving of Nature's secrets be? The discovery of God both within and without.

IF you wish to advance into the infinite, explore the finite in all directions.

IF you desire refreshing contemplation of the Whole, you must discern the Whole in the smallest of things.

IN the infinite the same events repeat themselves in eternal flux, and the thousandfold vault of the heavens powerfully conjoins with itself, and then the joy of life streams out of all things, out of the smallest and out of the greatest of stars, and all urgency, all conflict, is eternal rest in God the Lord.

Das Leben wohnt in jedem Sterne:
Er wandelt mit den andern gerne
Die selbsterwählte, reine Bahn;
Im innern Erdenball pulsieren
Die Kräfte, die zur Nacht uns führen
Und wieder zu dem Tag heran.

Nachts, wann gute Geister schweifen,
Schlaf dir von der Stirne streifen,
Mondenlicht und Sternenflimmern
Dich mit ewigem All umschimmern,
Scheinst du dir entkörpert schon,
Wagest dich an Gottes Thron.

Aber wenn der Tag die Welt
Wieder auf die Füße stellt,
Schwerlich möcht er dirs erfüllen
Mit der Frühe bestem Willen;
Zu Mittag schon wandelt sich
Morgentraum gar wunderlich.

Life dwells in every star: each gladly, with all the others, follows its pure self-chosen path; in the centre of the earth's globe throb the powers that move us into night and again into day.

At night, when good spirits wander abroad and wipe the sleep from your brow, and the eternal universe gleams round you in moonlight and glittering stars, you feel already disembodied and dare to approach the throne of God.

But when day puts the world on its feet again, your aspiration would be hard for it to fulfil, even with the best will of the morning; already the dreams of daybreak are most oddly transformed at noon.

Wär nicht das Auge sonnenhaft,
Die Sonne könnt es nie erblicken;
Läg nicht in uns des Gottes eigne Kraft,
Wie könnt uns Göttliches entzücken?

DER PANTHEIST

Was soll mir euer Hohn
Über das All und Eine?
Der Professor ist eine Person,
Gott ist keine.

Wie einer ist, so ist sein Gott;
Darum ward Gott so oft zu Spott.

Was der Mensch als Gott verehrt,
Ist sein eigenstes Innere herausgekehrt.

Ich habe nie mit euch gestritten,
Philisterpfaffen! Neiderbrut!
Unartig seid ihr wie die Briten,
Doch zahlt ihr lange nicht so gut.

If the eye were not sun-like it could not see the sun; if we did not carry within us the very power of the god, how could anything god-like delight us?

THE PANTHEIST

What are your gibes about the One and the Whole to me? A professor is a person; God is not.

As a man is, so is his God; that is what has often turned God to ridicule.

What man reveres as God is his own innermost being turned inside out.

I have never argued with you, you envious brood of philistine priests! You are as ill-mannered as the English, but you don't pay nearly so well.

WOLLTE Gott die Menschen belehren,
Mußt er ihnen nicht den Rücken kehren;
Und sollten sie auf ihr Bestes passen,
Mußt er sicht nicht schlecht behandeln lassen.

NIEMAND soll ins Kloster gehn,
Als er sei denn wolhl versehn
Mit gehörigem Sündenvorrat,
Damit es ihm so früh als spat
Nicht mög am Vergnügen fehlen,
Sich mit Reue durchzuquälen.

DER Gotteserde lichten Saal
Verdüstern sie zum Jammertal;
Daran entdecken wir geschwind,
Wie jämmerlich sie selber sind.

«WAS heißt du denn Sünde?»
Wie jedermann,
Wo ich finde,
Daß mans nicht lassen kann.

IF God wanted to instruct mankind, he needn't have turned his back on them; and if he wanted them to heed what was best for them, he needn't have let them treat him so badly.

LET no one go into a monastery unless he is well equipped with a suitable store of sins, to ensure that he shall never lack the pleasure of tormenting himself with remorse.

GOD's earth, this great shining room, they darken to a vale of misery; thereby at once revealing what miserable wretches they are themselves.

'WHAT's your definition of sin, then?' The same as anyone's: whatever I find someone unable to stop doing.

DAS ist eine von den alten Sünden;
Sie meinen: Rechnen, das sei Erfinden.

Und weil sie so viel Recht gehabt,
Sei ihr Unrecht mit Recht begabt.

Und weil ihre Wissenschaft exakt,
So sei keiner von ihnen vertrackt.

«WAS ist denn die Wissenschaft?»
Sie ist nur des Lebens Kraft.
Ihr erzeuget nicht das Leben,
Leben erst muß Leben geben.

ZIERLICH Denken und süß Erinnern
Ist das Leben im tiefsten Innern.

ANGEDENKEN an das Gute
Hält uns immer frisch bei Mute.

Angedenken an das Schöne
Ist das Heil der Erdensöhne.

Angedenken an das Liebe,
Glücklich! wenns lebendig bliebe.

Angedenken an das Eine
Bleibt das Beste, was ich meine.

THAT'S an old besetting sin; they think calculating is inventing. And that because they have been right so often, their wrong-headedness is right-minded. And that because their science is exact, none of them can be crazy.

'WHAT is science, then?' It is only the energy of life. None of you can beget life; only from life can life come.

LIFE in its deepest essence is a delightful thinking and a sweet remembering.

REMEMBRANCE of what is good keeps us high in spirit. Remembrance of what is beautiful is the salvation of mortal men. Remembrance of what is dear will be happiness, if it remains alive. Remembrance of the One is still the best thing I know.

ICH träumt und liebte sonnenklar;
Daß ich lebte, ward ich gewahr.

HAST du es so lange wie ich getrieben,
Versuche wie ich das Leben zu lieben.

WER recht will tun, immer und mit Lust,
Der hege wahre Lieb in Sinn und Brust.

WAS auch als Wahrheit oder Fabel
In tausend Büchern dir erscheint,
Das alles ist ein Turm zu Babel,
Wenn es die Liebe nicht vereint.

GLÜCKSELIG ist, wer Liebe rein genießt,
Weil doch zuletzt das Grab so Lieb als Haß verschließt.

DU sollst mit dem Tode zufrieden sein,
Warum machst du dir das Leben zur Pein?

I WAS dreaming and loving clear as day; I realized that I was alive.

IF you've been at it as long as I have, try to love life as I do.

IF you want always to do right, and to enjoy doing it, then let true love fill your mind and heart.

WHATEVER truths or fables you may find in a thousand books, it is all a tower of Babel unless love holds it together.

HE is happy who tastes the unmixed joy of love; for the grave closes in the end over both love and hatred.

YOU will have to be content with death, so why make your life a misery?

LEBENSREGEL

Willst du dir ein hübsch Leben zimmern,
Mußt ums Vergangne dich nicht bekümmern,
Und wäre dir auch was verloren,
Mußt immer tun wie neugeboren;
Was jeder Tag will, sollst du fragen,
Was jeder Tag will, wird er sagen;
Mußt dich an eigenem Tun ergötzen,
Was andre tun, das wirst du schätzen;
Besonders keinen Menschen hassen
Und das übrige Gott überlassen.

Eigenheiten, die werden schon haften;
Kultiviere deine Eigenschaften.

Überzeugung soll mir niemand rauben;
Wers besser weiß, der mag es glauben.

PRECEPT

If you want to make a good life for yourself, you must forget about the past, and even though you may have lost something, you must always behave like one new-born; you must ask: what does each day demand? and what each day demands, it will tell you; you must take delight in activity of your own, and you will then value the activity of others; above all you must hate no man, and leave all the rest to God.

You will always be stuck with your peculiarities; your qualities are what you must cultivate.

Let no one rob me of my conviction; if anyone knows better, let him believe it.

SPRUCH, WIDERSPRUCH

IHR müßt mich nicht durch Widerspruch verwirren!
Sobald man spricht, beginnt man schon zu irren.

DAS BESTE

WENN dirs in Kopf und Herzen schwirrt,
Was willst du Beßres haben!
Wer nicht mehr liebt und nicht mehr irrt,
Der lasse sich begraben.

«DIR warum doch verliert
Gleich alles Wert und Gewicht?»
Das Tun interessiert,
Das Getane nicht.

ALLES in der Welt läßt sich ertragen,
Nur nicht eine Reihe von schönen Tagen.

SAYING AND GAINSAYING

YOU needn't confuse me by contradicting! One cannot begin to speak
without beginning to err.

NOTHING BETTER

IF there is confusion in your head and in your heart, what more do you
want! A man who no longer loves and no longer errs should have himself
buried straight away.

'BUT why, for you, does everything at once lose all its value and impor-
tance?' Doing is interesting; what's done is dull.

ANYTHING in the world can be endured, except a series of wonderful days.

287

WER aber recht bequem ist und faul,
Flög dem eine gebratene Taube ins Maul,
Er würde höchlich sichs verbitten,
Wär sie nicht auch geschickt zerschnitten.

ANNONCE

«EIN Hündchen wird gesucht,
Das weder murrt, noch beißt,
Zerbrochene Gläser frißt
Und Diamanten scheißt».

Es ließe sich alles trefflich schlichten,
Könnte man die Sachen zweimal verrichten.

WER sich nicht nach der Decke streckt,
Dem bleiben die Füße unbedeckt.

WER mit dem Leben spielt,
Kommt nie zurecht;
Wer sich nicht selbst befiehlt,
Bleibt immer ein Knecht.

IF a man is a real lazy sluggard, a roasted pigeon could fly into his mouth and he would indignantly decline it unless it were skilfully carved as well.

ADVERTISEMENT

'WANTED: a small dog that neither growls nor bites, can eat broken glass and can shit diamonds.'

EVERYTHING could be very nicely arranged, if one could only do things twice over.

IF one does not lie according to the blanket, one's feet will be left uncovered.

A MAN who plays with life will never get anywhere; a man who cannot command himself will always be a slave.

«Wer ist ein unbrauchbarer Mann?»
Der nicht befehlen und auch nicht gehorchen kann.

Was ist ein Philister?
Ein hohler Darm,
Mit Furcht und Hoffnung ausgefüllt.
Daß Gott erbarm!

Wer immerdar nach Schatten greift,
Kann stets nur leere Luft erlangen:
Wer Schatten stets auf Schatten häuft,
Sieht endlich sich von düstrer Nacht umfangen.

Dem ist es schlecht in seiner Haut,
Der in seinen eignen Busen schaut.

Was hat dir das arme Glas getan?
Sieh deinen Spiegel nicht so häßlich an.

Ganz und gar
Bin ich ein armer Wicht.
Meine Träume sind nicht wahr,
Und meine Gedanken geraten nicht.

'What is a useless man?' One who can neither command nor obey.

What is a philistine? A hollow gut, stuffed with fears and hopes. Merciful God!

A man who is always snatching at shadows can never grasp anything but empty air; he who piles shadows upon shadows for ever will finally find himself enveloped in night and darkness.

It's an uneasy man who peers into his own mind.

What has the poor glass done to you? Don't give your mirror such a dirty look.

I really am a poor miserable wretch. My dreams aren't true, and my thoughts don't come to anything.

Suche nicht vergebne Heilung!
Unsrer Krankheit schwer Geheimnis
Schwankt zwischen Übereilung
Und zwischen Versäumnis.

Gehts in der Welt dir endlich schlecht,
Tu, was du willst, nur habe nicht recht.

Komm her! wir setzen uns zu Tisch;
Wen möchte solche Narrheit rühren!
Die Welt geht auseinander wie ein fauler Fisch,
Wir wollen sie nicht balsamieren.

Und was bleibt denn an dem Leben,
Wenn es alles ging zu Funken,
Wenn die Ehre mit dem Streben
Alles ist im Quark versunken.

Und doch kann dich nichts vernichten,
Wenn, Vergänglichem zum Trotze,
Willst dein Sehnen ewig richten
Erst zur Flasche, dann zur Fotze.

Seek no cure where there is none! Between leaping without looking, and letting opportunities slip, the grievous secret of our sickness is suspended.

If things end by going badly with you in this world, do anything you like except be in the right.

Come along, let's sit down to dinner; how can one be upset by such idiocy! The world is disintegrating like a rotten fish; let's not embalm it.

And what good is life, then, any longer, when it has all gone up in smoke — when all honour and all ambition have gone down into the rubbish-heap?
 Nevertheless you are proof against everything if, in defiance of change and decay, you perpetually direct your desires firstly to the bottle and secondly to the cunt.

Ja, schelte nur und fluche fort,
Es wird sich Beßres nie ergeben;
Denn Trost ist ein absurdes Wort:
Wer nicht verzweifeln kann, der muß nicht leben.

Gut verloren – etwas verloren!
Mußt rasch dich besinnen
Und neues gewinnen.
Ehre verloren – viel verloren!
Mußt Ruhm gewinnen,
Da werden die Leute sich anders besinnen.
Mut verloren – alles verloren!
Da wär es besser, nicht geboren.

Gott grüß euch, Brüder,
Sämtliche Oner und Aner!
Ich bin Weltbewohner,
Bin Weimaraner;
Ich habe diesem edlen Kreis
Durch Bildung mich empfohlen,
Und wer es etwa besser weiß,
Der mags woanders holen.

Yes – carry on cursing and fulminating; things will never get any better. For consolation is a ridiculous word: if one cannot despair, one need not live.

Property lost – something lost! You must think again quickly and win it afresh. *Honour* lost – much lost! You must win fame, and then people will think differently. *Courage* lost – everything lost! Better then not to have been born.

God save you, my brethren, with all your -isms and schisms! I am a citizen of the world, and a man of Weimar. I have established myself by culture in this choice society; and if anyone knows a better place, let him go to it.

DEN ORIGINALEN

Ein Quidam sagt: «Ich bin von keiner Schule;
Kein Meister lebt, mit dem ich buhle;
Auch bin ich weit davon entfernt,
Daß ich von Toten was gelernt.»
Das heißt, wenn ich ihn recht verstand:
Ich bin ein Narr auf eigne Hand.

Vom Vater hab ich die Statur,
Des Lebens ernstes Führen,
Vom Mütterchen die Frohnatur
Und Lust zu fabulieren.
Urahnherr war der Schönsten hold,
Das spukt so hin und wieder;
Urahnfrau liebte Schmuck und Gold,
Das zuckt wohl durch die Glieder.
Sind nun die Elemente nicht
Aus dem Komplex zu trennen,
Was ist denn an dem ganzen Wicht
Original zu nennen?

TO ALL WHO ARE ORIGINAL

A certain So-and-so declares: 'I belong to no school, I go a-whoring after no living master, and nothing could be further from me than to have learnt anything from the dead.' That is to say (if I have understood him aright): I am a fool after my own fashion.

From my father I get my stature and serious conduct of life; from mother dear my blithe nature and my *penchant* for telling stories. Great-grandpapa was one for the girls, and that has left one or two traces in me; great-grandmama was fond of jewellery and gold, and I daresay I have that under my skin. So if one is such a complex of inseparable elements, is there anything at all in the poor fellow that can be called original?

Gern wär ich Überlieferung los
Und ganz original;
Doch ist das Unternehmen groß
Und führt in manche Qual.
Als Autochthone rechnet ich
Es mir zur höchsten Ehre,
Wenn ich nicht gar zu wunderlich
Selbst Überlieferung wäre.

Das Alter ist ein höflich Mann:
Einmal übers andre klopft er an;
Aber nun sagt niemand: Herein!
Und vor der Türe will er nicht sein.
Da klinkt er auf, tritt ein so schnell,
Und nun heißts, er sei ein grober Gesell.

Wer dem Publikum dient, ist ein armes Tier;
Er quält sich ab, niemand bedankt sich dafür.

I should be glad to break free of tradition and be original right through; but that is a big undertaking and leads to much vexation of spirit. As a genuine earth-native I should regard it as a supreme point of honour, if I were not so strangely a tradition myself.

Old age is a polite gentleman: he knocks more than once at the door, but of course nobody says 'Come in!' And he doesn't want to be left standing outside. So he lifts the latch and quickly enters; and then people say he is an ill-mannered fellow.

The servant of the public is a poor brute; he wears himself down and gets thanks from no one.

TRÜGE gern noch länger des Lehrers Bürden,
Wenn Schüler nur nicht gleich Lehrer würden.

MICH nach- und umzubilden, mißzubilden
Versuchten sie seit vollen fünfzig Jahren;
Ich dächte doch, da konntest du erfahren,
Was an dir sei in Vaterlandsgefilden.
Du hast getollt zu deiner Zeit mit wilden,
Dämonisch genialen jungen Scharen,
Dann sachte schlossest du von Jahr zu Jahren
Dich näher an die Weisen, Göttlich-Milden.

HÄTTE Gott mich anders gewollt,
So hätt er mich anders gebaut;
Da er mir aber Talent gezollt,
Hat er mir viel vertraut.
Ich brauch es zur Rechten und Linken,
Weiß nicht, was daraus kommt;
Wenns nicht mehr frommt,
Wird er schon winken.

I SHOULD be glad to go on bearing a teacher's burdens, if only one's pupils didn't at once become teachers.

THEY have tried for fully fifty years to copy me, reshape me, and misshape me; I really think that should have taught me what role I play in my native land. One has acted the madman in one's time with a wild young crew of demonic geniuses; then gradually, from year to year, one has grown nearer to the wise and the divinely gentle.

IF God had wanted me different, he would have built me differently; but by endowing me with talent he has entrusted me with a lot. I use it left and right, not knowing what will come of it; when it is no longer any use, I'm sure he'll let me know.

DEMUT

SEH ich die Werke der Meister an,
So seh ich das, was sie getan;
Betracht ich meine Siebensachen,
Seh ich, was ich hätt sollen machen.

NEHMT nur mein Leben hin in Bausch
Und Bogen, wie ichs führe;
Andre verschlafen ihren Rausch,
Meiner steht auf dem Papiere.

TEILEN kann ich nicht das Leben,
Nicht das Innen, noch das Außen,
Allen muß das Ganze geben,
Um mit euch und mir zu hausen.
Immer hab ich nur geschrieben,
Wie ichs fühle, wie ichs meine,
Und so spalt ich mich, ihr Lieben,
Und bin immerfort der Eine.

HUMILITY

WHEN I look at the works of the masters, I see what they did; when I look at my own bits and pieces, I see what I ought to have done.

PLEASE take my life as a whole, for that is how I lead it. Other men sleep off their follies; mine remain in black and white.

I CANNOT divide life, cannot divide what is within and what is without; I must give all of you the whole, if I am to live with you and with myself. I have always written just what I felt, just what I thought; and thus, my dear friends, I split myself up and remain always one and the same.

«Du kommst nicht ins Ideen-Land!»
So bin ich doch am Ufer bekannt.
Wer die Inseln nicht zu erobern glaubt,
Dem ist Ankerwerfen doch wohl erlaubt.

Der Zeitungsleser sei gesegnet,
Der liest, was heute mir begegnet.

Ich wünsche mir eine hübsche Frau,
Die nicht alles nähme gar zu genau,
Doch aber gleich am besten verstände,
Wie ich mich selbst am besten befände.

Ich, Egoist! – Wenn ichs nicht besser wüßte!
Der Neid, das ist der Egoiste;
Und was ich auch für Wege geloffen,
Aufm Neidpfad habt ihr mich nie betroffen.

Den Dichter könnt ihr mir nicht nehmen,
Den Menschen geb ich euch preis;
Auch der darf sich nicht schämen,
Greift doch an euren Steiß.

'No admission for you to the Land of Ideas!' Well, I'm known on its shores anyway. If one is not aiming at conquest of the islands, I suppose one may be permitted to cast anchor.

Blessings upon the newspaper-reader who reads what is happening to me today.

I should like a pretty wife who would not be too particular, but who at the same time would understand best what suited me best.

I, an egoist! – What will they say next! It's envy that's the egoist; and whatever ways I may have walked in my time, you've never caught me in Envy Street.

You can't stop me being a poet, and you can say what you like of me as a man; the man needn't be ashamed either; just you feel your own rumps.

WENN ich dumm bin, lassen sie mich gelten;
Wenn ich recht hab, wollen sie mich schelten.

WAS soll ich viel lieben, was soll ich viel hassen?
Man lebt nur vom leben lassen.

GESELLSCHAFT

AUS einer großen Gesellschaft heraus
Ging einst ein stiller Gelehrter zu Haus.
Man fragte: Wie seid Ihr zufrieden gewesen?
«Wärens Bücher», sagt' er, «ich würd sie nicht lesen.»

MAN könnt erzogene Kinder gebären,
Wenn die Eltern erzogen wären.

ICH kann mich nicht bereden lassen,
Macht mir den Teufel nur nicht klein:
Ein Kerl, den alle Menschen hassen,
Der muß was sein!

WHEN I am silly they approve of me; when I am right they take me to task.

WHY should I love so much, why should I hate so much? One only lives by letting live.

SOCIETY

A QUIET scholar once left a large party and went home. He was asked: 'How did you like it?' 'If they were books,' he said, 'I should not read them.'

CHILDREN might be born well-brought-up, if the parents were well-brought-up themselves.

I REALLY cannot be persuaded – please just do not belittle the Devil! A fellow hated by the whole human race – he surely must be somebody!

Am Jüngsten Tag, vor Gottes Thron,
Stand endlich Held Napoleon.
Der Teufel hielt ein großes Register
Gegen denselben und seine Geschwister,
War ein wundersam verruchtes Wesen;
Satan fing an, es abzulesen.

Gott Vater, oder Gott der Sohn,
Einer von beiden sprach vom Thron,
Wenn nicht etwa gar der Heilige Geist
Das Wort genommen allermeist:

«Wiederhols nicht vor göttlichen Ohren!
Du sprichst wie die deutschen Professoren.
Wir wissen alles, mach es kurz!
Am Jüngsten Tag ists nur ein Furz.
Getraust du dich, ihn anzugreifen,
So magst du ihn nach der Hölle schleifen.»

Was ich nicht weiß,
Macht mich nicht heiß.
Und was ich weiß,
Machte mich heiß,
Wenn ich nicht wüßte,
Wie's werden müßte.

On the Day of Judgement, Napoleon the hero at last stood before God's throne. The Devil was holding a great catalogue against him and his hangers-on, full of strangely heinous doings; Satan began to read them out.

God the Father or God the Son, one or other of them, spoke from the throne – or maybe it was even the Holy Ghost who did most of the talking:

'Don't repeat all that in Our Divine hearing! You talk like a German professor. We know it all – cut it short. It's worth no more than a fart on the Day of Judgement. If you dare attack him, you can drag him off to Hell.'

I lose no sleep over what I don't know. And I should lose it over what I do know, if I didn't know how it's bound to turn out.

«Wie hast du an der Welt noch Lust,
Da alles schon dir ist bewußt?»
Gar wohl! Das Dümmste, was geschicht,
Weil ich es weiß, verdrießt mich nicht.
Mich könnte dies und das betrüben,
Hätt ichs nicht schon in Versen geschrieben.

Dichter gleichen Bären,
Die immer an eignen Pfoten zehren.

Jüngling, merke dir, in Zeiten,
Wo sich Geist und Sinn erhöht:
Daß die Muse zu *begleiten*,
Doch zu *leiten* nicht versteht.

Hier liegt ein überschlechter Poet.
Wenn er nur niemals aufersteht!

«Manches können wir nicht verstehn.»
Lebt nur fort, es wird schon gehn.

'How can you still enjoy the world when you know everything already?'
Certainly! The silliest things that happen don't annoy me, because I know
about them. And I might be saddened by one or two things, if I hadn't
already written poetry about them.

Poets are like bears, always gnawing their own paws.

Young man, remember, at times of exaltation of mind and spirit, that the
Muse can be a *companion*, but not a *guide*.

Here lies a really bad poet. Let's hope he'll never rise again!

'There are a number of things we can't understand.' Just carry on living,
you'll learn in time.

Iм Auslegen seid frisch und munter!
Legt ihrs nicht aus, so legt was unter.

Durch Vernünfteln wird Poesie vertrieben,
Aber sie mag das Vernünftige lieben.

Hast deine Kastanien zu lange gebraten;
Sie sind dir alle zu Kohlen geraten.

All unser redlichstes Bemühn
Glückt nur im unbewußten Momente.
Wie möchte denn die Rose blühn,
Wenn sie der Sonne Herrlichkeit erkennte!

Ja, das ist das rechte Gleis,
Daß man nicht weiß,
Was man denkt,
Wenn man denkt;
Alles ist als wie geschenkt.

Be bold and resolute in interpretation! If you can't work it out, then work
something into it.

Ratiocination drives Poetry away; but she is a friend of what is
reasonable.

Your chestnuts have been roasting too long; you've cooked them all into
cinders.

All our most honest toil succeeds only in unconscious moments. For how
would the rose blossom if it were aware of the splendour of the sun!

Yes, one is on the right track when one does not know what one is
thinking when one is thinking; everything is handed to one, as it were.

«WIE hast dus denn so weit gebracht?
Sie sagen, du habest es gut vollbracht!» –
Mein Kind! ich hab es klug gemacht:
Ich habe nie über das Denken gedacht.

«WOHL kamst du durch; so ging es allenfalls.»
Machs einer nach und breche nicht den Hals.

NICHTS vom Vergänglichen,
Wie's auch geschah!
Uns zu verewigen,
Sind wir ja da.

«ZU Goethes Denkmal was zahlst du jetzt?»
Fragt dieser, jener und der. –
Hätt ich mir nicht selbst ein Denkmal gesetzt,
Das Denkmal, wo käm es denn her?

'HOW did you get so far, then? They tell me you have achieved great things!' My child! I went about it wisely: I have never thought about the process of thinking.

'SO you've got by! Well, you managed it, anyhow.' Just you try to do it, and not break your neck.

NO more about things that perish, no matter how they perished! We are here, after all, to make ourselves eternal.

'WHAT are you contributing now for Goethe's memorial?' asks this man and the next man and the other man. If I hadn't set up a memorial for myself, where would my memorial come from?

Was der Dichter diesem Bande
Glaubend, hoffend anvertraut,
Werd im Kreise deutscher Lande
Durch des Künstlers Wirken laut.
So im Handeln, so im Sprechen
Liebevoll verkünd es weit:
Alle menschlichen Gebrechen
Sühnet reine Menschlichkeit.

URWORTE. ORPHISCH

ΔΑΙΜΩΝ, *Dämon*

Wie an dem Tag, der dich der Welt verliehen,
Die Sonne stand zum Gruße der Planeten,
Bist alsobald und fort und fort gediehen
Nach dem Gesetz, wonach du angetreten.
So mußt du sein, dir kannst du nicht entfliehen,
So sagten schon Sibyllen, so Propheten;
Und keine Zeit und keine Macht zerstückelt
Geprägte Form, die lebend sich entwickelt.

May the faith and hope which the poet entrusted to this volume* be sounded abroad throughout German lands by the actor's art. Lovingly, in action and speech, proclaim it thus far and wide: for all human frailties, pure humanity atones.

FIRST AND LAST WORDS. ORPHIC
Destiny

Even as the sun and planets stood, to salute one another, on the day you entered the world – even so you began straightway to grow and have continued to do so, according to the law that prevailed over your beginning. It is thus that you must be, you cannot escape yourself – the Sybils and Prophets said the same thing long ago; and no time nor power can destroy the shape that has been impressed upon evolving life.

* These lines were inscribed in a presentation copy of *Iphigenia on Tauris* which Goethe sent to an actor in 1827.

ΤΥΧΗ, *Das Zufällige*

Die strenge Grenze doch umgeht gefällig
Ein Wandelndes, das mit und um uns wandelt;
Nicht einsam bleibst du, bildest dich gesellig,
Und handelst wohl so, wie ein andrer handelt:
Im Leben ists bald hin-, bald widerfällig,
Es ist ein Tand und wird so durchgetandelt.
Schon hat sich still der Jahre Kreis geründet,
Die Lampe harrt der Flamme, die entzündet.

ΕΡΩΣ, *Liebe*

Die bleibt nicht aus! – Er stürzt vom Himmel nieder,
Wohin er sich aus alter Öde schwang,
Er schwebt heran auf luftigem Gefieder
Um Stirn und Brust den Frühlingstag entlang,
Scheint jetzt zu fliehn, vom Fliehen kehrt er wieder:
Da wird ein Wohl im Weh, so süß und bang.
Gar manches Herz verschwebt im Allgemeinen,
Doch widmet sich das edelste dem Einen.

Chance

And yet these stern bounds are obligingly transgressed by an element of change which moves with us and around us; one does not remain in isolation, one is moulded in society and falls in with the ways of others. Life falls out sometimes this way, sometimes that; it is a trifle, and thus it is trifled away. Already the circle of the years has quietly completed itself: the lamp awaits the kindling flame.

Love

And sure enough, it comes. The god, who once soared from the ancient wilderness up into heaven, plunges down thence towards us like a bird on airy pinions and flutters around our heads and breasts all through the spring day; at times he seems to withdraw, but he returns from his withdrawal; then our anguish is delight and our tremor is sweetness. Many a heart wanders and is lost in too general a love; but the noblest devotes itself to one object alone.

ΑΝΑΓΚΗ, *Nötigung*

Da ists denn wieder, wie die Sterne wollten:
Bedingung und Gesetz; und aller Wille
Ist nur ein Wollen, weil wir eben sollten,
Und vor dem Willen schweigt die Willkür stille;
Das Liebste wird vom Herzen weggescholten,
Dem harten Muß bequemt sich Will und Grille.
So sind wir scheinfrei denn, nach manchen Jahren
Nur enger dran, als wir am Anfang waren.

ΕΛΠΙΣ, *Hoffnung*

Doch solcher Grenze, solcher ehrnen Mauer
Höchst widerwärtge Pforte wird entriegelt,
Sie stehe nur mit alter Felsendauer!
Ein Wesen regt sich leicht und ungezügelt:
Aus Wolkendecke, Nebel, Regenschauer
Erhebt sie uns, mit ihr, durch sie beflügelt,
Ihr kennt sie wohl, sie schwärmt durch alle Zonen –
Ein Flügelschlag – und hinter uns Äonen!

Necessity

And then, once more, what the stars have decreed comes to pass – the condition, the law is imposed; and all our will is a mere willing of what we were bound to do, and before this will caprice is dumb; what we have loved most dearly is angrily driven from our hearts, and wish and whim submit to hard compulsion. Such then is our illusory freedom – after many years we are still faster bound than at the start.

Hope

And yet the dread gate in this imprisoning brazen wall can be unbolted, though it stand firm as ancient rock! There is a Being that moves, lightly and untrammelled, lifting us with her out of cloudy skies, fog and showers of rain, giving us wings: you know her well, she roves from zone to zone: one wing-beat, and aeons lie behind us!

UM MITTERNACHT

Uм Mitternacht ging ich, nicht eben gerne,
Klein, kleiner Knabe, jenen Kirchhof hin
Zu Vaters Haus, des Pfarrers; Stern am Sterne,
Sie leuchteten doch alle gar zu schön;
 Um Mitternacht.

Wenn ich dann ferner in des Lebens Weite,
Zur Liebsten mußte, mußte, weil sie zog,
Gestirn und Nordschein über mir im Streite,
Ich gehend, kommend Seligkeiten sog;
 Um Mitternacht.

Bis dann zuletzt des vollen Mondes Helle
So klar und deutlich mir ins Finstere drang,
Auch der Gedanke willig, sinnig, schnelle
Sich ums Vergangne wie ums Künftige schlang;
 Um Mitternacht.

AT MIDNIGHT

Aт midnight I would walk, rather unwillingly, as a very little boy, along past that churchyard to father's, to the parson's house; star upon star, how beautifully they all shone, at midnight.

Then, later, far back in life, when I was going to my beloved, drawn by her compulsion, the stars and the northern lights would be at war above me, and as I went and as I came I sucked in happiness with every breath – at midnight.

Until at last the full moon's radiance penetrated my darkness so clearly and plainly, and thought willingly, meaningfully, swiftly embraced the past and the future; at midnight.

TRILOGIE DER LEIDENSCHAFT

AN WERTHER

NOCH einmal wagst du, vielbeweinter Schatten,
Hervor dich an das Tageslicht,
Begegnest mir auf neu beblümten Matten,
Und meinen Anblick scheust du nicht.
Es ist, als ob du lebtest in der Frühe,
Wo uns der Tau auf Einem Feld erquickt
Und nach des Tages unwillkommner Mühe
Der Scheidesonne letzter Strahl entzückt;
Zum Bleiben ich, zum Scheiden du erkoren,
Gingst du voran – und hast nicht viel verloren.

Des Menschen Leben scheint ein herrlich Los:
Der Tag wie lieblich, so die Nacht wie groß!
Und wir, gepflanzt in Paradieses Wonne,
Genießen kaum der hocherlauchten Sonne,
Da kämpft sogleich verworrene Bestrebung
Bald mit uns selbst und bald mit der Umgebung;

TRILOGY OF PASSION

TO WERTHER

ONCE again, much-lamented shade, you venture out into the daylight, encountering me in freshly flowering meadows, and are unabashed to see me. It is as if you were alive again in those early days when the same field's dew refreshed us both, and after the day's unwelcome toil the departing sun's last ray enraptured us. I was destined to remain, you to depart; you went on ahead of me – and have missed very little.

One might think oneself happy to be allotted a human life; how sweet the day seems, and the night how splendid! And planted in a paradise of delight, we have scarcely begun to enjoy the magnificent and lofty sun when a confused impulse at once comes into conflict now with ourselves and now with our environment; neither harmonizes with the other as we would wish;

Keins wird vom andern wünschenswert ergänzt,
Von außen düsterts, wenn es innen glänzt,
Ein glänzend Äußres deckt ein trüber Blick,
Da steht es nah – und man verkennt das Glück.

Nun glauben wirs zu kennen! Mit Gewalt
Ergreift uns Liebreiz weiblicher Gestalt:
Der Jüngling, froh wie in der Kindheit Flor,
Im Frühling tritt als Frühling selbst hervor,
Entzückt, erstaunt, wer dies ihm angetan?
Er schaut umher – die Welt gehört ihm an.
Ins Weite zieht ihn unbefangne Hast,
Nichts engt ihn ein, nicht Mauer, nicht Palast;
Wie Vögelschar an Wäldergipfeln streift,
So schwebt auch er, der um die Liebste schweift,
Er sucht vom Äther, den er gern verläßt,
Den treuen Blick, und dieser hält ihn fest.

gloom gathers without when the light is shining within, and a bright external prospect is hidden from the clouded gaze – thus happiness is at hand, and we fail to recognize it.

Yet now we think we have grasped it! A woman's sweet shape casts a strong spell on us; the young man, happy as in the flower of childhood, steps forth in the spring and is himself the spring – he is delighted, astonished, wonders who can have done this to him; he gazes round, and the world is his. Impulsive haste draws him afar, neither walls nor palaces constrain him. As birds that fly round wooded peaks, so he hovers, circling round his beloved; from the airy heights, ready to swoop down, he seeks her loving glance, and it holds him captive.

Doch erst zu früh und dann zu spät gewarnt,
Fühlt er den Flug gehemmt, fühlt sich umgarnt.
Das Wiedersehn ist froh, das Scheiden schwer,
Das Wieder-Wiedersehn beglückt noch mehr,
Und Jahre sind im Augenblick ersetzt;
Doch tückisch harrt das Lebewohl zuletzt.

Du lächelst, Freund, gefühlvoll, wie sich ziemt:
Ein gräßlich Scheiden machte dich berühmt;
Wir feierten dein kläglich Mißgeschick,
Du ließest uns zu Wohl und Weh zurück.
Dann zog uns wieder ungewisse Bahn
Der Leidenschaften labyrinthisch an;
Und wir, verschlungen wiederholter Not,
Dem Scheiden endlich – Scheiden ist der Tod!
Wie klingt es rührend, wenn der Dichter singt,
Den Tod zu meiden, den das Scheiden bringt!
Verstrickt in solche Qualen, halbverschuldet,
Geb ihm ein Gott zu sagen, was er duldet.

But having first been warned too soon, and then too late, he feels his
flight hindered, feels himself ensnared. To see her again is happiness, to
part from her is grievous, to see her yet again gives him even greater joy,
and years are requited in a single moment; but at the last a cruel farewell
lies in wait for him.

You smile, my friend, and with feeling, as is appropriate; for a departure
full of horror has made you renowned. We commemorated your lament-
able fate, and you left us behind you, for better or for worse. And then
once more we were drawn along an uncertain labyrinthine path of passion:
for us there is complicated oft-repeated anguish, and finally the departure
– the parting which is death! How touchingly poets sing, evading the mor-
tal blow of this separation! Entangled in such torments, and themselves
half to blame, may some god grant them the voice to tell of what they must
endure.

ELEGIE

Und wenn der Mensch in seiner Qual verstummt,
Gab mir ein Gott zu sagen, was ich leide.

WAS soll ich nun vom Wiedersehen hoffen,
Von dieses Tages noch geschloßner Blüte?
Das Paradies, die Hölle steht dir offen;
Wie wankelsinnig regt sichs im Gemüte! –
Kein Zweifeln mehr! Sie tritt ans Himmelstor,
Zu ihren Armen hebt sie dich empor.

So warst du denn im Paradies empfangen,
Als wärst du wert des ewig schönen Lebens;
Dir blieb kein Wunsch, kein Hoffen, kein Verlangen,
Hier war das Ziel des innigsten Bestrebens,
Und in dem Anschaun dieses einzig Schönen
Versiegte gleich der Quell sehnsüchtiger Tränen.

Wie regte nicht der Tag die raschen Flügel,
Schien die Minuten vor sich her zu treiben!
Der Abendkuß, ein treu verbindlich Siegel:
So wird es auch der nächsten Sonne bleiben.
Die Stunden glichen sich in zartem Wandern
Wie Schwestern zwar, doch keine ganz den andern.

ELEGY

And if tormented humanity is dumb,
some god has given me the voice to tell of what I suffer.

What have I to hope from this reunion, from the still unopened blossom of this day? The gates of paradise and of hell stand open for me; with what hesitancy my mind is moved! – Yet now begone, misgivings! She appears at the heavenly threshold, and one is lifted up into her arms.

And thus one was received into paradise, as if worthy of an eternity of beautiful life; not a wish, not a hope, not a desire remained – here was the goal of one's innermost aspiration, and in the vision of this unique beauty the fountain of one's passionate tears at once was dried.

How swiftly Day beat his wings, and seemed to drive the minutes before him! The kiss at evening, a faithful bond, a token that thus it should remain when the next sun rose. The hours moved softly by; like sisters indeed they resembled each other, yet none was quite like the rest.

309

Der Kuß, der letzte, grausam süß, zerschneidend
Ein herrliches Geflecht verschlungner Minnen.
Nun eilt, nun stockt der Fuß, die Schwelle meidend,
Als trieb' ein Cherub flammend ihn von hinnen;
Das Auge starrt auf düstrem Pfad verdrossen,
Es blickt zurück, die Pforte steht verschlossen.

Und nun verschlossen in sich selbst, als hätte
Dies Herz sich nie geöffnet, selige Stunden
Mit jedem Stern des Himmels um die Wette
An ihrer Seite leuchtend nicht empfunden;
Und Mißmut, Reue, Vorwurf, Sorgenschwere
Belastens nun in schwüler Atmosphäre.

Ist denn die Welt nicht übrig? Felsenwände,
Sind sie nicht mehr gekrönt von heiligen Schatten?
Die Ernte, reift sie nicht? Ein grün Gelände,
Zieht sichs nicht hin am Fluß durch Busch und Matten?
Und wölbt sich nicht das überweltlich Große,
Gestaltenreiche, bald Gestaltenlose?

The last kiss of all, cruelly sweet, tearing asunder a splendid tissue of intertwining desires. The foot, in faltering haste, now flees that threshold, as if a fiery cherub drove it hence; the eye stares frustrated on a darkling path, and when it looks back the gate is still closed.

And now the heart is imprisoned within itself, as if it had never opened, never known those blessed hours at her side when it vied in radiance with all the stars of heaven; and vexation, remorse, self-reproach, a burden of anxiety, now weigh it down, and sultry weather surrounds it.

Is there not still the world? Are rocky cliffs no longer crowned with holy shadows? Does the harvest not ripen? Does a green countryside of bushes and fields not lie along the river? and does the great transcendent vault not still fill itself with shapes and empty itself of them again?

Wie leicht und zierlich, klar und zart gewoben
Schwebt, seraphgleich, aus ernster Wolken Chor,
Als glich' es ihr, am blauen Äther droben
Ein schlank Gebild aus lichtem Duft empor!
So sahst du sie in frohem Tanze walten,
Die lieblichste der lieblichsten Gestalten.

Doch nur Momente darfst dich unterwinden,
Ein Luftgebild statt ihrer festzuhalten;
Ins Herz zurück! dort wirst dus besser finden,
Dort regt sie sich in wechselnden Gestalten:
Zu Vielen bildet Eine sich hinüber,
So tausendfach, und immer, immer lieber.

Wie zum Empfang sie an den Pforten weilte
Und mich von dannauf stufenweis beglückte,
Selbst nach dem letzten Kuß mich noch ereilte,
Den letztesten mir auf die Lippen drückte:
So klar beweglich bleibt das Bild der Lieben
Mit Flammenschrift ins treue Herz geschrieben.

How lightly and delicately, clearly and tenderly fashioned, like a hovering seraph, from amid the stern chorus of the clouds, up yonder against the blue sky a slender figure of bright haze rises, as if it were her own! It was thus that you saw her blithely dancing, the loveliest shape of all.

But do not presume to hold fast an airy image in her stead for more than a few moments; return into your heart, for there you will more readily find her. There she lives and moves in changing forms: though ever one, she takes on many aspects – a thousand times different, and ever more dear.

How she waited by the gates to receive me, and from then on increased my rapture step by step, and even after the last kiss hastened after me and caught me, to press the last of all upon my lips – this image of my darling, clear and active, is inscribed with letters of fire upon my faithful heart.

Ins Herz, das fest, wie zinnenhohe Mauer,
Sich ihr bewahrt und sie in sich bewahret,
Für sie sich freut an seiner eignen Dauer,
Nur weiß von sich, wenn sie sich offenbaret,
Sich freier fühlt in so geliebten Schranken
Und nur noch schlägt, für alles ihr zu danken.

War Fähigkeit, zu lieben, war Bedürfen
Von Gegenliebe weggelöscht, verschwunden,
Ist Hoffnungslust zu freudigen Entwürfen,
Entschlüssen, rascher Tat sogleich gefunden!
Wenn Liebe je den Liebenden begeistet,
Ward es an mir aufs lieblichste geleistet;

Und zwar durch sie! – Wie lag ein innres Bangen
Auf Geist und Körper, unwillkommner Schwere:
Von Schauerbildern rings der Blick umfangen
Im wüsten Raum beklommner Herzensleere;
Nun dämmert Hoffnung von bekannter Schwelle,
Sie selbst erscheint in milder Sonnenhelle.

Upon my heart, which preserves itself for her and her within itself, steadfast as tall battlements; which rejoices for her sake in its own continuance, knows itself only when she makes herself known, feels itself liberated by such well-loved bonds, and now has no beat but of gratitude to her for everything.

Its power to love, its need for love in return, had burnt out and vanished away, but at once I found again the glad impulse to hope and to make plans, to take decisions and quick action! For if love has ever inspired lovers, it did so most delightfully to me:

and that was her doing! – How heavy and irksome a burden of inward disquiet lay upon my mind and body: images of dread wherever I looked, in the waste land of the stifled empty heart! And now hope dawns on a familiar threshold: she herself appears in a mild radiance of sunlight.

Dem Frieden Gottes, welcher euch hienieden
Mehr als Vernunft beseliget – wir lesens –
Vergleich ich wohl der Liebe heitern Frieden
In Gegenwart des allgeliebten Wesens;
Da ruht das Herz, und nichts vermag zu stören
Den tiefsten Sinn, den Sinn: ihr zu gehören.

In unsers Busens Reine wogt ein Streben,
Sich einem Höhern, Reinern, Unbekannten
Aus Dankbarkeit freiwillig hinzugeben,
Enträtselnd sich den ewig Ungenannten;
Wir heißens: fromm sein! – Solcher seligen Höhe
Fühl ich mich teilhaft, wenn ich vor ihr stehe.

Vor ihrem Blick, wie vor der Sonne Walten,
Vor ihrem Atem, wie vor Frühlingslüften,
Zerschmilzt, so längst sich eisig starr gehalten,
Der Selbstsinn tief in winterlichen Grüften;
Kein Eigennutz, kein Eigenwille dauert,
Vor ihrem Kommen sind sie weggeschauert.

To the peace of God, which (we read) brings here on earth a blessedness
that passes all understanding, I may compare the tranquil peace of love in
the presence of the object of all our love; then the heart rests, and nothing
can trouble that deepest sense, our sense of belonging to her.

In the clear depths of our soul there springs an impulse to give ourselves
freely, in gratitude, to something higher, purer, and unknown, and thus to
unriddle the eternal Unnamed; this we call piety. It is in this high blessed-
ness I seem to participate when I stand before her.

Before her gaze as before the might of the sun, before her breath as be-
fore warm breezes of spring, cold long-unyielding self-regard thaws and
melts away; no self-will, no self-interest can endure – they wilt and dissolve
at her coming.

Es ist, als wenn sie sagte: «Stund um Stunde
Wird uns das Leben freundlich dargeboten.
Das Gestrige ließ uns geringe Kunde,
Das Morgende – zu wissen ists verboten;
Und wenn ich je mich vor dem Abend scheute,
Die Sonne sank und sah noch, was mich freute.

Drum tu wie ich und schaue, froh verständig,
Dem Augenblick ins Auge! Kein Verschieben!
Begegn ihm schnell, wohlwollend wie lebendig,
Im Handeln seis, zur Freude seis dem Lieben.
Nur wo du bist, sei alles, immer kindlich,
So bist du alles, bist unüberwindlich.»

Du hast gut reden, dacht ich: zum Geleite
Gab dir ein Gott die Gunst des Augenblickes,
Und jeder fühlt an deiner holden Seite
Sich augenblicks den Günstling des Geschickes;
Mich schreckt der Wink, von dir mich zu entfernen –
Was hilft es mir, so hohe Weisheit lernen!

It is as if she were to say: 'Hour by kindly hour, life is offered to us; our yesterdays have left little record behind, and we are forbidden to know our tomorrows; and if ever, at evening, my heart misgave me, the setting sun still shone on sights that made me glad.

'Do then as I do, and face the Moment, with joy and understanding, and without procrastination! Meet it quickly, with a good and lively will, whether in action or in pleasure. Beloved, be only where you are and be wholly there – be ever childlike, and you will then be all things, and be unconquerable.'

You may well say so (I thought): by some god's favour, the grace of the moment attends your glance, and in your sweet presence, in the twinkling of an eye, every man feels himself fortune's favourite; but to me has come the terrible moment of banishment from you – of what use can it be to me to learn such lofty wisdom!

Nun bin ich fern! Der jetzigen Minute,
Was ziemt denn der? Ich wüßt es nicht zu sagen;
Sie bietet mir zum Schönen manches Gute,
Das lastet nur, ich muß mich ihm entschlagen.
Mich treibt umher ein unbezwinglich Sehnen,
Da bleibt kein Rat als grenzenlose Tränen.

So quellt denn fort und fließet unaufhaltsam;
Doch nie gelängs, die innre Glut zu dämpfen!
Schon rasts und reißt in meiner Brust gewaltsam,
Wo Tod und Leben grausend sich bekämpfen.
Wohl Kräuter gäbs, des Körpers Qual zu stillen;
Allein dem Geist fehlts am Entschluß und Willen,

Fehlts am Begriff: wie sollt er sie vermissen?
Er wiederholt ihr Bild zu tausendmalen.
Das zaudert bald, bald wird es weggerissen,
Undeutlich jetzt und jetzt im reinsten Strahlen;
Wie könnte dies geringstem Troste frommen,
Die Ebb und Flut, das Gehen wie das Kommen?

*

I am far from you now. This present minute – what does it demand? I cannot tell. It offers me many good and lovely things; they are only a burden, which I must renounce. An irresistible longing drives me hither and thither; unending tears are my only counsel.

Flow on then, tears, and flow unquenchably – though you could never still this fire within me! Already my heart is torn by a terrible frenzy, by a hideous life-and-death struggle. There may be herbs that can heal the body's pain, but one's mind lacks the power to will or to decide,

or to grasp the very idea of being without her. A thousand times it evokes within itself her image, which is sometimes slow in coming and sometimes snatched away – now indistinct and now radiantly clear. How can this yield the slightest comfort, this ebb and flow, this going and coming?

*

Verlaßt mich hier, getreue Weggenossen!
Laßt mich allein am Fels, in Moor und Moos;
Nur immer zu! Euch ist die Welt erschlossen,
Die Erde weit, der Himmel hehr und groß;
Betrachtet, forscht, die Einzelheiten sammelt,
Naturgeheimnis werde nachgestammelt.

Mir ist das All, ich bin mir selbst verloren,
Der ich noch erst den Göttern Liebling war;
Sie prüften mich, verliehen mir Pandoren,
So reich an Gütern, reicher an Gefahr;
Sie drängten mich zum gabeseligen Munde,
Sie trennen mich, und richten mich zugrunde.

AUSSÖHNUNG

D IE Leidenschaft bringt Leiden! – Wer beschwichtigt,
Beklommnes Herz, dich, das zu viel verloren?
Wo sind die Stunden, überschnell verflüchtigt?
Vergebens war das Schönste dir erkoren!
Trüb ist der Geist, verworren das Beginnen;
Die hehre Welt, wie schwindet sie den Sinnen!

Leave me here, faithful comrades! leave me alone amid rocks and marsh and moss! Hold to your course! To you the world lies open, the earth is wide, the heavens splendid and great; examine, investigate, collect details, and slowly spell out Nature's mystery.

I have lost the whole world, I have lost myself – I who but lately was the darling of the gods. They put me to the test, they gave me Pandora with her abundant store of blessings and greater abundance of danger. They pressed me to the bountiful lips – they sunder me from them, and destroy me.

RECONCILEMENT

Passion brings pain! – Who shall soothe you, anguished heart that has lost too much? Where are the hours that melted away all too swiftly? In vain you were granted a vision of supreme beauty! One's mind is dulled, one's purposes confused; and the world's splendour, how it fades away before one's senses!

Da schwebt hervor Musik mit Engelsschwingen,
Verflicht zu Millionen Tön um Töne,
Des Menschen Wesen durch und durch zu dringen,
Zu überfüllen ihn mit ewger Schöne:
Das Auge netzt sich, fühlt im höhern Sehnen
Den Götter-Wert der Töne wie der Tränen.

Und so das Herz erleichtert merkt behende
Daß es noch lebt und schlägt und möchte schlagen,
Zum reinsten Dank der überreichen Spende
Sich selbst erwidernd willig darzutragen.
Da fühlte sich – o daß es ewig bliebe! –
Das Doppel-Glück der Töne wie der Liebe.

PARIA

DES PARIA GEBET

Grosser Brahma, Herr der Mächte!
Alles ist von deinem Samen,
Und so bist du der Gerechte!
Hast du denn allein die Brahmen,

But now, on wings of angels, music comes forth and rises, making a million notes intertwine, penetrating man's innermost being, filling him to overflowing with eternal beauty: his eyes fill with moisture and feel, with sublime longing, the divinity of music and of tears.

And his heart thus lightened straightway notices that it is still alive and beating, and wishing to beat and in pure gratitude to offer itself up in willing requital for this too generous gift. It was then that one felt – oh, that it could be for ever! – the double joy of music and of love.

PARIAH

THE PARIAH'S PRAYER

Great Brahma, Lord of the Powers! All creatures were engendered by thee, and for this reason thou art just! Didst thou, then, create only the

Nur die Rajahs und die Reichen,
Hast du sie allein geschaffen?
Oder bist auch dus, der Affen
Werden ließ und unsresgleichen?

Edel sind wir nicht zu nennen:
Denn das Schlechte, das gehört uns,
Und was andre tödlich kennen,
Das alleine, das vermehrt uns.
Mag dies für die Menschen gelten,
Mögen sie uns doch verachten;
Aber du, du sollst uns achten,
Denn du könntest alle schelten.

Also, Herr, nach diesem Flehen,
Segne mich zu deinem Kinde;
Oder eines laß entstehen,
Das auch mich mit dir verbinde!
Denn du hast den Bajaderen
Eine Göttin selbst erhoben;
Auch wir andern, dich zu loben,
Wollen solch ein Wunder hören.

Brahmans, only the Rajahs and the rich, these alone? Or didst thou, too,
give life to apes and to creatures like us?

We cannot be called noble: for all that is vile is ours, and we only in-
crease by what others find deadly. This, indeed, is true for men, and they
may well despise us; but thou – thou must honour us, for thou couldst find
fault with everyone.

Therefore, Lord, after this supplication, bless me and make me thy
child; or create some being who will connect even me with thee! For even
for the dancing-girls thou hast raised up a goddess; and we too, to praise
thee, wish to hear of a similar miracle.

LEGENDE

Wasser holen geht die reine
Schöne Frau des hohen Brahmen,
Des verehrten, fehlerlosen,
Ernstester Gerechtigkeit.
Täglich von dem heiligen Flusse
Holt sie köstlichstes Erquicken –
Aber wo ist Krug und Eimer?
Sie bedarf derselben nicht.
Seligem Herzen, frommen Händen
Ballt sich die bewegte Welle
Herrlich zu kristallner Kugel;
Diese trägt sie, frohen Busens,
Reiner Sitte, holden Wandelns,
Vor den Gatten in das Haus.

Heute kommt die morgendliche
Im Gebet zu Ganges' Fluten,
Beugt sich zu der klaren Fläche –
Plötzlich überraschend spiegelt,
Aus des höchsten Himmels Breiten
Über ihr vorübereilend,
Allerlieblichste Gestalt

THE LEGEND

The pure and beautiful wife of the lofty Brahman – the revered and irreproachable, most grave in his justice – walks to fetch water. Daily she brings most precious refreshment from the sacred river – but where are her jug and pitcher? She does not need them. Since her heart is at peace and her hands virtuous, the moving liquid element solidifies into a splendid crystal ball; and this she carries, full of joy, morally untainted, gracious in her demeanour, home to her husband.

Today, early in the morning, she comes in prayer to Ganges' waters, and stoops over the clear surface: suddenly, unexpectedly, they mirror – speeding by above her from the heights of the wide heavens – the most enchanting noble shape of a young man, created by the primordial beautiful

Hehren Jünglings, den des Gottes
Uranfänglich schönes Denken
Aus dem ewgen Busen schuf.
Solchen schauend, fühlt ergriffen
Von verwirrenden Gefühlen
Sie das innere tiefste Leben,
Will verharren in dem Anschaun,
Weist es weg, da kehrt es wieder,
Und verworren strebt sie flutwärts,
Mit unsichrer Hand zu schöpfen:
Aber ach! sie schöpft nicht mehr!
Denn des Wassers heilige Welle
Scheint zu fliehn, sich zu entfernen,
Sie erblickt nur hohler Wirbel
Grause Tiefen unter sich.

Arme sinken, Tritte straucheln,
Ists denn auch der Pfad nach Hause?
Soll sie zaudern? soll sie fliehen?
Will sie denken, wo Gedanke,
Rat und Hilfe gleich versagt? –
Und so tritt sie vor den Gatten;
Er erblickt sie, Blick ist Urteil,
Hohen Sinns ergreift das Schwert er,

thought that rises from the god's eternal bosom. Seeing him, she feels her
innermost deepest being seized by confusing emotions; she wishes to gaze
on at this sight; she dismisses it, but it returns; and in confusion she
reaches out her uncertain hands to draw water; but alas! she can no longer
draw it! For the water's holy wave seems to retreat, to recede, and she sees
beneath her only dreadful eddying gulfs.

Her arms sink, her steps stumble; is this indeed her homeward path?
Shall she hesitate? shall she run away? Can she try to think, when thought
and counsel and help all fail her? – And thus she comes before her husband;
he looks at her, his look is judgement; in high determination he seizes his

Schleppt sie zu dem Totenhügel,
Wo Verbrecher büßend bluten.
Wüßte sie zu widerstreben?
Wüßte sie sich zu entschuldgen,
Schuldig, keiner Schuld bewußt?

Und er kehrt mit blutigem Schwerte
Sinnend zu der stillen Wohnung;
Da entgegnet ihm der Sohn.
«Wessen Blut ists? Vater! Vater!» –
Der Verbrecherin! – «Mitnichten!
Denn es starret nicht am Schwerte
Wie verbrecherische Tropfen,
Fließt wie aus der Wunde frisch.
Mutter! Mutter! tritt heraus her!
Ungerecht war nie der Vater,
Sage, was er jetzt verübt!» –
Schweige! schweige! 's ist das ihre! –
«Wessen ist es?» – Schweige! schweige! –
«Wäre meiner Mutter Blut!!!
Was geschehen? was verschuldet?
Her das Schwert! ergriffen hab ichs;
Deine Gattin magst du töten,
Aber meine Mutter nicht!

sword and drags her to the Hill of the Dead, where criminals pay the price with their blood. Could she resist? could she exculpate herself, guilty as she is, though without knowledge of guilt?

And with bloody sword he returns in meditation to his silent house; there his son meets him. 'Whose blood is this? Father! father!' 'Hers, the criminal's.' 'That cannot be! For it is not sticking to the sword as the drops of criminals' blood do; it is running as if fresh from the wound. Mother, mother! come forth! My father was never unjust: tell me what he now has done.' 'Be silent! be silent! it is hers!' 'Whose?' 'Be silent! be silent!' 'My mother's blood!!! What has happened? What was her offence? Give me your sword! I have it in my hand. You may kill your wife, but not my

In die Flammen folgt die Gattin
Ihrem einzig Angetrauten,
Seiner einzig teuren Mutter
In das Schwert der treue Sohn.»

Halt, o halte! rief der Vater,
Noch ist Raum, enteil, enteile!
Füge Haupt dem Rumpfe wieder,
Du berührest mit dem Schwerte,
Und lebendig folgt sie dir.

Eilend, atemlos erblickt er
Staunend zweier Frauen Körper
Überkreuzt, und so die Häupter –
Welch Entsetzen! welche Wahl!
Dann der Mutter Haupt erfaßt er,
Küßt es nicht, das tot erblaßte;
Auf des nächsten Rumpfes Lücke
Setzt ers eilig, mit dem Schwerte
Segnet er das fromme Werk.

Aufersteht ein Riesenbildnis.—
Von der Mutter teuren Lippen,
Göttlich-unverändert-süßen,
Tönt das grausenvolle Wort:
Sohn, o Sohn, welch Übereilen!

mother! A wife follows her only-wedded spouse into the flames, and a
loyal son follows his only-beloved mother on to the sword.'

'Stop, oh, stop!' cried the father. 'There is still time, go quickly, quickly!
Fit the head to the trunk again, touch her with your sword, and she will
follow you alive.'

Breathlessly hastening, he sees with astonishment the bodies of two
women lying one across the other, likewise the heads – oh, horrible choice!
Then he seizes his mother's head, and does not kiss it, dead and pale as it is,
and hastily sets it on the stump of the torso nearest to it; with his sword he
blesses this work of piety.

And a gigantic shape rises to life again. From his mother's dear lips,
changelessly divine and sweet, he hears words of horror: 'Son, oh son!

Deiner Mutter Leichnam dorten,
Neben ihm das freche Haupt
Der Verbrecherin, des Opfers
Waltender Gerechtigkeit!
Mich nun hast du ihrem Körper
Eingeimpft auf ewige Tage:
Weisen Wollens, wilden Handelns
Werd ich unter Göttern sein;
Ja, des Himmelsknaben Bildnis
Webt so schön vor Stirn und Auge—
Senkt sichs in das Herz herunter,
Regt es tolle Wutbegier.
Immer wird es wiederkehren,
Immer steigen, immer sinken,
Sich verdüstern, sich verklären:
So hat Brahma dies gewollt.
Er gebot ja buntem Fittich,
Klarem Antlitz, schlanken Gliedern,
Göttlich-einzigem Erscheinen,
Mich zu prüfen, zu verführen;
Denn von oben kommt Verführung,
Wenns den Göttern so beliebt.
Und so soll ich, die Brahmane,
Mit dem Haupt im Himmel weilend,
Fühlen, Paria, dieser Erde
Niederziehende Gewalt.

what reckless haste! There is your mother's corpse, and beside it the head of a wanton criminal woman, a victim of the rule of justice! You have now engrafted me on to her body in perpetuity. Among the gods I shall be wise in my intentions and uncontrolled in my actions; yes, the image of that son of heaven floats in such beauty before my face and eyes, but when it penetrates down to the heart it arouses a mad fury of lust. It will continue to return, and for ever be rising and sinking, darkening and filling with light, for thus Brahma has willed. For it was he who commanded those slender limbs, that divine unique manifestation, to test me and seduce me; for seduction comes from above, if the gods so please. And thus I, a Brahman, though my head remains in heaven, must feel, as a Pariah, the earth's downward-drawing power.

Sohn, ich sende dich dem Vater!
Tröste! – Nicht ein traurig Büßen,
Stumpfes Harren, stolz Verdienen
Halt euch in der Wildnis fest;
Wandert aus durch alle Welten,
Wandelt hin durch alle Zeiten
Und verkündet auch Geringstem:
Daß ihn Brahma droben hört!

Ihm ist keiner der Geringste –
Wer sich mit gelähmten Gliedern,
Sich mit wild zerstörtem Geiste,
Düster, ohne Hilf und Rettung,
Sei er Brahma, sei er Paria,
Mit dem Blick nach oben kehrt,
Wirds empfinden, wirds erfahren:
Dort erglühen tausend Augen,
Ruhend lauschen tausend Ohren,
Denen nichts verborgen bleibt.

Heb ich mich zu seinem Throne,
Schaut er mich, die Grausenhafte,
Die er gräßlich umgeschaffen,
Muß er ewig mich bejammern:
Euch zugute komme das.

'Son, I send you to your father! Console him! Let no dismal penance, obstinate inertia or proud merit-earning imprison you in the wilderness; wander forth through all worlds, journey through all ages, and proclaim, even to the least of men, that Brahma in heaven hears him!

'To him, none is the least of men – as anyone, whether Brahman or Pariah, may feel and learn who with palsied limbs or wild distraught mind, from a darkness where there is no help or rescue, turns his gaze upwards: there a thousand eyes are burning, and a thousand ears calmly listening, before which nothing is hidden.

'If I raise myself to his throne, and he beholds me, thing of horror that I am, whom he has so hideously transformed, he cannot but pity me for ever; and may this be to the advantage of all of you. And I will counsel

Und ich werd ihn freundlich mahnen,
Und ich werd ihm wütend sagen,
Wie es mir der Sinn gebietet,
Wie es mir im Busen schwellet.
Was ich denke, was ich fühle –
Ein Geheimnis bleibe das.

DANK DES PARIA

Großer Brahma! nun erkenn ich,
Daß du Schöpfer bist der Welten!
Dich als meinen Herrscher nenn ich,
Denn du lässest alle gelten.

Und verschließest auch dem letzten
Keines von den tausend Ohren;
Uns, die tief Herabgesetzten,
Alle hast du neu geboren.

Wendet euch zu dieser Frauen,
Die der Schmerz zur Göttin wandelt!
Nun beharr ich, anzuschauen
Den, der einzig wirkt und handelt.

him in friendship, I will tell him in fury, what my mind dictates, what rises swelling in my heart. As for what I think and feel, let that remain a mystery.'

THE PARIAH'S THANKSGIVING

Great Brahma! now I see that thou art the creator of the worlds! I name thee as my Master, for no one is without value before thee.

And even to the lowest of us thou closest none of thy thousand ears; we, who are so deeply despised, have all been given new life by thee.

Turn your prayers, all of you, to this Lady whom suffering has transformed into a goddess! I now shall persist in the contemplation of him who is the sole source of all events and actions.

[BEI BETRACHTUNG VON SCHILLERS SCHÄDEL]

Im ernsten Beinhaus wars, wo ich beschaute,
 Wie Schädel Schädeln angeordnet paßten;
 Die alte Zeit gedacht ich, die ergraute.
Sie stehn in Reih geklemmt, die sonst sich haßten,
 Und derbe Knochen, die sich tödlich schlugen,
 Sie liegen kreuzweis, zahm allhier zu rasten.
Entrenkte Schulterblätter! was sie trugen,
 Fragt niemand mehr, und zierlich tätge Glieder,
 Die Hand, der Fuß, zerstreut aus Lebensfugen.
Ihr Müden also lagt vergebens nieder,
 Nicht Ruh im Grabe ließ man euch, vertrieben
 Seid ihr herauf zum lichten Tage wieder,
Und niemand kann die dürre Schale lieben,
 Welch herrlich edlen Kern sie auch bewahrte.
 Doch mir Adepten war die Schrift geschrieben,

[ON CONTEMPLATING SCHILLER'S SKULL]

In the solemn burial-vault I gazed at skull upon skull, all fitly ranged, and thought of olden times that had turned grey. There they stand, wedged together in rows, that once were at enmity, and rough bones that once clashed in mortal combat lie crosswise, tame in this their resting place. See, shoulder-blades wrenched apart! What did they carry? No one cares now; and graceful active limbs – a hand, a foot – lie scattered and out-of-joint and dead.

So you lay down in vain, you weary ones, and they would not let you rest in the grave; you have been driven out and up again to the light of day, and no one can love the dried-up shell, however splendid and noble a kernel it once enclosed.

Die heilgen Sinn nicht jedem offenbarte,
 Als ich inmitten solcher starren Menge
 Unschätzbar herrlich ein Gebild gewahrte,
Daß in des Raumes Moderkält und Enge
 Ich frei und wärmefühlend mich erquickte,
 Als ob ein Lebensquell dem Tod entspränge.
Wie mich geheimnisvoll die Form entzückte!
 Die gottgedachte Spur, die sich erhalten!
 Ein Blick, der mich an jenes Meer entrückte,
Das flutend strömt gesteigerte Gestalten.
 Geheim Gefäß! Orakelsprüche spendend,
 Wie bin ich wert, dich in der Hand zu halten?
Dich höchsten Schatz aus Moder fromm entwendend
 Und in die freie Luft, zu freiem Sinnen,
 Zum Sonnenlicht andächtig hin mich wendend.
Was kann der Mensch im Leben mehr gewinnen,
 Als daß sich Gott-Natur ihm offenbare?
 Wie sie das Feste läßt zu Geist verrinnen,
 Wie sie das Geisterzeugte fest bewahre.

But the writing that would not reveal its holy sense to every man was written plain for me, the adept, when in the midst of this stiff crowd I caught sight of one shape of priceless beauty, so that in this cold narrow chamber of decay I felt refreshed and liberated and warmed, as if a fountain of life had welled up from death.

With what mysterious delight I was filled by its outline, by the divinely conceived traces it still preserved! This was a sight that transported me to the shores of that swelling sea from which ever more perfect forms perpetually pour. Oh secret vessel, fountain-head of oracles! how am I worthy to hold you in my hand? And piously rescuing this supreme treasure from decay, I reverently return to the open air and sunlight, there freely to muse.

What more can life give to man than that Nature-which-is-God should reveal herself to him? she who causes firm matter to dissolve into spirit, and firmly preserves what spirit has engendered.

aus den CHINESISCH-DEUTSCHEN
JAHRES- UND TAGESZEITEN

SAG, was könnt uns Mandarinen,
Satt zu herrschen, müd zu dienen,
Sag, was könnt uns übrig bleiben,
Als in solchen Frühlingstagen
Uns des Nordens zu entschlagen
Und am Wasser und im Grünen
Fröhlich trinken, geistig schreiben,
Schal auf Schale, Zug in Zügen?

WEISS wie Lilien, reine Kerzen,
Sternen gleich, bescheidner Beugung,
Leuchtet aus dem Mittelherzen,
Rot gesäumt, die Glut der Neigung.

So frühzeitige Narzissen
Blühen reihenweis im Garten.
Mögen wohl die Guten wissen,
Wen sie so spaliert erwarten.

from THE CHINESE-GERMAN BOOK OF
HOURS AND SEASONS

SAY, what is there left for us, mandarins weary of ruling and sick of
serving – say, what should there be left for us to do in these spring days,
but to abjure the court life of the North, and here by the water's edge, under
the green trees, to drink gaily and write with wit – to drain cup after cup,
to trace line upon line?

WHITE as lilies, pure candles, starlike, modestly bowing – from their
hearts in the centre glows the red-rimmed radiance of love.

Thus early narcissi bloom in rows in the garden. No doubt, in their
goodness, they know who it is they are waiting for, so neatly arranged.

ZIEHN die Schafe von der Wiese,
Liegt sie da, ein reines Grün,
Aber bald zum Paradiese
Wird sie bunt geblümt erblühn.

Hoffnung breitet leichte Schleier
Nebelhaft vor unsern Blick:
Wunscherfüllung, Sonnenfeier,
Wolkenteilung bring uns Glück.

DER Pfau schreit häßlich, aber sein Geschrei
Erinnert mich ans himmlische Gefieder,
So ist mir auch sein Schreien nicht zuwider.
Mit indischen Gänsen ists nicht gleicherlei,
Sie zu erdulden ist unmöglich:
Die häßlichen, sie schreien unerträglich.

ENTWICKLE deiner Lüste Glanz
Der Abendsonne goldnen Strahlen,
Laß deines Schweifes Rad und Kranz
Kühn-äugelnd ihr entgegen prahlen.

WHEN the sheep leave the meadow, there it lies, pure green; but soon it will bloom into a many-coloured paradise of flowers.

Hope spreads bright misty veils before our eyes: may happiness come to us with the parting of the clouds, a fulfilment of wishes, a feast of the sun!

THE peacock's scream is ugly, but when I hear it I think of the bird's divine plumage, and so I do not mind its screaming. With Indian geese it is quite otherwise; it is impossible to tolerate them – they scream unbearably, the ugly things.

UNFOLD the brilliance of your lusts in the golden rays of the sun as she sets; let the round glorious diadem of your tail rise boldly, making many eyes at her. She will take them for flowers, and search for them in the green

Sie forscht, wo es im Grünen blüht,
Im Garten überwölbt vom Blauen;
Ein Liebespaar, wo sies ersieht,
Glaubt sie das Herrlichste zu schauen.

DÄMMRUNG senkte sich von oben,
Schon ist alle Nähe fern;
Doch zuerst emporgehoben
Holden Lichts der Abendstern!
Alles schwankt ins Ungewisse,
Nebel schleichen in die Höh;
Schwarzvertiefte Finsternisse
Widerspiegelnd ruht der See.

Nun am östlichen Bereiche
Ahn ich Mondenglanz und -glut,
Schlanker Weiden Haargezweige
Scherzen auf der nächsten Flut.
Durch bewegter Schatten Spiele
Zittert Lunas Zauberschein,
Und durchs Auge schleicht die Kühle
Sänftigend ins Herz hinein.

of the garden, overdomed with blue; but if she comes upon a pair of lovers, she will think them the most splendid spectacle of all.

DUSK has come down from above, and all that is near is already far off; but first the evening star has stood forth, high and radiant! Everything drifts into uncertainty; mists steal upwards; the still lake mirrors black gulfs of darkness.

Now in the eastern sky there is a hint of moonlight and moonglow; the branching hair of slender willows toys with the near-by water; through the play of moving shadows a tremulous lunar magic shines, and through the eye a soothing coolness steals into the heart.

«MICH ängstigt das Verfängliche
Im widrigen Geschwätz,
Wo nichts verharret, alles flieht,
Wo schon verschwunden, was man sieht;
Und mich umfängt das bängliche,
Das graugestrickte Netz.» –
Getrost! Das Unvergängliche,
Es ist das ewige Gesetz,
Wonach die Ros und Lilie blüht.

FRÜH, wenn Tal, Gebirg und Garten
Nebelschleiern sich enthüllen,
Und dem sehnlichsten Erwarten
Blumenkelche bunt sich füllen;

Wenn der Äther, Wolken tragend,
Mit dem klaren Tage streitet,
Und ein Ostwind, sie verjagend,
Blaue Sonnenbahn bereitet;

'I FEAR the insidiousness of this hateful theorizing, in which nothing seems permanent, everything flees, and whatever one sees has already disappeared; and the dread grey-spun web enmeshes me.' – Do not lose heart! That which does not pass away is the eternal law by which the rose and the lily bloom.

IN early hours, when the valley and the hills and the garden divest themselves of veils of mist, and the cups of flowers fill themselves with many colours, so longingly awaited;

 when the air, carrying clouds, vies with the bright daylight, and an east wind, dispersing them, prepares a path of azure for the sun –

Dankst du dann, am Blick dich weidend,
Reiner Brust der Großen, Holden,
Wird die Sonne, rötlich scheidend,
Rings den Horizont vergolden.

DEM AUFGEHENDEN VOLLMONDE

WILLST du mich sogleich verlassen?
Warst im Augenblick so nah!
Dich umfinstern Wolkenmassen,
Und nun bist du gar nicht da.

Doch du fühlst, wie ich betrübt bin,
Blickt dein Rand herauf als Stern!
Zeugest mir, daß ich geliebt bin,
Sei das Liebchen noch so fern.

So hinan denn! hell und heller,
Reiner Bahn, in voller Pracht!
Schlägt mein Herz auch schmerzlich schneller,
Überselig ist die Nacht.

you will then, as you gaze in delight, raise a pure and thankful heart to the great and good goddess; and the sun will glow redly as it sinks away, encircling the horizon with gold.

TO THE RISING FULL MOON

WILL you leave me already? You were so near to me a moment ago! Cloud-masses overshadow you and now you are gone.

And yet you feel how sad I am, your gleaming edge peeps over like a star! You bear me witness that I am loved, however far away my darling may be.

Move onward then, radiant and ever more radiant, on your pure course, in your full splendour! Though my heart beats faster and hurts, there are no words for the blessedness of this night.

DER BRÄUTIGAM

Um Mitternacht, ich schlief, im Busen wachte
Das liebevolle Herz, als wär es Tag;
Der Tag erschien, mir war, als ob es nachte –
Was ist es mir, so viel er bringen mag?

Sie fehlte ja! mein emsig Tun und Streben
Für sie allein ertrug ichs durch die Glut
Der heißen Stunde; welch erquicktes Leben
Am kühlen Abend! lohnend wars und gut.

Die Sonne sank, und Hand in Hand verpflichtet
Begrüßten wir den letzten Segensblick,
Und Auge sprach, ins Auge klar gerichtet:
Von Osten, hoffe nur, sie kommt zurück.

Um Mitternacht, der Sterne Glanz geleitet
Im holden Traum zur Schwelle, wo sie ruht.
O sei auch mir dort auszuruhn bereitet!
Wie es auch sei, das Leben, es ist gut.

THE BRIDEGROOM

At midnight, I slept, and my heart, full of love, lay awake in my bosom as if it were day; the day came – and to me it seemed dark as night: what is day to me, however many gifts it may bring me?

For she would not be among them! – For her sake only I endured my busy activity and effort through the hot burning hours; and how my life was refreshed in the cool evening! This was my good reward.

The sun went down, and plighted hand in hand we saluted the last gleaming benediction; and our eyes, as we met each other's clear gaze, said: Hope on, for from the east it will return.

At midnight – the brightness of the stars guides me in a sweet dream to the threshold of where she lies. Oh, for me too may a resting-place there be ready! Let life be as it will, yet it is good.

GOETHE

VERMÄCHTNIS

[An Marianne von Willemer]

Vor die Augen meiner Lieben,
Zu den Fingern, die's geschrieben –
Einst mit heißestem Verlangen
So erwartet wie empfangen –
Zu der Brust, der sie entquollen,
Diese Blätter wandern sollen;
Immer liebevoll bereit,
Zeugen allerschönster Zeit.

aus FAUST

(Part II, lines 4634–65)

[GESANG DER ELFEN]

Wenn sich lau die Lüfte füllen
Um den grünumschränkten Plan,
Süße Düfte, Nebelhüllen
Senkt die Dämmerung heran,

A LEGACY

[TO MARIANNE VON WILLEMER]

To the eyes of my darling, to her fingers that wrote them, to the heart
from which they poured, these letters – once so ardently and passionately
awaited and received – now shall return: ever ready full of love, to bear
witness to the loveliest time of all.

from FAUST

[SONG OF THE ELVES]

When all about the green-surrounded glade the air grows rich and mild,
sweet fragrance and veils of mist descend with the dusk, and it softly

Lispelt leise süßen Frieden,
Wiegt das Herz in Kindesruh,
Und den Augen dieses Müden
Schließt des Tages Pforte zu.

Nacht ist schon hereingesunken,
Schließt sich heilig Stern an Stern,
Große Lichter, kleine Funken
Glitzern nah und glänzen fern,
Glitzern hier im See sich spiegelnd,
Glänzen droben klarer Nacht;
Tiefsten Ruhens Glück besiegelnd
Herrscht des Mondes volle Pracht.

Schon verloschen sind die Stunden,
Hingeschwunden Schmerz und Glück;
Fühl es vor: du wirst gesunden!
Traue neuem Tagesblick!
Täler grünen, Hügel schwellen,
Buschen sich zu Schattenruh,
Und in schwanken Silberwellen
Wogt die Saat der Ernte zu.

whispers sweet peace, rocks the heart like a child to rest, and closes day's
door upon the eyes of this weary mortal.

Night has fallen here already; star joins with star in holy array, great
luminaries and little sparkling lights glitter from near by and shine in the
distance; they glitter here, mirrored in the lake, and shine up there in the
clear night sky; and sealing the joy of deepest repose, the moon's full
splendour reigns.

Already the hours are spent, and pain and joy have passed away; feel
now, before it happens, that you will be healed! Trust the new day's
dawning! Valleys grow green, hills loom forth, bushes appear on them
with shade for resting, and in rippling silver waves the crops swell towards
harvest.

Wunsch um Wünsche zu erlangen,
Schaue nach dem Glanze dort!
Leise bist du nur umfangen,
Schlaf ist Schale, wirf sie fort!
Säume nicht, dich zu erdreisten,
Wenn die Menge zaudernd schweift!
Alles kann der Edle leisten,
Der versteht und rasch ergreift.

(Part II, lines 4679–727)

[FAUST BETRACHTET DEN SONNENAUFGANG]

DES Lebens Pulse schlagen frisch-lebendig,
Ätherische Dämmerung milde zu begrüßen;
Du, Erde, warst auch diese Nacht beständig
Und atmest neu erquickt zu meinen Füßen,
Beginnest schon mit Lust mich zu umgeben,
Du regst und rührst ein kräftiges Beschließen,
Zum höchsten Dasein immer fortzustreben. –
In Dämmerschein liegt schon die Welt erschlossen,
Der Wald ertönt von tausendstimmigem Leben;

Gaze, to gain your every wish, at the brightness there appearing! You are but lightly enthralled; sleep is a husk – cast it off! Hasten into bold adventure, while the common herd wanders hesitantly to and fro! There is nothing a noble spirit cannot achieve, if he understands and seizes his opportunity.

[FAUST CONTEMPLATES THE SUNRISE]

LIFE'S pulses beat again, with living freshness, in clement salutation to the ethereal dawn; earth, you have lasted out this night as well, and new-revived lie breathing at my feet, beginning to surround me with delight already, stirring, stimulating me to strong resolve: never to cease to strive towards supreme existence. In the half-light the world already lies revealed; life sings in the forest with a thousand voices; long clouds lie spilled in and

Talaus, talein ist Nebelstreif ergossen,
Doch senkt sich Himmelsklarheit in die Tiefen,
Und Zweig und Äste, frisch erquickt, entsprossen
Dem duftgen Abgrund, wo versenkt sie schliefen;
Auch Farb an Farbe klärt sich los vom Grunde,
Wo Blum und Blatt von Zitterperle triefen:
Ein Paradies wird um mich her die Runde.

Hinaufgeschaut! – Der Berge Gipfelriesen
Verkünden schon die feierlichste Stunde;
Sie dürfen früh des ewigen Lichts genießen,
Das später sich zu uns herniederwendet.
Jetzt zu der Alpe grüngesenkten Wiesen
Wird neuer Glanz und Deutlichkeit gespendet,
Und stufenweis herab ist es gelungen –
Sie tritt hervor! – und, leider schon geblendet,
Kehr ich mich weg, vom Augenschmerz durchdrungen.

So ist es also, wenn ein sehnend Hoffen
Dem höchsten Wunsch sich traulich zugerungen,
Erfüllungspforten findet flügeloffen;
Nun aber bricht aus jenen ewigen Gründen
Ein Flammenübermaß, wir stehn betroffen:

out of the valleys, but heavenly brightness is penetrating deeper down, and branches and boughs, freshly revived, have risen into sight out of the misty chasm where they slept submerged; and bright colours detach themselves one after another from the depths, where flowers and leaves have been dripping with tremulous pearls: all round me, a paradise comes into being.

Let me raise my eyes! – The mountains' giant peaks herald already the most festive hour: they are privileged to enjoy in advance the eternal light that will later descend here to us. Now on to the green-sunk mountain meadows new radiance and clarity is poured, and it all moves down triumphant step by step: the sun emerges! – and alas, already dazzled I turn away, pain piercing my eyes.

Thus, then, it is when longing and hope have ardently striven towards a supreme wish, and find the portals of fulfilment flung wide open: but then there bursts from these eternal depths an overwhelming excess of flame,

Des Lebens Fackel wollten wir entzünden,
Ein Feuermeer umschlingt uns, welch ein Feuer!
Ists Lieb? ists Haß? die glühend uns umwinden,
Mit Schmerz und Freuden wechselnd ungeheuer,
So daß wir wieder nach der Erde blicken,
Zu bergen uns in jugendlichstem Schleier.

So bleibe denn die Sonne mir im Rücken!
Der Wassersturz, das Felsenriff durchbrausend,
Ihn schau ich an mit wachsendem Entzücken.
Von Sturz zu Sturzen wälzt er jetzt in tausend,
Dann abertausend Strömen sich ergießend,
Hoch in die Lüfte Schaum an Schäume sausend.
Allein wie herrlich, diesem Sturm erсprießend,
Wölbt sich des bunten Bogens Wechseldauer,
Bald rein gezeichnet, bald in Luft zerfließend,
Umher verbreitend duftig-kühle Schauer!
Der spiegelt ab das menschliche Bestreben.
Ihm sinne nach, und du begreifst genauer:
Am farbigen Abglanz haben wir das Leben.

and we stand amazed: we sought to kindle the torch of life, and we are
engulfed in a sea of fire – what fire! Is it love? or hatred? embracing, burn-
ing us, with terrible alternation of pain and joy – so that we turn back
again to earth, looking for youth's most virginal veil to hide in.
 So let the sun remain behind me! This waterfall that rages down the
crag, I watch it with increasing delight. From fall to fall it rolls, pours
down now in a thousand and now ten thousand currents, roaring and
foaming, foaming high into the air. But how splendidly, springing out of
this tempest, stands the many-coloured rainbow's arch of changing per-
manence – now clearly outlined, now melting into air, and scattering mist-
cool showers all round it! This rainbow mirrors man's endeavours. Reflect
on this, and you will understand more clearly that it is in a reflected
splendour of colour that our life consists.

(Part II, lines 7249–312)

[FAUST AM PENEIOS]

PENEIOS (*umgeben von Gewässern und Nymphen*):
 Rege dich, du Schilfgeflüster!
 Hauche leise, Rohrgeschwister,
 Säuselt, leichte Weidensträuche,
 Lispelt, Pappelzitterzweige,
 Unterbrochnen Träumen zu!
 Weckt mich doch ein grauslich Wittern,
 Heimlich-allbewegend Zittern
 Aus dem Wallestrom und Ruh.

FAUST (*an den Fluss tretend*):
 Hör ich recht, so muß ich glauben:
 Hinter den verschränkten Lauben
 Dieser Zweige, dieser Stauden
 Tönt ein menschenähnlichs Lauten.
 Scheint die Welle doch ein Schwätzen,
 Lüftlein wie ein Scherzergötzen.

[FAUST BY THE RIVER PENEIOS]

PENEIOS (*surrounded by tributaries and nymphs*): Stir, you whispering sedges! Breathe softly, brother and sister reeds; murmur, light willow branches; lisp, trembling sprays of poplar; speak to my interrupted dreams! For the dread of a coming storm, a hidden all-shaking tremor wakes me from my stream's placid sliding.

FAUST (*coming to the river*): Unless my ears deceive me, I think that behind the close-mingling foliage of these branches and shrubs I hear a sound as of human voices. For the water is like a chattering, the breezes like a delightful jesting.

NYMPHEN (*zu Faust*): Am besten geschäh dir,
Du legtest dich nieder,
Erholtest im Kühlen
Ermüdete Glieder,
Genössest der immer
Dich meidenden Ruh;
Wir säuseln, wir rieseln,
Wir flüstern dir zu.
FAUST: Ich wache ja! O laßt sie walten,
Die unvergleichlichen Gestalten,
Wie sie dorthin mein Auge schickt!
So wunderbar bin ich durchdrungen!
Sinds Träume? sinds Erinnerungen?
Schon einmal warst du so beglückt.
Gewässer schleichen durch die Frische
Der dichten, sanft bewegten Büsche,
Nicht rauschen sie, sie rieseln kaum;
Von allen Seiten hundert Quellen
Vereinen sich im reinlich-hellen,
Zum Bade flach vertieften Raum.
Gesunde, junge Frauenglieder,
Vom feuchten Spiegel doppelt wieder
Ergötztem Auge zugebracht!

NYMPHS (*to Faust*): You would do best to lie down and refresh your weary limbs in this coolness, enjoying the rest you can never find; we shall murmur and ripple and whisper to you.
FAUST: But I am awake! Oh let them continue, these incomparable shapes, these images projected by my eyes! How wonderful is the sensation that floods through me! Are these dreams? are they memories? I have known this joy once before.

Through the fresh, dense, softly-stirring undergrowth, waters move stealthily, unmurmuring, scarcely rippling; from all around a hundred streams converge in this pure, clear, shallow, bathing pool.

Women's limbs, young and healthy, mirrored in the moist surface, are doubly displayed to my delighted eyes! I see then a happy company of

Gesellig dann und fröhlich badend,
Erdreistet schwimmend, furchtsam watend;
Geschrei zuletzt und Wasserschlacht.
Begnügen sollt ich mich an diesen,
Mein Auge sollte hier genießen;
Doch immer weiter strebt mein Sinn.
Der Blick dringt scharf nach jener Hülle:
Das reiche Laub der grünen Fülle
Verbirgt die hohe Königin.

Wundersam! auch Schwäne kommen
Aus den Buchten hergeschwommen,
Majestätisch-rein bewegt,
Ruhig schwebend, zart gesellig,
Aber stolz und selbstgefällig:
Wie sich Haupt und Schnabel regt! –
Einer aber scheint vor allen
Brüstend kühn sich zu gefallen,
Segelnd rasch durch alle fort;
Sein Gefieder bläht sich schwellend,
Welle selbst, auf Wogen wellend,
Dringt er zu dem heiligen Ort. –

them bathing, swimming boldly or wading timidly, finally shrieking in a watery battle.

With those I should be content, and look my fill here; but my mind presses on further and further. My keen gaze seeks to pierce that screen of leaves: that rich foliage of abundant verdure hides the lofty queen.

Wonderful! swans too come swimming from the little inlets, with an unspoilt majestic motion, floating calmly, in tender companionship yet proud and conscious of their beauty: how they move their heads and their beaks!

But one of them seems more self-admiringly audacious than all the rest, and sails swiftly through the midst of them all; his feathers billow and swell, and himself a wave, undulating on waves, he penetrates to the sacred place.

341

Die andern schwimmen hin und wider
Mit ruhig glänzendem Gefieder,
Bald auch in regem prächtigen Streit
Die scheuen Mädchen abzulenken,
Daß sie an ihren Dienst nicht denken,
Nur an die eigne Sicherheit.

(Part II, lines 9506–73)

[FAUST UND HELENA IN ARKADIEN]

DIE Gaben, diesen hier verliehen –
An jeglichen ein reiches Land! –
Sind groß und herrlich: laß sie ziehen!
Wir halten in der Mitte stand.

Und sie beschützen um die Wette,
Ringsum von Wellen angehüpft,
Nichtinsel dich, mit leichter Hügelkette
Europens letztem Bergast angeknüpft.

Das Land, vor aller Länder Sonnen,
Sei ewig jedem Stamm beglückt,
Nun meiner Königin gewonnen,
Das früh an ihr hinaufgeblickt,

The others swim to and fro, with calmly glistening plumage, and
soon, too, in lively splendid strife, they distract the timid maidens and
make them forget their office, thinking only of their own safety.

[FAUST AND HELEN IN ARCADIA]

THE gifts I have bestowed on these – a rich domain to each of them! – are
great and glorious; let them depart! We shall take up our stand in the centre.
And they will vie with each other in defending this peninsula, surround-
ed by leaping waves, which a slender chain of hills connects to Europe's
last branch of mountains.
May that land, which outshines all other lands, be blessed for every race
for ever – that land, now conquered for my queen, which long ago gazed
up at her,

Als mit Eurotas Schilfgeflüster
Sie leuchtend aus der Schale brach,
Der hohen Mutter, dem Geschwister
Das Licht der Augen überstach.

Dies Land, allein zu dir gekehret,
Entbietet seinen höchsten Flor;
Dem Erdkreis, der dir angehöret,
Dein Vaterland, o zieh es vor!

Und duldet auch auf seiner Berge Rücken
Das Zackenhaupt der Sonne kalten Pfeil,
Läßt nun der Fels sich angegrünt erblicken,
Die Ziege nimmt genäschig kargen Teil.

Die Quelle springt, vereinigt stürzen Bäche,
Und schon sind Schluchten, Hänge, Matten grün.
Auf hundert Hügeln unterbrochner Fläche
Siehst Wollenherden ausgebreitet ziehn.

Verteilt, vorsichtig-abgemessen schreitet
Gehörntes Rind hinan zum jähen Rand;
Doch Obdach ist den sämtlichen bereitet:
Zu hundert Höhlen wölbt sich Felsenwand.

when amid the whispering reeds of Eurotas she broke radiant out of her shell, dazzling the eyes of her lofty mother and of her sister and brothers.

To you alone this land now turns, offering you its richest blossom; the earth belongs to you, but oh, give preference to your native land!

And on the jagged mountain-range's ridge the sun's shafts may fall coldly, but now among the rocks patches of green show forth, and the goat can gobble a meagre portion.

The spring gushes, streams mingle and rush downwards, and glens and slopes and pastures are green already. On the interrupted surface of a hundred hills you can see woolly flocks moving far and wide.

Here the horned cattle walk, evenly distributed, with careful precision, to the very edge of the sheer drop; but there is shelter ready for all of them – the curving cliff provides a hundred caves.

343

Pan schützt sie dort, und Lebensnymphen wohnen
In buschiger Klüfte feucht-erfrischtem Raum,
Und, sehnsuchtsvoll nach höheren Regionen,
Erhebt sich zweighaft Baum gedrängt an Baum.

Altwälder sinds! Die Eiche starret mächtig,
Und eigensinnig zackt sich Ast an Ast;
Der Ahorn, mild, von süßem Safte trächtig,
Steigt rein empor und spielt mit seiner Last.

Und mütterlich im stillen Schattenkreise
Quillt laue Milch bereit für Kind und Lamm;
Obst ist nicht weit, der Ebnen reife Speise,
Und Honig trieft vom ausgehöhlten Stamm.

Hier ist das Wohlbehagen erblich,
Die Wange heitert wie der Mund,
Ein jeder ist an seinem Platz unsterblich:
Sie sind zufrieden und gesund.

Und so entwickelt sich am reinen Tage
Zu Vaterkraft das holde Kind.
Wir staunen drob; noch immer bleibt die Frage:
Obs Götter, ob es Menschen sind!

There Pan protects them, and life-giving nymphs dwell in the moist fresh spaces of wooded ravines; and crowded trees thrust up their branches in longing for higher regions.

There are primeval forests! The mighty oak-tree stands rigid, with stubborn forking limbs; and the generous maple, heavy with sweet sap, plays with its burden as it soars cleanly upwards.

And in the quiet shady zone warm mother-milk wells up in readiness for child and lamb; fruit, the ripe fare of the plains, is at hand, and honey drips from the hollow tree-trunk.

Here well-being is hereditary; there is gladness in their faces and their lips; each of them is immortal in his place; they are contented, they are healthy.

Thus under this pure day their sweet children grow to strength of fatherhood. We watch amazed, our question still unanswered: are these gods, or are they men?

344

So war Apoll den Hirten zugestaltet,
Daß ihm der schönsten einer glich;
Denn wo Natur im reinen Kreise waltet,
Ergreifen alle Welten sich.

So ist es mir, so ist es dir gelungen;
Vergangenheit sei hinter uns getan!
O fühle dich vom höchsten Gott entsprungen!
Der ersten Welt gehörst du einzig an.

Nicht feste Burg soll dich umschreiben!
Noch zirkt in ewiger Jugendkraft,
Für uns zu wonnevollem Bleiben,
Arkadien in Spartas Nachbarschaft.

Gelockt, auf selgem Grund zu wohnen,
Du flüchtetest ins heiterste Geschick!
Zur Laube wandeln sich die Thronen:
Arkadisch frei sei unser Glück!

Apollo among the shepherds was fashioned to resemble them, so that
one of the most beautiful of them had his likeness. For in a region where
pure Nature reigns, all worlds intermingle.

And this have I, and this have you achieved; let us put the past behind
us! Oh, feel yourself to be the offspring of the highest of the gods! for to
none but the first of worlds do you belong.

No fortress shall circumscribe you! This land still stands, a zone of
everlasting youthful vigour, to offer us delightful sojourn: Arcadia, in
Sparta's neighbourhood.

Lured to live on a blessed soil, you have escaped into the fairest of
destinies! Our thrones are transformed into an arbour; may our happiness
be Arcadian and free!

(Part II, lines 9992–10038)

[SCHLUSSCHOR DER DIENERINNEN HELENAS]

EIN TEIL DES CHORS:

Wir in dieser tausend Äste Flüsterzittern, Säuselschweben
Reizen tändelnd, locken leise wurzelauf des Lebens Quellen
Nach den Zweigen; bald mit Blättern, bald mit Blüten über-
 schwenglich
Zieren wir die Flatterhaare frei zu luftigem Gedeihn.
Fällt die Frucht, sogleich versammeln lebenslustig Volk und
 Herden
Sich zum Greifen, sich zum Naschen, eilig kommend, emsig
 drängend,
Und wie vor den ersten Göttern bückt sich alles um uns her.

EIN ANDERER TEIL:

Wir, an dieser Felsenwände weithinleuchtend-glattem Spiegel
Schmiegen wir, in sanften Wellen uns bewegend, schmeichelnd
 an;
Horchen, lauschen jedem Laute, Vogelsängen, Röhrigflöten,
Sei es Pans furchtbarer Stimme: Antwort ist sogleich bereit.
Säuselts, säuseln wir erwidernd, donnerts, rollen unsre Donner
In erschütterndem Verdoppeln, dreifach, zehnfach hintennach.

[FINAL CHORUS OF THE FOLLOWERS OF HELEN]

PART OF THE CHORUS: We shall dwell in the whispering tremor, the
murmurous motion of these myriad boughs, and softly entice the
fountains of life, playfully charm them to rise from the roots to the
branches; and we shall adorn now with leaves, now with copious
blossoms these floating tresses that freely thrive in the air. When the
fruit drops, the people with their flocks will at once crowd round to
snatch it and taste it; quickly they will come, busily they will throng,
and all bow down around us as before the primal gods.

ANOTHER PART: We, moving in gentle waves, shall closely caress the
smooth far-shining surfaces of these cliffs: we shall listen, we shall hearken
to every sound, whether bird-song or reed-pipe flute or the fearful voice
of Pan, and be ready at once with our answer. When the wind sighs we
shall sigh back; when there is thunder, our thunders shall roll in deafen-
ing repetition, a triple or tenfold reply.

EIN DRITTER TEIL:
Schwestern, wir, bewegtern Sinnes, eilen mit den Bächen weiter;
Denn es reizen jener Ferne reichgeschmückte Hügelzüge.
Immer abwärts, immer tiefer wässern wir, mäandrisch wallend,
Jetzt die Wiese, dann die Matten, gleich den Garten um das Haus.
Dort bezeichnens der Zypressen schlanke Wipfel, über
 Landschaft
Uferzug und Wellenspiegel nach dem Äther steigende.

EIN VIERTER TEIL:
Wallt ihr andern, wos beliebet: wir umzingeln, wir umrauschen
Den durchaus bepflanzten Hügel, wo am Stab die Rebe grünt;
Dort zu aller Tage Stunden läßt die Leidenschaft des Winzers
Uns des liebevollsten Fleißes zweifelhaft Gelingen sehn.
Bald mit Hacke, bald mit Spaten, bald mit Häufeln, Schneiden,
 Binden
Betet er zu allen Göttern, fördersamst zum Sonnengott.
Bacchus kümmert sich, der Weichling, wenig um den treuen
 Diener,
Ruht in Lauben, lehnt in Höhlen, faselnd mit dem jüngsten
 Faun.

A THIRD PART: Sisters! ours is a more mobile spirit, and with the brooks
we shall hasten onwards; for those far-off richly covered hills entice us.
Ever deeper downwards we shall meander, watering now the meadow,
then the pastures, then the garden round the house: yonder its place is
marked by the slender tips of the cypresses, which soar skywards above
the landscape and banks and watery surface.
A FOURTH PART: You others may wander where you please: our rustling
shall encircle the hill so thoroughly stocked with green propped vines.
There, every hour of every day, we shall watch the wine grower's passion,
his loving diligence and its uncertain outcome. Now he hoes, now he
digs, now he piles earth, prunes and binds, and prays to all the gods and
to the Sun-god most of all. Effeminate Bacchus takes little thought for
his faithful servant, but rests in arbours, lolls in caves, flirting with the
youngest of the fauns. He has constant supply of all he ever needed for

Was zu seiner Träumereien halbem Rausch er je bedurfte,
Immer bleibt es ihm in Schläuchen, ihm in Krügen und Gefäßen,
Rechts und links der kühlen Grüfte, ewige Zeiten aufbewahrt.
Haben aber alle Götter, hat nun Helios vor allen,
Lüftend, feuchtend, wärmend, glutend, Beerenfüllhorn
 aufgehäuft,
Wo der stille Winzer wirkte, dort auf einmal wirds lebendig,
Und es rauscht in jedem Laube, raschelt um von Stock zu Stock.
Körbe knarren, Eimer klappern, Tragebutten ächzen hin,
Alles nach der großen Kufe zu der Keltrer kräftgem Tanz.
Und so wird die heilige Fülle reingeborner, saftiger Beeren
Frech zertreten: schäumend, sprühend mischt sichs, widerlich
 zerquetscht.
Und nun gellt ins Ohr der Zimbeln mit der Becken Erzgetöne;
Denn es hat sich Dionysos aus Mysterien enthüllt,
Kommt hervor mit Ziegenfüßlern, schwenkend Ziegen-
 füßlerinnen,
Und dazwischen schreit unbändig grell Silenus öhrig Tier.
Nichts geschont! gespaltne Klauen treten alle Sitte nieder,
Alle Sinne wirbeln taumlig, gräßlich übertäubt das Ohr.

his half-drunken dreamy musings, in wine-skins, jars, and vessels, to
right and left in the cool vaults, stored from time immemorial. But at
last – when all the gods, and the Sun above all, by giving air and mois-
ture and warmth and fire, have heaped the grapes' horn of plenty to the
brim – the scene of the wine-grower's silent labour comes suddenly to
life, and all around it there is a rustling and crackling among the leaves
from vine to vine. Baskets creak, pails rattle, hods groan as they are all
carried to the great vat where the lusty treaders will dance. And thus the
sacred bounty of pure-bred succulent grapes is insolently trodden under-
foot and mixed, foaming and spurting, into a crushed misshapen mass.
And now the ear is pierced by the brazen clamour of cymbals; for
Dionysus has unveiled himself from mysteries, and comes forth accom-
panied by goat-footed satyrs and satyresses, tossing and swaying, and
among them the long-eared beast of Silenus brays with unruly stri-
dency. Nothing is to be spared! Cloven hooves trample all decency
down; all the senses whirl and reel, the ear is deafened with hideous din.

Nach der Schale tappen Trunkne, überfüllt sind Kopf und
 Wänste;
Sorglich ist noch ein- und andrer, doch vermehrt er die Tumulte:
Denn um neuen Most zu bergen, leert man rasch den alten
 Schlauch!

(Part II, lines 11288–303)

[LIED DES TÜRMERS]

ZUM Sehen geboren,
Zum Schauen bestellt,
Dem Turme geschworen,
Gefällt mir die Welt.
Ich blick in die Ferne,
Ich seh in der Näh,
Den Mond und die Sterne,
Den Wald und das Reh.
So seh ich in allen
Die ewige Zier,
Und wie mirs gefallen,
Gefall ich auch mir.
Ihr glücklichen Augen,
Was je ihr gesehn,
Es sei, wie es wolle,
Es war doch so schön!

Drunkenly they grope for their cups, their heads and bellies filled to
overflowing; here and there someone has misgivings, but only swells
the tumult; for old wine-skins are quickly emptied when the grape's
new juice is stowed!

[SONG FROM THE WATCH-TOWER]

I WAS born for seeing, I am employed to watch, I am bound by my oath
to this tower, and I love the world. I look into the distance and see, as from
near by, the moon and the stars, the forest and the deer. And in all of them
I see the eternal adornment; and as the world delights me, so I delight
myself. Oh, happy eyes, whatever you have seen, let it be as it may be, it
has been so beautiful!

349

(Part II, lines 11844–89)

[DIE ANACHORETEN]

CHOR UND ECHO:
Waldung, sie schwankt heran,
Felsen, sie lasten dran,
Wurzeln, sie klammern an,
Stamm dicht am Stamm hinan.
Woge nach Woge spritzt,
Höhle, die tiefste, schützt.
Löwen, sie schleichen stumm-
freundlich um uns herum,
Ehren geweihten Ort,
Heiligen Liebeshort.

PATER ECSTATICUS (*auf- und abschweifend*):
Ewiger Wonnebrand,
Glühendes Liebeband,
Siedender Schmerz der Brust,
Schäumende Gotteslust!
Pfeile, durchdringet mich,
Lanzen, bezwinget mich,
Keulen, zerschmettert mich,

[THE ANCHORITES]

CHORUS AND ECHO: Woods wave about us, crags bear down heavily
upon them, roots clutch and embrace, trunk stands close to trunk. Wave
after wave of spray is flung; profoundest cavern protects us. Lions creep
round us, quiet and friendly, honouring this sanctified place, this holy
refuge of love.

PATER ECSTATICUS (*floating up and down*): Fire of eternal delight, burn-
ing bond of love, pain seething in my heart, divine rapture foaming!
Arrows, pierce me; spears, compel me; clubs, break me to pieces;

Blitze, durchwettert mich!
Daß ja das Nichtige
Alles verflüchtige,
Glänze der Dauerstern,
Ewiger Liebe Kern!

PATER PROFUNDUS (*tiefe Region*):
Wie Felsenabgrund mir zu Füßen
Auf tieferm Abgrund lastend ruht,
Wie tausend Bäche strahlend fließen
Zum grausen Sturz des Schaums der Flut,
Wie strack, mit eignem kräftigen Triebe,
Der Stamm sich in die Lüfte trägt:
So ist es die allmächtige Liebe,
Die alles bildet, alles hegt.

Ist um mich her ein wildes Brausen,
Als wogte Wald und Felsengrund,
Und doch stürzt, liebevoll im Sausen,
Die Wasserfülle sich zum Schlund,
Berufen, gleich das Tal zu wässern;
Der Blitz, der flammend niederschlug,
Die Atmosphäre zu verbessern,
Die Gift und Dunst im Busen trug:

lightnings, flash through me! That this unreality may indeed all dissolve
into nothingness, let the lasting star shine, the everlasting kernel of love!
PATER PROFUNDUS (*at a lower level*): As this rocky chasm at my feet rests
its weight on a still deeper chasm; as a thousand glittering streams flow
towards the foaming flood's terrible fall; as by its own strong impulse
the tree trunk soars straight into the air – even so it is the almighty Love
that forms and cherishes all things.
 All round me there is a wild roaring, as if the forest and the rocky
abyss were shaking; yet the copious water is full of rushing love as it
pours down into the ravine, for it is its task at once to water the valley.
The lightning whose flame struck down must purify the atmosphere,
which was harbouring poisonous vapours. They are messengers of love!

Sind Liebesboten! sie verkünden,
Was ewig schaffend uns umwallt.
Mein Innres mög es auch entzünden,
Wo sich der Geist, verworren-kalt,
Verquält in stumpfer Sinneschranken
Scharfangeschlossnem Kettenschmerz!
O Gott, beschwichtige die Gedanken,
Erleuchte mein bedürftig Herz!

(Part II, lines 12032–75)

[GRETCHEN VOR DER MATER GLORIOSA]

CHOR DER BÜSSERINNEN: Du schwebst zu Höhen
 Der ewigen Reiche;
 Vernimm das Flehen,
 Du Ohnegleiche,
 Du Gnadenreiche!
MAGNA PECCATRIX (*St Lucae VII, 36*):
 Bei der Liebe, die den Füßen
 Deines gottverklärten Sohnes
 Tränen ließ zum Balsam fließen
 Trotz des Pharisäerhohnes,

They tell of the eternal creative force whose motion surrounds us. May it also kindle a fire within me! for my mind, confused and cold, is tormented in the bondage of the dull senses, in a close-riveted agony of chains. Oh God, set my thoughts at rest, give light to my needy heart!

[GRETCHEN BEFORE THE MATER GLORIOSA]

CHORUS OF PENITENT WOMEN: Thou who art soaring high in the realms of eternity, oh hear our supplication, thou peerless one, thou who art full of grace!
THE WOMAN WHOSE SINS WERE MANY (*Luke vii: 36*): By the love that shed tears and balm on the feet of thy God-transfigured Son, despite the

Beim Gefäße, das so reichlich
Tropfte Wohlgeruch hernieder,
Bei den Locken, die so weichlich
Trockneten die heilgen Glieder –

MULIER SAMARITANA (*St Joh. IV*):
Bei dem Bronn, zu dem schon weiland
Abram ließ die Herde führen,
Bei dem Eimer, der dem Heiland
Kühl die Lippe durft berühren,
Bei der reinen, reichen Quelle,
Die nun dorther sich ergießet,
Überflüssig, ewig helle
Rings durch alle Welten fließet –

MARIA AEGYPTIACA (*Acta Sanctorum*):
Bei dem hochgeweihten Orte,
Wo den Herrn man niederließ,
Bei dem Arm, der von der Pforte
Warnend mich zurückestieß,

Pharisee's scorn; by the vessel that so richly poured out a sweet fragrance; by the tresses that so softly dried those holy limbs –
THE WOMAN OF SAMARIA (*John iv*): By the well where once long ago Abraham sent his herd to water; by the pitcher that was privileged to touch and cool the Saviour's lips; by the pure abundant fountain that now wells up from that place and flows to overflowing through all the worlds around it, radiant for ever –
MARY OF EGYPT (*Acta Sanctorum*): By the holy sanctuary where the Lord was laid to rest; by the warning arm that thrust me back from the door;

Bei der vierzigjährigen Buße,
Der ich treu in Wüsten blieb,
Bei dem seligen Scheidegruße,
Den im Sand ich niederschrieb –
ZU DREI: Die du großen Sünderinnen
Deine Nähe nicht verweigerst
Und ein büßendes Gewinnen
In die Ewigkeiten steigerst,
Gönn auch dieser guten Seele,
Die sich einmal nur vergessen,
Die nicht ahnte, daß sie fehle,
Dein Verzeihen angemessen!
UNA POENITENTIUM (*sonst Gretchen genannt, sich
anschmiegend*):
Neige, neige,
Du Ohnegleiche,
Du Strahlenreiche,
Dein Antlitz gnädig meinem Glück!
Der früh Geliebte,
Nicht mehr Getrübte,
Er kommt zurück.

by the forty years' penance faithfully performed in the desert, and by
the blessed words of farewell I wrote in the sand –
THE THREE IN CHORUS: Thou who refusest not thy presence to great
sinners, thou by whom the reward of repentance is enriched and raised
into eternity – grant to this dear soul also, who forgot herself but once
and had no thought that she was sinning, thy fitting pardon!
ONE OF THE PENITENTS (*formerly called Gretchen, approaching closely*):
Oh, bow down, thou peerless one, thou who are full of brightness, bow
down thy face graciously to my joy! He whom I loved long ago, he is
clouded no longer, he is coming back!

(Part II, lines 12104–end)

CHORUS MYSTICUS

ALLES Vergängliche
Ist nur ein Gleichnis;
Das Unzulängliche
Hier wirds Ereignis;
Das Unbeschreibliche,
Hier ists getan;
Das Ewigweibliche
Zieht uns hinan.

CHORUS MYSTICUS

ALL transient things are but a parable; the inaccessible* here becomes actuality; here the ineffable is achieved; the Eternal-Feminine draws us onwards.

* Or perhaps 'the insufficient'; but Goethe is probably using *unzulänglich* here (as he occasionally does elsewhere) in the sense of *unzugänglich*.

INDEX OF FIRST LINES

MORE ABOUT PENGUINS, PELICANS
AND PUFFINS

For further information about books available from Penguins please write to Dept EP, Penguin Books Ltd, Harmondsworth, Middlesex UB7 0DA.

In the U.S.A.: For a complete list of books available from Penguins in the United States write to Dept DG, Penguin Books, 299 Murray Hill Parkway, East Rutherford, New Jersey 07073.

In Canada: For a complete list of books available from Penguins in Canada write to Penguin Books Canada Ltd, 2801 John Street, Markham, Ontario L3R 1B4.

In Australia: For a complete list of books available from Penguins in Australia write to the Marketing Department, Penguin Books Australia Ltd, P.O. Box 257, Ringwood, Victoria 3134.

In New Zealand: For a complete list of books available from Penguins in New Zealand write to the Marketing Department, Penguin Books (N.Z.) Ltd, Private Bag, Takapuna, Auckland 9.

In India: For a complete list of books available from Penguins in India write to Penguin Overseas Ltd, 706 Eros Apartments, 56 Nehru Place, New Delhi 110019.

Goethe in the Penguin Classics
FAUST
(in two volumes)
Translated by Philip Wayne

Goethe's activities as poet, statesman, theatre director, critic, and scientist show him to be a genius of amazing versatility. This quality is reflected in his *Faust*, which ranks with the achievements of Homer, Dante, and Shakespeare. The mood of the play shifts constantly, displaying in turn the poet's controlled energy, his wit, his irony, his compassion, and above all his gift for lyrical expression. *Faust*, which Goethe began in his youth and worked on during the greater part of his lifetime, takes for its theme the universal experience of the troubled human soul, but its spiritual values far transcend mere satanism and its consequences.

also published:

ELECTIVE AFFINITIES
Translated by R. J. Hollingdale

ITALIAN JOURNEY
*Translated by W. H. Auden and
Elizabeth Mayer*

THE PENGUIN BOOK OF
GERMAN VERSE

Edited by Leonard Forster

The Penguin Book of German Verse is the first attempt for
many years to provide an anthology of German lyric poetry
for the English public at large. Professor Forster's presenta-
tion is fresh and contemporary, and his range of selections
extends from the Minnesingers – the German equivalent of
the Troubadours – to established writers alive today. The
prose translation at the foot of each page – a feature of
Penguin anthologies – has encouraged him to include not
only medieval poets, who would otherwise be difficult for
readers equipped only with modern German to enjoy, but
also some writers in dialect whose poems provide variety
and exhibit a characteristic side of German literature.

Professor Forster has also given liberal space to the poets
of the seventeenth century whose work has only compara-
tively recently come into favour in Germany itself and who
correspond roughly to the English Metaphysical poets, and
he has supplemented his choice from that age with a handful
of unforced folk-songs. For the later half of the book he has
drawn freely on the acknowledged great: Goethe, Schiller,
Hölderlin, Heine, Morike, George, Rilke, Hofmannsthal,
Trakl, Benn, and Brecht.

CLASSICS IN TRANSLATION
IN PENGUINS

☐ *Remembrance of Things Past* **Marcel Proust**
☐ Volume One: *Swann's Way, Within a Budding Grove* £7.50
☐ Volume Two: *The Guermantes Way, Cities of the Plain* £7.50
☐ Volume Three: *The Captive, The Fugitive, Time Regained* £7.50

Terence Kilmartin's acclaimed revised version of C. K. Scott Moncrieff's original translation, published in paperback for the first time.

☐ *The Canterbury Tales* **Geoffrey Chaucer** £2.50

'Every age is a Canterbury Pilgrimage . . . nor can a child be born who is not one of these characters of Chaucer' – William Blake

☐ *Gargantua & Pantagruel* **Rabelais** £3.95

The fantastic adventures of two giants through which Rabelais (1495–1553) caricatured his life and times in a masterpiece of exuberance and glorious exaggeration.

☐ *The Brothers Karamazov* **Fyodor Dostoevsky** £3.95

A detective story on many levels, profoundly involving the question of the existence of God, Dostoevsky's great drama of parricide and fraternal jealousy triumphantly fulfilled his aim: 'to find the man in man . . . [to] depict all the depths of the human soul.'

☐ *Fables of Aesop* £1.95

This translation recovers all the old magic of fables in which, too often, the fox steps forward as the cynical hero and a lamb is an ass to lie down with a lion.

☐ *The Three Theban Plays* **Sophocles** £2.95

A new translation, by Robert Fagles, of *Antigone, Oedipus the King* and *Oedipus at Colonus*, plays all based on the legend of the royal house of Thebes.

PLAYS IN PENGUINS

☐ Edward Albee *Who's Afraid of Virginia Woolf?*　　£1.60
☐ Alan Ayckbourn *The Norman Conquests*　　£2.95
☐ Bertolt Brecht *Parables for the Theatre (The Good Woman of Setzuan/The Caucasian Chalk Circle)*　　£1.95
☐ Anton Chekhov *Plays (The Cherry Orchard/The Three Sisters/Ivanov/The Seagull/Uncle Vania)*　　£2.25
☐ Henrik Ibsen *Hedda Gabler/Pillars of Society/The Wild Duck*　　£2.50
☐ Eugène Ionesco *Absurd Drama (The Rhinoceros/The Chair/The Lesson)*　　£2.95
☐ Ben Jonson *Three Comedies (Volpone/The Alchemist/Bartholomew Fair)*　　£2.50
☐ D. H. Lawrence *Three Plays (The Collier's Friday Night/The Daughter-in-Law/The Widowing of Mrs Holroyd)*　　£1.75
☐ Arthur Miller *Death of a Salesman*　　£1.50
☐ John Mortimer *A Voyage Round My Father/What Shall We Tell Caroline?/The Dock Brief*　　£2.95
☐ J. B. Priestley *Time and the Conways/I Have Been Here Before/The Inspector Calls/The Linden Tree*　　£2.50
☐ Peter Shaffer *Amadeus*　　£1.95
☐ Bernard Shaw *Plays Pleasant (Arms and the Man/Candida/The Man of Destiny/You Never Can Tell)*　　£1.95
☐ Sophocles *Three Theban Plays (Oedipus the King/Antigone/Oedipus at Colonus)*　　£1.95
☐ Arnold Wesker *The Wesker Trilogy (Chicken Soup with Barley/Roots/I'm Talking about Jerusalem)*　　£2.50
☐ Oscar Wilde *Plays (Lady Windermere's Fan/A Woman of No Importance/An Ideal Husband/The Importance of Being Earnest/Salomé)*　　£1.95
☐ Thornton Wilder *Our Town/The Skin of Our Teeth/The Matchmaker*　　£1.95
☐ Tennessee Williams *Sweet Bird of Youth/A Streetcar Named Desire/The Glass Menagerie*　　£1.95

PENGUIN BOOKS OF POETRY

THE PENGUIN POETRY LIBRARY

● ● ●